AMBER CASSIDY

FIRST CHANCE

First edition

ISBN: 979-8-9890036-7-9

This book was professionally typeset on Reedsy.
Find out more at reedsy.com

Preface

I've been imagining Lochlan's story since nearly the beginning of the Chance Encounters Series, and it's been one of my favorites to write so far. He's a gruff man of few words, until he isn't.

This is a slow burn -slower than the other stories, but I think Lochlan and Jo's story is worth the wait… But, don't worry, once the spice hits, *it hits*.

Enjoy!

Chapter One

Jo

"Don't smile the entire time, you're not auditioning. But smile at appropriate times so you seem equal parts sincere and endearing," my muttered words echo around the interior of my BMW. My scattered thoughts cannot be contained inside my head.

My Ballet Pink manicure taps rhythmically against the steering wheel, not to the beat of the song playing through my speakers, but matching the jitters coursing through my veins. A flutter of nerves that has only increased the closer I get to my destination.

"Let him know how important this is, but don't seem desperate." *No one cares about your problems, Jo. Not like you do.* A notorious bit of advice from my mother.

"**Your destination is on the left,**" my navigation quips, cutting through my compulsive rehearsing.

I turn off the pavement onto a dirt drive, braking in front of the black metal gates looming before me. The entrance is as ominous as the rumors about this place, Second Chance Sanctuary. A privately owned black bear rehabilitation center that has become animal and human-centered.

The sanctuary was created to help the high concentration of bears in the Blue Ridge Mountains. Residents know to keep their trash locked up and their eyes peeled on the roadways, but the bears are still subjected to encroachment and the carelessness of humans.

They're known to be hit by vehicles, poached by hunters, and the victims of the occasional accident reported by the timber companies.

According to an online article I read from years back, Mr. Dane hired ex-cons to help him take care of the black bears when the business was in trouble. The news of it went statewide when he started hiring newly released felons and repeat offenders before they fell through the cracks.

Information about this place is aloof. Other than the occasional smear article, there isn't information released to the public. Hence the ominous rumors.

I don't believe rumors. I've been subjected to enough of them to know that relying on facts is much more efficient. Facts don't lie. Facts don't have any ulterior motives. Facts cannot be swayed by an agenda.

My foot relaxes on the brake, letting my bumper creep forward a few feet until the tall wrought iron bars start moving. The hinges creak loudly from effort and years of use as the gate opens.

There's a moment of hesitancy. Brake or accelerate. Forward or backward. Once I go through these gates, everything changes. I'm taking steps to change my life.

Forward.

The gravel and dirt mixed terrain isn't ideal for my luxury sedan, and I feel each rock under my tires as the loose bits in my car rattle and sway dramatically until I brake again.

I'm not sure where to go. There's an old farmhouse to my right and a large barn to my left with various outbuildings scattered about. They're all mismatched and unidentifiable.

The largest barn is gray metal and looks the newest. The one next to it has to be no less than 100 years old, with its missing boards and deteriorating facade. The other buildings are smaller, probably not classified as barns, but I'm not sure what the criteria is. I should Google it later.

No, not important.

What is important is the giant man stalking towards me. I hardly give myself time to shift into park before scrambling out of my car.

His dark hair is long, curling across his temples wildly and past his ears. His beard is unkempt, hanging below his chin. His eyes, though... They're as dark as his scowl.

Hi, I'm here for my interview. No.

Hello, my name is–

"This is private property," he states, thunderously cutting off my internal dialogue. His deep voice reverberates through me like an earthquake, throwing me off balance.

That wasn't part of my rehearsed conversation, and I don't have a quick response. "Oh, yes. I mean, I know," I mutter, stepping awkwardly from around my car.

"What's your business here?"

My business?

"I'm here for an interview?" I can't stop it from coming out in the form of a question. It seems like the appropriate response, but his stance doesn't relax. His hands stay sturdy, balled into fists across his chest.

"Must be a mistake, there are no jobs for you here." He turns his back on me and starts walking away before even

3

giving me a chance to respond.

"I got an email to be here at 1:00!" I shout after him, and his feet stop so suddenly that it kicks up the dirt, making dust particles catch the sunlight all around him.

"Seiver!" He yells to someone out of sight, and he doesn't wait to see if he's been heard before turning back to me.

"I don't know what your game is, but you don't belong here," his deep voice states plainly. His eyes flick from my car and back to me, giving me a steely once-over.

I'm wearing a knee-length pencil skirt, white blouse, and interview-appropriate heels. This is the average attire for a person looking for a job. I checked.

"I'm here for an interview," I repeat because I can't seem to string together any other rational response to his aversion to me.

"You need something, boss?" An older man comes half-jogging, half-limping, over toward us. His tawny skin wrinkled from years under the sun.

"This woman thinks that she is here for an interview. Would you know why?" He asks with such an accusatory tone that even I'm afraid to hear the response.

"Well, I don't know, boss. The only resume we got was for a guy named Jo. I emailed him to set up an interview like you told me."

"That's me." I raise my hand as if there is anyone else around. "I'm Jo. JoAnna, actually."

Both their heads swivel, one look of innocent curiosity, and one is a full-blown glare. I wish I was talking to the curious old man, but it looks like Mr. Glare is the one in charge.

"We don't hire women."

"Excuse me?"

"This isn't a place for women. The gates will open automatically on your way out." He turns, giving me his back again, with no chance to respond. My gut sinks.

This guy is going to ruin everything I had planned.

"Can I speak to the real boss?"

His shoulders stiffen at my question, but he doesn't turn around; he only tilts his head in my direction. "The real boss?"

"Yes. Mr. Dane."

He rolls his shoulders before stalking toward me slowly like a hungry predator. He keeps walking until his tall frame is blocking the glare of the sun from my face. "I am Mr. Dane."

What?

"No, Mr. Dane is older." This Mr. Dane cocks his head slightly, looking at me as if for the first time.

"My grandfather?"

"So you're?"

"Lochlan Dane, his grandson. The only boss here, according to his obituary."

No.

Mr. Dane is dead. The man I thought I was meeting with. The one that is specifically part of my plan.

And that means I am having a conversation with *the* Lochlan Dane.

I know the name, but I've never seen a photo. Besides, nothing could do him justice. The aura emanating around him is as sinister as the stories about him. All of which are rumors. I think.

It doesn't matter. He's not giving me a chance. I'm not going to get the job here. Avoiding his gaze of terror, I reach into my purse and retrieve my sunglasses, pushing them onto my face before looking up at him again.

"I apologize for wasting your time then. Have a nice day."

His stance doesn't falter as I turn on trembling knees, crossing the gravel lot to get back in my car. My heels are as adept at this terrain as my tires, but it doesn't matter. I won't be back.

I'm sliding into my seat as gracefully as I can in this skirt when someone whistles from across the yard. "Is that the Princess of North Carolina?" The words bounce around in my head, but I'm an expert at ignoring catcalls.

"What the hell did you just say?" Lochlan growls to whoever said it, but I tune out the conversation.

I need to leave. The trundles of nerves have transformed into bubbles of devastation over how this day unfolded. I thought this was it, my clean break.

I reverse, flipping my car back toward the gates to get the hell out of here, but before I can accelerate forward, a large palm smacks down on the roof of my car, making me jump.

Lochlan's staring into my window, waiting, but all I can focus on is his eyes. Deep blue, almost navy, glaring at me as if he can see straight through into my soul.

He's close enough now that I can see the details of the raised white scar that starts at his temple and travels down, disappearing under his beard. It's precise, but not surgical, and he's likely had it for years.

After a momentary silent standoff, I unthaw myself from my frozen state and roll my window down.

"Is he right? Are you the Governor's daughter?"

"Former Governor. But, yes," I admit begrudgingly.

His whole frame stumbles back a step, but his eyes never leave mine. He doesn't say another word, but I can feel the tear that leaked from my eye is about to escape the coverage of my sunglasses.

I accelerate.

His silhouette fills my rear view mirror as I exit through the black gates and flee back down the mountain.

Chapter Two

Jo

I've never felt such nerves walking into my favorite coffee shop, but after I ran away from Second Chance Sanctuary last week, I received a very gruff voicemail from Mr. Dane asking if I could meet with him.

He insisted it be somewhere public and not at the sanctuary, somewhere I was comfortable. Unfortunately, the only place I am semi-comfortable is on my college campus. It's the only place where there aren't eyes on me.

He's impossible to miss sitting in the corner, even though his back is to me, looking out the big open window overlooking the square. It's the main cross-traffic area for students going to their classes, and the crowd favorite lunch spot on nice days like today.

He doesn't have a drink in front of him, but I order one of my own anyway before uneasily making my way over to him. I practiced a hundred different things to say when I showed up today, but none of them make their way from my throat as I sit down across from him.

His attention turns to me slowly, like he already knew I was here, but he doesn't say anything as he studies me. We sit in silence across from each other until it gets uncomfortable, which isn't very long at all.

"Jo!" One of the regular baristas walks over with my iced Churro Espresso Latte with extra caramel drizzle.

"Thank you, Hannah." I smile warmly at her when she glances at Lochlan nervously. We aren't personal acquaintances, but after ordering my drink from her a couple of times a week, I looked forward to seeing a friendly face at school.

I can sense her worry about the company I'm meeting with.

Lochlan doesn't look like he belongs on a college campus. This is a diverse school with a multitude of ethnicities, social classes, and ages. It isn't his mature appearance that I would guess is somewhere around mid-thirties; it's the black cloud he walks around under.

His hands are stuffed into the pockets of his plain black hoodie as he returns to assess the world outside instead of looking at me or Hannah. "I'll be right over there if you need anything else, Jo." She smiles sincerely, returning to the coffee counter.

"You didn't order anything?" I break the silence, speaking to him for the first time.

"No."

"Okay. So..."

I didn't initiate this meeting. The trajectory of this conversation should be led by him. That's the unspoken societal norm.

"You go to school here?"

"I'm studying to get my Master's Degree."

"In what?"

"Engineering."

His eyes widen ever so slightly. "Impressive."

"Thank you."

I tend to pick up on the tiniest of changes in facial expressions that others might not notice because certain cues help me prepare for where the conversation might go, but he's incredibly difficult to read as the silence continues.

"Why did you want to work at Second Chance Sanctuary?" He finally asks.

"I have experience in Public Relations."

"A Bachelor's Degree, I know. I read your resume after you left. You didn't mention that you were still in school or any work history. It's all volunteer work."

"I've had trouble with employment based on who I am."

"The Governor's daughter?"

"Former Governor."

"Wouldn't everyone like to hire the Princess of North Carolina?"

That dreaded nickname. My father has been known as the Governor of North Carolina for most of my life. He has held office in this state in some capacity longer than any other official.

He started as a mayor in the capital of the state, then did two non-consecutive terms as Lieutenant Governor before doing two non-consecutive terms as Governor.

If he didn't hold the office, then he was either running his campaign or maintaining a good reputation for the House or the Senate. He is and will forever be known as the Governor, as if he holds celebrity status.

Our family is treated as royalty in the worst way. Gossip, scandal, and unlimited notoriety. I have been primed and polished from infancy to showcase our family name in an ungodly light.

After I won Miss North Carolina Teen when I was 16, my "Princess of North Carolina" title stuck.

"You didn't want to hire me," I state blandly. The initial fire I had to get the job has completely dissipated.

"Because you're a woman."

"You don't think women are capable enough to work with you?"

His brows furrow deeper than they had been previously, since there seems to be a permanent scowl on his face. "No, that's not why."

"Then, why?" I cross my arms over my chest. I have the sudden urge to stomp out of here, but decorum tells me otherwise. I know my butt will be planted in this seat until it's socially acceptable to leave.

"What do you know about SCS?"

"It's a rehabilitation sanctuary for black bears and felons."

"So, you see my reasoning." He stares at me pointedly, expecting me to understand him without having to actually explain.

"I'm not afraid of black bears."

He huffs, leaning back in his seat and rubbing his hand across his forehead. "The bears aren't the problem. They rarely are."

"All of my research told me that you only hire non-violent felons. You don't trust them around a woman?"

"I hire men who have been convicted of non-violent crimes. Men who have a plan to better their lives. I don't know every detail of their past. I don't know what type of temperament they're capable of when a pretty piece of meat is dangled in front of their face. There is no guarantee that they can't be violent."

"Did you just call me a piece of meat?" I think now would be an appropriate time to leave.

"I know bears. I've worked with black bears my entire life. I can guess what they'll do when subjected to external forces. I cannot guess it as accurately with the men that come through my gates. They don't behave like bears. It's safer for you to steer clear."

"Then why am I here?"

"Because of your father."

"My father?"

"I owe him a debt from a long time ago. This might be my only chance to fulfill it."

"So I can have the job?"

"There are rules."

"Like?"

"You can only be on the property during set times. Only in the big house. You can't wander around by yourself or go into the barns. *No* socializing with the workers. And, you always have to be within arm's reach of your phone when you're working. If you aren't reachable, I'll assume there is trouble."

I'm analyzing each point as quickly as he's speaking, but my brain is already telling me what it wants. "Okay, I'll do it."

He holds his hands up to stop me. "I'm not done. I can't promise it will work out. I'm not making you sign a contract, but you need to understand that if the rules aren't being followed or I feel like there is any risk to your safety, I'll pull the plug and you're out."

"You act like I'll be walking into war."

"Someone wants to shut us down. Every other week, we're

getting threatening letters, fences damaged, or harassed in some way, and it's escalating. I need to get cameras and security up and running across the entire property. It could cost half a million dollars that I don't have, and I don't know how to get it. The funding we get from the state covers basic needs for operation, and that's it."

He sits silently as I ponder that. I knew the position was for a part-time Assistant/PR, but I didn't know why it was needed. It seems like Lochlan is in over his head.

"So, the sanctuary is dangerous?"

"Yes."

"I'll still do it."

He clenches his hands together on the table as if he is disappointed with my answer. As if he was hoping he'd scare me away.

"Do you know who I am, Jo?"

It's the first time he's spoken my name since meeting me. "Yes, I know who you are."

"About my past?"

I nod.

"And, you still want the job?" He asks the heavily loaded question and watches me closely for my answer.

"Yes."

Chapter Three

Jo

It took me 24 years to get my first job, and now I feel like my real life is beginning.

This is exactly what I needed, a place isolated from my family where I can be myself. None of their judgment or critiques can follow me here, not behind these gates.

As soon as I step out of my car, Lochlan is waiting on his front porch. I tiptoe excitedly to the front steps, avoiding letting my heels sink into the dirt. His eyes travel the length of me from head to toe before taking a deep breath and shaking his head.

Okay... Maybe I'll still face some critiques here, but I love wearing heels, and not even Lochlan Dane can stop me.

"This is where you can report every day, or every other day. I'll only need you for about twenty hours a week. You can pick what works best for your schedule, but you have to tell me ahead of time and stick to it." He holds the front door ajar with an outstretched arm, waiting for me to walk in before him.

"Thanks," I mutter softly as I squeeze past him. There's plenty of room, but he's so large in this normal sized house that it feels like he's looming over me. In my heels, I'm about six feet tall, but I'm still only to his chin.

There's a straight wooden staircase directly in front of the door, leading upstairs. To the right is a modest but outdated living room, and to the left is the kitchen, which is where he leads me. His head nearly brushes the top of the door frame, but he doesn't duck as if years of the same routine tells him he won't hit it.

The brown oak cabinets match the oak table sitting off to the side. The refrigerator and stove look straight out of a sitcom from the 70's. It looks like someone's grandparents' house, in every stereotypical way.

"The computer is in here, and I keep all the paperwork in these drawers." He pulls out a stack of mail from the built-in above the kitchen table. "I'd like you to go through the mail and my emails regularly, throw away the junk, and prioritize the rest. The bills are always the number one priority," he sighs.

"Bills, emails, mail. What else?" I ask with too much gusto, and he notices, looking at me peculiarly. I don't care, it's my first day and I'm so excited.

"Well, I'm not asking you to be an accountant, but if there is any way you can crunch some numbers, find areas that we can decrease spending, or a way to make a profit. I've been racking my brain for months now and can't find a way out of the hole we're in."

"How much of a hole?"

"We're operating at the base level, enough to function. There isn't any extra. My grandfather started this place when things were simple and cheaper. Now, food for the bears, materials, and the equipment we need cost almost triple what they used to."

"How much are your workers making?"

"They only make minimum wage, but they live here for free, get two meals a day provided."

"Like prison?" The words leave my mouth before I have a chance to think about it, and his face darkens.

"No, not like prison. They're free men here. They choose to be here to get a leg up with employment experience and some savings before getting thrown into the real world. They can come and go as long as they do their jobs. They get a bonus once their parole is up. Most of them use it to buy a car or put a down payment on a place to live once they leave. They follow my rules because they want to stay, not because they have to."

"I'm sorry, I didn't mean anything by it."

He doesn't respond right away, turning in a half circle and swiping a hand over the back of his neck. "Follow me, I'll show you around the property so you know the basics."

I trace his steps back out of the house when he stops suddenly. "Upstairs is off limits. You can go anywhere on the main level and the porch. Not upstairs," he says over his shoulder, not waiting for me to confirm.

I follow him across the dirt lot toward the outbuildings, wobbling slightly when I hit the gravelly spots. The only indication he notices is how his strides shorten, slowing his pace.

"The main barn is the bunkhouse. The guys live here, dorm style. Shared kitchen and living space, but their beds are quartered off and private." He doesn't open a door to show me inside, he continues walking down the alleyway between all the buildings. "This is where we keep the vehicles." He opens the door, showing me a few mismatched work trucks not likely from this decade and a couple more small all-terrain vehicles. Aside from a shiny red motorcycle in the corner and a green Ford Bronco, they're all dirty and well-used.

"We keep all the bear supplies in here." He shows me inside a smaller building, leading me into the depths this time. "Food and medical supplies. GPS collars, if we need them."

"They don't wear collars all the time?"

"No, only if they need regular medical intervention or supervision. They have over 100 acres here to roam freely. Our goal is to keep it as close to their natural habitat as possible."

"How do you keep them contained?"

"A fence runs around the entire property. My grandfather spent most of his time here making sure every inch was fenced in. Mostly to keep people out and away from his animals."

"But it's not working now?"

"It's an old fence," he says wearily. "We don't have eyes everywhere. If we could see the breach right away, they wouldn't have time to mess with anything."

"And, that much surveillance over that distance and up in these mountains is expensive. Got it." All the pieces are coming together, and where his problem lies. This is a not-for-profit company that needs big profits, and fast.

He nods, leading me out of the building and back up toward the house. "What about that far building?" I point down past the others, the one he didn't show me.

"It's where we keep all the strays." I raise my eyebrow at

him, so he continues. "People see the word sanctuary and use it as a dumping ground. We find all sorts of animals abandoned at our gate. Dogs, chickens, goats, and worse. They stay over there, away from the bear enclosures until we find them a new, permanent home."

"How do you get to the bears?"

"Trails cut through the woods and lead to the bear fences at each corner. North, South, East, and West are how we navigate them. It's a grid that'll always lead you back here eventually. Not *you*, specifically. You shouldn't go near the enclosures for any reason."

My mood deflates, but I try to hide it. The glimpse of the fence that I can see is just past the main yard and barns through the tree line.

"This barn is completely off limits. It's an original, been on the property for as long as my family has owned it, but it's a death trap. Don't even stand near it if the wind is blowing."

I chuckle until he glares at me seriously. Oh, not a joke.

"There she is, Second Chance Sanctuary's newest employee," a man says, rounding the corner of the bunkhouse to cut us off.

"Frank, I told you to stay scarce." Lochlan levels him with a sinister look, but the guy doesn't budge.

"We were just curious, is all. The guys wanted to say hi." He smiles innocently but with too many teeth. A wolf in sheep's clothing.

"They're all right inside, aren't they?"

"Yep."

Lochlan lets out a sharp whistle and then stands silently, and reluctantly, while six more guys stumble out through the doorway. "Alright, get it out of your system. Go ahead."

A chorus of hellos and introductions come my way all at once, indistinguishable from one another. A few cheeky smiles and one or two bored expressions.

"Nice to meet all of you, I look forward to working here," I respond sincerely.

"These are the Second Chance parolees. They will leave you alone at all times. They've been informed of the consequences if they choose to disobey." He looks pointedly at them before turning back to me. "All communication goes through me. Do not engage with them. Are we clear?"

"Yes." The longer he looks at me, the more my heart thunders in my chest. He's so intense all the time, but standing here in front of all these guys is the first time I feel the weight of what I'm doing. I'm the only woman among eight grown men.

"Curtis, go grab Hayes and Seiver. Might as well get all the introductions out of the way. The rest of you, get back to work."

Correction: 10 grown men.

"Come back up to the house, they'll find us." He ushers me forward, making sure he stays between me and the rest of the men at all times. "Those the shoes you're going to wear every day?" He asks suddenly.

"No, that would be ridiculous. They only match certain outfits."

He huffs but doesn't say anything else. It takes the entire walk back to the front porch for me to realize that he probably wasn't referring to the specific shoes I was wearing, but rather the heels themselves.

I don't bring it up again, though. I don't feel like explaining my love of shoes to him, or how my mother always insisted that leaving the house in anything but a perfect outfit was doing our family a disservice.

All of our outfits were to be hand-picked by her or a trusted stylist, tailored to precision, and never replicated. I've ignored that last rule as an adult, mixing and matching pieces to eliminate the wastefulness of it all. My mother turns her nose up at me anytime she notices.

She's been doing that since I was a child, making it abundantly obvious anytime she disapproved. There was no such thing as kids' clothing to her, no characters or sequins, I looked like a politician's daughter since birth.

Her disappointment was palpable the moment I hit puberty and went from adolescence straight into womanhood. My hips widened and my chest grew too quickly for her liking, and she made sure to point out every imperfection on my skin.

Every dress fitting included a healthy dose of ridicule and degrading remarks. She was 5'2 and 100 pounds on her wedding day, and she's never let me forget it. My father and brother both tower over her, each of them a few inches over 6 feet. She could never wrap her head around having a daughter who was nearly as tall as the boys and not as light as a feather.

My shoes are the one size that has never faltered. No matter how old I am, or how bloated I get, or the amount of sweets I eat will not change my shoe size.

However, the one item of clothing that doesn't give me anxiety to try on makes me a mockery for other reasons.

A man like Lochlan would never understand something like that. I could wear a pair of my tallest stilettos and still not rival his height. He would never worry about people making fun of him for being too tall, not like I have.

"Having second thoughts?" His deep voice startles me, as I'm staring unfocused across the property. When I turn towards him, he's closer than I realize. I have to crane my neck upward to look him in the face.

"No, I appreciate the opportunity to work here, Lochlan. Thank you again."

He doesn't respond, he's looking at me like he's trying to figure me out. Most people don't ever accomplish that, nor have they tried.

The older man from my failed interview comes around the house and climbs the porch steps slowly. "Miss Jo, I'm glad to meet you properly this time. I'm sorry about all that trouble from before."

"Oh, it's no problem at all. Seiver, right?" He smiles at my correct guess of his name, and I swear there is a faint flush on his weathered skin.

"He's been here a long time. He was friends with my grandfather before I was ever born," Lochlan informs me. "If you have questions or need anything and I'm not around, then Seiver is a good person to ask. He knows the ins and outs of this place as well as I do."

"Boss man has tried to get me to retire, but I'll wait and do that when I'm dead. I like this place too much." Seiver bumps his fist against Lochlan's shoulder, earning a glare, but I can see there isn't much heat behind it.

"Seiver and Hayes are the only two that work here without a commitment to the state. They aren't on parole and have freedoms the other guys don't. I just can't get rid of them."

"You'd be even more miserable if we weren't around, boss," a man says from behind us at the bottom of the porch steps.

Hayes, I assume.

He is younger than Lochlan but looks just as intense. I guess that's normal for someone who has been to prison.

The tattoos scattered down his arm are all in black ink with snip-its of more visible under the collar of his white T-shirt. He's lean with muscle, stealthy even, and even though he's as foreboding as Lochlan, he's not nearly as wild or rugged looking.

Hayes's dark blonde hair is buzzed short and tapered on the sides, and his smile is charming.

Lochlan is a brute force of nature.

"Hayes started here as one of the first parolees that we worked with. Once he was free and clear, he decided to stay on to help out. He keeps an eye on the guys when I'm not around. He knows what I expect, and they respect him. If any of them give you any trouble and I'm not around, go to Hayes. He'll take care of it." Lochlan looks at me seriously, letting me digest that information. I glance at Hayes, and he winks at me, but it's not flirtatious. It's a confirmation.

That rock in my gut settles heavier. I wanted to dip my toe into the real world, but I think I accidentally stepped into the deep end here.

Chapter Four

Jo

"Lochlan, this is terrible. It's not going to work," I admit, pacing back and forth in his kitchen.

"I warned you," he reminds me.

"I know, but no one can work under these conditions. I don't know how you've survived this long."

"I avoid it," he shrugs, shaking the mouse of his computer for the twentieth time. We've spent an hour attempting to log into his email because the computer lagged so long while booting up.

It's only my second day on the job, and I'm ready to throw the ancient device out the window.

"My laptop is in my car, I'll use it while I'm working. I'll accomplish everything ten times faster."

He sighs and leans against the counter. His air of confidence is completely different in here, around the paperwork, compared to how he holds himself outside in front of his men. He doesn't act like he has everything under control in here like he does outside.

"You're asking me to do a job here, and I can't do it on this computer. Let me use my laptop, it's no problem, really."

"Fine." I move to go get it, and he holds up his hand to stop me. "I'll get it. Where is it?"

"It's in my backpack, in the passenger seat." He nods and goes outside to retrieve it, and I move his notepad of logins and passwords over to the kitchen table from the computer desk.

"Why is your backpack so heavy?" He asks, setting it in one of the empty chairs.

"I have all my textbooks in there." I pull out my laptop and fire it up while he stands a few feet away watching me.

"Why don't you leave them at home?"

"In case I need them."

"You need all of your books every day?"

"Well, no. Not usually."

He looks at me curiously, but doesn't push it. We've only exchanged surface-level conversations for the past two days, nothing past the information I need to do my job here. A part of me is bursting to tell him the real reason that I needed this job, but only because I have no one else to talk to about it.

"Oh my God," I mutter once I'm logged into his account.

"What?"

"You have thousands of unread emails."

"I hate being on the computer."

"Why don't you check them on your phone, then?"

"I use a flip phone."

"You, what?!"

He pulls out his phone from his back pocket and flips it open to prove his point, and I can't pick my jaw off the floor. I didn't know they even sold those anymore. I knew he was older than me, but that's practically elderly of him.

24

"Okay, on your to-do list. Buy a new phone, buy a new computer. Pronto."

"Get me the money for a security system and I'll make those my next priorities," he mutters, unconvinced.

"Once you have a security system, you'll be able to watch live footage from your phone, open and close the gate on command, track people, bears, anything and everything," I argue.

"Fine." He pulls out a sticky note and writes, 'get smartphone.'

I snatch the pale yellow paper from his hand before he sticks it to his "bulletin board," which is a corner of his counter with six other sticky notes with random to-do items. I cross out smartphone and write, 'iPhone'.

"If you're going to get a new phone, you should keep up with the times." I hand the paper back with the sticky end attached to the tip of my finger.

"Now I know how the guys feel when I'm up their asses," he mumbles, sticking the note to the counter.

Maybe I should be offended, but I'm not. This is exactly why I am here and what I'm good at. Before I decided to pursue engineering, I knew how to organize and run things like the best of them. Parties, charities, and campaign events. I didn't want to do it for the rest of my life, but I strived to be the best at it regardless.

"My parents don't know I'm going to school for engineering," the words blurt out of my mouth before I can stop them after a few minutes of silence.

"Why?" He grunts. Most of his conversation with me is one-syllable responses, but I've gotten used to it.

"They wanted me to go into Political Science, but I didn't

want to. We compromised on Public Relations for my undergrad, but when it was time to apply for grad school, I went behind their backs and changed my major. That's why I carry all my books in my book bag. I don't want them to know because they'll make me quit."

"Why?"

"They didn't want me to go to grad school at all. They said it was a waste of time."

Lochlan's furrowed brow deepens, and he crosses his arms. "Because?"

I've said too much, I know it, but the way he's looking at me makes me want to spill my guts. He looks like he'll be mad at me for keeping a secret from him, even though we're nowhere near that level of familiarity.

My mother assumes I'll be someone's housewife, and my father can't grasp that I would do anything that doesn't benefit him.

"It's silly, just differing opinions. I'll tell them eventually," I say instead, trying to reverse out of the pothole I just stepped into. His eyes darken, but he doesn't press me further.

"Leave your books here." He walks out of the kitchen and out of the house without a farewell, cutting off our conversation completely.

I go back to checking his email and sorting through what needs immediate attention and what can be deleted, but my mind can't erase the way his eyes looked when I told him about my parents. It was disapproval.

I don't want him to think that I'm a liar or can't be trusted. No more conversation regarding my personal life. I'm here to get a paycheck, and that's it.

* * *

Over the next few weeks, it's more of the same. I go through emails, respond to what I can, and leave notes for Lochlan to fill me in on later. I pay bills and have organized all of his paperwork.

As I'm reading through the mail that he left on the table, I notice 'URGENT' stamped on one of the envelopes. It's from a Mayor Randall Porter with Langston's seal, the city just down the mountain.

That can't be good.

I slice open the envelope and start reading, piecing the information together as best as I can.

—

To whom it may concern:

Current records show your rehabilitation license has expired. A reinstatement application will need to be submitted and approved by the relevant licensing authority. Failure to do so or practicing while the license is expired will lead to disciplinary action.

State and Local agencies need copies of your records, or further action will be taken.

Submit documentation by the date posted.

—

Yep. Not good. The date posted on the header is for three days from now.

I should tell Lochlan about this asap, but I never leave the house. I park right out front, walk inside, and stay inside the entirety of my time working. He told me not to wander around, but this seems really important.

Walking across the gravel lot outside is getting more

difficult now that we've had rain. The dirt is softer, even muddy in some spots. I have to dodge and leap to avoid sinking into the ground and ruining my shoes.

I find a particularly dry gravelly spot and stop before I reach the big barn and the other outbuildings. I don't actually know where Lochlan is.

He told me not to go into the bunkhouse. He also said the old barn is off limits, so that helps narrow down my options, but it only gets muddier the farther I get from the house.

"Something I can help you with, ma'am?" A man's voice startles me as he steps out of the bunkhouse. It's a young guy, maybe even younger than I am. He has a hat on and a hooded sweatshirt, but I can see fingerless gloves covering his hands. It's not cold enough for gloves, but they also don't look equipped for cold weather. The material is almost spandex, looking like compression socks would be.

"I'm looking for Lochlan."

"He's out mending fences, I can get him on the radio for you." He pulls out an old-fashioned handheld radio and starts talking, but I'm distracted by his hands. The exposed parts of his fingers are scarred and discolored.

He notices where my attention is, and he turns his back. The heat rises in my cheeks with embarrassment. It's rude to stare. I know better than that. I should apologize, but that would only draw more attention to something he clearly doesn't want to be seen.

"And, I thought boss man had you locked away in that house of his." Another guy walks out of the bunkhouse, and I recognize him as Frank, the guy I saw on my first day.

"I've been pretty busy," I respond politely. I don't feel the same ease around Frank as I do the younger one.

"I'm surprised a pretty thing like you would want to work with a man like *Lochlan*," he clicks his tongue, enunciating his name like a curse word, and not taking the hint that I'm trying not to engage with him.

"Everything has been great so far."

"You're not worried about the allegations."

"I don't know what you mean."

He smirks at me. He knows that I know what he means. "You let me know if he gives you any trouble, sugar." He winks, and it's the least endearing thing ever.

I know about Lochlan Dane's past, and I'd still choose to be alone in a room with him over this guy any day.

"Frank, leave her alone. He's on his way, he said to meet him at the house," the younger guy says, stepping around Frank.

"Aren't you a good boy, Curtis. Maybe he'll give you a cookie." Frank scoffs but doesn't leave.

"I'll walk you up there," Curtis murmurs, ignoring Frank, and I'm glad not to be left alone.

"Thank you. I appreciate your help," I tell him quietly as I struggle up the slight hill of the dirt lot.

"It's none of my business, but I agree with the rule about us leaving you alone. Some of them are a little rough around the edges, Frank especially."

"I shouldn't have left the house. It's my fault."

"You shouldn't have to work in exile. There are enough good ones here, we'll keep an eye on you. Don't worry." He stops and doesn't follow me up the steps of the porch. "We're not allowed in the house."

"Oh, okay. Well, thank you again."

"He'll be here any minute, I'll make sure Frank isn't going

to bother you. Have a good day, ma'am."

"You can call me Jo."

"Alright, Jo. See you around." He nods his head, and I watch him walk back to the bunkhouse.

"I told you to stay in the house," Lochlan's voice comes from behind me. He must've come in the back way. The porch wraps all the way around, so he was able to sneak up on me.

He's wearing a worn pair of work pants and a dark long-sleeved shirt smeared with dirt. He stuffs faded work gloves into his back pocket and looks at me expectantly.

"I have something important for you to see." I hold up the envelope, and he looks at it only a moment before returning his gaze to me.

There's a standoff, neither of us acknowledging that I broke the rule about wandering. He glances at my shoes and sees the mud before inhaling deeply, exasperated by me.

"What's so important?"

"There's an urgent notice about renewing your rehab license. It'll need to be put in the mail by the end of the day."

He blinks a few times and then walks into the house without a word.

When I catch up to him in the kitchen, he's ringing out a damp paper towel. "Sit."

My butt plops into a chair immediately.

"Here." He hands me the paper towel and proceeds to open and shut a few drawers in the built-in cabinet next to the table. I'm still holding the wet towel when he glances at me. "For your shoes."

"Oh, thanks." I wipe the drying mud off the edges of my

tan pumps before cleaning the thin heel.

He sets a stack of certificates down on the table next to me and leaves again without saying goodbye, which I'm becoming quite accustomed to. So when he pops back up behind me a few minutes later, it makes me jump.

"Take off for the day," he says after my heart returns to normal rhythm and I seal the envelope.

"Are you sure? I was just going to drop it off when I left at 5."

"I need to fix something on the opposite side of the property, and I can't trust that you'll stay inside for the next few hours."

"I didn't go down by the barns for fun, I was looking for you because this seemed important."

"That's the third urgent notice I've received this year. They keep losing my paperwork, conveniently."

"I didn't know."

"Doesn't matter. I don't need my guys distracted by the Princess of North Carolina strutting around."

That smacks me right in the face. Hearing that nickname come out of his mouth so unprovoked rips right through me.

That's how he sees me? Even after all of the hard work I've been putting in...

"Fine. See you tomorrow afternoon." I gather my things quickly and shut my laptop a little too hard. I don't know if he notices, but he doesn't say anything.

I leave without looking back.

Chapter Five

Jo

It's been raining nonstop since yesterday, and the drive into SCS is thick with mud.

When I pull into my usual parking spot in front of the old farmhouse and step out of my car, my foot pauses, floating in the air. There is a large square paving stone directly under my foot that wasn't there yesterday. There are multiple, making a path from my car to the porch steps that is completely mud-free.

Did he do this for me?

When I go into the kitchen, there isn't any sign of him, but there's a new sticky note attached to the table.

Working fences all day. Call if you need me.

Okay, I get it. Don't go looking for him, just call his dinosaur cell phone.

Lochlan is hardly a conversationalist, but sitting in here alone for hours at a time is getting old. I don't have many friends or many reasons to socialize that aren't politics related, and these sticky notes are stagnant to stare at.

Still, I'd rather be here than at my parents' house when I'm not at school. I walk on eggshells around my family, not

32

wanting to do anything that could be critiqued. The way I dress, what I'm eating, or if I say the wrong thing. God forbid I have an opinion on anything.

It's easier to be invisible.

I could never live up to my older brother anyway. Conrad is running for Governor this year and has been deemed the most eligible bachelor in the state. If only they knew how unappealing he truly is.

He is my father's mini-me, and I've always been the black sheep. No matter how hard I tried, I was never good enough for any of them. The only reason I entered the beauty pageant world as a teen was because I thought if I started winning, they'd be proud, but it only drew harsher opinions.

My father was concerned about his image, my brother always told me that I looked hideous, and my mother made sure to point out every dress that didn't fit me in excruciating detail.

"What's wrong?"

I jump out of my skin hearing a voice from behind.

"Jesus, Lochlan. How are you so big and so quiet at the same time?" I bury my head back into my hands, not expecting an answer from him. "I thought you'd be out all day," I mumble into my palms.

I hear him open the fridge and rummage through it before closing the door. He starts making a sandwich, silently answering why he's here.

His back is to me, and I take my chance to look at him uninhibited. His shoulder blades flex as he's making his food, his muscles visible even through the fabric of his shirt. He wears nearly the same thing every day. Carhartt pants, Carhartt shirt or hooded sweatshirt, and his hair is always slightly unkempt as if he lets it air dry after his shower and doesn't touch it again.

Seeing his socked feet on the kitchen linoleum makes him less intimidating, knowing that he took the time to remove his dirty work boots before coming into his home.

I have no idea what it would be like to live in a place that's been in my family for so long. Lochlan clearly lives in the house that his grandfather lived in; it's homey and full of memories from the past.

I've snooped around some and seen the photographs on the mantle in the living room. His grandparents' wedding photo sits in the center, surrounded by old family photos of even older generations.

The TV is dusty and as old as the kitchen appliances, and there are a few large paintings, but no other decor.

I'm so lost in thought I forget to avert my gaze when he turns around. "Did you want something?" He asks with a mouth full of food.

"No, I had a salad for lunch." He visibly cringes and continues over to the table to sit down.

I'm hyper-aware of him being so near me. It's a kitchen table meant for six people, but his legs are so long that they take up more space than the average person. I continue working on my computer, trying to ignore his presence just as he's ignoring mine.

"Thank you for the paving stones," I mention quickly, before I lose my nerve. He grunts in response. Typical.

"Would it be okay if I stayed an hour late? I have a paper to finish and I'm afraid I'll run out of time before it's due if I wait until I'm back home."

"Sure."

"Thanks."

We go back to sitting in silence, and I conclude that it will be the extent of my social interaction for the day. I had class this morning, but I was in and out without talking to any of the other students.

Once they figured out who I was, they all avoided me like the plague. A known conservative father and a liberal college don't exactly mix. Not that I could convince them that I despise my father for far more reasons than they ever could.

"What does 'School Field Trip' mean?" He asks suddenly, looking at one of the sticky notes I left for him on the counter.

"I was brainstorming ways that you could earn more money. I thought maybe partnering with schools to do educational visits might help generate a little profit, but a lot of good publicity."

"No."

"What, why?"

"This isn't a petting zoo."

"Well, I know. I knew not to suggest opening it to the public." He throws daggers in my direction as if I suggested it anyway. "But education is so important. Helping new generations of kids learn the importance of conservation and wildlife management could be helpful in the long run."

"Who would willingly let their kids around a bunch of ex-cons and wild bears?"

"The bears are in an enclosure. The ex-cons... Well, that might be something we'd have to work around."

"No. One brat sticking their hand through the fence, and this whole place could get shut down. These bears aren't typically aggressive, but they're animals, and this is their home. They aren't here to be gawked at," he argues. He's not

35

yelling at me, but he's passionate enough in his inflection that I know this isn't a fight I'll win.

"So, no private parties, then?" I cringe even saying the words, but it was my last idea. He harrumphs and stalks out the back door.

Back to the drawing board, I guess.

* * *

Another week goes by, and I still don't have any more profit-inducing ideas, but today I've ventured out onto the porch to enjoy the weather. It's getting warmer in the mountains, and the sun's been out more, drying up most of the mud puddles.

Hayes walks by and does a double-take when he sees me. "Everything alright, Jo?"

"Yeah, I was just getting a little cabin fever being stuck inside."

"Hmm. Must be contagious in that house."

He doesn't elaborate before he joins me on the porch. I don't remember if Lochlan's rules included not talking to Hayes, but he initiated the conversation, not me.

"This is Loch's favorite chair, don't tell him I'm sitting in it," he says after he plops down in a sturdy rocking chair.

"I've never seen him sit in it."

"He sits out here at night after all the work is done."

"What work exactly? He's always pretty vague about what he's doing."

"Mostly securing the fences and fixing everything that's broken. We check the entire property every day to make sure there aren't any holes or damage. We also try to get a visual on all the bears every couple of days to make sure they're doing alright. They like to hide, so it can get tricky, but with what's been going on, Lochlan insists on having eyes on them as often as possible."

"The harassment, you mean?"

"The fence has been cut intentionally a couple of times. It seems like someone is trying to encourage the bears to get loose, but we keep them comfortable enough here that they aren't eager to run. Normally, human intervention is discouraged, but none of these bears have any business going back out to the wild."

"I read about that online. You have a couple that have been hit by cars, right?"

"Three. Dodie is missing his front leg because of it. Rocko and Minnie had enough internal damage that they were hospitalized, and then the vets didn't think they'd survive being reintegrated back to where they came from."

"I'm glad they could come here."

"Mr. Dane always had a soft spot for the bears, but they were Mrs. Dane's favorite animal."

"Did you know him well? Mr. Dane?"

"I did. I was here a couple of years before he died. I felt like I knew him before I ever met him, though. Loch always talked highly of him before he got out of prison."

"You and Lochlan were in prison, together?"

He looks at me thoughtfully, probably deciding how much he wants to tell me. "He was my cellmate for two years before he got out. I stayed in a couple more years, but we stayed in contact. He insisted I come work with him here."

"Why haven't you left?" He smiles slyly at my question.

37

"I'm sorry, was that rude to ask?"

"No, it's okay. I get it." He shrugs. "I've got it good here. It's given me a chance to get back on my feet and then some. Lochlan saved my life, though, and I haven't had it in me to abandon ship, yet." He looks somber after answering, staring off into the distance.

"Hayes, get back to fucking work," Lochlan shouts from the other side of the porch. Hayes just smiles and jumps to his feet dramatically.

"Yeah, yeah. I guess I will. See you later, Jo. Don't let the mean old bear boss you around," he whispers loud enough for Lochlan to hear. The bear flips Hayes off as he walks away.

"I came out to get some fresh air. Hayes just happened to walk by," I explain, even though Lochlan didn't ask.

"It is a nice day." He sits down in the rocking chair that Hayes abandoned. He motions, offering for me to sit down, but I wave him off.

"I've been sitting all day."

He nods and continues looking out over the property.

"Hayes doesn't seem afraid of you like some of the others."

"They seem afraid of me?" He tilts his head, watching me closely.

"Well, yeah, kind of."

"Good." There's a long pregnant pause. "Are you afraid of me, Jo?"

"Afraid, no. Intimidated, yes," I answer honestly.

"Good."

I roll my eyes at his response, and he smirks. "You must not be that intimidated," he adds.

I don't know why, but his amusement makes me blush. I

have to turn away from him so he doesn't notice. Miraculously, he starts speaking again unprovoked. "Hayes and I go back a long way. He has no reason to be afraid of me."

"He mentioned that you were cellmates," I admit cautiously.

"I had been in prison a long time already when he got locked up." I hold my breath while he continues, urging his admission. "He was young, pissed off. Despite how different our situations were, I completely understood him. He's the only person here with a violent background. I should have told you that from the beginning, in case you looked up his record, but I trust him."

"What kind of violence?"

"He beat someone nearly to death." A small gasp escapes me, but Lochlan continues. "It was a grown man, and he deserved it. He's never hurt a woman, just like I haven't."

There it is.

The elephant in the room since the very first day I came here. Lochlan Dane's notorious past.

18 years ago he was convicted of First-Degree Forcible Rape.

Chapter Six

Jo

"I had already been in prison for almost 8 years when I met Hayes. It took some heart-to-heart after he found out what I was in for to convince him that I was innocent. After a few days in the infirmary for both of us, he decided he could believe me."

I'd be more concerned except Lochlan seems amused by their history. "And, what about him? Did he try to convince you that he was innocent, too?"

He scoffs. "No, he took full accountability for what he did. I think he was kind of proud of it, honestly. He lived by a code, and I liked that about him."

"He said that you saved his life."

"I spent two years with him before I got out. There's a bond that can't be broken when you go through something like that with someone," he mutters.

"10 years in prison…" I mutter in disbelief.

"Your father exonerated me a year before my sentence was up. Cleared my record." He registers my unchanging expression. "You knew that, though, didn't you?"

"I did know, yes."

"And, you still wanted to work here."

"Yes."

"Why?"

I hesitate, staring back out across the yard for a moment. "I saw the job posting online, and I don't judge people before I know them. I did my share of research before I applied, and I knew what I was getting into."

His eyes narrow imperceptibly, and unconvinced, but he doesn't question me further. He's looking at me so closely, and I'm almost afraid he can see straight through to what I'm hiding.

"I need to run to the junkyard to find a part," he states suddenly. "Will you come with me?"

His dark ocean eyes carry a depth of wisdom beyond his years. He's trying to call my bluff, to see if I really trust him or not. He's testing me.

When I don't respond right away, though, he relents. "I'm not willing to leave you here unattended. Either come with me, or you can take off for the day," he adds.

"No, I'll go with you." Going home for the day is absolutely not what I want to do.

He seems surprised as he gets up to go get his truck. He pulls the green Bronco right up to the porch steps, leaving it idling as he gets out and comes to my side. When he offers his hand, helping me step over the damp dirt at the bottom of the porch and opening my door for me, heat creeps up my neck at his gesture.

The car is well-kept and the engine runs smoothly, but it's like stepping back in time. The front bucket seat has slightly worn leather, and the stick shift juts straight up out of the floor. It almost feels silly to only buckle a single lap belt in

41

the front seat of a car in this day and age.

"How long have you had this?" I ask halfway down the mountain to break the silence.

"It was my grandfather's baby, he bought it to surprise my grandmother for one of their anniversaries. I don't think she really gave a shit but he would have been buried in it if he could've," he admits in amusement, but with licks of sorrow.

There's a beat of silence because I honestly don't know what to say. I'm not always great at figuring out the right words. "What do you need from the junkyard?" I ask, changing the subject instead.

"One of the tractors needs a new seat."

I've never been to a junkyard, and I'm not sure how it works, but I imagine a fenced area with rottweilers like in the movies.

And, when we arrive, I'm not far off. We walk into a tiny little building with a single countertop and a couple of tires hanging on the walls, and an old TV mounted in the corner. There's a thick smell of gasoline and sweat.

I keep my hands clasped together so I don't accidentally touch anything.

"What can I help you with, Mr. Dane?" The man behind the counter is most likely the culprit of the smell. His clothes are stained to the point of filth, and his hair is slicked back, not likely with gel.

"Any Ferguson tractors back there?" Lochlan asks the guy whose name tag says 'Jerry' scrawled across it in Sharpie.

"Might have a few. Tractors are parked in the far back corner." He nods his head to a side door that I assume leads to the actual "junk yard."

"Thanks." Lochlan starts that way, glancing briefly to make

sure I'm following.

"Your girl can keep me company though," he winks at me, and I'm not sure I stopped my face from twisting.

Lochlan turns to him, eerily slow, and Jerry balks. "It was just a joke, man."

Without a word, Lochlan ushers me in front of him and out the door, mumbling something along the lines of, "…beat fuckers off with a stick."

"What did you say?" I ask, not thinking I heard him right.

"Nothing."

"Do you know him? He knew your name?"

"People tend to know who I am around here, unfortunately. I used to wear my hood up everywhere I went, but it didn't matter. Not enough guys around here my height to fool anyone."

"You shouldn't have to hide."

"*Shouldn't* and *have to* don't belong in that sentence together, darlin'," he drawls, his voice haunted by the past.

Despite all of my mixed feelings about Lochlan Dane and his grumpiness, my cheeks still heat when he calls me that. It's a common term of endearment in the south, so common that it's impersonal. But, I'm afraid that I like it.

We walk past old vehicles in every variety, a couple of old tow trucks, piles and piles of trashed parts, but thirty minutes later, we leave empty-handed with a promise from creepy Jerry that he'll keep an eye out for what Lochlan needed.

Once we're back at the sanctuary, I start to go back inside, but he stands motionless by the truck for several seconds.

"Everything alright?"

"I think one of the tires is going flat." He cocks his head slightly and curses. "I must've run over a screw at the

43

junkyard."

He calls Hayes, who joins us shortly, and they work together to pull off the damaged tire and put on the spare.

I've never seen anyone jack a car up or lift a tire, or the way muscles flex when they do those things…

Watching men work is a new interest of mine as I sit on the porch steps, admiring the view.

"Hey, girl," Seiver says from beside me, suddenly, making me jump out of my skin. "Woah, sorry."

"No, it's okay. I was… Distracted," I say as Lochlan lifts the old tire and puts it in the back of the Bronco. Seiver snorts at my obvious discomfort.

"I used to be able to do that too, ya know." He bounces his bushy eyebrows in a corny way, making me laugh.

"Do what?" Lochlan asks as he walks toward us, wiping his hands with a rag.

"Nothing." I glance at Seiver, and he smirks, but doesn't say anything.

"I can't believe you took the Bronco out and didn't take me," Hayes huffs from behind him. "I've only been asking for two damn years."

"You'll survive."

"Let me drive it."

"No."

"I know I'm not as pretty as Jo, but damn." Hayes feigns annoyance.

"No one is as pretty as Jo," Seiver adds.

I bump the ornery, sweet old man with my shoulder. "You're my favorite," I whisper, making him smile.

"Incoming," Hayes says suddenly.

I look up at the same time Lochlan looks away from me

and to the four-wheeler approaching us.

"Boss, sorry to interrupt, but there's something you've gotta see," one of the workers says.

"What is it, Jordy?"

Jordy glances at me before looking back at Lochlan silently. He doesn't want to say it in front of me. He's one of the more clean-cut guys, hardly appearing as someone who works a labor-intensive job because of his well-kept demeanor.

"Jo, stay inside the rest of the day. Let me know when you leave." Lochlan meets Jordy at the four-wheeler, and they speak to each other in hushed tones before they all take off across the yard in a direction I haven't been yet.

I piddle around for an hour inside before I'm supposed to be done for the day, but I can't seem to make myself leave. It's getting closer to summer, so the days are longer. Lochlan told me I wasn't allowed to be here at night, but the sun is setting later each day.

He walks in through the back door into the kitchen sometime after 6:30 and skids to a stop when he sees me sitting at the table with my textbooks.

He backpedals, dropping a small shoe box on top of the washer near the back door. "Don't look in that," he mutters as he passes by me to get into the refrigerator.

Well, now all I want to do is look in the box.

Why is it a secret?

"Are you planning to stay much longer?" He asks gruffly, downing a can of beer in nearly one drink.

"I'm about to leave, I just wanted to get some studying done before I went home."

"I'm heading out in about twenty minutes, be gone by then." He's climbing the stairs before I can respond. Not even a

45

minute later, I hear the pipes in the ceiling and assume he started the shower.

Being in his home while he's showering feels like an invasion of privacy. I don't think twice before stuffing all of my materials back into my backpack and slinging it over my shoulder, but I still hesitate to leave.

What's in the box?

The water is running steadily upstairs as I tiptoe to the back door and crack the lid of the box with the tip of my acrylic fingernail.

I gasp, dropping the lid and running before I have a chance to process what I just saw.

Animal heads. Two cats, a rabbit, a bird, and a raccoon.

Cold, foggy eyes, stained fur, and their tongues loose from their mouths. A horrifying display of cruelty despite there not being blood in the box. I shouldn't have looked.

I've been sitting in my car way too long, gripping my steering wheel, when I hear the front door shut. I look up as Lochlan locks eyes with me, the shoe box in his hand.

I shift into reverse, getting the hell out of here before I have to admit to Lochlan that I didn't listen to him.

Where is he taking it?

It consumes me the entire drive to my parents' house.

I should just ask him, but I don't want to tell him that I looked.

I'm so distracted by my thoughts that I forgot my brother would be here for dinner tonight. I see his car as I pull up the driveway to the old white colonial mansion. Black shutters and red doors make it look wicked and charming all at once.

"It's rude to be late," my mother greets me sourly as I walk in through the doors. Her short artificially blonde bob is styled impeccably, and her navy chiffon dress swings around her calves ever so properly.

"I'm not coming to dinner, I already ate."

"Of course, you did. You're expected at the dinner table. Pick at a salad for all I care." She stalks off across the foyer, click-clacking in her shiny silver heels. "You need more highlights in your hair, make an appointment at the salon," she adds before she walks through the doors to the parlor. I'm sure my father and brother are in there having a glass of scotch.

She's always hated my brown hair and insisted that I start bleaching it when I was barely 12. Every time I try to go for a more natural balayage, she never fails to mention how it's not blonde enough.

Unfortunately for her, my boring chocolate brown eyes can't be changed as easily. If it were acceptable, she'd insist I wear colored contacts.

I reluctantly follow her into the parlor because if I don't, then I'll never hear the end of it. As expected, my brother is sitting in a chair across from my father while my mother scolds one of the house staff.

"I have a campaign speech on Friday, JoAnna, you're expected to be on time," my brother says without bothering with any fake niceties first.

"I wasn't planning to attend."

"You have to, it's proper."

"Don't talk to me about proper, Conrad," I throw back at him with more spite than I ever afford anyone. My older brother is the only person in the world who can make me so mad.

He squints his eyes at me, and I know he's fighting all of

his internal demons begging him to behave as immaturely on the outside as he is on the inside. He's nearly ten years my senior but has never grown up. This run for Governor is the biggest acting performance I've ever seen.

"JoAnna, you'll be at the speech," my father states without question. He's not to be defied, he's made that clear my entire life.

"I have class." *I don't have class.*

He sets his glass down with a loud clunk on the table beside him, making my chest tense. "Skip it."

"Yes, sir."

"Good. Now that we're all in agreement, let's eat."

* * *

On Friday afternoon, when I pull up to the farmhouse, there is a porch full of people. All the parolees are standing in front of Lochlan as if they're having a meeting, but the conversation completely dies off when I get out of my car.

"Now, *that* is the Princess of North Carolina. I thought we got swindled," Frank croons boldly.

Despair overtakes me as I climb the porch steps, making me hang my head.

I had to wear the outfit that my mother picked out for my brother's speech tonight. I have to leave as soon as I finish working and go straight there. My normally work appropriate clothing is already more dressed up than is needed for this place, but today I am wearing a bright red fit and flare dress that hits above my knees and strappy nude heels.

"Frank, I'll rip your fucking tongue out if you talk to her like that, again. Address her with respect." I look up as Lochlan shoves Frank down the porch to make him leave out the back way. I can only imagine my cheeks rival the color of my dress.

"I have an event later," I mumble to no one in particular.

"You do look like a princess, ma'am. Respectfully," Curtis adds, dipping his head after Lochlan smacks the back of it as he walks by.

"Anyone else?" Lochlan asks, obviously annoyed by the disturbance. There's a chorus of "no's" before he turns his back to walk inside. Jordy slips me a thumbs up, but Lochlan must sense it because he snaps his head to the side, and everyone scatters like flies.

I, unfortunately, have to follow Lochlan into the bear cave and I know he's going to be pissed that I made a scene. Now, I'll get the silent treatment the rest of the day.

"If you're here trying to get male attention, then you can get lost. I don't tolerate that shit," Lochlan snaps as soon as we're in his kitchen. He's pacing back and forth, rubbing his hand across his face.

"What?"

"I'm not an idiot, Jo. You're the same age as some of those guys. They see a beautiful woman and they lose their fucking minds. If this is some game to you, then it ends here."

"That isn't fair."

He shrugs, not backing down from his accusation, and something inside of me boils up until it spills over.

"I didn't dress like this for them. I didn't even dress like this for myself, but I'm not going to apologize for the way that I look. If they can't control themselves, then that's on them.

49

Or, you, since you act like you can't control them!" This inner fury is coming from somewhere else but I'm unleashing it all on Lochlan because he chose the wrong day to be an asshole.

"I'm following all of your rules and I'm doing a damn good job despite winging it half of the time because you want nothing to do with me. Adding new rules because I'm too pretty is low even for you."

The silence that fills the room is suffocating. There seems to be a beat of uncertainty in his eyes, and I think he might apologize. "Maybe it's best if you leave."

Of course, I should have expected this. He warned me that he'd fire me at any given issue, and here we are.

"You know what? I think you're right." I'm out the front door in seconds, flinging my backpack into my car with enough force to rattle the interior. He steps out onto the porch as my car catapults a dirt cloud into the air as I speed away.

Chapter Seven

Jo

Fuck my life. I've burned all of my bridges.

I'm type A to the extreme. I plan everything, make lists, write addendums for my lists, and choose my battles wisely. Yet today of all days, I've blown up every single connection that I have. I have nowhere to go. I refuse to go home, and I have no one else.

It's almost midnight as I idle in front of the gates to Second Chance Sanctuary. I'm way more uncertain about driving through them now than I was the first time I was here.

I shouldn't be here, it's late, and he told me not to be here at night but, I've already pissed him off once today.

How much worse could it get?

My feet are aching so badly by the time I park and turn my car off that I rip my shoes off and chuck them into the backseat. I'll just curl up in my seat and get some rest somewhere I feel safe. I can figure out my life tomorrow. I'll come up with a plan, I'll–

"What the hell are you doing here?" Lochlan barks at me through my window, forcing my eyes wide. It's so dark I didn't even see him come outside.

"I didn't have anywhere else to go," I admit, pitifully, my voice barely sounds real as it escapes through the crack I made in the window.

He stares at me with those dark eyes that are always filled with so much conviction. So much anger. But this time they look filled with sorrow.

"Come have a seat on the porch." He didn't phrase it as a question, and it doesn't seem like he's giving me a choice as he steps back, giving me space to open my door.

I don't necessarily want to get out of my car just to be scolded, but it's better than being told to get the hell off his property.

He holds my door open as I climb out of the car, letting the cool paving stones bite at my bare feet. I don't rush to get to the porch, accepting the discomfort after the day that I've had.

Lochlan trails me until I get to the rocking chairs and then indicates for me to sit in the chair next to his. There's a short glass sitting next to his seat, a finger of amber liquid in it that is dark enough to be bourbon.

We sit next to each other in silence for so long that a chill whispers across my skin, and I hug myself to ease it.

"You can't sleep here in your car," he says suddenly as if all this time he's been trying to figure out what to say and that's what he came up with.

He stands up, and I think that's the end of the conversation, but he only snatches a jacket from inside the doorway to drape over me. It smells like he's worn it a few times, but clean like men's soap with a slight twang of cigar smoke. He either smoked one a while ago, or he's been around someone who has.

I like it.

"I was hoping to be gone before you woke up. I thought maybe you wouldn't notice." I tuck the jacket up under my chin, burrowing deeper into it.

"You don't know what time I wake up."

I huff. He always says what I expect, but not at all at the same time. "You're right, I was just hoping to avoid making you mad at me."

"I'm not mad at you, Jo."

"Really? Had me fooled."

He sighs and downs the rest of his drink. "I'm sorry about earlier."

"It's okay."

"No, it's not."

"You're right, it's not."

"Then why did you say it was okay?" The question rumbles from his chest roughly, but with hesitant curiosity.

"I don't know, that's what you say when someone apologizes."

"Don't do that."

"What?"

"Don't tell me what you think I want to hear. I need the truth from you if this is going to work."

"You mean I'm not fired?"

"I didn't fire you. You fled out of here like a bat out of hell." His analogy makes me laugh softly. "I'll have ruts from how you peeled out of here." That makes me laugh harder, my head falls back, resting against the top of the rocking chair. It's shorter than his, made for a woman.

"I looked in the shoe box," I finally admit after holding it in for days, staring at the ceiling of the covered porch.

"I know."

"How?"

"The lid was tipped."

He knew, but he never said anything. He didn't get mad at me. "Sorry for looking."

"I'm sorry for making you feel uneasy around me."

"It's not– I wasn't–"

"No, you were. You didn't feel like you could tell me the truth because you were afraid I'd get angry. I don't want you to feel like that."

"I'm not afraid of you, remember?"

"Right. Just intimidated." He sighs. "I'm used to working around men. I don't give a shit if they're scared of me, I prefer it. But that doesn't go for you. I want you to listen to me because I'm your boss, not because you're afraid of how I'll react."

"A healthy level of respect for authority."

"Yes, exactly," he exclaims, and it makes me laugh again.

"I need to get a second job. I might have to change my schedule around."

"Why?"

"My parents found out about school. They're pissed."

"So?"

"It's too late to change my major, or I'd have to start over, not that I'd want to, and they said I have to quit if I want to continue living under their roof. Which is such a manipulation tactic because they think I have nowhere else to go. Exactly as they've planned it," I mumble.

"What do you mean?"

"My parents want me at their beck and call. They didn't ever want me to attend grad school, and they've never wanted me to work. Or, allowed it.

"They've spent the last 24 years of my life grooming me to be the perfect political pawn. I want a life, and they don't want to let me go, so I'm going behind their backs."

"Jesus Christ, Jo. What the hell kind of family drama are you getting me mixed up in? Your father doesn't even know you work here?"

"No."

"Fucking hell," he mumbles.

"When he finds out he's not going to be happy."

"I hired you because I thought I was doing good by your family, because your father helped me."

"I know. I'm sorry." I squeeze my eyes shut, curling deeper into his jacket in case it's the last bit of warmth I have before he kicks me to the curb.

"But it sounds like your father is a jackass."

A sob rips from my throat after processing what he said. "I only need to play nice until September. I told him that if he forces me to quit school, then I'll refuse to participate in my brother's campaign, and I'll start leaking family secrets. His image is everything despite how imperfect he is."

"You're going to blackmail your father?"

"It's the only way to win against a man like him."

"Remind me not to mess with you," he mutters, and I grin. *He has no idea.* "You can stay here."

My smile drops. "What?"

* * *

"This is my grandmother's old studio." He flips on the lights to what I thought was a detached garage this whole time. I've parked my car twenty feet away from it for over a month.

The small interior is filled with stacks of painted canvases. A small bistro table sits off to the side of a micro kitchen. It's only one counter with a single tub sink under a small window. A small toaster oven and two cabinets.

"It's not much, but it's livable. There's a twin bed and a small bathroom behind that curtain. My grandfather renovated this so she had somewhere to paint, but she hated it. She preferred painting upstairs in the house where there were more windows. So it turned into storage and then his room when he was in the dog house."

I look at him curiously. "They loved each other like crazy, but they fought like cats and dogs. Pops always said that she was the love of his life and the biggest thorn in his side." He looks so wistfully lost in thought, I almost want to touch him, pat his arm, or squeeze his shoulder in some sort of silent support. Instead, I bury my hands into his jacket that I wrapped myself in before we walked down here.

"They sound wonderful," I murmur into the quiet space.

"They were." He clears his throat and turns to look at me. "There will be more rules if you stay here."

Of course, there are.

"Let me guess. Don't talk to the guys. Don't make noise. Don't bug you unless I'm working." I tiptoe around the room with my bare feet on the hardwood floor. It only takes a few steps to cover the space between the door and the kitchen. One car could barely even fit in this space.

"Don't make friends with the guys. Don't wander around, especially at night. If you need to go outside after dark, text me first. If you're on the property, then I need to know. If you leave, I need to know. Keep this door locked at all times. Your phone needs to be on you, and you need to answer if I call you."

"This is crazy, Loch-"

"That shoe box was left by people who want to hurt this place, Jo. Those animal heads were a threat. No one here has been harmed yet, but I'm not taking that risk with you. None of my parolees have stepped out of line yet, but they also haven't had the chance." He looks at me pointedly so I understand. "I'm not risking that with you. Do you hear me?"

"Yes." He's a commanding presence anytime I'm near him, but being near him in such a small space is suffocating. His aura is all-consuming in a way that I'm not used to.

Even when I don't want to look at him, I catch myself glancing in his direction, but when his full attention is directed at me, it's hard to meet his stare head-on.

His gaze dips to my bare feet and travels slowly back up to the oversized fleece covering more of me than my dress did, and he sighs. "If you want to stay here, then it's temporary, so you can focus on school. You do your job and you keep your head down."

"Okay."

"Go home. Get your stuff and come back in the morning. I'll have it cleaned up."

"I can help you."

"No, I've got it." He grabs a stack of paintings and heads out the door, but I'm transfixed by the one that's left leaning against the wall. It's an oil-painted landscape like the one in his living room, except it's the view from the porch. The sunrise is streaming over the property, with the light slicing through the gaps of the old abandoned barn.

It's a warm and peaceful, but intricately detailed view of the place that seems so stagnant. A woman's perspective of a place completely overrun by men. It's beautiful.

"Can I keep this one in here?" I ask once he returns.

He picks it up and inspects it thoughtfully before hanging it on the wall. The entire length of the wall has a track running across it with hooks to hold the canvases like an artist's workshop.

"Thank you, Lochlan."

He shrugs, still looking at the painting. "No problem."

"No, I mean thank you for letting me stay here."

"Everyone needs a chance in life. This is yours, so don't let it go to waste." He continues lofting stacks of paintings out the door, not even glancing at me after that loaded statement.

He's right, though, I'll never get another opportunity like this to get out of my parents' grip. I have to make it count.

* * *

The next day, when I arrive at my new home, there are paving stones creating a path from my door, along my new parking spot, and all the way to Lochlan's porch. He's either being considerate of my less-than-functional footwear, or he's marking the exact areas within my bounds.

The door is unlocked when I try it, and I open it to a completely different space. All the paintings are gone except the one hanging on the wall. The counters and floors are wiped down, there are fresh sheets on the bed, and the curtains above the kitchen sink are pulled open.

I was here by 10 am; he had to have been working at this all night. It's perfect.

"Is this all you have?" Lochlan asks from behind me, holding my giant overstuffed suitcase as if it's a bag of feathers.

"Yes, I told my parents I was moving out, but convinced them to let me leave the majority of my clothes in my old room."

"How'd you do that?"

"Well, if they want me to be the perfect accessory at all of my brother's campaign events, then I'll still need to be able to access my wardrobe. They'd never risk me not showing up, or worse, showing up in something less than perfect."

"You have a weird family."

"Oh, I know. I've been taught from an early age that appearances are everything. Show the perfect face and people will throw money at you."

He looks at me dumbly, it's clearly not a lesson he was ever taught, rightly so.

"Wait! That's it! You should come to these events!"

"No."

"Yes, Lochlan, it's perfect. Half of these events are charity-oriented. Everyone networks to gain more support for their cause. Second Chance Sanctuary just needs more investors and more donations. That's how I can help!" I'm so excited I'm nearly bouncing where I stand. It's perfect, I don't know why I hadn't thought of it before.

"No."

That's why. "Can you just think about it?"

"No."

"Lochlan..." He turns his back on me before I can continue.

"No!" He's already out the door and walking back to his house.

Okay... Back to square one.

Chapter Eight

Jo

Lochlan's house feels different now that I live next door. It's always been an extension of him, but only during work hours. I don't know how he fills his time on the weekends, or even during the evenings, other than sitting on the porch with a glass of whiskey.

Now that I have more of an opportunity to catch him in his natural habitat, I feel tempted to snoop. The itch to go upstairs nags at me every time I walk through the front door, even though it's strictly off limits. What doesn't he want me to see?

The possibilities are endless when you come from a family like mine with a million skeletons in their closets, but even though Lochlan is the one with a notorious reputation, his moral code is titanium.

I tear myself away from the enticing pull of his home and make two loops around the wrap-around porch before I see Curtis off in the distance, pruning some sort of tree.

"Hi, Curtis." I wave across the yard, and he glances around before throwing his hand up in response. I take that as my invitation.

"What are you doing?" I ask as I tiptoe across the grass towards him. He looks visibly put off by my approach.

"Um, I'm getting the trees ready so they produce more when the fruit is ready."

"What kind of fruit?" He clearly knows he isn't supposed to be talking to me, but I've backed him into a corner, and it'd be rude to ignore me at this point.

"Persimmons."

"Oh, I'm not familiar."

"It's for the bears. They go crazy for it, but the tree won't produce for another couple of months." He glances past me, busying himself again.

"What are you doing?" Lochlan barks from behind me.

"Nothing," I say at the same time Curtis says, "Almost done, boss."

Lochlan crosses his arms and looks at me, but doesn't scold me like I know that he wants to. "I can't sit inside all day," I argue, even though he didn't say anything yet. "It's beautiful out. Even prisoners get yard time."

Curtis gasps from behind me and grabs his tools before rushing away from the ticking time bomb.

"Prisoners do what they're told or they're thrown in solitary confinement," he counters, stepping close enough to block the sun from my face.

"Speaking from experience?" I clap a hand over my mouth as soon as the words come out. Why did I say that?

"You can hang out in the yard or on the porch," he growls. "Don't go down by the barns. That's final." He stalks off, and I'm still standing there with my hand over my mouth when Jordy runs past me.

"JO! We got a new drop off at the gates, come look!"

Lochlan only made it a few steps away from me, and I'm close enough to hear him sigh, but I'm too excited to be included in something, so I take off across the dirt lot with the other guys before he can tell me not to.

"It's a donkey!" The guy named Arizona yells to everyone as we make it to the entrance.

"No, it's a mule," Rain corrects. He's the first one that I realized uses a nickname instead of his real name. Trying to keep them all straight has been a challenge.

"Does this mean we're cowboys, now?" Curtis asks.

Lochlan and Hayes respond, "No," in tandem.

Its brown fur twitches as it stands as far from the gate as it can with a rope tied taut around its neck.

"Seiver, take it down to the barn with the rest of the strays. Everyone else, get back to work."

"It's Sunday…" I utter out of pure boredom.

"Animals don't give a shit if it's the weekend, they still need cared for. Fences need checked, bears need fed, and vehicles need repaired. You're the only one not working today, darlin'."

"Fine, give me a job." I chase after him, somehow managing to keep up with his long strides.

"No."

"I have to earn my keep, boss."

He whips around. "You don't call me, boss. They call me, boss."

I don't know why that matters, but it's not the point of this conversation. "Give me something to do and I'll do it."

"Fine. Go clean the work truck."

Wash a truck? That seems easy enough. I jog straight over to where they keep the trucks parked and skid to a stop. The only truck parked in its spot is a flat-bed rust bucket and the shiny green Bronco. The Bronco is in pristine condition.

The flat bed is caked in dried mud.

* * *

My waterlogged fingers are burning from scrubbing so hard. My back is so stiff that a sharp biting pain radiates through me if I move too hard, but I did it. I cleaned the truck until it was spotless and the sun disappeared from the sky.

I'm proud of myself despite the menial job Lochlan gave me. He was testing me, and I definitely passed.

"Where have you been?" He asks me as I approach the house.

"I cleaned the work truck?" Can't he see the dirt crusted up my arms and legs?

"It's dark, you shouldn't be out here alone."

"Of course, I'm doing something wrong. My mistake," I snap, stomping past him. "You are so frustrating, you know that?" I yell over my shoulder when I realize that he's following me. "You told me to do a job and I did it. I just about killed myself to do it perfectly, too. But you're still mad."

"Dammit, Jo. I'm not mad. I'm trying to keep tabs on you so I don't have to worry about your well-being!"

"Stop worrying! No one wants to talk to me, they'll hardly look at me because they're so damn scared!"

"You chose this, I'm not forcing you to be here."

"I know!" I slump onto the porch steps. "I just don't want

to be trapped in the guesthouse by myself," I add pitifully, hanging my head in my hands.

I don't need friends, I've gone long enough without them, but it'd be nice if anyone would socialize with me besides the grumpy man in front of me.

A rugged growl erupts from him, forcing my head up. "Go take a shower and get dressed, meet me right here in 30 minutes. Go!" He demands, stomping inside his own house.

I don't give myself even a minute to question it before I take the fastest shower I've ever taken and pull on the most casual sun dress I own.

I'm ready and waiting before my half hour is up when Lochlan walks out of his house. He must've just showered, too. I'm drawn to the scent of his soap as he comes near me.

He starts walking across the dirt lot towards the bunkhouse without instruction, expecting me to follow, and I do, skipping merrily behind him. I don't know what we're doing, but I'm happy to be included.

"Behave," he warns gruffly before holding the door open to the bunkhouse. Everyone's voices fall silent as I enter.

It's a wide-open barndominium with a living area in the middle. Two large sectionals square off in front of a massive flat screen TV. Behind that is a pool table and a large table that resembles something from a school cafeteria.

One side of the barn has a spacious kitchen, and the other side looks like dormitory showers, or something you'd see in a locker room.

Stairs lead up to a second level that contains the bunks. They're private but open at the same time.

"You need something, boss?" Ryker asks. He's another parolee that I don't know very well. He asks the question as if it's unusual that he's here.

"Jo's bored, someone entertain her."

I gape at him, throwing me under the bus. Hayes cackles from the other side of the room. "We were just about to run a table tournament, you in Loch?" He eyes his friend knowingly, and I can't help but watch the interaction.

Hayes is so friendly, it's hard to believe he beat someone badly enough to go to prison. Lochlan seems more susceptible to committing a crime like that with his glowing personality.

"Sure," Lochlan grunts, planting himself on the sofa.

"Jo's on my team," Hayes adds, and Lochlan's eyes narrow.

"I'm sorry, team for what?"

"Billiards, single elimination, winner stays on," Curtis enlightens me while Hayes and Lochlan continue their stare off.

"I've got the boss, then," Seiver yells from somewhere in the kitchen, and before I know it, everyone's standing around the pool table laughing and shouting as the teams take turns.

Someone hands me a beer at some point, but I only let it get warm in my hand, pretending to sip on it occasionally so no one notices. I watch Lochlan run the table once it's his and Seiver's turn. Sinking most of their colors with ease.

They win twice before it's mine and Hayes' turn to play and determine the winner. The pool stick looks too big in my hand compared to how Lochlan holds his. Each shot is solid and precise, he never slips up.

"Alright, listen. I'll break, rack up as many as I can to give us a head start. Then you can show me what you got," Hayes whispers.

My eyes are stuck over his shoulder on Lochlan and the

way he's watching us. The scar on his cheek is much more visible under the fluorescent lights in here, making him look as scary as he acts.

"Wait!" Seiver shouts before Hayes breaks. "There's always a wager. What's the bet?"

Hayes looks up at Lochlan from his shooting stance, a silent conversation happening between them.

"No, bet," Lochlan answers. The entire room erupts in complaint. Apparently, this is an important topic.

"Fine. Jo, what do you want to bet?" Hayes asks.

"Umm. I don't know, what's normal?"

"Last time I lost, Lochlan made me run through the bear enclosure naked," Arizona admits.

"No, I made you run through the enclosure. You were drunk and took your clothes off on your own," Lochlan argues, and a couple of people start cracking up.

It's so odd to see this side of him. There is still a line between him and the men who work for him, but there's also camaraderie that I've never witnessed.

"I don't think I want to do that," I admit.

Lochlan looks at me flatly. "You're not going near the fences, Jo. I don't care if these morons get hurt." More people laugh. Must be a guy thing.

"What do you want from Lochlan, Jo?" Hayes asks more specifically.

A mischievous grin graces my lips. "I want you to agree to come to the events with me this summer to raise money for the sanctuary."

The room goes silent as Lochlan's glare turns deadly. "And, if I win?"

"Then I'll stop bending the rules and listen like a good little girl."

I wasn't expecting such a reaction, but you could hear a pin drop with everyone holding their breath, waiting for Lochlan's response.

His stare burns straight through me as if he can see my heart thundering in my chest.

"Deal." His voice raises the little hairs on the back of my neck.

Hayes breaks, and all the balls go rolling in different directions. "We're stripes," he announces, and the game begins.

Chapter Nine

Jo

Hayes sinks four balls before missing the corner pocket and giving our opposing team a turn, and I'm feeling even better about our chances when Seiver lines up a shot and misses by a millimeter.

His ball knocks one of mine right in front of a side pocket, and I tap it in no problem.

Unfortunately, my next options aren't great, and I don't want to look like a fool in front of all these guys. I take my time, circling the table before deciding on the 10-ball into the front corner pocket.

I have to lean deep over the table to line up my shot, but as I find the center of the cue, Lochlan zips a short whistle through his teeth. Everyone backs up, giving me a wide berth.

I don't think it was intentional, but it throws off my trajectory, putting my focus on the man standing opposite me across the table and not the stripe I'm aiming at.

I miss.

He smirks as I stand up, but it's hardly noticeable aside from the slight crinkle around his normally serious eyes.

Lochlan confidently sinks five solids before missing, and

that's only because he was going for a double on the last two.

"Shit," Hayes mumbles.

It's just a game, but my body is tingling with nerves. I don't like to lose, but I also think Lochlan attending charity events with me will truly benefit the sanctuary, and this is the only way to convince him to do it.

Hayes takes his turn and puts the 15-ball in the side pocket, but misses our last stripe. He curses again under his breath, and I know that's a bad sign.

"Seiver, don't fuck this up," Lochlan threatens lightly before Seiver makes one and misses one.

One stripe left.

One solid.

And, the 8 ball.

I chalk the end of my stick for no other reason than luck. I'm not confident in my skills here, especially when my ball is on the opposite side of the table from the cue ball and the 8-ball is in between.

Okay, Jo. Don't hit the 8-ball. Don't hit the 8-ball. My stick punches the cue ball and…

I hit the 8-ball.

"No!" I gasp as it rolls closer to the side pocket. If it falls in, then I lose.

It rolls to the very edge of the green felt and stops. My head thunks down on the top rail, and I take a deep breath before standing up.

It's not over yet, but it feels like it is. All Lochlan has to do is hit his 4-ball in and finish with the black.

As he lines up his shot on the 4, Hayes leans over and whispers in my ear, and I catch Lochlan's gaze shifting to us. He makes his shot anyway.

"I can't do that," I whisper back to Hayes.

"It'll work, I promise," he insists, stepping back.

A desperate woman will do desperate things...

As Lochlan leans over to fire on the 8-ball and win the game, I step to the side and directly into his line of sight. His dark eyes flick to mine quickly before lining up on the corner pocket directly in front of me.

My fingertips hit the skin of my left thigh, and his stick freezes mid-strike. As my hand moves upward, his eyes follow it, snapping to my face when I catch the hem of my flowy skirt and drag it higher.

A few whistles and innocent catcalls ring out around me, but I'm locked in on Lochlan. He's trying to focus, but a magnet can only resist its opposing force for so long. His pupils darken as he lines up his shot again, and just as the fabric of my sundress hits my upper thigh... He shoots.

And, misses the black ball completely.

The cue ball rolls toward the corner pocket, depositing into the hole with a *thunk*, and the entire room erupts in cheers.

I win.

He stands up without tearing his gaze from mine, and my skirt falls from my hand.

He's pissed.

Everyone is congratulating me, but I can't stop looking at him. I'm paralyzed watching him back away from the table and turn to go out one of the back doors.

"I knew it would work," Hayes jokes from beside me.

"I think I made him mad, Hayes." I look at him worriedly and he cocks his head at me.

"You don't see it, do you?"

"What?"

"He's not mad." Right at that moment we both hear the muffled, but loud, "FUCK!" roared just outside the barn walls. "Okay, maybe he's pissed about losing the bet, but that's because he's hidden out behind these gates for so long. Going around people who might know who he is, or worse, insist he's someone he's not, is his nightmare."

"Oh." Lochlan walks back through the back door of the bunkhouse and locks onto target immediately. "No, I think he is mad at *me*, Hayes."

"That man doesn't have the ability to be mad at you." I snap my neck to look at him because clearly, he is not referring to the same person that I am. "He was in prison surrounded by men for ten years, and then 8 more here. He doesn't know how to talk to you," he finishes in a whisper as Lochlan approaches us.

"Let's go, I'll walk you to the guesthouse." He grabs the still-full can of beer out of my hand, and his eyebrows scrunch briefly in confusion before setting it down on the nearest table.

"Good game, Loch," Hayes smirks.

"Fuck you, Jensen." Lochlan starts walking and I take the queue to follow him.

He doesn't know how to talk to you. I don't believe Hayes, but the best way to prove the theory is to test it. "I'm sorry for beating you in front of the guys," I say from behind him, and he skids to a stop.

"No, you're not."

"Okay, you're right. I'm glad I won, not because I wanted to beat you, but because I think I can really help make a difference here if you let me."

He starts walking again, slowing his pace so I can keep up.

"I'm still not sure it's a good idea," he mutters.

"I'll be with you every step of the way. I won't let you down, I promise." We're stopped in between our respective houses, lit only by a floodlight across the lot.

"Fine," he agrees, and I squeal in delight, grinning like a kid while he stares at me unmoving.

"Thank you, Lochlan." I clap my hands together gently, and he looks more uncomfortable with my obvious excitement. "And, thank you for letting me hang out with you guys."

He opens and shuts his mouth, but nothing comes out.

"That's when you say, you're welcome, Jo."

"You're welcome," he mumbles, making me grin harder.

Maybe Hayes is right, I'm a foreign object to Lochlan, and he doesn't know how to deal with me.

I bounce a few steps away towards my door and spin in a circle because I'm in such a good mood.

"Goodnight, Lochlan." I smile at him, and this time he's paralyzed, staring at me silently until I step inside and shut my door.

I slump against the cool surface and sigh. I did it. I'm going to help him get the money he needs for the security system, we're going to keep the bears safe, and I'm doing a damn good job at my first job ever.

This is the best day of my life!

* * *

The calendar slides an inch down the front of the refrigerator before I right it and add another magnet. It's filled with important dates and reminders for Lochlan about the business, and I added all the events I'd like to attend over the summer.

"What the hell are these?" Lochlan asks as he comes through the back door, noticing the hot pink sticky notes I replaced the boring yellow ones with.

"If you insist on communicating by ancient means, then I need to add a little excitement to it." I straighten my calendar again, and it draws his attention to the floral pattern I've picked. He grumbles and drops down into the kitchen chair to take his boots off.

"There's a Memorial Day Charity Banquet that I want to be our first event. It's honoring veterans and service members."

"I'm not a veteran."

"It's for everyone to attend, fundraise, and donate. Plus, your grandfather was a veteran."

"How'd you know that?"

How do I know that?

"His service photo is framed in the living room."

"Fine." He starts looking over some of the papers I left out for him as I tap my pointer finger against the space bar on my laptop.

He leans back in his chair and raises his arms over his head to rub his hands through his hair as he sighs, somehow making him look larger. He's wearing a plain gray T-shirt today and clings to his arms at the largest part of his bicep. I've never noticed that before. Or, how the material stretches across his chest when he raises his arms.

He has jagged bolts of black lightning tattooed on his forearm, scattered across his skin, ending just above his wrist. If you aren't looking closely enough, it looks vascular... Like ink in his veins.

"How often do you leave this place?"

"I go pick up feed twice a week, go buy new tools, and machinery. I drive hours in any direction to retrieve the bear when one needs to be transported here." He shrugs like, "What else do you want from me?"

"I meant, do you ever go anywhere for fun?"

"I don't have fun," he states plainly, and I roll my eyes, but unfortunately, I believe him.

"It's going to be a long summer," I mumble, turning my attention back to my laptop.

"I'm sure you'll make it interesting," he mutters, getting a beer from the fridge. It's only 3 pm.

"Are you done working for the day?"

"I'm never done working." He harrumphs, noticing me eyeballing his drink. "Don't worry, I've cut back recently," he says right before downing the rest of the can.

He grabs a water bottle next and sticks it in his back pocket, turning to snatch his boots off the floor before leaving out the back door.

Almost as soon as the backdoor latches shut, someone knocks on the front door.

There's no peephole, only small window cutouts toward the top of the wooden door. When I glance out, I see Frank at the same time that he sees me. He smiles, waiting for me to open the door. Which I do, reluctantly.

"Hi, Frank. Lochlan isn't here."

"Oh, I know. He was out on the other side of the property last I saw." His smile doesn't slip, but it makes me uneasy. He's never done anything to make me feel afraid of him, but he's bolder than the other guys. He says what's on his mind a little too easily.

"Actually, he was ju–" I try to correct him, but he interrupts, cutting me off.

"I was coming back from a beer run, and I wanted to invite you to the bunkhouse tonight for a fire."

"Oh, um, I don't know if I should." It seems innocent enough of a request, but Lochlan's voice echoes in my head. *No socializing. Behave.* "All the guys will be there?"

His mouth twitches in amusement. "Yes, ma'am. Of course."

"Maybe," I utter, shifting my weight and preparing to close the door, but he leans in, resting his forearm on the door jam.

"Frank, what the hell are you doing up here?" Lochlan's voice booms from the other side of the porch.

"Just getting back to work, boss." He tips his head to me and scurries down the porch steps by the time Lochlan gets to me.

"What did he want?"

"He invited me to a bonfire at the bunkhouse later. Will you be there?"

He contemplates my question, glancing toward Frank's retreating form. I watch his brow deepen into a furrowed glare. "I'll be there."

* * *

There's a pep in my step as I skip down to the bunkhouse in my new cute ankle boots. As I get closer, I can smell the wood burning and see the smoke rising around the back.

When I round the corner, all of the chatter hushes and

everyone looks at me. "Our pool champ is back," Hayes breaks the silence, pulling a chair near the fire and offering it to me.

There's a moment of awkward energy until the conversation picks back up, and I'm left wondering why.

"Hey, Boss! I thought you were taking off tonight?" Someone says suddenly. Lochlan appears around the corner of the barn like a cloud of smoke, silently blending into the night.

"Decided to stay back," he says, pointedly, cutting a look at Frank. He glances at me and Hayes next to me, a silent conversation happening between them while everyone else continues with their own.

"I thought you didn't have fun?" I ask him once he sits down a few feet away on the other side of Hayes.

"He doesn't. He leaves to take care of business," Hayes says, smirking at his friend. Lochlan shakes his head and ignores him. Once again, leaving me to interpret some cryptic social exchange.

Women aren't like this. They are usually over-sharers even with strangers. Prying information from anyone here is painful. I'm still trying to get all of their first and last names straight because they act like there's some mysterious code name they have to follow.

"Is this like our first big team bonding?" Ryker asks, earning a few groans of annoyance.

"No."

"Well, come on, now. We hardly know our girl," Frank says, setting a beer down on the arm of my chair without asking if I want one.

"Not your girl," Lochlan growls.

"It's okay, I can tell them a little bit. I'm going to drag you all around all summer to network, so we might as well be friendly," I say directly to Lochlan, and he grits his teeth subtly but ignores me.

"My name is JoAnna Montgomery, Jo for short, because only people who don't really know me call me by my full name. I'm 24 years old, and studying for my Master's in Biomedical Engineering with an interest in prosthetics. My favorite food is ice cream. I love watching movies. I have a collection of ten DVDs that I cherish and take everywhere."

"Damn. She's smart and pretty," Ryker says. Curtis kicks the leg of his chair in warning as if he had said something offensive.

I don't mind, I've had to work hard for both titles to be true.

"They call me Spock because I sold fraudulent Star Wars memorabilia to a museum. A hundred grand worth," he admits, and a couple of people laugh. "I don't even like sci-fi movies, so I didn't realize the nickname doesn't make sense until it had already stuck."

"I'm Rain because they caught me in a strip club throwing around fake currency. Making it rain," he adds proudly.

Okay... This has turned into a nickname and rap sheet show-and-tell, but they're being open, and I don't want to stop their momentum.

In the corner of my eye, I see Lochlan dig around in a cooler and pull out a white seltzer can. He hands it to Hayes, who puts it on my chair after removing the beer can that's still sitting unopened.

"I'm good at stealing cars," Ryker says when it's his turn.

"Not good enough, apparently," Arizona jabs. "I embezzled

money. And, I'm from Arizona." He makes a motion like 'hence the nickname'.

I open the seltzer at the same time Lochlan opens the beer he just swapped me.

"They call me Hawk because I was the lookout during a bank robbery... But, failed at it." The next guy says, making everyone laugh again.

"My name is Jordan, my friends call me Jordy. I got mixed up selling drugs, but I'm four years sober this summer," he admits proudly.

Rain claps him on the shoulder, and Jordy blushes, making me smile hard. I'm so proud of these people that I hardly know.

"Curtis?" Jordy deflects the attention, passing the imaginary speaking stick.

"Um, I'm from here in Langston. I never went to prison, but I went AWOL to attend my grandmother's funeral and got involved with a bad crowd. They got me hooked on fentanyl and strapped a bomb to me." He laughs humorously like a man who has coped with his trauma, but my jaw drops.

Poor Curtis.

"My buddy Jesse struck a deal with the military after he found out about this place. Once I got out of rehab, I committed to five years here instead of getting a dishonorable discharge and jail time. Still got these as evidence of what happened." He holds up his arms to show his scars before quickly covering them again with his sleeves.

"Proud of ya, kid," Seiver says, and Curtis nods in shy acknowledgment.

"Frank?" Seiver prompts.

"Drugs," Frank admits, not elaborating.

"Me, too. I'm sober 40 years," Seiver admits proudly, before lifting his can to take a drink. "From drugs," he clarifies with a wink in my direction, and it makes me chuckle.

"Boss, your turn," Frank prompts, and everyone falls silent.

Chapter Ten

Jo

The crackling of the fire and the cicadas vibrating in the trees behind us grow louder as the anticipation of what's to come weighs on us all. The stare down between Lochlan and Frank is more intense than the fire burning at the epicenter of this.

"She already knows, Frank. You can quit your games."

My cheeks warm. Why am I being brought into this?

"No games. We're all sharing, thought you'd like a turn." He doesn't even bother with his usual greasy smirk.

"Take a walk," Lochlan demands. Hayes grips the arms of his chair beside me, and I curl further into my chair like it will protect me from whatever is about to happen.

Frank stands from his seat, tossing his drink into the fire, causing a burst of embers before choosing reason and stalking inside.

"I'll make sure he goes to bed," Seiver says, following him into the barn. Lochlan and Hayes exchange a glance, but both visibly relax.

"Don't worry about it, Jo. He's drunk," Curtis tells me softly, attempting to ease the tension in the air.

"And, we're not drunk enough," Rain quips, and the rest of them laugh. Just like that, the bonfire resumes.

More than an hour of talking and staying clear of anything particularly serious goes by. It's chaotic and hilarious, and the most fun I've had in my entire life.

"Jo, why are you here?" Arizona asks me suddenly, drawing most of the attention to me. One set of dark eyes that I can feel burning into the side of my face.

"What do you mean? I needed a job?"

"No, I mean, why are you here with us? And, not out on a date with your boyfriend?"

"I guess I would be if I had a boyfriend," I giggle as he slumps in his seat further, both of us clearly feeling our alcohol content.

"I've got some friends back home if you're looking. No criminal history. Let me know." He raises his can to clink my nearly empty one. My third nearly empty one.

"No, thanks. I've been set up enough for one lifetime."

"What do you mean?" Jordy asks, tearing his eyes off of Arizona.

"My mother has arranged two engagements for me. Neither of which I consented to and had to bend over backwards to get out of." His eyes go wide, and I throw my head back and laugh. When my neck lolls to the side, my throat constricts.

Lochlan's staring into the fire with such hatred that I'm concerned for the well-being of the crushed can in his hand. I glance at Hayes beside me, and he's looking at the fire with a smirk on his face. Except his amusement fades as soon as Arizona directs his attention to him.

"Jensen, do you have a woman out there somewhere?"

"I do."

"Why the hell are you here, then?"

"Because she thinks I'm a ghost."

Back to the cryptic riddles that I cannot interpret with a buzz. "I think I need to go to bed," I stand suddenly, not able to contain a yawn. Three other people mimic me.

"I'll walk her back," Lochlan announces, standing from his chair. Everyone else sits.

"I don't need an escort."

"Non-negotiable."

We match pace all the way back to the big house in complete silence. "See uneventful. You could have stayed down there with them," I finally say as it's time to split paths, except I wobble slightly on one of the paving stones. He steps forward to steady me, but I correct my footing before he can. "I was just testing you."

He scoffs and shakes his head. "What am I going to do with you?" He mumbles it to himself before walking up the porch steps. "Go inside."

"I'm going."

"Lock your door," he adds when I continue standing in my doorway, looking at him.

"Ayay, Cap'n." I salute him as I shut my door, and barely catch him shaking his head at me. Maybe I'm drunker than I thought.

I just need a snack. My favorite thing in the world is a late-night treat.

Except that the basket of snacks I keep on my little counter is empty, other than a few sad granola bars. And, my mini fridge only has cans of sparkling water.

My bare feet scamper across my path to Lochlan's front door and I twist the knob hesitantly, tiptoeing to the kitchen once I'm inside. I'll be in and out quickly; he won't even realize I've been here.

Freezer. Freezer. Freezer. I stick my face into the icy air, then groan in disappointment.

"No ice cream in there," he says from behind me, making me jump.

"How'd you know I was looking for ice cream?"

"Wild guess." He's leaning against the door frame, watching me as I shut away my hopes and dreams of a sweet treat.

He's still in his same clothes from earlier, but he looks more casual now with no boots and his hair even more askew than normal. He looks tired, but not like he had been about to go to sleep.

"Who only keeps frozen vegetables in their freezer?" I continue my mission to find something to cure my buzz, and he watches as I open and close various cabinets, inspecting the contents within.

"Someone who needs an ice pack on a semi-regular basis."

"Why not buy ice packs?" I ask as I find his whiskey cabinet, sighing as I shut the door. He only shrugs in response.

His crossed arms barely move as he lifts a hand to point above my head, and I follow the path to the cabinet above the fridge. I don't bother to confirm before pulling one of the kitchen chairs over and stepping onto the seat. He watches on silently, letting me embark on my journey.

"Girl Scout cookies?" I ask in astonishment, pulling out one of the green boxes.

"And, Boy Scout popcorn. Marching band chocolate," he adds.

"You didn't strike me as a sweets guy."

"I'm not. That's my poison." He points to the whiskey

cabinet. "But, I can't walk past those damn booths without letting them rob me."

"Aw, Lochlan Dane is a philanthropist." He rolls his eyes as he comes over to steady the back of the chair as I transfer my loot to the countertop.

I plop down on the counter once I'm done and crack open the thin mints. My knees nearly brush his knuckles where they grip the chair.

He seems very concerned that I'm going to fall off this counter and hurt myself, but I am absolutely not that intoxicated.

"Should I expect to be ransacked like this regularly?"

"Yes." I bite into my cookie and sigh happily. "But I'm celebrating because I had a big exam today and I aced it."

"Of course, you did."

"Are you calling me smart?"

"No."

I finish my cookie slowly. "You totally are. That is the sweetest thing I've ever heard you say."

He shakes his head in exasperation. "Do me a favor, will ya?"

"Maybe."

"Don't drink with the guys unless I'm there." He watches me lean my head against the side of the fridge, pondering his request.

"I'll think about it."

"What am I going to do with you?" He mutters again, except this time he's close enough to hear that it's not a rhetorical question. I think he's really trying to figure me out.

"How did you get this scar, Lochlan?" He's close enough that I could reach out and touch it, but I don't dare.

He looks at me for so long, contemplating his next words, but I don't care. I'm lost in the depths of his tortured eyes. Without the permanent furrow in his brow, I can see how beautiful they are, but still so mysterious.

They leave me longing to find out every secret he keeps locked inside his hard head. I want to listen to all his burdens.

Just as his lips part and I think he might give me a straight answer, the front door slams open and we both jump.

"LOCH! FIRE!" I don't even know who screams the words or how I end up on the porch, but suddenly I'm standing atop the front steps watching an inferno engulf the old barn. It's ablaze, burning so hot that I have to shield my eyes from the light.

"Did you call 911?"

"They're ten minutes out," Hayes explains between bursts of talking into his handheld radio. There are guys dragging hoses toward the burning structure and others moving anything that they can out of its wake.

"Why aren't they spraying the fire?" I yell as I watch them hosing down the building next to the old barn.

"It's too hot, all we can do is keep it from spreading." Hayes doesn't take his eyes off the scene as he answers my panicked question.

"Fuck! How did this happen?" Lochlan roars, stomping toward the chaos. I start after him, being pulled by a magnet, when he whips around and stops me. "Stay!" He yells, making me flinch.

Even with all of the commotion, he's visibly distraught, noticing my body language. He takes a step toward the fire but immediately backtracks to where I'm standing immobile.

He threads his giant hands into my hair on either side of my

86

head and whispers into my ear, "Stay on the porch, please."

And then he's gone, running into the disaster zone while I stand motionless, wondering how this happened.

* * *

The smoke-filled air lingers, blocking all the early morning light. No one got any sleep, and all the guys are covered in a fine layer of ash.

"The fire chief definitely thinks it's arson," Sheriff Malec explains with a vacant look in his eyes. "We've seen something like this before."

"Where was Frank?" Lochlan asks Seiver.

"He was in the bunkhouse all night." Seiver shrugs.

"They'll keep investigating," Jackson explains. "I'm putting all my effort into finding out who likes starting fires around here."

Lochlan nods his head stiffly, clearly full of rage over this situation. He turns and walks away, silently dispersing the rest of the group.

"Hey, give me a minute." Jackson tugs on my elbow, pulling me to the side.

"Why didn't you tell me you were staying here?"

"It's a new development." The Sheriff and I haven't known each other very long, but his protective instincts have already umbrella'd over my life. Even though our situation is atypical, I appreciate his concern.

We talk for a few minutes in hushed tones before I catch Lochlan's glare from across the yard. "I need to get some sleep, I'll talk to you soon." I hug him before walking away, but he calls after me.

"You're sure about this, right?"

"Yes, I'm sure," I confirm with a smile, heading back to the guesthouse as he leaves in his cruiser.

My hand turns the door knob when I'm ambushed from behind by Mr. Grumpy.

"What the hell was that?"

"What?"

"If there's some weird shit going on between you and the Sheriff then you need to leave it off my property."

"Define weird?"

"Don't start with me, Jo."

"I'm a grown woman, and I don't need to explain all the details of my life with you."

"Like shit you don't."

We're exhausted, the night took a toll on us, and neither of us can curb the escalation happening.

"What, Lochlan? What do you want from me? Should I go back to being scared to breathe in front of you, or are we past that? Because that was miserable."

He scoffs. "Miserable for you? You make me feel like I'm back in fucking prison!"

There's a heavy beat of silence as I process his angry words.

I step back.

Then another step.

And, I slam my door right in his mean face.

God, what is wrong with me?

Why do I keep putting effort into people who don't care about me?

Because I have no one, and the pain of that is worse than

anything Lochlan could say to me.

No one cares about your problems, Jo.

My mother's voice nags in my head and forces a sob out of my throat. What is so terrible about me?

"Jo, open the door." Lochlan's voice penetrates my break-down, but it only lets the tears in my eyes loose as I slump to the floor. *"I'm sorry. Shit, Jo. I'm sorry."*

"Go away," my voice cracks, and I cry harder.

I crawl to the tiny single stall shower and raise my hand high to crank the handle. With my knees to my chest, I sit on the cold tile floor, fully clothed, and let the water beat down on me until the stench of smoke dissipates from my hair.

By the time I make it to my bed, I'm a shivering, exhausted shell of a person.

Chapter Eleven

Jo

I refuse to leave the guesthouse until 8 am on Monday.

When I do, I'm wearing my favorite tan pencil skirt, white blouse, and my strappy nude heels. My blonde hair is perfectly blown out and curled, my makeup is impeccably done. I even broke out more of my jewelry to dress myself up.

The best cure to having my spirit crushed into a million pieces is to look like it never happened at all.

I walk into Lochlan's empty kitchen by 8:01 and start packing up all of the textbooks I had left piled on the table. When I hear the backdoor open, I scramble, shoving them into my backpack.

"I wasn't expecting you so early," Lochlan says from the doorway. I don't look up, avoiding eye contact while I struggle to zip my bag.

"I'm only grabbing my stuff, I'm on my way out."

"Jo, I need to apologize," he starts, but I cut him off.

"No, you don't. I wanted to be friends with you, but you drew a line. You're my boss, and I will respect that."

"I shouldn't have said what I said."

"But you did." I throw my bag over my shoulder and step toward the front door.

"You're leaving?" He exhales roughly.

"I have to go return these books to campus and get my new ones for the summer semester. I'll be back this afternoon to get some work done." I give him my fakest, cheeriest smile. "Enjoy your day."

Each step of my heels across the hardwood floors is echoed by his boots behind me, following me to the front porch.

He watches me get in my car, and I watch his form disappear in my dust cloud as I leave.

* * *

Two weeks go by, and I'm still firm in my decision to keep my distance from Lochlan. Aside from a few words every day to communicate what needs to be done for the sanctuary, I haven't spoken to him or any of the guys.

When I'm not at school or in Lochlan's kitchen, I'm studying or working on my Master's thesis.

I've organized every single piece of paper in his filing cabinet, I've set up auto-pay on every bill that I can, and I've written out the checks that need to be signed for the things still being paid the old-fashioned way.

I shouldn't have to converse with Lochlan about anything for at least six months at this rate.

"Are you done for the day?" He asks from behind me as soon as I shut my laptop.

"Yeah, I have to take my car in for an oil change."

"I can do it."

"No, it's okay. I couldn't ask you to do that." *Wouldn't ask.* I walk out onto the porch, but he follows me.

"Let me change your oil."

I don't know why he wants to, but I've been dreading hanging out in some greasy auto shop. I'm almost two thousand miles overdue.

My fingers fidget with my key fob until he holds his hand out for them.

"Okay," I concede. "Thanks." I hand him my keys as he saddles past me.

"I'll take it down to the garage if you want to ride down with me," he announces when he notices me standing in the same spot.

"Oh, um. Sure." I climb into my passenger seat, immediately regretting it as he shuts the door behind me and walks to the driver's side. My little BMW is way too small, and he's way too big.

He takes up so much space that our bodies are within inches of each other, and I'm hyper aware of it.

My brain has replayed how it felt when he threaded his fingers into my hair the night of the fire every time I close my eyes to go to sleep…

I'm so deprived of any type of intimacy that I'm touch-starved.

But, here he is, so close to me that I could rest my head on his shoulder if I wanted to. I don't want to, not with someone who thinks it's a chore to deal with me.

Like he's back in prison…

It was admittedly the worst ten years of his life, and I'm comparable. The pain of that is still as sharp as it was the moment he said it, and it makes the air in here suffocating.

But, I'm desperate to keep this job and to have a place to stay that my father can't touch, so I have to endure it.

"You can sit over here." Lochlan points to a short rolling stool before he lifts my hood and pulls out the oil dipstick. He wipes it clean, sticks it back in, and then pulls it out again to check the level. "You're pretty low."

"My parents' assistant used to keep track of all the upkeep on the family vehicles. But, once I moved out, I lost all special treatment."

He looks at me briefly, "I'll fill your windshield wiper fluid, too. Hayes knows more about cars, he can make sure everything else is running right."

"Oh, no, that's okay, I didn't mean to–"

"You're a part of this place now. We'll take care of it," he insists, pumping the jack to raise my car, flexing the corded muscle along his bicep.

Part of this place.

A tingle emerges behind my nose and travels higher, making my eyes glossy.

"You okay?" He asks after I raise my head to ward off the unshed tears.

"I think the fumes in here are getting to me."

He opens a side door to encourage more ventilation, but it only makes the moisture in my eyes worsen.

"Did you always know that you'd live here? Follow in your grandfather's footsteps?" I ask, trying to distract myself.

"The day my mother dropped us off on his doorstep to take off for a more exciting life, my grandparents never hesitated to treat us as their own. They were my parents, and I knew I'd spend the rest of my life repaying them for their generosity."

"Us?"

"I have a little sister. Becky."

"She didn't want to work here?"

He scoffs, "Hell no. She couldn't wait to leave. She loved my grandparents, too, but she was a free spirit like our mom was. She traveled for a few years before she came back to help my pops out after my grandmother died, and I was in prison. As soon as I got out, I told her to take off. I couldn't let her life suffer because of my shit. She settled down and has a family now."

"You never wanted a family?" I ask hesitantly. His eyes go distant, and I know I asked the wrong question.

"No."

I don't think he's telling me the truth, but I let it go. He's my boss. Not my friend.

"What about you? What's next once school's finished?" I'm surprised he asked me a question; I was expecting all conversation to cease.

"I don't know. I thought about touring different universities in different parts of the country and maybe pursuing a PhD or another Master's degree."

"Damn."

"I enjoy learning."

He raises his hands in a "I'm not judging" way.

"What about a family?" He asks, and my cheeks heat.

"I want to get married, but no family."

He tilts his head in surprise.

"My family didn't exactly give me a good example of family life. I'll pass," I add, defusing the questions I see stewing in his brain.

"My sister is coming over for dinner," he says while

lowering my car to the ground. "You should come. She'll also insist," he adds under his breath.

* * *

"Uncle Lochy!!" The little girl with beaded braids in her hair screeches out the window of a red SUV, scrambling out of the car and jumping into his arms as soon as they park.

"Eminem." He presses a kiss on top of her head. "It's been too long."

"Who is this?" She asks, smiling sweetly at me. I'm not great with kids' ages, but I'd guess she's 7 or 8.

"This is Jo, she works here."

"Jo, huh? And here I thought this place was a cockpit," a woman with a blonde pixie cut says.

"Jo, this is Tessa, my sister's wife. And, my sister, Becky." His sister looks a lot like him. Tall with dark hair, French braided down her back. "And their pet velociraptor, Emory."

"I'm not a velociraptor, Lochy. I'm a princess." She points to the glittery butterfly and flower clips in her hair to prove her point.

"You're right, I'm sorry."

"Are you able to stay for dinner?" His sister asks, and Lochlan glances at me like 'told ya'.

"I invited her already. She's staying in grandma's old studio," he explains, and I watch her eyes widen briefly before she recovers.

"Hmm, interesting," Becky smirks, but turns around to grab something from her backseat. "I brought pizza, take these."

She plops three boxes in his arms and walks ahead of us into the house.

"She never fails to make herself right back at home," he mumbles.

Chapter Twelve

Jo

T hey're so normal.

It's like watching bees buzz around a hive, except the little girl, Emory, is at the center. Her mom carries over a slice of pizza and drops it on her plate, her other mom pulls paper towels from the roll beside the sink and divides them out among us while Lochlan lets his niece talk his ear off.

I somehow gathered that they own a brick oven pizza shop and that they've been together since college. Becky is Mommy, Tessa is Momma.

I can hardly take a bite of the pizza sitting in front of me, even though it looks incredible. I don't want to blink and miss a moment of this when it's better than anything I could have imagined a normal family could be.

Because they love each other.

"Jo, can you teach me how to do pretty makeup like you?" Emory asks, focusing everyone's attention on me suddenly.

"Oh, um," I don't know how to respond because I don't want to step on any toes, but I don't want to reject her either.

"Emory has been obsessed with all the glamorous things

since she saw her first play on Broadway over spring break," Tessa says, twirling Emory's pigtail around her finger playfully.

"My moms aren't very good at girly stuff even though they're both girls." She rolls her eyes in an exasperated kid way that makes them both laugh.

"Jo was Miss North Carolina." The hive goes silent at Lochlan's announcement.

"Miss Teen," I correct him.

"A beauty queen!" Emory squeals, smushing her hands to her cheeks.

Embarrassment fills me, and I'm not entirely sure why. I'm used to that information about me being made known, but I guess I'm used to being mocked for it.

"I would love to teach you makeup, Emory." I smile at her genuinely, and she erupts in another squeal, clapping her hands.

An hour later, I'm seated cross-legged on the floor in Lochlan's living room with my makeup bag, teaching Emory how to apply eye shadow in the most age-appropriate way I can.

She, of course, wanted to use the boldest and most sparkly colors, and I would never tell her no.

She giggles endlessly, using her fingertips to smear pink blush across my cheeks, and I don't need to look in the mirror to know it's probably the best I've ever looked.

"Am I beautiful?" She asks, but her attention is directed at the small lighted mirror sitting on the coffee table, and to the man standing in its reflection behind us.

Lochlan's leaning casually against the wall with his arms folded across his chest, watching in amusement.

"You're the most beautiful girl in the world, Eminem." Her smile widens at his sweet words, and my heart does a little skip. The man who makes men scurry in fear is wrapped around this little girl's finger.

"What about Jo?" She asks innocently, but he's already studying the streaks of purple above my eyes, the fingerprints of blush, and the glitter that glosses my lips. He looks longer than necessary, and I can only imagine the response he's trying to articulate to avoid hurting his niece's feelings.

"Beautiful," he forces out.

"Jo, can you do my nails like yours, too?" She asks, tearing my attention from Lochlan's piercing stare.

"I might have some nail polish somewhere, but I get these done at a nail salon. It's called acrylics."

"I want acrylics," she pouts, and it makes me laugh.

"It's bad for your real nails. You should wait until you're much older," I suggest, seeming to appease her.

"When I'm older, I'm going to be a veterinarian," she exclaims proudly, over-enunciating the word only slightly.

"That's amazing. You love animals?"

"Yep! I'm going to rescue all the animals and bring them here to take care of them. Lochy said I can do whatever I want since I was hand-gifted in a basket to run this place."

"What do you mean?"

"I'm the only stray he's ever kept," she states proudly.

"She gets it all. The sole inheritor," Lochlan explains. "Becky and Tessa adopted her after she was abandoned at the front gate. She was only one year old, buckled into a car seat in the middle of March."

I gasp, but Emory doesn't look the least bit affected. She must know this story well.

How can people be so cruel?

Leaving a baby in the elements, not knowing if they'll be safe or cared for. It's unimaginable.

It's not fair.

"I'm sorry, I need some air." I jump up from my seat and run to the front porch before collapsing to my butt on the porch steps.

The heel of my palms dig into my forehead, trying to understand this cruel world. It's only a few minutes later that Becky comes out of the house and sees me sitting alone.

"I don't know what your story is, Jo, but this place is really good for giving second chances. My brother can be a bonehead, but I'm glad he's letting you help him."

"He didn't want to hire me."

"Can you blame him? He has trust issues with women." She snorts, knowing it's an understatement. "He's also fiercely protective of his own."

"He warned me not to make friends with any of the guys and plenty of other things, but I keep screwing up. I keep making him mad. Even when I don't know why."

"I meant what I said, he's a bonehead, but he also sees you as someone to protect now. He'll do that in the only way he knows how, even if it doesn't make sense." Her cryptic advice reminds me of Lochlan.

"Well, he's definitely hard to interpret sometimes." I laugh when she does.

"Thank you for helping him here. And, Emory. I think she's going to talk about meeting a beauty queen all week at school." She stands up, noticing them coming out of the door, Lochlan right behind them.

"She's wonderful. It was nice meeting all of you." I smile

as Emory comes from behind and snakes a hug around my neck.

"Bye, Miss Jo. I'll see you next time!"

Once they say their goodbyes and leave, the air is thick with Lochlan's presence.

"You alright?"

What a silly question. I'm never alright, not truly. "I'm fine."

"No, you're not." He sits down next to me for only a second before he shifts a few feet to the side to lean against the porch railing instead, as if he can't stand to be near me.

"Hearing about Emory being abandoned just upset me, I guess."

"Becky and Tessa were newly married, still figuring things out, but they knew they could give her a good life. It worked out."

I nod, not really sure what to say.

"What's really bugging you?"

"Nothing, I'm fine. Thanks for inviting me to dinner."

* * *

Fresh spray tan, fresh coat of matching paint on my fingers and toes, and a new white dress to wear on the biggest weekend of summer. Tonight's charity event will host all the biggest businesses and prominent families. Charities and politicians of all statuses will mingle and negotiate for their cause.

And, it's my job to make it look like Second Chance Sanctuary belongs there just as much as everyone else.

"Lochlan, are you ready?" I yell as soon as I open his front door, stopping so hard my shoes pinch my toes when I see him thumping down the stairs.

The man attempting to button the cuff of his black dress shirt is not the Lochlan Dane I know.

His hair is still long but trimmed and styled back so it's not obscuring his face. There's a rogue curl falling down over his forehead that looks perfectly imperfect.

His beard is gone, but he's not completely clean-shaven. There's enough stubble to leave a shadow, and you can see an indented white scar that curves along his chin and disappears underneath.

But, most surprising is a mustache that matches his features impeccably.

It's trimmed precisely along his top lip, not too long on the sides or unfitting in any way.

I've never felt drawn to that style of facial hair, but I've never seen it look so right. He has always been attractive, I'm not blind, but at this moment, I realize how attracted I am to *him*.

My heart thunders erratically as I cope with my spiraling thoughts... *I'm attracted to my boss.*

His thick fingers struggle with the tiny buttons, and the veins in his forearms strain as I blink at him.

"I only own this shirt and one tie. I wore them to my grandfather's funeral." He holds up a gray and black striped tie that I didn't notice he was holding. My tongue is thick in my throat, and I can't come up with thoughts to put into

102

words.

Black hair, black shirt, dark denim wranglers, and cowboy boots. He's a tall, dark, and dangerous southern gentleman.

He's still holding his tie, looking at me expectantly. "Jo?"

"No tie." I throw it over the banister and fix the top button on his shirt so it hangs open just enough to show a peak of his sun-tanned skin, but not the dark chest hair hiding just beneath.

The testosterone oozing off of him is authentic and natural to his environment. He's a man who has nothing to prove to anyone, but he's doing what's necessary to take care of this place that he calls home.

I'm already less nervous about how tonight will go because he'll be with me.

"I like your haircut," I finally admit, softly, buttoning the cuff at his wrist for him, and hiding away the ink of his tattoo just barely.

"Hayes insisted."

"He works on cars and does haircuts?" I straighten his collar, making sure it's creased just right, purposefully letting my fingers linger longer than necessary.

"He did my tattoos, too." *Plural.*

He has more than one. That means the lightning bolt is the only one I can see.

"He does everything, then?" I tease.

"He does everything because he's good at everything." He huffs in an annoyingly proud big brother way. Not that I know what that's like, but it makes me smile regardless.

"Are you nervous?" My hands smooth the imaginary wrinkles across his chest, giving me an excuse not to look him in the eyes.

103

"No," he lies. I can tell. "Are you?"

"No," I admit, truthfully. "This is your world behind these gates, but my world is out there. I can play the game with the best of them," I smile and look at him finally, but he's staring at me fiercely.

My hands are motionless, resting on his chest.

"Let's go." I clap them against him playfully, pretending that my touch was only friendly.

And, not at all curious.

Chapter Thirteen

Lochlan

Every nerve ending in my body is screaming at me to get up and hightail it out of this packed banquet hall. The noise of surface-level conversation vibrates my eardrums in a painful way.

I've never been in a room with this many people in it, and for good reason. Every head turned my way, or pair of eyes that catch mine makes the boulder on my chest weigh down on me further.

Most of them probably don't know who I am, but it only takes one person to whisper a lie about me for the whole room to go abuzz with suspicion.

He's a sex offender.

Lie.

He was in prison.

True, but they never include that I was falsely accused.

I heard he paid off a judge.

I've never had the type of money to sway people with money. Not like the people in this room.

As soon as we arrived at the doors, Jo was pulled away to go speak to people she knew. She encouraged us to find our table, and we took it. Seiver, Arizona, and Jordy are the lucky ones tonight. She suggested that bringing some of my guys to the events would be helpful, and I can't for the life of me tell that woman no.

I've tried. Many times. But somehow she still twists my arm behind my back without ever touching me.

Except for today. Today she touched me.

"Do you want another one, boss?" Jordy asks, pointing to my empty glass. This place is too sophisticated to serve beer in a can.

"If you see this empty, fill it up."

He fake salutes me and gets up to go to the bar, and I scan the hall for the hundredth time, looking for–

Her.

My eyes find her on the opposite side of the vast room, skirting her away around people and tables as expertly as if she were dancing.

A serene smile graces her lips that only grows wider anytime someone grabs her attention with a word or a wave. But her eyes, those rich brown eyes that fill you with warmth every time she looks at you...

It's excruciating when she looks at anyone but me with them.

She carries herself so elegantly, her head always high and on a swivel, blissfully approachable. Everyone in the room is drawn to her. Necks bend to watch her walk by in those shoes that accentuate every muscle in her tanned legs. Light was invented to catch the thickness of her thighs, hitting perfectly below the hem of her dress.

A dress that hugs every curve on her body in a way that has brought grown men to their deaths for centuries.

You can see the moment when stray eyes catch a glimpse of the bouncing blonde hair flowing down around her in waves as she passes by.

Everyone strains to watch a gorgeous woman striding across the room, hoping she'll head toward them.

Does she even realize what men would do to have a woman like her choose them in a room full of people?

To have her look at them with her full attention despite the chaos surrounding her. To have that smile be directed right at them because no one else deserves it.

She's a commanding presence, dominating the attention of every single person in this room. She's crossing the room looking for someone, some lucky motherfucker who doesn't deserve her time or–

Oh. She's looking for me.

Her pretty, bright eyes lock onto mine, and I see her dial in on me. Those long lashes squint as her eyes crinkle, an excited smile forming on her glossy pink lips. The single dimple that forms at the top of the apple of her cheek when she's really happy makes it hard to breathe.

God dammit, she's the most beautiful woman I've ever seen.

I've tried to get used to it, but I can't. It knocks me off my feet every time I look at her.

"You guys! I've been looking for you everywhere!" She chirps so enthusiastically that everyone within a 50-mile radius grins. She's an enigma that everyone wants a piece of.

20 years ago, I would have assumed I'd be lucky enough to marry a girl like her. 18 years ago, I thought I had met the woman I was going to spend the rest of my life with.

Then everything came crashing down around me.

Eight years ago, I stepped foot outside of the prison walls and swore I'd never fall for a woman's lies again.

Turns out I wouldn't have the opportunity anyway.

I would be recognized in a grocery store and watch a young mother shield her babies away from me as if I were a monster.

I would have a polite conversation with someone in public and then be avoided the next time I saw them because they had finally heard the rumors about me.

I was stained.

Damaged goods.

No one wanted to be dragged into the depths of hell that was my new reality, anyway.

Even being near me is a risk to Jo's reputation.

Normally, I'd stand at her approach, a gesture hardwired into my brain as a man who was raised to respect women, but my frame would only draw attention to our association.

I stay seated.

My existence is bleak, and she has so much to look forward to; I don't want my disease to spread.

"I already have two companies that have vowed to donate to Second Chance Sanctuary," she tells us proudly.

"Vowed? What does that mean?"

"It means they'll go to work on Monday morning and tell their assistant to write a check." She winks, making Jordy and Arizona cheers her with their drinks across the table.

She glances around like she's looking for a chair, and I kick Seiver's seat, encouraging him to go take a trip to the bar. He takes the hint humorously, raising his arms as he stands. "I need to stretch my legs. Can I get ya a drink, Jo?"

"Vodka-water with a lime wedge, please." She takes his seat before noticing all of our grimaces. "It's not that bad."

"You don't like beer, but you like that?"

"I like beer."

I look at her curiously. I thought she was tipsy the night we played pool, but she had barely had a sip when I took her can. I assumed it's because she wasn't a fan of the taste.

"It has too many calories," she adds.

"Jesus Christ," I mutter to myself. She has the most perfect body I've ever seen, and she's worried about calories.

"Trust me, if you had someone mocking you relentlessly the moment you hit double-digit sizes, you'd watch what you consumed, too."

"Aren't all adults double-digit sizes?"

She snorts. "Not women's sizes. I needed a ten by the time I was 20, and my mother held an intervention and told me to get liposuction."

"I don't know what any of that means."

She rolls her eyes at me but doesn't elaborate.

"That person right there." She leans near me, pointing across the room toward the stage. "They own all the biggest hospitals in the state."

Someone at the table next to us side-eyes me and Jo, and I instinctively, but reluctantly, put a couple more inches of space between us.

"And that woman is Miss North Carolina. She lost to me during the Miss Teen pageant and hates my guts. Even though I stopped competing she talks shit about me every time we're in the same room."

She leans closer again, completely oblivious to what people might think of her association with me, and whispers. "That's my brother, Conrad."

Beside the tall, slender man she's pointing to is someone

I recognize. "That's our Mayor, Randall Porter. He showed up the day after my grandfather died with his mother and offered to buy my property."

"Wow, no wonder he wants to be in cahoots with my brother. Seedy politicians always gravitate toward each other."

"You really think that about your own brother?"

"I don't think... I *know* he's rotten. He takes after–"

"Your father," I interrupt, seeing the tall politician walk into the room.

"Have you met him?"

"No. I've only seen photos." Everything he did to exonerate me was done through lawyers and heaps of paperwork. "Will you introduce me?"

"Oh, um. I don't know if that's a good idea..."

"I need to shake his hand, Jo. He saved my life." She glances back and forth between me and her father, looking unsure.

"Okay, but let me do most of the talking. I don't think he's going to be who you think he is," she mutters under her breath.

I'm too overwhelmed to register why she's biting her lip. My focus is entirely in my own head, determining what I should say to the man who listened to my grandfather's pleas to free me.

It's like static in my ears, drowning out all the other noise around me.

"JoAnna, I'm happy you saw reason and decided to join us tonight," the well-dressed but pensive woman beside him says. There is hardly any resemblance, but I assume it's her mother.

"Mom, Dad," she ignores her mother's comment, "This is

Lochlan Dane, he wanted to introduce himself."

I look down on the man by a few inches, but I watch him size me up regardless. There is obvious scrutiny on his face, but nothing that tells me he recognizes my name. I see the moment he looks at the scars on my face and the judgment that passes over him.

"Sir, it's an honor to meet you, finally." I hold out my hand to shake his, needing this moment to erase all the years of pressure I've built up thinking about this interaction.

He grabs my hand but doesn't shake it. "How exactly do you know my daughter?"

"He's my boss, Dad. I'm interning at Second Chance Sanctuary." *Interning?*

He drops my hand without giving me a chance to say anything, without actually shaking it.

"Second Chance Sanctuary? Never heard of it."

"It's for school."

I finally register how slumped her shoulders are and how the vibrant woman is wilting right in front of me.

"This is ridiculous," her mother snips.

"We had a deal," Jo argues, looking at her father pointedly.

"I hope your boss knows how important this election is for your brother, JoAnna," he says directly to her as if no one else is present, talking down to her in a way that I'd never accept from anyone at the sanctuary. Anyone, period.

"I'll give it the same level of concern that any of you have ever given me." As soon as the words leave her mouth, she looks surprised that she said them and clears her throat.

Her mother glares at me for the briefest moment before returning her attention to her husband. "Honey, this is a family matter. Let's discuss this later."

"Was there something else, then?" Her father asks, redirecting his attention back to me. This is the part where I should say thank you. I should praise his kindness for getting me out of prison.

"No." I turn my back on him and walk away, but not before hearing him scoff. I clear the doors and grab the handrail along the stairs to keep myself from doubling over.

The gnawing pit in my stomach has turned to fiery anger.

"I'm so sorry, Lochlan," Jo says, busting through the doors behind me. "I ruined it. You didn't even have a chance to talk to him."

"Stop," I sigh.

"No, it's my fault, they were too focused on scolding me and-"

"Jo, stop!" I snap at her, and she slams her mouth shut.

"I wasn't going to stand there and kiss his ass after hearing the way he spoke to you."

"But," she starts before I cut her off.

"All the stuff you've told me and the way he treated you in front of me after he knew I was your boss." I shake my head. "That's not a man who gets my respect, Jo."

"Oh my God." She leans against the railing next to me and closes her eyes, tipping her head up to the night sky.

"What?"

"He's horrible. He's the most horrible person I've ever met in my entire life, and you're good. You are too good for him. I knew you'd never like him," she admits, a freeing smile overtakes her face. "No one ever believes me."

She thinks I'm good?

"I would have believed you."

"Maybe, but I had to let you come to the conclusion on

your own. I couldn't crush your idea of him. Not without cause."

"Your parents treating you like shit is enough cause for me." She's standing so close to me that I have to look down to speak to her. Her big, fawn eyes stare at me in relief as if weight has been lifted off her chest.

If she keeps looking at me like that, I'll go inside and kick the Miss Teen runner-up's ass just to keep her smiling.

And that is why I need to stay away from Jo Montgomery.

Chapter Fourteen

Jo

I wouldn't consider this evening a win, but it wasn't a complete failure either. I secured donations and relationships with several people interested in helping the rehabilitation efforts of the bears and the parolees.

I felt confident and in my element advocating for these men who have become my friends. Well, coworkers. Lochlan has been kinder to me, but I won't overstep.

He looked to be in genuine pain the entire event. By the time I found them at their table, he looked like he was being tortured. As far as I know, nobody had even spoken to him.

"Hey, boss. I need nicotine. Can you stop at the carryout?" Arizona asks on our way back from the function.

We're close enough now, there is only one possible place left to stop before we head up the mountain to the sanctuary. It's a mediocre gas station with a lackluster food counter that's treasured like the royal palace because it's the only one for miles.

"I'm not a fucking taxi driver. It's late, we're not stopping." Arizona and Jordy both groan. Seiver chuckles.

We continue driving in relative silence, other than the

radio, while I inventory the snacks I have in the guesthouse. I was so busy getting ready for the event tonight that I hadn't gone to the store to stock up.

"You want something?" He asks me suddenly.

"Oh, it's okay. We don't have to stop."

He pulls into the gas station anyway. "Go on, I'll fill up while we're here."

Jordy and I enter a silent race and rush the doors, barely managing to squeeze through at the same time, giggling like kids.

I like him a lot. He's always positive and ready to laugh. He's easy to talk to, unlike most men.

We both head toward the candy aisle, but while I'm deciding what I might want, I watch his head follow Arizona across the other aisle. "I think I might want some chips," he announces unnecessarily.

"Then go get your chips." I smile at him, and he nods, walking over to where Arizona is filling his hands with snacks. He offloads some of what he's holding, and they walk over to check out together.

I try not to be jealous. One day, I'd like the simple friendship and innocent flirting. The butterflies before a first date. The anticipation of that first hug, first kiss.

I want roses strewn across the bed. A white knight and glass slippers.

I want someone who wants me for everything I am, and nothing that I'm not.

Someone who doesn't mind my ice cream obsession.

I've wandered over to the freezer section, but can't decide if I want my usual favorite or a new seasonal flavor.

The door chimes as someone exits, and I assume that means

my time is up. Jordy and Arizona are probably already back in the truck and Lochlan's going to be pissed that he has to wait on me.

The freezer door swings closed, and I take a step to my right, but there are two guys standing at the end of the aisle. They're not paying attention to me, but they're blocking my lane to the checkout.

I pivot to the left to go up the other aisle, but when I go toward the checkout again, they're standing there, looking at me.

"Excuse me, I just need to get by." I motion to the front counter as if they don't already know.

"We don't see much like you around here," the older guy says, widening his stance.

He doesn't look like he has any interest in letting me by, but unfortunately, it's so ingrained in my DNA to be polite to people, I have a hard time telling anyone they're making me uncomfortable.

Luckily, it doesn't matter.

Lochlan comes through the door before I have a chance to deter them. He doesn't glance around and notice the confrontation; he was locked in on it the moment his feet hit the welcome mat.

His icy glare gets closer to the two men until he's standing right at their backs. "Do we have a problem?" The eerie timber of his voice raises the baby hairs at the nape of my neck.

The two men part like the Red Sea, dispersing to separate aisles without a word, or daring to look at Lochlan. I don't blame them.

If I were them, I'd be scared, too.

He jerks his head in a "come on" motion and I jet past him with my two silly pints of ice cream.

"Do you want me to stick around until they leave?" Lochlan asks the cashier over my head. She's an older woman who should definitely be retired; her thin gray hair is pulled back in a low ponytail, and she has sparkly blue fingernails that match her eye shadow.

"Don't you worry about them. They're pests, but they don't have enough balls between the both of them to actually bother a woman." She laughs, rasping from her lungs like a long-time smoker. "I'd kick their asses anyways."

"I know you would," Lochlan says, with a small smirk on his face. It's a comfortable interaction, he's familiar with her. He throws a twenty on the counter before she tells me the total. "Let's go," he mumbles to me without waiting for change.

It isn't until I'm back in the truck that I can feel the tension rolling off his shoulders in waves. No one dares to speak as if the tiniest spark and the cab will combust.

The silence follows us until we're through the gates of the sanctuary, and Lochlan drives down to the bunkhouse to drop the guys off. Seiver, Arizona, and Jordy get out of the backseat, and Lochlan follows. "Sit tight."

I watch him through the window as he grabs Arizona and Jordy both by the collar, reprimanding them harshly, but it's too muffled inside the truck to tell what he's saying. He tosses them away roughly and climbs back into the driver's seat as if nothing happened.

"What was that about?"

"Nothing."

"Oh, we're keeping secrets, then?"

"I don't know what you're talking about."

"Yes, you do. You talk in riddles. Big man use little words." I mock like a caveman as he parks the truck.

"Are you done?"

I get out and slam my door dramatically in response. Why does he have to make everything so difficult?

Every time I feel like I crack his shell a hairline, he comes along with super glue and seals any evidence of its existence.

"I told them that the next time they leave you alone in a fucking gas station, I'd bash their fucking skulls in."

His confession stops me just before I get to the guesthouse.

"Why would you tell them that? It's not their job to watch out for me? It was those other weirdos' fault."

"Their job is to do what I tell them to. And, if they're too dumb to realize that there could have been a worse outcome to what they did, then they need to be reminded not to be dumb asses."

"You're ridiculous."

"No, you're naive." His condescending words roll over me painfully.

He probably doesn't realize how close to home his comment hits. How being sheltered by my parents has set me back in life significantly. That's why I've worked so hard in school. I can control my knowledge, and no one can take it from me.

"Maybe I am naive, but they shouldn't be blamed for it. I'll apologize to Arizona and Jordy in the morning."

"You better fucking not."

"If you think I'm going to listen to you about this, then you're naive."

"You're the only person who gets away with this shit, Jo."

He curses under his breath and stomps up the porch steps.

"Lochlan!" I call after him.

"What?" He yells back, *fully* annoyed with me.

"Can you take my ice cream inside? They won't fit in my mini fridge."

He stomps back down the steps and over to me before I can take a step in his direction. "Give me the fucking ice cream."

"Thank you."

"You're welcome," he grumbles.

* * *

Jo: **The guys are having another fire on Friday**

Lochlan: **No**

Jo: **I didn't even ask a question**

Lochlan: **Answer is no**

Jo: **Can I go?**

Lochlan: **No**

Jo: **URGGG!!**

Jo: **What else am I supposed to do all summer?**

Jo: **Are you ignoring me?**

Jo: **I'm going to the fire**

Chapter Fifteen

Lochlan

8 years ago...

The last chain link gate opens thunderously as I step through it with lead in my shoes. Ten years. It's been ten years since I've been outside of these prison walls.

The trees look different, the air feels crisper when you're breathing it in freely.

I'm afraid to take another step. As if one wrong move will get me thrown back into the hell I just escaped. All that I endured over the past decade was for nothing, and now my entire life is ahead of me, stained by my misfortune.

"Well, are you going to stand there gawking or are you going to give your old man a hug?" My grandfather's voice is like wind chimes and the creaking of a rocking chair on a summer day. Like home.

"Pops," I barely breathe the name out before his arms are around me, and the tears fall. I can't make another sound as I dampen his T-shirt. Ten long years without a hug from the man who means everything.

He should be standing here with my grandmother, but I'll never get the chance to hug her again.

We lost her while I was in this damn prison and I missed everything. I couldn't comfort my sister or support the man who raised me. I didn't get to say goodbye to the woman who was more of a mother to me than my own mom.

But I'm free now.

I have the chance to repay my grandfather for so many debts, but most importantly, for how tirelessly he fought to set me free. He drained his life's savings to get lawyers and special litigators. He hired private detectives and extra hands at the sanctuary to keep things running while he's been focused on all his efforts for me.

"I've got to tell you, Loch," he starts once we're nearly home, back up the mountain where I was raised. "This place probably isn't how you remember. Some things have gone to the back burner while I've been... Preoccupied."

"It shouldn't have been like this, Pops." I rub my hand across my head, the stubble scratching my palm. I've kept it short since the first week I was locked up. My size made a target, and one scuffle in the yard was all it took for me to eliminate any leverage they could get.

"Now, listen. Life can be a real pain in the ass sometimes. We don't always get the easy route; that's the way it is. You can't keep focusing on the past. We're moving forward the best we can. That's all we can do."

Keep moving forward.

How can I?

I lost everything in one day. My freedom, my good name, and the woman I thought would marry, have a family with.

Years of my life are gone, and I'll never get them back.

He pulls in through tall black gates that I've never seen before that connect to a perimeter fence on either side, lined with barbed wire along the top…

The entire property wasn't fenced in before, only the bear enclosures.

The barn is in rougher shape than I remember; the sliding doors are propped up on the sides and not attached to the tracks, boards are missing, and there are holes in the side and the roof. It looks ready to collapse.

The trucks parked in the grass with weeds growing up alongside them resemble a wasteland and not a farm. There used to be a chicken coop and goat pens, but they're empty. There aren't any animals that I can see.

"How are the bears?" I ask him as I survey the desolate property that once flourished.

"They're alright. We only have four right now. I haven't been able to travel to pick up any new rescues."

"Why not?"

"The trailer's busted. Can't keep it aligned."

"I have an idea for this place, Pops, but you have to trust me. It's going to take some time and an open mind."

"Son, I've got more faith in you than I've ever had in anyone, the Lord included. This place is yours, Loch. You do *whatever* you damn please and I'll support ya the best I can." He slaps my shoulder and walks toward the house that he and my grandmother shared for fifty years. The house I grew up in.

I'm going to make this place something for him. I'm going to keep it alive for him. Even as the looming black gates shut behind me and I'm trapped in another cage.

* * *

Damn, JoAnna Montgomery.

I've lived my life hidden away from the real world for years. I had accepted that I was destined to live in the shadows of society, avoiding glances or being recognized.

For eight years, any time I've had the itch for a little female company, I've made the conscious effort to travel far out of Rollins County to get away from anyone who might have an idea of who I am.

I don't expect much, and I definitely don't give a lot in return. An easy pick-up in a seedy bar. No names, no intimacy.

I prefer not to remember what their face looks like. I've taught myself how to stare straight through a woman without forming any opinion about their looks or retaining any memory of them.

But... Not tonight.

Every woman who looked in my direction was painfully disappointing.

Every smile that flashed my way was lacking.

No one compared to Jo.

It's a ridiculous problem to have because I'll never have a woman like Jo.

She's too young. Too innocent. She's the all-American sweetheart.

And, I'm the creature trapped behind the gates of Second Chance Sanctuary like all the other animals.

As I park my truck, failing in my mission for a little human connection, I feel more like a beast than ever.

I get out and stand in the moonlight, letting the weight of gravity crush me. 18 years ago, I never would have suspected my life would turn out this way, surrounded by people just as lost as me. Or worse, at night when I'm only accompanied by silence.

At least, it's usually silent.

Engines rev loudly as two trucks speed toward me from around the backside of what's left of the old barn. The flatbed comes barreling dangerously fast onto the gravel lot where I'm standing, blinding me with the headlights and blowing dust into my face before hitting one of the ruts in the dirt, and sending the truck airborne. All four wheels crash down at once, making the shocks groan painfully loud as the truck lands.

Ryker falls out of the passenger seat to his hands and knees, kissing the ground with his forehead. "Oh, sweet Jesus," he cries.

"What the fuck is this?" I yell at him before storming over to see who is driving. "Frank, you better have a damn good explanation."

"We heard people messing with the fences, went to investigate. Was just coming to let you know we missed 'em."

Rain, Arizona, Jordy run up from the other truck, looking more concerned than I'd expect for Ryker's well-being until the passenger seat tips forward. Curtis tumbles out of one of the side-facing jump seats, clutching his hand to his ribs.

"I'm sorry, boss. I'm sorry. We tried to get him to slow down." He stumbles to the side, and it's as if I've stepped into a pressure chamber.

My senses go numb, aside from a high-pitched ringing in my ears.

Because I see her.

She's clutching her head between her hands, hunkered down behind the driver's seat. She's terrified.

I can't hear Hayes and Seiver approach from the bunkhouse because a train whistle is splitting my eardrums from inside my head.

Chapter Sixteen

Jo

I haven't had very many instances of social peer pressure in my life. Mostly because I didn't hang out with enough of my peers to be persuaded into doing anything.

So when we were only one hour into the bonfire and heard tires peeling out along the west fences, my feet moved on autopilot when someone told me to climb in the work truck. Everyone was moving, going in that direction, and I followed.

There was none of my normal rational thought or careful planning. Before I knew what I was doing, I was facing Curtis in the backseat, and he was telling me to put my seat belt on with a worried look on his face.

Frank took off across the property, and I was holding on for dear life. It was like the worst roller coaster I could ever imagine. It was too dark to see out the windows, and without any anticipation of where we were going or what Frank had planned, I was getting bashed and banged against the back wall of the cab and the back of the driver's seat. Neither of which had padding for a blow.

Curtis was yelling at Frank to slow down, Ryker was echoing his pleading, but with more ad-libbed cursing and panic. I couldn't do anything but brace myself for the next impact.

All I could gather was that they saw a truck on the other side of the fence, and it took off once it saw us. Frank wanted to chase after it, but Arizona was driving the other truck and cut him off. I couldn't hear exactly what he said, but he called him a few choice words that set Frank off.

He slammed on the accelerator and we took off again. A scream ripped from my throat as my head slammed against the side window and bounced, smashing my cheek against the back wall.

Curtis unbuckled his seat belt and bounced as Frank hit a bump, crashing into the center console before leaning over me to shield my head from more damage. "Dammit, Frank. STOP THE TRUCK!"

"FINE!" He slams on the brakes, and it feels like the entire truck is going to explode into pieces as he crashes to a stop.

It's too silent as Ryker frantically claws his seat belt off and leaps from his seat. That's when I hear a very distinct growl that makes me want to curl into my seat further and cry.

He's mad.

Big mad.

"I'm sorry, boss. I'm sorry. We tried to get him to slow down." Curtis's voice is hollow in my ears as he gets further away from me. I can't look. I can't look.

I have to.

My eyelids crack open one at a time, but I don't have to search for what I'm looking for at all. Lochlan is standing directly in my line of sight, staring at me through the passenger side door.

His eyes are wide with fury, but his jaw is set, locked so

127

tightly I can see the muscles working the side of his face. He lunges suddenly, his frame blocking all the light from the moon as he grabs Frank by his shirt and forcefully drags him out of the driver's seat. As soon as he's through the passenger door, he's launched into the dirt.

He hardly has a moment to cry out in pain when Lochlan grabs him by the back of the neck like a rag doll and throws him against the porch steps as if he weighs nothing, brutally knocking the wind out of him.

Then he's on him.

His fist connects with Frank's cheek, bouncing his head against the wooden boards. The impact of the second punch makes his neck snap to the side with a sickening crunch.

I brace myself for the third blow and the damage it will inevitably cause, but it never comes.

His forearm drives into his chest, pinning him down as the other hand grips his throat. "You're done. You're fucking done. I should kill you," his voice thunders, rattling my bones.

He is going to kill him. Even with how dark it is, I can see the redness of Frank's face turning purple. His eyes are bulging with exertion to breathe, and the fear that he might not be able to again.

He's going to kill him.

And no one is doing anything. Everyone is watching on like spectators while I'm frantically searching for the answer to this problem. No one is reacting at all until my eyes catch Hayes's.

"Loch." His voice calls out after he tears his gaze from mine. "LOCH!" He barks louder, finally drawing the angry man's attention. "That's enough."

Lochlan glares at him as they have a silent standoff, a

conversation among two people who have known each other for a decade, but Lochlan still doesn't loosen his grip.

Frank's eyes flutter, and my hand covers my mouth, but a squeak escapes.

"You're scaring her," Hayes says quietly, but I read it on his lips and watch as Lochlan's furious attention latches onto me, still in the truck.

His wild eyes glare at me as if I'm the next victim before loosening his grip on Frank and pushing himself up and off of him.

When he straightens to his full height, it's like he's standing taller and wider, filled with adrenaline. His hands flex at his sides, his muscles twitching as if he's still contemplating homicide, and I can't breathe.

"Get his shit, take him to the closest rat infested motel, he's not welcome here anymore. I'll deal with the rest of you tomorrow," his deep voice instructs calmly. The shift is so sudden, I'm sure I imagined it, but everyone starts moving around him, silently obeying his command.

No one is surprised at all by tonight's turn of events.

Within 60 seconds, Frank is moved from the steps, and everyone has disappeared.

Aside from Lochlan.

His steps are heavy as he approaches the truck, not looking at me until he braces himself between the door frame and the back of the passenger seat, his midnight eyes roaming over me. There isn't a trace of anger in them, but I'm still afraid to speak.

"Are you okay?"

I don't realize how bad I'm shaking until I try to shrug. My whole body is shivering, but I know I'm not cold.

"Are you afraid of me, Jo?" He asks the question he's asked once before, but not after seeing something like this.

"No," I force through my chattering teeth.

My fingers feel thick as I try to release the seat belt from my waist, not adept enough to push the button and pull simultaneously. I press and pull, press then pull, not quite getting it each time until his calloused hand covers mine, blanketing my fingers in warmth.

"Let me." He unbuckles it easily, letting the belt fall to either side of me.

"Come on." His hand retreats, but I snatch it before it gets away, needing to hold on to his steadying force.

He studies my two hands grasping his before pulling me from my seat, and balancing me as my feet touch the ground.

"You're hurt," I murmur as the moon illuminates the blood on his knuckles.

"I'm fine."

"I'm sorry, Lochlan. I don't know why I got in the truck, I shouldn't have," my voice shakes as I fight to keep my tears at bay. I feel so stupid.

"Jo..." He says my name softly, and I have to crane my neck to look up at him directly.

My teeth chatter as I stare at him, waiting for my punishment. Instead, his right hand raises hesitantly and cradles the side of my head tenderly. My hair's thick and I can hardly feel him, but I want to.

I lean into his palm, and his eyes flare.

His mouth parts as if to say something, but when his hand shifts like he might touch my cheek, I hiss in pain. "Ouch."

"Dammit. Why didn't you tell me you were hurt?"

"I didn't realize I was." I touch the spot on my jaw just

below my ear and cringe. The skin's rubbed raw from hitting the inside of the cab.

"I'll fucking kill all of them." He pulls away to storm down to the bunkhouse, but I interlock my fingers in his, forcing him to stop and look at me.

"It's not their fault. I got in the truck willingly. Curtis and Ryker just didn't want me to go alone. Curtis tried to shield me the best he could. It was my fault for going to the fire in the first place. I should have listened to you."

"Yes, you should have."

"I'll listen next time, I'm sorry." I drop his hand, wrapping my arms around my torso and fleeing to the guesthouse.

I don't expect him to follow me, but when I turn to close the door, he's still watching me, and a part of me wishes I didn't have to be alone tonight.

* * *

I slip on my black stilettos, struggling to clasp them because I can't bend properly. This dress is fitted from my chest to my thighs with a boning that makes it hard to breathe when I sit down, but it does wonders to enhance an hourglass figure.

The deep maroon color brings out the brown in my eyes, much to my mother's dismay. That's why I picked it.

We have a big event tonight. The richest companies from all over the state will be there, which means their foundations will be looking for ways to spend money. Not because they're feeling charitable, but because they want the tax write-offs.

If all goes well, I'll get closer to our goal fund, and Lochlan will be able to get the security system he needs. He's already started spending some of the money on better fencing, but the bulk of it will need to go toward the camera system.

Once I have that accomplished, I might feel worthy of something.

Unfortunately, the thought of completing the goal and not being needed here anymore leaves me feeling empty.

Jo: Are you almost ready?

Jo: Do you have a big mirror?

Lochlan: Give me five minutes.

We haven't spoken since the other night. Other than floating around each other, and a few surface-level words exchanged.

There have been subtle attempts to check on the scrape under my ear, but other than that, we've both pretended nothing happened.

Lochlan: Ready.

As soon as I walk into his house, I see a standing full-length mirror in the living room that wasn't there before. Its intricate oak frame matches most of the other furniture, but this is definitely not something I've seen here.

"Did you carry that down the steps?"

"Yes." He's wearing dark jeans and the same black shirt as last time.

"I could have gone up." He always said the upstairs was off limits but carrying a heavy ass mirror down here seems a bit dramatic.

"Are you almost ready?" He asks, ignoring my statement.

"I just need my dress zipped the rest of the way." I back towards him and flip my hair over my shoulder to expose my zipper, then wait.

And, wait.

"Lochlan? Can you zip my dress?"

He doesn't respond, but I feel a tug on my zipper. He pulls the tab as far as it will go, then hesitates.

"Clasp the piece at the very top, and then it should zip the rest of the way," I explain breathlessly after feeling the faintest touch of his fingers against my spine.

I don't think I've ever had a man do this, but I don't have many options. Unless we stop at the carryout at the bottom of the mountain, I won't see another woman until we get to the event.

The smell of his shaving cream lingers in the air and fills my senses. Even though he's behind me, I feel him all around me.

My eyes find his furrowed brow of concentration in the mirror's reflection as he pulls the zipper to the clasp. He holds it there briefly, squeezing his eyes shut before taking a step back and walking out the front door without another word.

Chapter Seventeen

Lochlan

18 years old...

"Pops, can I borrow your Bronco?" I smooth out my white dress shirt again, even though I spent an hour ironing it.

"Hell no, why do you need my truck?" He doesn't look up from where he's whittling a stick with his favorite pocket knife.

"It's my anniversary. I want to take Bethany to a nice restaurant."

"I thought you guys were keeping your relationship a secret?"

"I'm 18, she turns 18 in a few months. Her daddy can't stop us forever."

"So you're going to drive up to her daddy's house in my vintage Bronco and tell him to fuck off with his rules and hope he doesn't smash my hood in with a golf club? No way in hell. Drive one of the work trucks."

"Pop."

"No. I'm your elder and I know better than you. This night is going to end in disaster. You never should have gotten involved with a girl who comes from such a strict family."

"But, I love her."

He stands up from his favorite rocking chair and hands me the stick he was working away on and his pocket knife. "I'm sure you do, son. I'm sure you do."

He stops just before he walks through the front door and turns back to me. "We don't always get what we want in life, I hope you know that."

* * *

Her sweet smell followed me onto the porch. I don't know if it's perfume or hairspray, but it lingers wherever she goes. I appreciate that it does, but it's hard to pretend I'm not entranced.

"You said it takes over an hour to get there," I yell back into the house. The event starts in 45 minutes.

"Well, it's not acceptable to be right on time. Are the guys ready?" She yells back.

"They're waiting on you." She insisted everyone attend, so we'll have to take multiple vehicles.

"If I were surrounded by women, this would not be an issue," she grumbles as she walks out of the house, hooking big dangly earrings in her ears.

She looks like a damn movie star.

Her thick hair is in big, bouncy waves, she's bronzed all over, and her dark purple dress contours the lines of her body distinctly. Lines I've studied from afar, thoroughly.

It's hard to tear my eyes off of her.

The top is tight, pushing her chest out liberally but not

135

indecently, and the thin fabric at the bottom is draped in layers, ending mid-thigh in my favorite place.

My eyes keep traveling down her legs because I can't help but get a good look at every inch of her while she rambles on about the testosterone-filled hellscape she's in. Her skin is shimmering from whatever lotion she used, and her shoes...

One of her shoes isn't clasped.

The two pieces dangle loosely around her ankle.

"I can take a couple of people in my car, so you guys don't have to cram into two trucks. You can follow me, and–"

I bend to one knee on the step below her, threading the loop to hook the strap and secure it properly before I realize she's stopped speaking entirely.

Having my hands on her ankle and being this close is severely intimate, like zipping up the back of her dress.

Being close to her is a test in strength.

I'm her boss. I'm 12 years older than her.

Those facts remain the same no matter how badly I want her.

Or, how desperately I want her to run her fingers through my hair and pull me closer, burying my face between her sexy ass thighs and letting me breathe in her true scent...

Fucking hell.

"I didn't want you to trip," I explain, clearing my throat and standing back up, but not without letting my fingers linger on her ankle a second longer than necessary. "I'll go grab the guys."

I'm nearly sprinting to the bunkhouse to get away from her with my fists clenched at my sides, hoping her lotion stuck to my hands.

If I'm lucky, it will embed itself into my skin, that way I

can actually have a piece of her.

My fingers unclench, and I'm staring at the same rough skin I've always had. Hardened by years of not wearing gloves when I work.

The hands of a man who has beaten men nearly to death and cared for the dangerous animals we rescue.

Hands that aren't worthy enough to touch her.

"Spock's staying back to keep an eye on things," Hayes says, snapping me from my thoughts.

"Has anyone heard from Frank?"

"No, last we checked, he is still at the motel we dropped him at, but I don't think he's brave enough to try anything. It'd be a hike to get back up here just to fuck with us when he doesn't have a vehicle."

"All this shit started not long after he got here."

"I know, but if he was involved, he would have to have someone helping him out, and so far, there haven't been signs of that. All we can do is wait." Hayes whistles into the bunkhouse and everyone starts our way. "I tried to get them in their best shirts. I know you don't want to embarrass her."

"I never said that."

He side-eyes me. "Right."

"Not all of us can be a pretty boy like you, Jensen." That's a stretch of a statement because Hayes is every bit as rough around the edges as me but he knows how to dress. He takes pride in his haircut and his tattoos. His Indian motorcycle is never dirty.

"Luckily, for you, it seems like Jo isn't into pretty boys."

"What the fuck does that mean?"

"I'm used to deflecting female attention, but she hasn't so much as bat an eyelash at me."

137

"I think your callousness towards women is screwing with your brain. I told her she can't involve herself with you guys."

"Us guys, specifically? Or are you included in that?" He smirks, backing toward the house where he will inevitably offer to ride with the woman I can't stop thinking about because he knows I can't.

"Shut the fuck up."

"Yes, boss." He laughs loudly when I flip him off in response.

Chapter Eighteen

Jo

Everything is going perfectly. I've set up my basket for the silent auction, and I've spent an hour sprinkling hints to potential donors to bid on a private tour with the bears.

I broke the news of my plan to Lochlan as soon as we arrived here, and he was furious. Of course, I expected it.

He didn't tell me to take it off the table, but he did grumble something and storm off.

I know where the tables are that I reserved for Second Chance Sanctuary, so he won't be far, but I haven't been brave enough to go apologize. He already can't stand to be near me half the time.

As I round a table to go talk to another potential bidder, I see my parents and freeze. I told them I wasn't available tonight because I hoped this event would be big enough not to be seen.

My brother is behind them, and I watch his eyes squint as he locks in on me. He leans in to talk to his campaign manager, Austin, but I turn and book it the other direction.

I'm halfway across the room when I hear his voice behind

me. "JoAnna."

"Not today, Austin." He's been my brother's best friend for years, and I haven't been able to stand him for an equal amount of time.

"Your brother and parents expect you to join them," he says, still following behind me as my legs move on autopilot, trying to get away.

"I'm not able to join them. I'm working."

"Working? Did you decide to become a cocktail waitress?" He snorts at his own crude joke. As if making fun of the working class is hilarious.

"I work for Second Chance Sanctuary."

"What's that?"

"It's a black bear rescue." I stop walking, turning on him so he's forced to stop, too. "Now, if you will excuse me."

"It's required that you be seen with your family." His tall, lanky figure is dressed in a suit worth more than most people's entire wardrobe, and it makes him even more off-putting because of it.

"I don't care. Have a nice night," I dismiss him, turning to walk away.

I thought he got the hint, but as I reach the table where the guys are sitting, he speaks again. "JoAnna, this is not negotiable," he states harshly, just as I lock eyes with Lochlan.

How embarrassing that I have to be scolded by one man in front of another man who's probably waiting patiently to scold me as well.

I spin on my heels to face him. "I'm sitting at the table I reserved for Second Chance Sanctuary. My family is on their own."

He looks over my shoulder and visibly shows his disgust

at my friends. They're all in their Sunday best, and I want to punch Austin in the face for looking down on them.

"These people are bad for Conrad's image."

I can feel Lochlan's attention locked in behind me like a solar wave, fueling me.

"I don't care about his image!" I protest loudly, earning a couple of nosy looks in my direction.

Hayes is watching us from his seat, throwing glances between the man in front of me and the man behind me, whom I can't see, but I'm sure is scowling because I've dragged more of my drama into his hemisphere.

"JoAnna, this is ridiculous." Austin's freckled face is growing red with frustration. "Come on," he demands, grabbing my elbow.

The air shifts as four grown men stand up from the table.

I jerk my arm out of his grip, absorbing the energy from the people on my side. "I said, I'm sitting here."

"There isn't even an available seat," he mutters, trying to save himself from the wrath of the real men behind me.

Without bothering to look, my hand finds the top of Lochlan's shoulder, and with absolutely no strength and the slightest pressure from my palm, the giant of a man lowers to his seat. "I don't need a chair." One step and I'm between his legs, planting my ass on his muscular thigh.

What the hell am I doing?

It doesn't matter. I have to commit. I wrap my arm around the back of his neck and lean into his hard chest, attempting to look as comfortable as I can during this awkward situation.

Austin's stare drills into the back of my head as I keep my attention focused on Curtis and Seiver's wide eyes across the table. They follow my queue, though, and return to their seats, not uttering a word about how strange it is for me to sit on my boss's lap.

Hayes sits next, and I hope that means the coast is clear.

"Is he gone?" I whisper, not daring to look at Lochlan directly. Our heads are so close, though, he has to know I'm talking to him, but he's painfully still.

"He's gone," Hayes answers instead from beside me, and I breathe a sigh of relief, leaning further into Lochlan unintentionally.

He's granite beneath me, and I've never felt more foolish. He's made it clear so many times that he hates my shenanigans. He didn't want to come to these events in the first place, but I'm making a mockery of myself when I'm supposed to be helping the sanctuary.

I should move before he tosses me off, but his palm is so warm through the fabric of my dress, I can almost imagine what it would feel like to have his bare skin against mine.

The heat of that thought rises to my cheeks and the spot between my thighs that I try to ignore.

I'm sitting on my boss's lap, and all I can think about is the hard muscles along his back and the strength of his arm wrapped around my waist. I'm close enough to distinguish the smell of his soap from the shaving cream he uses.

And that he's drinking beer tonight.

"I'm sorry, I'll move, I'm probably crushing your leg." I brace myself to stand but my butt barely lifts an inch before I'm forced back down.

Lochlan's big hand cups my hip, firmly keeping me in place. "You're fine right here." His low, gravelly voice vibrates across my skin.

I look at him curiously, but his gaze is focused somewhere

across the room, as a speech starts. It's inappropriate to be sitting on his lap, but I feel trapped. If I try to stand up now, people will take notice because everyone else is seated. Finding and pulling up my own chair is out of the question.

So, I sit.

And, when I shift to adjust my seat against his firm quad, he pulls me a fraction of an inch closer, his hand drifting the same distance down my dress towards the exposed skin of my thigh.

He probably doesn't even realize he did it, and I'm over-analyzing every single point of contact. My knuckles have turned white clutching the small handbag in my lap.

The person speaking on stage finishes, and the next speaker replaces them, but I have no idea what's being said.

My fingers twitch, the tips barely brushing against the skin above his shirt collar before returning to the safety of his shirt, and at that exact moment, his fingertips graze the hem of my maroon dress, barely touching my skin.

Did he do that on purpose?

I'm a woman in STEM... I value you a good experiment of cause and effect...

I force my fingers to inch towards his neck again, fighting against my nerves to prove my theory by dragging my nails along the edge of his collar.

My knuckles glide across his skin, and I don't breathe, waiting for his reaction. It's only a moment before his hand inches further down my lap and the pads of his fingers dig into my skin.

The pounding in my ears is deafening as I flatten my palm against the back of his neck, cupping his warm skin.

The veins on the back of his hand flex as he covers the

space of my exposed thigh entirely with his hand.

My heart threatens to burst from my chest as my gaze shifts to his face, but his unfocused eyes are still lost across the banquet hall.

His stone-cold expression stays averted as I squeeze the back of his neck, but I know he's with me because, without hesitation, his fingers dig into my thigh, gripping it with desperation.

Everyone else in the room disappears until all I can see is him.

Someone tries to get my attention, but I can't stop looking at him.

His hooded eyes turn to me, finding my lips first before moving gradually upward. From an outward perspective, it would appear that he just turned his attention to me, but I know he's been focused on me this entire time.

He's as consumed by this as I am.

He doesn't say a word as he raises two fingers, signaling something to someone out of my line of sight.

I'm afraid that if I look away from him, he'll disappear, and so will this moment.

The endorphins coursing through my veins are making me high. I've never been high, but I imagine this is what it feels like. I'm floating on a cloud of ecstasy, embraced in a warm hug as my skin tingles from my scalp to the tips of my toes.

The fire deep in my belly is burning me from the inside out.

You can probably see the flush of my cheeks through my makeup, but I don't care. I don't care what anyone in this room says about me. I could be getting cross looks from every direction, but for the first time in my life, I couldn't care less what anyone else thinks.

Only what he thinks.

Something is set down on the table beside us, and I hear the crack of a can opening before he lifts it to my bottom lip.

"Drink," he orders, watching my mouth as he waits for me to obey.

My lips part a fraction, and the icy aluminum meets my mouth in a kiss, making my eyes flutter closed when he tips it into my mouth. The crisp liquid coats my tongue as the cold beer travels down the back of my throat and into my stomach.

When my eyes blink open, the can is gone, but his mouth is directly in front of me.

A shiver zips down my spine, and his arm hugs me tighter.

"Cold, darlin'?" He rumbles, sending warmth to my very core.

"No."

His hand twitches against my thigh again, gripping me harder, and I become overly aware of how damp my panties are.

If he keeps touching me, he'll feel how turned on I am through his damn jeans.

But I can't think straight enough to care.

Instead, I do something I've been imagining since our first event when he trimmed his hair, and twine my fingers into the loose curls at the nape of his neck, letting my nails scratch the base of his scalp.

His nostrils flare, and his eyes squeeze shut briefly as his whole body inhales roughly, letting the breath out just the same. Then his fingers flex, inching closer to the soft flesh between my thighs.

Entering dangerous territory.

Nearing the line of public indecency.

And, outright scandalous.

But, every fiber of my being that has always done the right thing, played by the rules, and been a well-behaved girl wants him to go further. I want to know what it feels like to have his rough, callused hands caress the skin where no one has been before...

I want him to touch me.

My knees spread on their own command, widening the gap between my thighs mere millimeters...

His entire body goes rigid.

Dousing me with a bucket of ice water.

What the hell am I doing?

The noise in the room returns at full volume, screaming at me, reminding me that I am, in fact, in a room full of some of the most influential people in the state.

I'm sitting on my boss' lap at a charity auction ready to whore myself out for a glimmer of pleasure.

I'm a disgrace.

"I'm sorry. I'm so sorry," I utter, jumping up from his lap, nearly taking the tablecloth with me.

"Jo," he starts, but I'm already running away.

Running and making an absolute spectacle of myself.

The double doors break apart as I push through them, sucking in lungfuls of the humid night air.

"Jo!" Lochlan shouts after me as my feet hit the parking lot.

I start running again.

"Jo! Stop, dammit." He wraps an arm around my waist, lifting me clear off the ground and forcing a squeal from my throat.

"No, please let me go," I cry woefully.

He sets me down but doesn't release my waist. I'm too mentally weak to stop myself from slumping against his hard chest.

"Please don't say anything, Lochlan. I'm embarrassed, let's just forget it happened and move on."

"You have nothing to be embarrassed about. I need to apologize."

"No."

"Yes, dammit. I know better." He spins me so I'm facing him. "You're a beautiful woman," he opens his mouth to say something else, then shuts it and shakes his head to clear it. "I forgot for a moment who I was."

"Who you are?"

"Your boss and a man with a terrible reputation. I'm a black hole that will ruin you if you get too close."

"I don't believe that," I whisper.

"You have to."

I shake my head, dismissing him. "You didn't do anything wrong. I initiated what happened in there, and then I got overwhelmed, I panicked."

"You tried to stand up, and I didn't let you. I made you uncomfortable, and it's my fault."

"No, God, Lochlan!" I screech into my hands. "I didn't want to stand up." The silence is pungent as I look up at him.

He's looking at me with so much confusion. He doesn't know what to say to stop the train wreck happening in front of him.

"I need to leave. I need to go." I fumble around in my tiny clutch, trying to yank my keys from the cramped space as I approach my car.

He's right behind me, though, snatching them from my hand as soon as they're out.

"You're upset. I'll drive you home."

"You drove here with them." I motion to the building where the guys still are, and that sends a new wave of dread through me. "Oh my God! I can't believe they just witnessed that."

"No one cares. They won't say a word about it. I'll make sure they don't," he assures me, but it doesn't matter. The embarrassment is still hot on my skin. I've been programmed for too long to believe my behavior was egregious.

"What about the truck keys? They'll need them," I suggest as a last-ditch effort to get him to leave me alone.

He takes the keys out of his pocket and tosses them into the floorboard of the truck parked next to my car. "They'll figure it out."

Chapter Nineteen

Lochlan

There haven't been many moments in my life where I've struggled with restraint. The first time it happened was my first week in prison when I got jumped for the first time and nearly used all my pent up rage to kill the fucker.

I spent a day in the infirmary. He spent a month there.

Frank putting Jo in danger made me snap, and I'm not sure how far I would have taken it if Hayes hadn't called me off.

But the moment Jo sat in my lap, the chaos in my head was so unhinged I could hardly breathe.

The smallest lapse in control, and I was going to throw her over my shoulder and carry her out there.

Her touch is a miracle, but knowing I can't have my way with her is a curse.

The hold she has on me is deeply deranged.

I pull my hand off the steering wheel, glancing at my palm subtly before clenching it. Shimmer.

The lotion on her legs clings to me, forcing more of my impure thoughts about her to the surface while she sits beside me, mortified that the event took place.

"I've never done that before," she whispers suddenly, just loud enough to hear over the engine.

"What?"

"Sat on a man's lap."

"In public?"

Her silence lingers. "Not exactly."

I peek at her from the corner of my eye, and she's staring out the passenger side window, deep in thought.

"I've never been so close to a man. *Ever*," she finally admits.

I slam on the brakes harder than necessary at the red light, making us both jerk against our seat belts. "What?"

"I don't want to talk about it. I just needed you to know that I didn't freak out because of anything you did. I got overwhelmed. It was all me."

She did not just tell me she's never been with a man. I heard it wrong. There's no way.

"You've never had a boyfriend?" I can't hide the disbelief from leaving my mouth and sounding like an accusation.

"Been engaged twice against my will. No boyfriends allowed, though." She scoffs. "By the time I got to college, I was so inexperienced around boys that I didn't even try. I imagined that prince charming would come along and erase the awkwardness of it for me."

"I'm sorry."

"My mother convinced me that I had to look a certain way, act a certain way, to appeal to the male gaze. She ensured I looked like the ideal woman, suitable for marriage, but it was never for my own good. It was to secure a future connection to whoever I ended up marrying.

"I needed to save myself for marriage, but I didn't get any say on who the marriage was to. I needed to be able to impress my future husband but don't act flirtatious because they'll think you're slutty," she rambles on, firing herself up.

"God forbid I find someone who would actually want me for me. Not someone who wanted to up their political career. God forbid I find someone to give myself to who actually loves me," her voice fizzles out.

"You're young. You still have time."

She shakes her head. "No one has ever been able to see me for me. They see me for my father's connections, his money, my looks, or my brother's career ambitions. I'm just a pawn. I'll never be enough for anyone. I can only hope one day I'll find a guy who might actually fall in love with *me*," she states hopefully. I scoff from deep in my chest and her eyes turn to slits. "What?"

"That's stupid."

"Why?" She asks in offense.

"Because any man who spends a little time in your presence will fall in love with you, darlin'."

Her sad eyes twinkle brightly for a moment before she blinks it away. "It's not that simple."

"Why not?"

"Men want a family, and I can't have children."

If I weren't already parking in front of the house, I would have slammed on the brakes again. "What?"

"I found out just after I turned 19. Premature ovarian failure. My doctor said if they had caught it sooner, they might have been able to do an egg retrieval, but... No one knows. Except you, now. I made sure my parents didn't see my medical bills. They thought I went into surgery to remove a cyst." She rolls her eyes as she wipes a tear from her cheek.

"They didn't even bother driving me to or home from the

surgery center."

"Why didn't you want to tell them?"

"Because then they'd see me as damaged goods, and it'd be one more reason for them to look down on me. To them, I'll be useless if I can't have children."

"Jo..." Now I can imagine why Emory's story hit her so hard.

It's not fair that some of the worst people on the planet can reproduce, but a light like Jo can't physically have children if she wants them.

* * *

"Maybe you should slow down." I cringe slightly as she tips the second bottle of wine into her mouth. She started drinking from a glass, but apparently it wasn't efficient enough.

She said she needed a drink, and I convinced her to come inside because I didn't want her to be alone. Now, I'm worried she'll pass out.

"I mean, what's so wrong with me? Am I so terrible?"

"There is nothing wrong with you."

"Then why doesn't anyone want me? My family... A man... You."

She's drunk enough that she doesn't wait for a response from me.

"You can't wait to get rid of me. You told me I was worse than prison."

"No, I didn-"

She cuts me off. "I'm going to die alone." She tips the bottle back again, gulping loudly.

When I told her that being around her felt like prison, I meant it, but not in the way she thinks.

Her existence is torturous to be around.

I can't imagine a world without her in it, and yet the fact that I'm subjected to her presence is a twisted joke.

I want to be near her in every way, I only want to breathe the air that has graced her lips, but I can't.

I am a grown man, and I've lived multiple lives in my time on Earth. But nothing has come close to being here at the same time as Jo.

Every second of every day, I want to be near her, hearing her sweet voice or having her smile aimed my way, but I have to watch as her family ignores her.

I have to sit by and watch the fuckers who are meant to cherish her, abuse the gift they were given.

She is the sun their universe should revolve around.

She is the main character.

And, I can't have her.

Because I'm the seedy villain locked away in the sewer.

I'm the beast.

"I've never even seen a penis. Can you believe that? I mean I have, but not in real life." She hiccups.

She is *very* drunk. "Okay, I think it's time for bed."

She stands from my couch, wobbling slightly even though she tossed her heels over the arm a while ago. "I've never even been kissed properly."

I ignore every word coming out of her mouth. It's not helping the internal battle raging inside of me to show her how damn desirable she is.

"It's overrated," I grunt instead. I've never been particularly excited about kissing someone, it's more a means to an end.

"What, why?" She asks as she claws at the back of her dress, trying to get the zipper.

I can't tell her how enticing her lips are and how they would blow my opinion out of the water.

"Stop, let me get it." I unzip her dress halfway down her back, only intending to help her so she's not stuck in it, but she reaches behind herself and unzips it the rest of the way, letting it slip from her body.

"Jesus Christ." I spin around, facing the wall, before it hits the floor. "What the hell are you doing?"

"Sleeping," she mumbles. After a couple of seconds of silence, I break my neck looking over my shoulder.

She's lying on the couch with the flannel throw blanket I keep on the back. Her eyes are closed, and it already sounds like she's snoring and fast asleep.

Naked under my blanket... In my house...

Suddenly, the air is too thick to breathe, and I have to dash onto the porch to gasp for breath.

What the hell am I going to do with this woman?

Chapter Twenty

Jo

I've never been desperate for water like I am as soon as my eyes split apart and I stare directly into the stream of sunlight coming through the window.

Why didn't I close the curtain?

Wait.

The morning sun doesn't come in my window…

I shoot up, gasping as my brain pounds against my skull, and realize way too slowly that I'm in Lochlan's living room. On his couch.

A chill skates over my skin, and I glance down at my naked breasts, fully exposed. "Oh my God!" I gasp, covering myself with the blanket.

My dress from last night is folded neatly on the coffee table, beside it is a black T-shirt with the SCS logo on it.

I'm in Lochlan's house, but a part of me hoped he didn't know I was here. Beside the T-shirt is a bottle of water and a pink sticky note.

Drink the whole bottle. You'll need it.

I have made a mockery of myself more in the past twelve hours than I have in the past twenty-four years of my life.

Drunk on my boss's couch after sitting on his lap in a public setting. And, admitting to him that I've never been with a man. Ughhh.

Maybe I only dreamed it.

I hope I don't have to face him today. I can't handle it.

I sling the T-shirt over my head, thankful that it drapes to my mid-thigh, and I snag my dress and the water bottle. I have no clue where my shoes went, but it's only a few steps to the guesthouse. I've done it barefoot many times already.

Lochlan is probably hours into his day, but I tiptoe to the front door anyway, nervous to be caught. I just want to sneak home and ignore him the rest of the weekend.

The door creaks as it opens, and I watch the stairs expectantly, like he might come down them at any moment, holding my breath until my feet are on the porch and I can pull the door shut.

I exhale roughly as I spin around, and gasp from deep within.

All of them. They're all standing twenty feet away, having some sort of pow wow, staring at me in nothing but my boss's T-shirt. My back slams against the door as Lochlan's gaze catches mine and doesn't let go.

My hand struggles frantically for the door knob, twisting at the same time my body shoves the door back open so I can flee to safety inside.

Fuck my life.

He comes in a moment later while I'm sitting on the stairs with my head in my hands.

"I'm sorry," I mumble.

"For what?"

"For being a disaster."

"You're not a disaster. You're hungover, it happens."

"I look like a train wreck who just had a one-night stand," I speak directly into my hands, muffling my voice.

"Jo, look at me."

"No."

"You're too concerned by what people think. They didn't say a word about you coming outside in my T-shirt because they know better. Now, I can let them think you were wearing my clothes because you chose to spend the night here or I can tell them you got shit faced drunk and unzipped your dress before I could stop you, and snuggled onto my couch like a little cat."

"Are those my only two options?"

"I told them you weren't feeling good last night and fell asleep on my couch. No one in their right mind would assume you stayed here on purpose. Don't worry." He turns to leave.

"I'm worried about making you look bad."

His body goes stiff. "Why would you make me look bad?"

"It's unprofessional of me to be standing on your porch half-naked in front of all the guys. I wasn't trying to embarrass you."

"If you think for one second that *I'm* worried about that, then you haven't been paying attention."

"What do you mean?"

"A gorgeous woman walks out of my house looking like that… Embarrassed is not what I'm feeling. Trust me." He walks out of the house, letting the door slam behind him, leaving me slack-jawed.

Gorgeous?

157

* * *

I spent all of yesterday hibernating in my bed, too nauseous to eat and too dizzy to do anything but doze in and out of sleep. Today hasn't been much better, but I've managed to move to my little table to study.

Lochlan: How are you feeling?
Jo: Great
Lochlan: I don't believe you
Jo: Like hot garbage
Lochlan: Get some fresh air
Jo: No
Lochlan: Open your door.
Jo: No
Lochlan: Yes

I shove away from my laptop and answer the door, reluctantly. "What?"

"Do you have plans tonight?"

I glance back at my sad pile of textbooks, and he follows my gaze. "No, I don't."

"I want to show you something," he motions for me to follow him.

I shuffle after him in my oversized hoodie and pajama shorts, completely disregarding my physical appearance. I haven't put anything on my face but lotion since removing my crusty makeup yesterday morning, and my hair hasn't been washed. The messy bun on top of my head is authentic, not curated.

"Sit," he instructs as soon as we walk through his front door.

My body moves just enough to get me to the couch, and I plop down, leaning heavily against the back of it. I'm staring into the abyss of a black screen before I process what I'm looking at.

A BRAND NEW TV.

"Did you? When did you? Why?" I stutter as he comes back into the room. "Oh my. This is so exciting!" I clap my hands together before he can say anything, grabbing for the remote. Then pause. "I'm sorry, did you want to watch something in particular?"

He huffs a short laugh. "I got it for you. I wouldn't even know what to watch."

"For me?"

"Whenever you want, come over and watch your movies." He hits a button on the side of the TV, and a DVD player pops out. "No more depression cave."

"Lochlan," I utter happily before launching up and giving him the biggest bear hug around the neck. I'm too happy to care that I've never actually hugged him before or that he might not have wanted me to.

I'm too happy to care that I'm hugging a man who made me feel a lot of warm, tingly things two days ago.

I needed a hug.

"Thank you," I whisper genuinely. "This is the best gift ever."

"Go get a movie, Jo. I'll get your ice cream." His hands caress my back as he steps away, avoiding eye contact... Bashfully?

"I'm going to cry!" I take off with more energy than I've had in months, sprinting to the guesthouse to get one of my favorite movies.

I get it set up, and when he hands me a bowl of ice cream, I stare at it for a full minute. I don't think I've ever been this happy.

The smile stretches across my face as I look over at him sitting in the seat on the opposite side of the couch, then it morphs to confusion. "Are you eating cereal?"

"I don't like ice cream." He shrugs.

"I knew there was something wrong with you."

He rolls his eyes. "What are we watching?"

"This, Lochlan Dane, is Pride & Prejudice."

Chapter Twenty-One

Lochlan

"I don't get it."

"What do you mean?" She looks so genuinely concerned, I can't help but give her a hard time.

"She hated him. She told him to fuck off. Then she loved him because…" I raise my hands in confusion. "I don't get it."

"He was drawn to her from the very beginning. He looked at her in the ballroom. Did you see him look?"

"Then he called her ugly."

"He's a man, he was being dumb." I don't have time to be offended, or pretend to be, before she continues passionately. "He was in love with her. He helped her into the carriage, so he had a reason to touch her. His hand, did you see his hand?" She rewinds the movie to show me.

"I don't get it."

"Ahhh!!" She launches herself back onto the couch in distress and fake cries. "Did you enjoy it at all?"

I've never been someone who gets emotionally attached to fiction. I didn't watch much TV growing up, only read a few books, and didn't ever see a movie more than once. I could count on one hand the times I went to a movie theater.

"It was alright." But if Jo asked me to watch a movie with her every single night. My ass would be here, ready with the remote.

"I should probably go home now," she sighs, but doesn't move.

I should ask her to stay longer, but I won't.

"I'll walk you back."

"It's twenty feet away, I'll be alright." She laughs, climbing to her bare feet.

I'm not a feet guy; they've never been an exceptionally appealing part of a woman, but seeing her pad around without shoes on in my home touches something deep within me.

Don't get me started on all the sexy shoes she wears, strutting recklessly around this place. A sane man would have told her to stop wearing them because they aren't functional… But I'm not sane when it comes to her.

I follow her to the door because seeing her safe inside is not up for debate, and she spins suddenly, facing me in the doorway. "Thank you for tonight, Lochlan. It really got me out of my funk."

She's looking up at me so sweetly, full of hope and wonder. She's looking at me like she wishes I were the prince charming she's dreamed about.

I'm not.

"Jo, I-" I'm not sure what draws my attention away from her, a sound, a sixth sense, but my head jerks up, surveying our pitch black surroundings.

"Come back inside."

"Why?"

"Someone is watching us."

* * *

"Search the entire property and make sure there aren't any signs of trespassers. Starting now, we're taking shifts, and someone needs to be a lookout at all times."

"Is she okay?" Hayes asks, peeking past me into the house.

"She's fine." I stare at the dripping red letters on the side of the guesthouse.

'GET OUT'

I don't know if it has anything to do with her or if it's a bad coincidence, but the fact that someone was so close to us, to her, sets my skin on fire.

"Sheriff's here." Hayes lumbers away. He has even more bad blood with the police than I do.

"Jackson's here?" Jo asks from behind me. I haven't let her set foot outside my house since I suspected someone was on the property.

"Jackson? Are you that familiar with him?" I ask too defensively, making her step back. I haven't forgotten her hushed conversation with him after the barn fire.

"It's definitely paint, not blood. Any sign of foul play anywhere else?" Sheriff Malec asks as he steps onto the porch, immediately pinging his gaze between us, sensing tension.

"They came in, sent a message, and got out," I admit gruffly.

"And you're sure it was meant for you?" He asks me, but glances at Jo.

"This shit started before she got here."

"I need to cover all my bases."

"I'm sure you do." I don't like the way he looks at her. He can't wait to protect her like the savior she needs.

"Lochlan, he's just trying to help." She steps forward like she might grab my elbow, but I back up before she can. I don't need pity.

I'll never be the guy she needs.

"Maybe it's time you stayed somewhere else, Jo," Sheriff Malec suggests, ripping a knife through my gut.

"Yeah, maybe it is," I agree, and she flinches at my clipped tone. "I'm going to sweep the property one more time."

"Lochlan!" She yells after me.

I stalk off without looking back.

Chapter Twenty-Two

Jo

I'm staring blindly into stage lights, disassociating just to make it through hearing my brother talk for ten minutes. Hearing him schmooze people as if he is the best man to run this state's administration, but all I can think about is *him*.

I had the best evening of my life with Lochlan, and then everything shifted. I shouldn't be surprised, it seems like it always happens this way.

Every time I think we've turned over a new leaf, the same walls go back up, and I'm reminded how little companionship I have.

The hot and cold is exhausting. No matter how hard I work or how friendly we get, I seem to mess something up.

Jackson suggested I leave, and he agreed... Just like that. I thought we were past the miserable neighbor act. I know he was upset about someone being on the property, but I don't know why he took it out on me.

I haven't spoken to him. We've gone back to being strangers, floating around each other.

I didn't bother checking to see if he was attending tonight's event that I had circled on the calendar. There's no point in my searching the crowd for the people I've started to think of as friends.

Instead, I'm standing on a stage in front of 500 people like a show pig in a fitted dress, begging myself not to look as sour as I feel inside.

My mother's teeny tiny petite figure stands next to me, making me feel like an ogre in front of all of these cameras.

I don't want to be here.

I want to be with my people.

My people.

Second Chance Sanctuary has become a safe place to me despite how Lochlan acts, not this environment that my parents forced on me.

Applause erupts around me, but I can't force myself to clap for a man I'm not voting for. I keep my hands clasped in front of me and wait for my cue to exit the stage.

My brother takes his time smiling and waving at the cameras before strolling across the stage and down the only set of steps. Austin follows behind him, and then my parents. I start after them, standing motionless while conversation congests my only escape.

These frustrating, selfish people. Leaving me to be ignored as if I'm not here at all, even though they forced me to be here.

As if I don't have my own life or better things to do.

They'll make me stand here until my feet go numb and I topple over in exhaustion. I'm so tired of being invisible.

A shrill whistle interrupts my pity party.

I know that whistle.

"What are you doing?" I ask him, barely being able to bend

166

in my dress enough to talk to him, where he stands beside the stage.

"You look miserable." Lochlan holds his hands out in a come-hither motion. Surely he doesn't expect to lift me off the stage?

"Uh, I don't think that's a good idea."

"Jo, you can do this easily, or I can throw you over my shoulder and embarrass you in front of your friends."

I gasp in offense. "These people are not my friends."

Our eyes connect as my hands clasp the top of his shoulders and his envelop my ribs. I take a step off the stage, trusting him to catch me, but I don't come close to falling.

My shoe meets the floor gracefully as if there wasn't any distance between my steps at all.

The warmth of his hands slips from my sides as he turns to walk back toward the banquet tables, quickly cutting off our connection. He's clearing a path for me while simultaneously continuing the silent treatment from before.

Everyone moves out of his way like a school of fish sensing a shark. No one looks in my direction or waves me over for conversation. Nobody is trying to get anything from me because they're afraid to approach me.

I'm not invisible when I'm with Lochlan, not like I am to my parents, but I'm safeguarded.

I'm free.

I grab his forearm from behind before we reach the large round table, where I see everyone else is sitting. "Thank you for the rescue," I say as he turns his attention to me.

His eyes go to my hand on his forearm first and then to the crowd around us before landing on my face, but he looks anguished.

"The quicker we get the funds we need from the events, the quicker I can get my cameras and stop pretending to be someone I'm not."

"What?" My heart sinks in my chest.

"I don't belong here, Jo. Just like you don't belong at the sanctuary." My hand falls from his arm, and he turns away, walking away from me again like he did a couple of nights ago.

Everything feels heavy. My skin, my bones. I want to slump to the floor and forget the facade I always put on.

I'm so tired of not being good enough, but it doesn't matter because I have to continue on. I have to be the perfect daughter in a room full of people who don't know the faintest detail about me. I have to pretend to be a good sister.

I have to mingle and market Second Chance Sanctuary to people even though I'm being shoved out of the gates like an unwanted stray.

"Are you out of your mind, JoAnna?" My mother's voice attacks me from behind. "Being lifted off the stage. Sitting on *that* man's lap. It's despicable."

"I don't want to talk about this right now, Mom."

"Randall Porter told your brother about him. You're trolliping around with a *rapist*?" She spits the word at me.

"He's not. Daddy exonerated him."

"Your daddy will pick up a hooker off a turnpike. He has no critical thinking skills, clearly."

"Lochlan is a good man, but he's just my boss."

She scoffs and rolls her eyes. "Your boss. You're wasting everyone's time. Come back home, or we'll pull your school admission."

"Dad promised."

CHAPTER TWENTY-TWO

"I don't care what your daddy promised."

"If you don't let me get through school, I'll tell everyone about what Dad and Conrad did."

She recoils. How dare I put her precious family in the way of scandal?

"I wish you were never born," she sneers, stomping away.

I'm motionless while her nasty words sink in. Slowly letting the deep void in my heart overtake me.

Everything is too tight.

I can't breathe.

The crowd disappears as I snake my way through people without seeing them, desperate for an escape. I'm clawing at the neckline of my dress before I reach a long, dark hallway, pulling at it desperately for some relief.

I need more room to breathe.

It's too tight, I'm suffocating.

I burst through a doorway leading me to a balcony overlooking a garden, sucking in fresh air but it doesn't help.

My hands fight against the fabric, pulling, tugging, and I can't get it off. I can't reach my zipper.

The frustration turns to tears, and I'm hyperventilating as my panic attack consumes me.

It feels like a heart attack, it feels like–

"What's wrong?" Lochlan appears out of thin air because, of course, he does. He's always center stage as my life falls apart.

"I can't breathe. Get it off." I hug myself, desperately trying to calm down, but I can't catch my breath. "Lochlan, get it off!" I scream, and his hands find my zipper immediately.

He tugs the dress open, but it's not enough. The shapewear necessary for this dress is still squeezing my insides

169

painfully.

"What is this shit?" He grabs the spandex but hesitates.

"I can't breathe. I can't breathe."

Rippp.

He tears the material right down my spine and I suck in a chest full of air, dropping to my knees. I keep my head between my legs and take long drags of air, in and out.

"Hell, no wonder you couldn't breathe, it left indentations all over your back," he remarks, not having any idea why I'm actually falling apart.

"Why are you here? Why is it always you?"

He doesn't humor me with a response.

"You show up every time I'm a disaster. Why are you here?" I yell.

"I saw you run out of the banquet hall."

I clamber to my feet with unsteady knees, grasping my dress above my chest to keep it from falling off. "Just leave."

"I'm not leaving you like this."

"Go, please," I murmur, facing the balcony.

"Jo, let me–"

"NO!" I scream into the wind in front of me. I'm so tired of taking his emotional hand out, and then it being snatched away from me.

I'm so tired of being nothing.

After a long minute of silence, his black shirt is draped across my shoulders, and it takes all of my effort to keep the sound of my cry in.

I hear the doors click shut behind him as he leaves.

Chapter Twenty-Three

Jo

When the weight of life catches up to me, I have a hard time getting out of bed. Between juggling classes, work, my parents' drama, and my other complicated feelings, I feel the weight of the world on my shoulders.

It's as if all of my energy has been depleted, and I need a day to recharge in my depression cave, as Lochlan called it.

Today, all my life choices are catching up to me, and I haven't been able to move.

I'm wallowing in self-pity and inability to see light at the end of the tunnel when someone knocks on my door.

Someone.

I know it's Lochlan. No one else would be brave enough to visit me.

Like a corpse rising from the dead, I crawl out of bed and crack the door open. "What do you want?" I grumble.

He studies me for a moment like he's not sure where my chilly attitude is coming from. As if he isn't one of the culprits.

"The guys are going into town for the Independence Day

festival. Thought I'd tell you in case you'd be interested."

"What time are you leaving?"

"I'm not. I'm staying here."

"Oh, why?"

"They have a big fireworks show that sends a lot of noise and smoke up here. I stay back to watch over everything in case the bears get spooked."

Normally, I'd jump at the opportunity to get out, but going to a crowded festival doesn't sound as alluring as it would on any other day. The effort it would take me to get ready seems unachievable.

"Well, I'll probably stay back, too. Let me know if you need anything while they're all gone." I give him a considerate half smile and move to shut the door, but he stops me with a hand gripping the door.

He doesn't say anything as we stand silently holding the door. He wants to say something, but as usual, it gets locked away inside his head, and he doesn't enlighten me with it.

If he wants me to read his mind, I don't have the energy for it today.

"Bye," I whisper, pushing the door again. This time, he lets me shut it.

* * *

Lochlan: Meet me outside

It's been a couple of hours since he was at my door, and I've left his message unanswered for over ten minutes.

I shouldn't humor him. He has me all twisted up in my

head, but I'm still the same girl I was before I ever came here, desperate for a friend.

Jo: When?

Lochlan: Right now

Lochlan's sitting on his porch steps when I open my door, looking at me. He's holding a folded fleece blanket and a small plastic container.

"What are you doing?" I ask him skeptically.

"Will you take a walk with me?"

I'm hesitant to be near him after what happened last night, but I'm too curious not to follow him.

We walk in silence as he leads me down a path past the bunkhouse I've never followed. I've never explored the property because I'm not supposed to, and I never thought to ask Lochlan to guide me.

I catch him glancing at me a few times, and I think he might say something, but he doesn't. We only walk for a few minutes when the path opens into a field surrounded by trees. The clearing is overrun by little white flowers, but it isn't until I get closer that I see all the specks of red.

"Strawberries? Did you plant these?"

"No. I'm not sure how they got here, but every summer they grow like wildfire. We only see ripe berries for a few weeks before all the critters destroy them. The bears like them, too." He holds up the container he carried all the way here. "I thought you'd like to pick some."

"I've never picked wild anything before." My smile widens in excitement.

"They're smaller than you'd see at the grocery store, but they'll be sweeter too."

I pick a little berry and examine it in the fading sunlight.

It's bumpy and firm, but it's the richest color of red I've ever seen in nature.

"I have a lipstick I love that's almost this shade of red. I was so excited the first time I put it on, I felt so mature, but my mother told me I looked like a slut... I never did wear it again."

Talking to my mother last night stirred up bad memories. I place the strawberry in the container and look up to see the most startled expression on his face.

"The more you tell me about your family, the more I hate them."

"You don't even know the half of it," I scoff, but then laugh at the ridiculousness.

"I'd like to, if you want to tell me," he admits softly.

I fill the rest of the container, wishing I would stop gravitating towards him when he's so grumpy with me, but every time he blankets me in his warm presence, I can't seem to turn it away.

"It'd be a long story..."

"There's a spot I like to go on nights like this, when it's just me and the bears. Will you come with me?" He asks hesitantly.

There's a softness in his eyes that isn't usually there. A different type of sorrow that I'd never be able to turn away from, no matter how hot and cold he acts towards me.

He leads me to the farthest outbuilding, the one that contains all the bear supplies, but doesn't take me inside. Instead, he grabs a ladder propped up against the outside wall and leans it against the building.

"Are you afraid of heights?"

"I don't think so, but I've never climbed a ladder like this."

CHAPTER TWENTY-THREE

He chuckles and shakes his head. "Go on, I'll catch you if you fall."

I grab the metal rungs but hesitate before pulling my feet off the ground.

"Take your time. Three points of contact at all times. Hand, hand, foot, foot," he instructs from right behind me. I start to move, and he continues talking me through it softly. "Hand, hand, foot, foot. Good. Keep looking up. Hand, hand, foot, foot. You're almost there."

"Now, what?" My shaking knees don't know how to get off the ladder and onto the flat-ish roof without losing my balance and falling backward.

"Plant your hands at the top of the ladder to stabilize your body and step onto the roof. I'm right behind you. I won't let you fall."

"Not on purpose, but I'm heavy. I could bring us both down like dominoes." Now my wrists are trembling, and I feel like the whole ladder is shaking.

"I'd never let that happen, darlin'." The deep timber of his voice melts over me, convincing me to spur forward and hoist myself off the ladder, but more importantly, to get away from the jitters that nickname causes in my nervous system.

Once I'm on the roof, I don't know what to do with my body, freezing in a half-crouched stance.

"And, for the record." He steps onto the roof easily and lays the blanket down. "I could have carried you up the ladder, so assuming you could knock me over is an insult."

"Gravity doesn't apply to you?"

"I'm not talking about gravity," he says pointedly, setting the strawberries down in the middle of the blanket and sitting down himself.

Oh.

I look out over the roof to the view beyond. We're sitting right above the edge of the bear enclosures. I haven't been this close yet.

"Will they come over here?"

"Maybe. They roam a little, but they also pick their favorite areas and tend to frequent them." He shrugs, leaning back on his arm.

"You really do love them, don't you?"

He shrugs again. "I don't know if love is the right word. I respect them. They didn't choose to be locked up for the rest of their life. The least I can do is make sure they're comfortable and taken care of. This is their home."

"I bet your grandfather was proud of what you did here."

He scoffs. "I don't know why, but he always said as much."

"You are a good man, Lochlan. No matter how much you don't think so."

"You hardly know me, Jo."

"I know enough." I pick up a strawberry and bite into it, surprising myself with how sweet it really is. I suck the juice from the soft inside part, before biting it to the stem. It's the best strawberry I've ever had.

I glance up to tell him, but his eyes are trained on my mouth, watching me as I finish chewing my bite. I swallow thickly under his serious observation.

"I need to tell you about my past," he says suddenly. "I don't want you to have this false idea of me. I need you to know the truth."

"I already know–"

"No, I need to tell you the whole story. You're working your ass off to get donations for this place and I need you

176

to know who I am. People are seeing that you're associated with this place, with me, and I need you to have confidence in who you're representing."

"Okay." It doesn't matter what I say; he seems ready to purge his soul, and I'm guilty for wanting him to.

He sits up, rubbing his hands together across his knees like he's revving up his courage.

"I had just turned 18 and I thought I was in love."

Chapter Twenty-Four

Lochlan

18 years ago...

As soon as I turn onto Bethany's street, every house and yard in sight is lit up in red and blue flashing lights. Cop cars are parked on the curb in front of her house, and my heart rate picks up...

What happened? Did someone get hurt?

There are no ambulances, only cop cars. A few police officers mill about on her porch, but I don't see Bethany anywhere.

The thought of her being hurt stirs dread in my chest that I've never experienced.

I park my truck on the street as close as I can since the driveway is blocked and cut across the front lawns to get to her house.

As soon as the cop on her front stoop sees me, he startles, drawing his gun on me. "Don't fucking move, boy." My hands go up on instinct.

"I'm Bethany's boyfriend. I need to make sure she's okay."

"Oh, you've done enough, son." He moves towards me and motions to the ground with the barrel of his gun while two more cops provide backup.

I'm big for my age, my grandfather always warned me to respect the law because they'd be intimidated by my size. I'm complying, but they don't seem to care.

"Down on your stomach, now!"

I do as I'm told, lying face first in the muddy grass, staining my nice shirt. I thought tonight would be special, but now it'll be a night to remember for the worst reasons.

He cuffs my wrists behind my back, and I let him because this has to be a big misunderstanding. There must have been a robbery, and it will all get cleared up when Bethany and her parents see me.

Except when two of the cops work together to help me stand, I see Bethany's dad standing on the porch with his arms crossed. "Sir, what's going on? Is Bethany okay?"

"Don't ever speak her name, you vile son of a bitch!"

What? I knew he didn't approve of us dating, but what did I do to deserve this type of hate?

"Please, someone tell me what's going on! Call my grandfather! Please, someone help me!" I beg as they shove me into the back of a cop car. They ignore my pleas, pulling away from the house without explanation.

I strain my neck to get a glimpse of her window when I notice a silhouette.

She watches as the car I'm in gets further from her house.

* * *

"The next time I saw her was in the courtroom. She sat behind the District Attorney and accused me of rape.

"I couldn't believe it was happening. I thought I would marry this girl, and she was letting them destroy me. I was so angry, but at the same time, I had convinced myself it was all a mistake. Her father had to have put her up to it. She was still 17, but we had been dating on and off for two years, and it wasn't illegal.

"It wasn't until she was called to testify that my world fucking shattered. She swore under oath that I had forced myself on her after she told me that she wasn't allowed to date me."

I keep my focus on the moon because I'm not brave enough to look Jo in the face as I tell this story.

"She gave them details about my anatomy and how rough I handled her. She told them how afraid she was of my size. I'll never forget the betrayal I felt when she sat there in front of everyone and described a sexual encounter that we had, but twisted it into a non-consensual nightmare." I hang my head in my hands, recalling how sick it made me.

"They all took one look at me and assumed my guilt, but I didn't, Jo. I never…" I can't even finish my thought. Saying this out loud to her is painful.

"I believe you, Lochlan."

"I don't know why. No one has ever given me the benefit of the doubt." I shake my head.

"After I got sent to prison, and she was no longer a minor, it came out that she was pregnant. That's what started it all." Jo gasps beside me.

"Even after everything that happened, I still convinced myself that she was confused and scared. Her father was a mean man, but I made my grandfather promise to take care of her and the baby, despite what she had accused me of. If I had a child out there, I wanted it taken care of...

"He told me when it was born, but she wouldn't speak to my grandparents, and she eventually ran off with the baby."

"Oh my God. I didn't know."

"Pops spent his life savings to hire a private investigator to track her down. I spent 68 months in prison, not knowing if it was a boy or girl, what it looked like, what she named it."

"That must've been torture." She gazes at me in disbelief, but she hasn't heard the worst of it yet.

"Almost six years in, I finally found out it was a girl... But she wasn't mine."

Jo covers her shock with a hand over her mouth. There is nothing to be said when hearing a horror story like this anyway.

"It took years to get the paternity testing done, though. Bethany would refuse; her lawyers made our lawyer jump through every hoop, and she lived in a different state by that time. But even after the DNA test results were presented to the court, they wouldn't reevaluate my conviction. They were bogged down, no one wanted to reopen such a heinous case. I think the heartbreak of that is what killed my grandmother. They said it was a heart attack, but I know it was my fault.

"She never got to see me as a free man. I missed her funeral..."

"You shouldn't have had to go through that," she murmurs, settling some of the rage boiling back up inside of me.

"My grandfather didn't visit me for almost a year after she died. I didn't blame him for it. The stress of my situation and losing the love of his life was too much for him... But when he did come back, he had a letter.

"I guess Bethany sent it here, assuming my grandfather could get it to me."

"What did it say?"

"She admitted that she lied about everything. When she found out she was pregnant, she was terrified to admit the truth to her father, especially since she wasn't supposed to be dating at all. She was sleeping with a bunch of people, cheating on me. That broke my heart all over again because I really had loved her at the time." I shake my head at the memory.

"She admitted that blaming me for rape was an impulse decision because she felt trapped. She regretted it immediately, but she was too afraid of her father to tell the truth. She only wrote the letter to me because she had finally gone no contact with him after years in therapy."

"Still, she ruined your life," Jo says angrily.

"I know. I had to mourn the relationship that I thought I had with her. I mourned my normal life. I mourned a child that was never truly mine. It ruined me."

"But you got a second chance."

"It took my grandfather forever to get a meeting with your father. I couldn't believe it when he called to tell me it worked. I was exonerated. My charges were dismissed, and I wouldn't have to live with my name on some vile sex offender's list."

"Did he tell you about it? The meeting?"

"No, not really. We were so happy I was getting out of prison that we only spoke about the future." I glance at her as she bites her lips introspectively. "Why?"

"I need to tell you the truth about something, but I don't want you to be angry at me."

182

"Why would I be angry?"

"I've kept something from you."

My stomach sinks. After the betrayal I just spoke about, she thinks dropping another bomb on me is a good idea?

"Tell me, Jo."

"I knew your grandfather."

"What?"

"I met him that day, in the Governor's office. I was shadowing my dad for school in my sophomore year."

I stare at her fully, not having any idea where this is going.

"I listened to him talk about his grandson and how innocent he knew you were. I was moved to tears, hearing him advocate for you. No one in my life had ever been in my corner the way he was for you. He was the most genuine man I had ever met. I felt like I could see the honesty in his eyes, and I believed every word he said.

"He was in his military uniform, it was really sweet. He showed the letter to my father to prove your innocence, but I never knew what it said. All I knew was that my father was going to say no. He had no intention of exonerating you."

Chapter Twenty-Five

Jo

He stares at me in disbelief, but it's so dark now that it's shielding me from the intensity of it.

"I knew your grandfather was telling the truth. I knew you were innocent because he believed you were. He left the room, and my dad practically threw the file into the trash. I was horrified that he could be so cold-hearted."

"Jo…" He mutters, but I keep going.

"I threatened to tell my mother about his affair with his secretary if he didn't do what your grandfather asked. They had just recovered from his last affair, and he couldn't afford to get caught in a lie again."

Lochlan's mouth hangs open, listening to me spew my truth. It feels freeing to get this weight off my chest.

"He called your grandfather back in the room and stamped his approval to set you free. I could see how surprised he was, and when he looked at me, I think he realized what I had done… He was so thankful, he cried like a baby, and I did too."

"You… My grandfather…" he mumbles, still processing what he's hearing.

"I followed him into the hallway, and I told him that I wished I had someone in my life who loved me like he loved you." I lay back on the blanket and stare into the dark sky, warding off the burning in my eyes.

"He must've seen the pain in my eyes because he told me if I ever needed a safe place to go, he had a black bear sanctuary that was always open to rescues."

"You came here looking for him?"

"Yeah."

He lies back on the blanket beside me, and we sit in silence for a long time, staring at the blanket of stars above us. Long enough for the fireworks' booms to echo up the mountain and fall quiet again once the show is over.

"All this time, I thought your father saved me. I thought it was him who I owed a debt to. But it's you."

"You don't owe me anything. You were innocent, and you deserved to be free."

"I don't know how, but I'll pay you back for your faith in me, I swear."

I tilt my head to the side to look at him, and he's already looking at me, so seriously. His normally furrowed brow is even deeper. I want to reach out and smooth it with my finger as if it will take away his hurt.

"Your grandfather told me that I could come here for solace, and I think I've found it," I whisper now that he's so close. Our faces are still nearly a foot apart, but it feels like centimeters.

"What are you running from? What aren't you telling me?"

"My family."

"I know they're bastards, but there has to be more to it. A woman like you doesn't come to a place like this for no reason."

"I needed to be somewhere that my father couldn't reach. This place is so far off the map that I knew he couldn't sink his claws in and ruin it for me. And, I hoped that your grandfather would keep his promise. To keep me safe."

"I'll keep you safe, Jo."

"I know, that's why I put up with your grumpy attitude."

He scoffs, but a small smile tilts his lips, and I cherish it because I never know when I'll see the next one.

"Why didn't you tell me all of this from the beginning? From the first time you drove through these gates."

"I didn't want you to give me a job because of your grandfather or because of my dad. I was prideful enough that I wanted to earn it the old-fashioned way, but I was desperate and took the job anyway after you found out I was a Montgomery."

"I'm glad you took it."

"Me too." My eyes trace the scars on his face, still not knowing the story behind them. But as we sit in silence, only accompanied by the sound of the world around us, croaking toads, vibrating beetles, and the occasional grunt that I've convinced myself is one of the bears, I can't make myself ask.

I don't want him to have to share any more sad stories with me, not tonight.

"I can't believe he never told me my guardian angel was a teenage girl," he ponders out loud, looking back up to the sky.

"It was my father who signed the papers."

"Your father is a jackass. I won't give that man credit for a thing," he states seriously, making me smile.

He notices my amusement and his face softens instantly.

"It broke my heart when you told me he was dead, though,"

CHAPTER TWENTY-FIVE

I admit softly.

"I was so callous about it, too." He sighs, rubbing a hand across his face in regret. "He's buried here on the property. If you'd ever like to visit him."

"I'd love to."

Saying goodbye properly might give me closure, even though I only ever met the man one time. I spent years idolizing him in my head, hoping I'd see him again one day.

He talks me down the ladder and we take a different path I've never traveled, only guided by the moonlight and the occasional lightning bug.

"I still didn't get to see a bear."

"I'll make it happen soon, don't worry." He smiles softly, and the sight of it makes my stomach flutter. It does a flip when his knuckles brush the back of my hand as we walk side by side.

That small touch of his skin makes me ache to hold his hand again. Not because he's helping me unbuckle a seat belt or getting me out of an awkward situation, but because he's a man who wants to hold my hand.

I shouldn't have a crush on Lochlan. He's too old for me. He's given me every reason to dislike his presence and to be turned off by his grouchy demeanor, but I long to be near him every time he lets me.

"This is our family plot. My grandparents are buried together."

"Wow, I didn't realize people could be buried anywhere other than a cemetery." My knees sink into the cool grass in front of the giant granite headstone, my index finger tracing the engraving.

Henry & Alice Dane

"I bet your grandmother was wonderful, too." I wipe a tear from my cheek, trying to hide how silly I'm being. I hardly knew his grandfather and his grandmother, not at all, but it feels like a piece of me missed out on knowing them.

"She was," he speaks gently behind me, letting me have a moment.

I take my time, wiping loose pieces of grass and leaves that have fallen onto the smooth stone, shining it properly for two strangers. It seems like the least I can do.

"Thank you for bringing me here." When I stand and face him, the hard lines of his face are intense, watching me closely. It would probably put most people off, but it only makes me wonder what it would be like to bury my head in his chest, or to have his arms wrapped around me with that same intensity.

"Come on, it's late. I'll get you back."

I follow his lead even though I don't want to go back to my lonely guesthouse yet. The air is thick with the smoke he predicted would get caught in the mountains, and it makes the walk hazier than before. The footpath is eerie with fog, and I walk closer to Lochlan's side because of it.

An animal jumps in the brush alongside us, and I flinch, bumping into his arm. "Sorry," I mumble in embarrassment.

His hand brushes mine again, but I don't move away. Instead, I let my pinky graze his knuckles, waiting for him to pull back.

But he doesn't.

The pressure building in my chest is nearing volcanic. Every beat feels closer to my heart bursting as I wrap my littlest finger around his ever so gently.

I wait for a protest through the roaring in my ears, but

it never comes. He holds my pinky in his much larger one, walking me home under the moonlight.

Butterflies flutter through me, and I can't control the corners of my lips from lifting. It's silly. I shouldn't be so giddy, but it's the closest I've ever felt to being a character in one of my movies.

Until loud popping bursts through the silent night, echoing and bouncing off the trees all around us.

His hand envelops mine, pulling me to his chest and backing us into the cover of the woods.

Pop, pop, pop.

"Is that fireworks?" I ask breathlessly, the blood roaring in my ears is less romantic now.

Pop, pop.

"No." His head is high, listening closely to which direction the noise is originating. *Pop, pop, pop.* "Dammit."

"What?"

"I need to get you back to the house." He's still holding me tightly against him, but I can't enjoy the moment because of what he's telling me.

"And, then what?"

"Call 911. Tell them we're being shot at."

Chapter Twenty-Six

Lochlan

There aren't many people in this world who have the privilege to touch the fur of an adult bear. The dense black hairs that don't feel real when smoothed under your hand, and the giant paws tipped with dangerously long claws.

My palm caresses the tan snout of this bear as if to comfort him. He's too far gone to save and too hurt to fight.

Three bullet holes ripped through his innocent body, doing more damage than any animal like this should ever experience in the wild. All because he trusted me to keep him safe here.

The last few hours have been a blur; my memory of it is already slightly out of focus.

Her hands are on my chest, her frightened eyes pleading with me to stay with her.

"Run to the house, call the Sheriff."

"But, Lochlan..."

I rake my fingers into her hair like I crave doing every moment I'm near her. "Go, Jo," I beg, wishing I could touch her like this without needing to push her away.

She takes off from the end of the footpath, crossing over the gravel lot to get to the house. As soon as she hits the porch steps, I take off toward the gunshots.

"Lochlan," Hayes's voice snaps me out of my thoughts. "I called the vet, he'll be here in an hour."

I rise, barely managing to move a few feet away before bracing my back against the trunk of a tree. Hayes and Seiver watch me warily.

"The rest of them?"

"It took us a bit, but we got eyes on the other bears. There were no more injuries. The fucker who attacked us only left one victim."

"I need to check on Jo." I don't explain further, and they don't ask.

Headlights sweep past me as I drag my feet back to the house. The Sheriff brought back up and now there are too many damn people here.

I should be more concerned that I'm walking up to a member of law enforcement with blood staining my hands, but all I can focus on is how close Jo's standing at his side.

I chased down the truck shooting a shotgun into the bear enclosures without anyway to protect myself, hopped a fence to check on the wounded black bear who was minding his business until a selfish asshole decided to harm him, and slid my hands over the animal's body checking for injuries before I knew if he would react aggressively.

But I'm hung up on the way Jo is shaking like a leaf.

And, seeking comfort from someone else when I wish it were me.

"I'm fine. I promise, I'm fine," Jo assures the Sheriff as I approach them. He's looking at her so tenderly, it makes me hate the man who's been nothing but fair to me.

He sees me, but has to tear his eyes from her to really look at me. "Is that your blood?"

Jo gasps as she notices my hands.

"No."

"A person's?"

"No."

"The bears?" Jo cries, covering her face with her hands, sinking down onto the porch steps. The Sheriff looks at her again, and I can see his need to comfort her. I feel the need too, but neither of us moves.

If he touches her, I might go to jail tonight.

"Lochlan, what are we going to do?" Jo asks me as the chaos continues around us.

Cops are combing the property for evidence, more than one is confirming there are no weapons here, just because there are felons in their presence.

Someone shot a gun at us.

This is way worse than all of the other harassment. This was deadly.

Sheriff Malec excuses himself to speak to one of his deputies, and we both watch him walk away. Actually, I watch her watching him.

The thorns of jealousy lick at my spine. I can never offer her anything like that. An upstanding citizen, a reputation of gold.

"What can I do?" She asks me again, but when her hand brushes my elbow, the noise in my head becomes too much, and I snap.

"I don't know, Jo. Go ask the Sheriff!" I bark the words out, throwing my hands up in frustration, and her face drops.

The kind and eager woman who has bent over backwards for the greater good of this place stares at me in devastation before running back to the guesthouse.

The woman who gifted me the gentle touch of her hands earlier.

The woman who had faith in me before she ever met me…

I snuffed her light out, and it doesn't matter that I regret it immediately. The further she stays from me, the better.

The further she gets from this place, the better.

I drag myself up my porch, needing sleep, but even more, a drink.

Everything is imploding around me.

She didn't deserve it, she never does, but whenever I attempt to voice my thoughts, my emotionally dense brain hijacks my words.

It's not an excuse. She shouldn't have to put up with it.

She's my damn guardian angel. She saved my life by convincing her father to exonerate me, and I will spend the rest of it making it up to her.

I can't offer her much, but a nonvolatile workplace should be a start, even though my skin itches to feel hers against mine, again.

Her soft hand against mine, her fingers gripping the shirt above my chest. It was selfish to let her get so close, because having her close is dangerous.

This place is dangerous.

And, if I touch her again, I won't want to let her go.

* * *

The rocking chair tips back and forth as the property finally quiets down.

The vet came and sedated the bear, taking away his pain until he passed.

The guys are back in the bunkhouse.

Sheriff Malec is the last to leave; he usually is, always staying until the dust settles. I've always liked that about him, until recently.

He takes two steps up the porch and stops, leaning against the handrail. I give him credit, he's taking this seriously. His trunk is full of evidence bags.

"You going to be able to get some sleep?" He eyes the glass of whiskey in my hand but doesn't say anything about it.

"Probably not." He follows my gaze to the guesthouse.

"I can try to keep extra patrols in the area, but you know how it is. My men can only cover so much ground."

"I know." This isn't the Sheriff's problem. Whoever is doing this has made a personal vendetta against me, and I intend to handle it when the time comes.

"I told Jo it might be best to stay somewhere else, but she told me no." He shrugs.

"Stay where? With you?" The words come out of my mouth like a whip, but I keep them hidden behind my glass.

"Sure, wherever. Natalie and Dec would love to have her."

I met Natalie and her little brother last year when Dec hopped my fences to get away from some bad men. I knew the Sheriff was involved with them, but the way he was towards Jo made me think twice about his relationship status.

He has a woman at home, so why the special attention on mine?

Not mine.

194

"Natalie is big on family. She wants to get to know her more, but I think it will take time."

I know I haven't slept, but I also haven't even finished this drink, and this conversation should not be as confusing as it is.

"I'm not following."

"Did Jo not tell you?"

"Tell me what?"

I see the moment he takes pity on my confusion and chuckles. "Sorry, I assumed you knew. She's my long-lost sister. Half sister," he corrects.

The glass in my hand pauses midway to my mouth.

Fucking hell.

The Sheriff is her brother...

All the secret conversations. The concern. He wasn't interested in her because she's a beautiful woman. He was watching out for her because she's his sister.

I let my jealousy lash out unjustly, no matter all the other reasons she should stay the hell away from me, how I've treated her is even more despicable now.

"Your father is..."

"Old Governor Montgomery. I know," he confirms the ridiculousness. "No one knows, but I assumed she would have mentioned it since I've been out here so many times. And, tried to get her to leave multiple times." He meets my eyes. "Sorry, no offense."

"None taken," I answer honestly. From an outside perspective, I wouldn't want my sister living here either.

"We haven't been able to spend much time getting to know each other yet, but she swore up and down it was safe here. But more so, that she was safe with you. I'll take her word for

195

it, but I wouldn't mind hearing it from you, too." He states seriously, waiting for me to confirm.

There aren't enough words to express how safe that woman is with me. Not words that I'm legally allowed to say in front of a member of law enforcement.

"This is no place for someone as good as Jo, but while she's here, she's safe. That's a fuckin' promise."

I'm not letting her out of my sight.

Chapter Twenty-Seven

Jo

I'm staring directly at myself in the mirror, but my eyes won't focus on anything but my mother's face over my shoulder. The permanently curled upper lip is hardly noticeable after all of the Botox, but I see it every time she looks at me.

She refuses to age, and I can't wait to get older. I want the freedom that comes with maturity. The independence.

I don't want anyone to control me.

"Your breasts are too heavy; they sag." She pinches the under cup of my bra and pushes up. "I think we should call a surgeon."

"Yes, mother."

"If you would stop eating breakfast and lunch, you'd lose a few inches off your waist by summer," she remarks disgustedly.

"But, I would starve."

"Replace it with a green smoothie, don't be a pig."

"Yes, mother."

It's strange how time can heal parts of the brain that seemed irreparably damaged. Six months ago, my mother had her claws so deep in me that I couldn't take a bite of food without considering her disapproval.

Any article of clothing that touched my body had to pass

her inspection.

One cross look would send me running to my room to change before I ended up in tears and ruining my makeup. The makeup that she critiqued down to each pore.

There hasn't been a miracle cure, but I find myself thinking about her opinion less.

I got less blonde highlights in my hair this morning at the salon, and I haven't been able to stop checking my reflection.

It's taken twenty-four years, but I'm finally starting to look like me and not the prototype she wanted but could never quite get right.

There's a knock at my door suddenly, and I suspect it's another delivery from Lochlan. He's been leaving random gifts.

Gift isn't the right word. Peace offerings would be more apt.

The first time, it was a drawing, held in place by a rock, that his niece had drawn. A colored pencil portrait of us doing our makeup. It was cute, so I hung it on my mini fridge.

I didn't make any effort to thank him for it.

The next delivery was a box of Girl Scout cookies.

I ate them, but I didn't thank him for them either.

When I went into his kitchen to get a few hours of work done the other day, there was a pink sticky note on the whiskey cabinet with my name on it. He swapped all my sweets down low so I didn't need to use a chair. I threw the note away and never mentioned it.

The last delivery was a small pizza from his sister's pizza shop. The kind with my favorite toppings.

I haven't acknowledged him when I know he's sitting on the porch, and I definitely haven't asked to explore the property.

Not since he lashed out at me for the last time.

I'm starting to gain the tiniest shreds of self-worth, and he is not going to take them away from me.

I open the door expecting to see something on my little welcome mat, but instead I see men's boots.

For the briefest moment, I consider shutting the door in his face, letting him feel an inkling of how he treats me, but he sees my intention before I can follow through.

"Can I talk to you? Please."

He looks as dark and dangerous as usual, and undeniably handsome. "We have to leave for the event soon."

"I know. It'll only take a few minutes."

"Fine." I brush past him to sit on the porch steps because I do not want to be inside the guesthouse with him.

"Here." He grabs a jacket from inside the door before I can sit and lays it down on the top porch step so my black dress doesn't get dusty.

"Thanks."

"We both know that I need to apologize for my behavior the other night. I'm sorry for how I acted, and I'm sorry for not knowing what to say to fix it."

"You don't owe me an apology, Lochlan. You don't owe me anything."

"Of course, I do. I owe you everything."

"I don't want you to only be nice to me because I convinced my father to exonerate you."

"That's not what this is."

"Then what is it? Because I am so sick of feeling worthless."

"That's how I made you feel?" He looks devastated.

"Yes. Believe it or not, I have feelings. Being kind to me one second and then snapping at me the next hurts." I can't look at him while I speak, my head's twisted to the side, staring out across the property.

"Dammit, Jo. I'm sorry. I never meant to hurt your feelings, I'm just an idiot when it comes to you."

"Hayes said you didn't know how to talk to women." I laugh humorlessly.

"That's probably true, but you're on a-whole-nother level. I suffocate when I'm near you." He jets up from his seat on the steps and starts pacing back and forth, scrubbing a hand through his hair.

"Like you're in prison," I mutter.

He skids to a stop and looks at me. "No, not like I'm in prison. Like I don't have the privilege to breathe the same air as you."

"What?"

"You don't belong here, Jo. I stand by that, but it's not because you're not worthy of being here. It's because you are too damn good for this place. You shouldn't be running away from bullets or worried if one of the parolees will slip up. You shouldn't be out there begging for money for this place. Or, being propped up on stage for your family's sake when they treat you like crap. You shouldn't be subjected to all my shit." He points to his head, clarifying what he means.

That's the kindest thing he's ever said to me, but it sounds like he's about to fire me. "I like it here."

"But, you shouldn't."

"I don't know what you want from me."

"I want you to be happy and safe. I want you to be proud of the work you do here, and then I want you to leave it in your rear view mirror as fast as possible. Move on to bigger and better things."

CHAPTER TWENTY-SEVEN

"Okay…"

"I promised your brother I'd keep you safe, and I intend to keep that promise."

"My brother?"

"Sheriff Malec."

"He told you."

"Yeah. Why didn't you?"

I've wondered that many times, but I always concluded that it wasn't the time to share something so deeply life-altering for me.

"When I was a little girl, close to Emory's age, I had a pet bunny that I loved. She was all white except for a black spot around her nose and right eye. She was my best friend."

Lochlan stands silently, letting me purge myself.

"I came home from school one day, and she wasn't in her cage. I ran around for hours looking for her until I found her behind the pool house. My brother had killed her. Pulled her arms off, tuffs of fur out, and mutilated her with a stick… He stood next to me, laughing about it."

"What?" He throws his hands out as if he's outraged because Lochlan Dane has a moral code.

"I bawled my eyes out to my parents, and they didn't care. They swept it under the rug and told me to get over it… I knew then that I was alone. My family was the worst of the worst. I kept my head down and did my best to avoid trouble, to avoid Conrad, my entire life."

"Jesus Christ. I'm sorry, darlin'."

A sad sigh escapes me. "Until he abandoned a child," I admit, barely above a whisper.

Lochlan tips his head and squeezes his eyes shut, "Son of a bitch…" He mumbles.

"I found out two and a half years ago that he got a woman pregnant. She thought they were in a relationship, but he did not see it that way. When she told him that she was going to have a baby, he completely cut her off. Filed a restraining order based on nothing, blocked her from contacting him in any way. I was devastated that he would do something like that, but I wasn't surprised.

"Of course, when I protested his behavior, I became enemy number one. He was pursuing his career, he was the victim." I roll my eyes, remembering the stupid excuses my parents gave.

"That's a pathetic excuse for a man," Lochlan says, affirming my beliefs.

"I've never been brave enough to stand up to my father, but I looked him in the eye and told him what Conrad did was despicable. How could a man do that and still sleep at night?"

My father's face has aged over the years, the texture of his skin has roughened, and his wrinkles have gotten deeper. The youthfulness has faded from my memories, but I will never forget how he looked when the blood drained from his face in shame.

"He was stricken with guilt, and I knew immediately he had done the same thing."

Lochlan doesn't speak, urging me to continue as he sits down beside me.

"I spit into so many little tubes, putting myself on every genealogy website and DNA app. I waited almost a year before I finally got a match. I don't know why I didn't tell you. Maybe to protect Jackson's privacy." I shrug. "I always wondered why there was such a big gap between me and Conrad. Turns out my father had Jackson from an affair with the gardener during that time... He and my mother went through a rough patch because of it." I roll my eyes incredulously.

"Instead of doing the right thing, he cut off Jackson's mother, never claimed him, or supported them in any way."

"And Conrad's kid?"

"I get an allowance every month from a trust that will be paid out when I turn 25. I've been sending most of the money to the mother of Conrad's child. I wrote her a letter and told her that she could never speak about it, and I'd deny doing it, but I'd help her as much as I could until the baby turned three. Give her time to get on her feet, I guess. That's next year sometime, I'm not even sure when his birthday is."

"A boy?"

"I don't know his name, and it breaks my heart. I have a nephew, and I don't even know him. He doesn't know half of his family, but it's probably for the best. My family wouldn't deserve him anyway."

"Is that why you needed a job so badly?"

"I was running low on money and needed to make it look like I wasn't, so my parents didn't find out and retaliate. I was afraid of what they'd do if they found out I was helping them.

"But, once I turn 25, I'll be able to get all my money and take off. They'll never know what I did and they'll never see me again," I explain coldly. I've had plenty of time to come to terms with it.

"When do you turn 25?"

"The week after summer semester ends." I stand up from the porch steps and straighten my dress. "So, you can take this as my termination notice. I'll be out of your hair then, too."

Chapter Twenty-Eight

Jo

"I don't want you out of my hair," he admits right behind me, following me to the guesthouse. He stops in the doorway as if he's afraid to go further.

"You've made it clear that you do." I avoid eye contact by sitting down to finish my makeup.

"You don't understand."

"Try me."

"From here on out, I don't want there to be any confusion. I am your boss, you're my employee. That's all," he states seriously, stepping forward to look at me in the reflection of my little mirror. Except, his eyes are trained on my lips as I apply chapstick.

"You don't want me to come over and watch movies, or eat ice cream?"

"No, you can still come do that."

"Then I shouldn't walk with you around the property?" I ask, drawing a line of nude lip liner around my lips.

He steps closer, his gaze never wavering from my mouth. "You can walk with me."

"What exactly is it that you're wanting then?" I smear the

nude lipstick across my bottom lip, and his hands grip the back of my chair.

"Don't touch me," he pleads, finally forcing his eyes to mine in the mirror. "You can't touch me anymore."

"Oh." Embarrassment floods my system. "I'm sorry if I made you uncomfortable."

"Don't do that, don't take it for something it isn't. I'm drawing a boundary for your own good, trust me." He tears his attention from the mirror and drags his hands down his face.

"For my own good," I utter under my breath, focusing on the mirror long enough to hate the lip color I chose.

I pick up a makeup wipe to smear it off as he stares at me.

I avoid his gaze as I fiddle with my lipstick tubes, shifting them around, pretending to choose a new one so he doesn't see the confusion on my face. The hurt.

He sees me as a naive young woman, another person who refuses to let me make my own choices.

"I'll be ready in a few minutes. I need to find some jewelry, but it spilled in the bottom of my suitcase." I stand from my seat without picking a color, and he backs up as if the boundary he put up between us is physically in the room, keeping us separated.

He moves toward the door, and I think he's going to leave without saying anything, but he stops suddenly at the threshold.

"Wear the red lipstick," he suggests over his shoulder, disappearing from the doorway.

I pick up the gold tube and twist it in my fingers.

The red lipstick that I love but my mother hates.

She'd be disgusted.

A minute later, I hear his steps approaching my door again, but his voice reaches me before he does.

"This probably isn't helpful, but I have some of my grandmother's old jewelry if you want to look through it." He stops suddenly in my open door, noticing my red lips.

He opens his mouth to say something, and I hope he might compliment me, but he shuts it again before clearing his throat.

He's holding a wooden jewelry box I recognize from one of the shelves in the living room, and he pops it open as I step towards him. A gasp escapes me. "These are beautiful pieces."

Real gold and silver, gems of all sizes and colors, authentic turquoise. My eyes are drawn to a vintage gold cluster ring with tiny diamonds; the floral pattern is stunning and will match the earrings I already have in.

"Your grandmother had great taste. Is this okay?" I ask, slipping the ring onto my middle finger.

He nods subtly and doesn't say another word to me as we all pile into the trucks and go to the event.

He doesn't speak to anyone or even look in my direction.

I thought maybe the lipstick would push his boundary just a little, but it seems like it had the opposite effect. He's stepping further away.

We arrive at the estate where the event is taking place, and he disappears as soon as we walk through the doors.

It doesn't matter. This is work, and I have a job to do.

"JoAnna." My mother's stuck-up voice slumps my shoulders immediately. "Why on earth do you keep associating with those thugs?"

"They aren't thugs."

"They've been to prison," she hisses.

"So? Did you need something? I need to make my rounds." The red lipstick is giving me an edge of confidence that I did not have the last time I spoke to this woman.

"I need you to come with me." She gestures for me to follow her, but I don't move. "Really, JoAnna? When are you going to grow up?"

"What, Mom? What do you want from me?"

She waves someone out of sight over, and I sigh. "It's time to push for publicity before we get into the final months of your brother's campaign."

His campaign manager, Austin, walks through the crowd, approaching us, and I take a deep breath to curb my annoyance because my brother and father are right behind him. Great.

"What is going on?" I ask even though I really don't care to know.

"We need to make things official."

"What things?"

"In two weeks, Austin will propose at the Biltmore Gala."

Plates crash, water spills, and someone in the distance screams in terror. Except the room doesn't falter because it's all in my head.

This can't be happening again, not after how far I've gotten away from them.

"No."

"This isn't up for debate, your father approves. The perception will be excellent for your brother's image."

"What? That we're a big, happy family?" I screech, causing a few heads to swivel in our direction. My mother smiles politely, redirecting their attention and then gritting her teeth at me.

"Your brother isn't ready for marriage, but being associated with an engaged couple will boost his likability."

"He isn't ready? He's ten years older than I am!"

"JoAnna, you'll calm down this instance," my father demands.

"No," I cry out, stepping back as they team up in front of me, crowding me like evil invaders.

I'm trapped with my back against the wall, literally. My panicked gaze flits across the room until it latches onto the only eyes that blanket me in safety.

Looming over the crowd, his stature filters through all the chaos. He's facing a couple of people, but his focus is on me because he always finds me in a room. His brows furrow deeper as my internal temperature rises.

"We'll start spreading the word tonight that you two have been seeing each other. It's official," my mother quips haughtily.

"I can't be engaged to Austin."

"And, why not?"

My fingertips graze the gold ring on the middle finger of my left hand, and I take a deep breath, slipping it off and onto the finger to its left.

"Because I'm already engaged."

"WHAT!" The chorus of outrage rings out, but I can't pay attention to who is the angriest. All I can see is Lochlan's confused expression from across the room.

He has no idea what I'm about to do.

I'm so sorry. I plead with my eyes anyway, hoping that I can get away with using him to save myself one last time.

"I'm engaged to Lochlan Dane," I state boldly, preparing to

reap the consequences of my actions.

Chapter Twenty-Nine

Lochlan

Her beautiful painted lips turn down, further and further, and I can't control the rage burning inside me. Someone's upsetting her.

Her big, sad eyes are a magnet pulling me in because whenever she needs me, I'll come. It doesn't matter where we are or what I said earlier about boundaries. If Jo needs help, then I'll be the one to help her.

I barely take a step forward when all hell breaks loose. Bodies start crashing and bumping into each other as they're being pushed away from the commotion. The stem of it is the circle of people surrounding Jo by the terrace.

Party goers in their fancy suits and dresses are being directed hastily to another area, but my eyes are on her. The moment she flattens herself against the wall and squeezes her eyes shut in fear, I'm plowing against the flow of people to get to her.

Men wearing suits, who typically stay within her family's radius, are the first to challenge me. They raise their hands, attempting to push me back as if they'll keep me from her.

It doesn't stop me but it slows me down enough to see that

the epicenter of all this bullshit is Jo's father. He's screaming at everyone, including Jo.

My hands find the bodyguards' shoulders, and I shove, bulldozing them out of my way. They could be Secret Service for the President of the United States, and I wouldn't stop.

They'd have to shoot me before I let whatever is happening continue happening to that woman.

I'm within arm's reach of their group when Jo launches herself at me, wrapping her arms around my neck. "I'm sorry, Lochlan, I'm so sorry," she pleads before spinning around and flattening herself against my front.

"THIS! This lowlife is who you're marrying," her father yells, shoving her brother's campaign manager for simply being in his path. A large vase takes the secondary impact and topples, sending dirt and palm leaves scattering across the floor.

I can hardly process what I'm hearing.

"Lochlan is my fiancé, so you'll speak to him with respect or you'll never speak to me again."

Fiancé. Fiancé?

"Oh my word," her mother cries, fanning herself with a handkerchief dramatically.

Fiancé?

"This is going to look terrible for me, JoAnna, you selfish little bitch!" Her brother screams, and I've had enough despite my confusion.

"Don't fucking speak to her that way," I demand, pulling Jo back to stand beside me, away from her psychotic family.

Fiancé.

"No one asked you, neanderthal." Her brother spits at my feet, and it flips a switch in my brain. A huff of laughter escapes me, and Conrad balks.

I'll kill this fucker exactly like he killed Jo's bunny.

I take one step before a delicate hand on my chest stops me. "Take me home, please," she begs desperately. Her fingers grip the fabric of my shirt. "Please, Lochlan. Take me home."

My attention locks onto her pleading eyes, and I can't tear it away.

I can't tell her no. I never could.

"Okay." I grip her fingers in my hand, intending to tug her back into my side when my thumb brushes over my grandma's ring. My grandmother's *engagement ring*.

Jo didn't know that when she picked it out, and I didn't say anything.

She steps away from her family, keeping my hand in hers, and tugging me along. She's a small thing compared to me, but it takes no strength at all to walk me on the leash she has me on.

The party crowd has dissipated, but Hayes and the other guys are standing as close as they can to the excitement, waiting in the wings as backup. Hayes talks to me without speaking, asking if there is trouble, and I shake my head.

"Not yet," I mutter to him as Jo walks me past him. If he's surprised that she's pulling me like a dog, he doesn't act it.

It isn't until we're outside and Jo's safe that some of the noise returns and the blinders come off.

"What did I do? What did I do?" Jo cries, gripping the sides of her head in her hands, mussing her hair.

We're standing in the parking lot between the trucks while the guys hover a few feet away, pretending to give us privacy.

"Jo, what the hell was that?"

"They backed me into a corner. I panicked!"

213

"And you told them we were engaged?"

"Yes."

My knees go weak. I hoped I was wrong and that she didn't do what I think she did, that I was mistaking the word fiancé for something else.

"Are you out of your mind?"

"I didn't have a choice."

"A choice? A choice! You cannot pretend to be with a man like me, Jo."

"What do you mean?"

"It will ruin your life! I will ruin your life!"

"That's not true."

"Jesus. Do you know what people will say about you? What they already say about me? We can't let this rumor spread just because you're trying to stick it to your parents."

"Lochlan, it's not that."

"What is it then? Why are you doing this?"

"They did it again."

"What?"

"They were forcing another engagement on me." Her words make the blood in my veins run cold.

"To who?"

"Austin. My brother's best friend."

I turn around in the confined space and brace my hands on the top of the truck bed. This poor woman is trapped between the worst of two worlds. The one that her parents want to force upon her, and mine. The cold, dark cave that is my life.

"I told them that I couldn't marry Austin because I was already engaged to you. That's what caused the scene in there," she whispers guiltily. "I know it isn't fair to drag you into this, but you told me that you'd keep me safe."

"Of course, I will, but not like this. There has to be another way."

"There isn't. As long as I'm single, my mother will try to sell me off like a prize horse."

"So, what? We pretend that we're a couple, and then what?"

"I'll finish school, get my trust fund, and then I'll be gone. They won't have any hold over me."

"I don't know. I don't think I can do this. It's not right."

"You told me that you owed me, that you'd repay me for my part in exonerating you. This is it. This is what I want."

I owe her everything, but I can't ruin her life after she saved mine.

Chapter Thirty

Jo

The rain hasn't stopped all weekend, but when there is the smallest break in dark clouds overhead and the droplets stop pelting my tiny kitchen window, I move my pouting outdoors.

Of all the things I've hated about myself, my brain has never been on the list. I've always been able to take pride in school and how smart I am. Top of my class, the one to set the curve on tests, and the overall ease in learning new subjects.

Yet, I've never felt dumber in my entire life.

Lochlan hasn't spoken to me since he stormed away from me in the parking lot at the event. I rode home with Jordy, Seiver, and Curtis. All of whom are normally chatty with me, but didn't offer me a word of support or advice.

I've really wrecked things this time.

I kick the little pebbles that haven't succumbed to the mud, wandering across the gravel lot until I'm near the barns. I shouldn't go any further, I'm not supposed to.

Instead of turning around and heading back to where all my textbooks are laid out in my depression room, my feet stay stuck in the same spot. I can't move forward, and I don't

216

want to go back.

I tip my head back, staring into the dull gray sky, until the faintest of mists tickles my face. I should go back inside before my hair gets frizzy.

My feet pivot, and I watch the gates open to a shiny Audi SUV.

I turn back to the barns and bolt, dodging between two of the buildings because I know who drives that car.

It's only a moment before they're blaring the horn, and I hear the transmission shift into park. "JoAnna! I saw you!"

Very reluctantly, I emerge from my hiding spot. "What do you want, Austin?"

"I'm here to bring you home."

"What? No."

"Your parents informed me that I'm not to leave without you."

"That's not my problem. I'm not going anywhere with you."

"You don't have a choice. You need to come with me."

The door to the garage beside me flies open suddenly, banging into the metal siding and making me jump. Hayes steps out, glaring at Austin. He's holding a crowbar in his hand, looking too lethal for someone with his rap sheet.

"Who doesn't have a choice?" He asks with deadly composure, stepping up beside me.

I'm incredibly concerned that he intends to use that crowbar on Austin until he flips one end over the other in his hand like a bat, handing it to me.

He doesn't need it to cause serious damage. I can see it in his eyes, and that makes me more nervous.

Lochlan said he would never hurt a woman, but he didn't say he wasn't still dangerous or violent. I've seen how they handle situations here. There's a reason Hayes is the only person who can keep Lochlan in check.

Austin is visibly nervous being confronted by a man, and Hayes takes notice, crossing his tatted arms and smirking.

"She doesn't belong here, and if you try to stop me, then I'll make a call to get you thrown back in prison," he threatens.

"Is that so?"

"Parolees can't slip up."

"Well, it's a good thing I'm not on parole anymore."

Austin blanches. That must've been his only defense, and it just went up in smoke. "Doesn't matter. A criminal history is a criminal history."

"I'm not a man who cares much about that."

"You would go back to prison for her?" He scoffs.

"I'd go back to prison if it meant doing what's right."

Seiver pops through the doorway out of nowhere, "Me too."

Jordy comes around the corner. "I'd go back to."

My nose is burning as my vision starts to blur from tears forming in the corners of my eyes. I don't want any of them to get in trouble for me, but it humbles me that they'd be willing.

"You can't stay here and marry some man who has been to prison. It will ruin your brother's campaign."

In all honesty, I'm still not sure that Lochlan is going to go along with my scheme. He hasn't confirmed that he'd pretend to be my fiancé, but it's safer to let Austin assume things between Lochlan and me are real. So I keep my lips shut and let him fume.

"This is ridiculous." Austin's pale face is growing red and peaked at my silence. "You can't stay here with him."

"And, who's going to take her from me?" Lochlan's deep voice rumbles out of nowhere, making me gasp.

He approached without being seen in that elusive way he's perfected, stepping up and looming behind Austin, forcing the grown man to shrink in terror.

"This is private property. You don't belong here."

"I just– I was– I–" Austin stutters, scrambling away from the dangerous man he thinks is my fiancé.

"Get the fuck out and don't come back. Or, I'll make sure you *never* leave again," he threatens twistedly.

Austin jumps into his car and reverses before he gets his door shut, throwing mud with his tires as he flees.

Silence descends as my body trembles.

Lochlan approaches me, and I can't tear my eyes off of him, waiting to hear what he has to say about being dragged into more of my mess.

He tugs the crowbar from my grip, tossing it back to Hayes behind me. He jerks his head slightly, and I know that means everyone around us will disappear, leaving me alone with him.

"Are you okay?"

I nod shakily, unable to tear my eyes from his.

"That's not acceptable. People can't come here and threaten to make you leave."

"I'm sorry. I didn't know he'd have the nerve to come here," I rasp between breaths.

"No, Jo, you don't understand. No one gets to come here and threaten you. With anything. *No one* gets to touch you, I'll never let that happen." His dark eyes bore into mine, forcing me to understand.

"You're not mad at me?"

219

"I'm furious," he mutters, holding my face in his big hands to soften my chattering teeth. "But, as long as you're here, I'll do *whatever* you need me to if it means keeping you from their grasp."

"You mean you'll be my fake fiancé?"

"You know that I can't say no to you."

My cheeks grin against his rough palms, soothing me with his touch. "You've told me no plenty of times."

"Yet, somehow you keep getting away with shit." He sighs. "We'll keep up the charade until you get your trust. That's the deal."

"Okay, deal."

He inhales roughly as if he already regrets it and mutters, "Here we go."

* * *

"My favorite color is lavender. My favorite flowers are peonies."

"What color peonies?" He scratches his head as if he's cramming for a test he'll fail. We're on the porch, debriefing about our relationship against his will.

"It doesn't matter."

"Why does any of this matter? This is fake."

"But on the outside, it needs to look real. You need to know all the little details that couples should know."

He sighs roughly. "I know you like vanilla ice cream with chunks of chocolate and cookies, but not chocolate ice cream, and especially at night. You get your nails painted a different color every two weeks. The last time you did your hair, you came back looking different, and I finally realized you're not a blonde. I don't know what that means in terms of hair, but I noticed. You've been watching movies during the day while you work, when you think I'm not paying attention. You talk to yourself while you type, and all of your sticky notes are in half print-half cursive."

My jaw hangs open. "Wow."

"I've seen your textbooks when you leave them lying out, you're the smartest person I know, and we've been around each other for months, this won't be hard for you."

The smartest person he knows.

"I've never even had a boyfriend, pardon me if I'm a little intimidated." I turn my back on him and stare out across the property, ignoring his flattering comment.

"You're overthinking this."

"Of course, I am. That's what I do."

"Don't think of us as a couple." I turn to him to protest, but he continues, standing closer than he was a moment ago. "I'm a man, you're a woman. As long as you hover near me and brush your hand down my arm every couple of minutes, no one will question our... Familiarity," he murmurs, standing so closely that he has to look down to see me.

"Like this," I whisper, gripping the back of his bicep and letting my fingers fall gently to his elbow.

"Yes."

"Or, this?" My other hand raises to his chest, my palm flattening to mold to his sternum.

He doesn't confirm, but when I glance into his eyes, there's a storm raging.

He's told me that I'm a beautiful woman, gorgeous even,

but he's never admitted to being attracted to me. I always assumed men don't see me as a sexual being.

But, something in his eyes tells me more than his words ever have. At least, that's what I tell myself.

"Should I stop touching you, now?"

"Yes," he exhales the word, but stops my hand from leaving his chest with his own. He's a very confusing man.

"What if…" He's watching my mouth form my words so intensely that I can hardly complete my thought. "What if we need to do more than touch like this?" I swallow thickly as his brow furrows deeper. "What if we need to kiss?"

"Why would we need to kiss?" His low voice barely reaches my ears, even though we're close enough to do just that.

"No one bats an eye when a soon-to-be married couple shows a little PDA. It's expected," I murmur, my breath skipping when his head leans immeasurably closer.

"You want your first kiss to be fake?" He asks, his hand cupping the back of my neck to tilt my head closer, and my heart beats like a drum against my chest.

"Technically, my first kiss was in 7th grade with a boy named Theodore."

He grumbles deep from his chest as if he despises the thought. "Fine, your first kiss as an adult."

"Yes."

His face inches closer, near enough that my eyes flutter shut, until I feel his nose trace the line of my jaw, making me shiver. "I'm sorry, I can't."

He releases me suddenly and is gone before I can blink my eyes open.

Chapter Thirty-One

Lochlan

S he flits around in her sundress like a fairy through the grass, winning over the people I've grown up around my entire life. All of the people who abandoned me after I was falsely accused.

She insisted that the Rollins County Fair was a good place to practice being a couple, but she doesn't understand how easy it is to be infatuated with her.

She still thinks my reluctance to this engagement has anything to do with me when it's entirely because of her. She's beautiful and brilliant. She has a bright future ahead of her, and I'm terrified to ruin it for her.

My heart was screaming at me to kiss her, but my head knew how selfish it is to claim her lips when they aren't truly mine to claim. She deserves all of her firsts to be as special as she wants them to be.

I am in no way deserving of any of them.

"I heard some frat bros over there thirsting over your girl," Hayes says as he plops down on the picnic bench next to me. He's eating a giant cheeseburger. It's the fourth thing I've seen him with since we got here.

"Yeah, well, I don't blame them." I don't bother correcting him for calling her mine. I know she isn't mine, but I'll damn sure protect her like she is.

"Who knew Lochlan Dane would get engaged? I hope I'm your best man."

"Shut the fuck up, Jensen." I only use his first name when he's annoying me.

"This indifferent attitude is going to blow up in your face when she leaves."

"I know."

"Ah, there they go." He nods his head toward the two guys wearing khaki shorts and V-neck T-shirts snaking through the crowd to get to Jo. She's standing with Curtis and Jordy, but unfortunately neither of them look like much competition to cocky college kids.

"Should I go over there?"

"Let's see what happens," he murmurs in amusement.

The two guys approach, easily earning a few smiles from the woman who has an endless supply. It only takes a moment for me to see the corners droop slightly. She'll keep the appearance up because that's what she's been taught, but I can tell a real smile from a fake one. I've studied them closely.

"Oh, look at that good fiancé," he remarks when she lifts her left hand to show her engagement ring.

One of them nods his head at Curtis and Jordy, but she shakes her head no and turns to point at me. They all look in my direction, and I meet their stares head-on. Hayes waves with his fingers like the cheeky fucker he is.

Jo smiles.

That beautiful, beaming smile has me up and out of my seat

in one second flat like a magnet pulling me in. If she honors me with a look like that, then I'm taking full advantage.

By the time I get to her, Tweedle Dee and Tweedle Dumb have disappeared.

"They wanted to dance with me," she explains. There is a live band and an open grassy dance floor in front of the stage.

"And, you told them that the boogeyman was watching."

She rolls her eyes at me. "No, I told them my fiancé was right over there and I'd be dancing with him."

"I don't dance."

"Oh, right." She blinks away her disappointment quickly, but not quickly enough.

"But, I also don't share, darlin'." I grab her delicate wrist, pinning it to my chest. "If you want to dance, it'll be with me."

"Okay," she responds breathlessly, her blushed cheeks begging to be caressed. Kissed.

I'm not much of a dancer, but I can get by without stepping on her feet. A simple sway and one or two steps here and there are the extent of it. It doesn't matter, though, because all I care about is having her in my arms. Getting to hold her on purpose without a definite time limit is a privilege.

"Thank you for humoring me," she whispers sweetly, tilting her face up to look at me. I can't stop looking at her lips.

"I didn't want any other fuckers trying to dance with you."

"It was one guy and his friend. There's not exactly a line of people waiting to cut in."

"You're right, they all dispersed the moment I claimed you."

"You're so funny," she giggles in amusement, but I wasn't joking in the slightest.

I tip her chin up to look at me again, and her breath catches in her throat. "Darlin', you're sin in a sundress. Every man wants a piece of you, and I'm not exaggerating."

She looks startled by my statement as if she has no idea of her effect on men.

"But, not you?" She asks suddenly, forcing me to spin her so I have a second to formulate my answer.

"Especially me," I whisper into her ear after she spins back into my chest.

I shouldn't, but I let my mouth linger, dragging my lips along her cheek.

We stop swaying, stop moving entirely, while she digests my answer. Admitting how much I want her isn't a part of our deal, but I can't lie to her either, not with how unwanted she's felt her entire life.

"Then why wouldn't you kiss me?"

"Because your first kiss should mean something. It should be special, and I am not anything special."

"I think you're special." The world moves around us, but we're in our own bubble, her soft eyes gleaming at me with tenderness that I don't want.

Because it makes me want it too much.

I don't always get the chance to stand this close to her, to really see the intricate details of her face that I've appreciated from afar many times. The exact curve of her cheek and jaw, her supple lips painted red. There's something special about seeing your infatuation right in front of your eyes.

"Lochlan Dane?" A voice speaks from behind me, and I want to punch whoever it is for interrupting this moment.

"Ah, yes. I thought that was you," he says when I turn around. Randall Porter.

"What can I do for you, Mayor?" I ask gruffly as Jo saddles up next to me. I take full advantage of our scheme and pull her closer to my side.

"I was hoping to speak to you again regarding your property. I've heard that you're entering a new stage in your life." He gestures to Jo, which is odd since the news of our "engagement" is still mostly under wraps.

"I'm not interested in selling my property now or ever. No amount of discussion will change that."

"Well, I'm sure your new bride will want a say. She is from an affluent family after all, and she's used to a certain lifestyle."

"Excuse me–" I'm about to add a colorful name to my sentence when Jo interrupts.

"I've never been happier than I am now, with Lochlan and at the sanctuary. Whoever your source is, let them know that bribing us with money is not going to solve *anyone's* problem. Have a good day." She dismisses him by turning away and walking back toward the table where the guys are sitting without a second glance.

That's my girl.

Mayor Porter starts to say something else to me, but I silence him with a look, following Jo's lead through the dense crowd.

We end up piling around our single picnic table listening to the band. A couple of the guys keep taking turns going to the beer stand, and despite Jo's refusal any time someone offers her a cup, she keeps stealing sips from mine.

I don't mind.

Fake or not, I'm a selfish bastard, and I want her all to myself. I like it when she brushes against me when she's standing too close, and how she smiles at me first when she hears a song that she likes.

She leans into me where I'm standing against the wooden tabletop, lingering to avoid being bumped as someone walks by, and I drink it in. When it happens again, I notice her tense, and it isn't until I tip her chin to look at me that she relaxes.

"That guy brushed his fingers down my thigh," she admits.

Now, I'm fucking agitated.

"Who?"

She hesitates, searching my eyes for my intentions, but when I cock my head, urging her to tell me, she relents. "That guy in the white cut off."

A few minutes later, the guy returns our way with a cup of beer in his teeth and one in his left hand, leaving his right hand free, using the crowd as a distraction to cop a feel on countless innocent women.

Just before he passes Jo again, I snatch his hand away before he can let it brush across her hip. "Touch her again, or anyone else, and I'll rip your fucking hand off." The beer drops from his mouth and splatters all over the ground, but I don't flinch, squeezing his wrist until I near his bones' breaking points.

He nods frantically trying to get away so fast that he falls to his ass in the dirt as I let him go. I fake a step forward like I might snatch him up again, and he scurries off. "Scumbag," I mumble to myself as I turn back toward our table.

Jo looks at me like she's about to scold me. Instead, I scoop her up under her arms and set her gently on the tabletop so she's out of the way. "Don't," I warn her, before she tells me I was being over the top. "He deserved to get his ass whooped but there are children around."

CHAPTER THIRTY-ONE

Her eyes soften. "Thank you," she says gently, kissing my cheek.

Feeling her lips against my skin steals the breath from my lungs, but I'd choose another touch from her over oxygen.

I would jump off a cliff and swim through shark-infested waters for the opportunity to feel her lips against mine without repercussions.

"Oh, I'm sorry, I left a lipstick mark." She moves to wipe it off, but I catch her wrist before she can.

"Don't."

She looks at me curiously, trying to read my face. All it will tell her is how starved I am for her.

"Lochlan," she utters as I watch my name form on her lips.

My desperation for her is clawing up my throat. I could kiss her right now, and not a flicker of it would be fake. I could take her first real kiss from her, and she might not regret it, not right away, but if there is even a seed of doubt, then I'd never forgive myself.

She tilts her head, leaning towards me, and giving me the consent that I'm dying for, but I hesitate, letting the buzz of the crowd around us filter in and force me to my senses.

I can't kiss her. Not here, in front of all of these people, not for the first time.

Not ever.

My head dips, cutting off the connection between us, and I watch the rejection sweep over her face.

"I'm ready to go home," she utters flatly.

"I can take you," I start, but she holds up a hand to stop me.

"Can someone take me home?" She asks the table.

The poor guys look caught in a trap, blinking back and forth between us. I should argue and insist that I take her home, but I don't.

Hayes looks at me with pity in his eyes because he knows all about the torture in my head. I nod at him and step out of her bubble, letting her hop down off the table.

"Don't worry, my birthday is in a month, so this charade won't be a burden much longer." She turns and walks away as I throw my keys to Hayes, letting her go.

* * *

I knock on Jo's door for the third time, but she doesn't answer. I should leave her alone, but I can't go to sleep knowing that she's upset with me. She feels rejected, and I don't know how to make her understand that I'd choose her in every lifetime if I could.

It's just not possible for her to choose me in this one.

I sink down onto the porch steps when I see Hayes leave the garage. He usually stays up working on his bike even though it's in impeccable condition. He sees me and comes my way despite my lack of desire for company.

"What are you doing?"

"I wanted to talk to Jo, but she's ignoring me."

"I dropped her off an hour or so ago, she's probably asleep."

"I knocked."

"You could just tell her the truth, you know? How you really feel…"

"Not happening."

"It's like the blind leading the blind," he huffs, shaking his head.

"Yeah, and where's your woman, Hayes? Take your own advice or leave me alone." His eyes go cold, and I know I hit a nerve, but we're good at kicking each other's sore spots.

"This is ridiculous." He storms over to Jo's door and slams his palm against it. "Jo, open the door or I'm coming in. Lochlan wants to tell you that he's an idiot as if we don't already know!" He yells as I stomp up behind him, but he flings the unlocked door open before I can stop him.

It's dark, but she's not inside. Her bed is empty. "Where the hell is she? Hayes, where is she?" I panic, running up my front steps and flinging my front door open, hoping that she's on my couch. It's empty, too.

"Where is she?" I yell again, flood lights illuminate as some of the guys come out of the bunkhouse to investigate the commotion.

"Everybody split up, go look around the barns, maybe she's wandering around," Hayes orders.

"She's not supposed to walk around the property without me. What if someone took her?"

My best friend, the man I've known for a decade, doesn't have to say a word to answer my question. His eyes tell me that he knows what will happen...

If someone took her, I'll destroy lives to get her back.

Including my own.

Chapter Thirty-Two

Jo

An hour earlier...

I want to scream.

If I weren't JoAnna Montgomery, he would kiss me. He wouldn't be concerned about what it means.

He was right before, I don't want my first kiss to be fake.

I want him to kiss me because he wants to.

I want *him* to kiss me.

"What exactly is your plan, Jo?" Hayes asked as he was driving me home.

"What do you mean?"

"You trick everyone into thinking you're engaged, and then what?"

"I'm not trying to trick anyone, I'm just trying to escape my parents."

"Well, you've done that for the most part. You're here, you're almost done with school. I think you're putting too much emphasis on your parents' power over you."

"You don't understand."

"I do, more than you think."

He didn't elaborate, but maybe he's right, I'm giving my

parents too much power.

I sigh against the door jam of the empty guesthouse because I can't make myself go in. I wish Lochlan were here, despite how frustrating he is, I wish he was waiting for me on his porch, asking me to sit with him.

My steps take me across the gravel lot towards the bear fences. I've never gone this far before, I've never dared, but Lochlan isn't here and I want to see the bears. I have more free will now than I ever have, according to Hayes, and I'm tired of feeling trapped.

The dirt path is worn and flat from years of men working these fences and tending to these animals. The first tall fence I come to is about twice my height and not nearly as sturdy as I presumed it would be.

Now, I understand why they're working on them so often. Thin chain links connected by aluminum poles, and stabilized by wooden boards, are the only thing keeping me from danger.

I study the patchwork as I move down the path, peering into the darkened trees that are barely lit by the moonlight, determined to accomplish one goal tonight.

My feet are covered with dirt, and my toes are starting to blister against the thin strap of my heeled sandal by the time I make it to the end of the fence where it meets the exterior perimeter. The fence keeping people off the property is sturdier than the one keeping the bears in.

I can hear Lochlan's voice now. *Humans are always scarier than animals.*

I walk the path between the two fences until my feet hurt badly enough that I have to take my shoes off. The dirt is soft enough that I can walk barefoot easily.

I should turn around and go back, but for what?

To sit by myself inside? To study for tests that I know I'll ace?

To wait for Lochlan to come home and ignore me?

Grunting startles me suddenly, and I freeze. It's somewhere close, but it's difficult to see without a light. I hold my breath, waiting to hear the direction of the sound when a loud snuff draws my eyes to ten feet down the fencing, just on the other side.

One of the bears is standing right next to the fence, face to the ground, nibbling on the undergrowth. He hasn't raised his head to look at me, but his ears twitch like he's alert.

They're probably used to people being around Lochlan and the parolees, but I'm still not trying to make it mad.

Its indifference urges me forward, tiptoeing until I'm nearly in front of it on the other side of the flimsy chain link fence. I watch in fascination as the moonlight reflects off the giant bear's shoulder blades as he eats. His dark coat is camouflaged expertly with his surroundings.

I'm not entirely informed on bears, but it does seem odd that it's not paying me any attention. I take another step forward to test his observation skills when the pad of my foot crunches something beneath it.

The bear grunts but doesn't stop eating.

It almost feels like dried mulch under my feet, but that can't be right. When I pull my phone out to shine it on the ground, the bear rears back on his hind legs suddenly, startled by the light. It roars loudly, throwing me back on my ass and I land right on my tailbone.

It takes off into the dense trees, but I stay on the ground, stunned. *That* was the animal I was expecting.

Despite my thundering pulse and aching butt, I start feeling around on my hands and knees for my shoes and my phone that flew from my hands when I fell. I'm feeling a lot less confident about being out here alone, now.

I find my phone at the same time my palms roam over the crunchy ground, and I use it to investigate the tan pellets littering the path between the fences.

I don't know what it is, but it looks like it was thrown over the fence, and the bear was eating it. A knot forms in my gut because I know deep down that I just discovered something bad.

I shove the pellets into the pocket of my dress and forget my shoes, running back towards the house. Except, it's so dark that it's hard to see where I'm going, and at some point I miss my turn, or take the wrong one. I'm not sure how many paths lead to and from the enclosures.

It's taking longer than it should to find my way back to the barns, but I'm not worried about it. Not until I hear shouting and multiple engines running like they've fired up the four-wheelers.

It's late, something bad must've happened.

Finally, my path ends near the last barn where they keep the strays. The mule that was abandoned at the beginning of the summer is standing in his open stall window, staring at me as he chews on some hay.

I blow out a deep breath, admitting my exhaustion. That was a bit too much adventure for me.

The alleyway between all the outbuildings isn't as smooth as the one through the woods, and I don't have my shoes to traverse over all of the gravelly bits.

I still hear people shouting, but I can't make myself move

to find out what's going on.

Rain runs out from behind the other building, nearly plowing me over in surprise. "Oh, fuck! What are you doing out here?" He asks, staring at me in obvious concern.

I don't have a good answer for him, so I just shrug.

"Boss, I've got her. She's down by the strays," he relays into his radio, still eyeing me up and down. I must look worse than I thought.

"He's got the whole mountain looking for you, girl."

"What? Why?"

"He thought someone snatched you up."

I don't have a chance to respond when three people come sprinting down the alleyway towards us. Lochlan, Hayes, and Jackson.

Oops, I think I'm in trouble.

"What happened? Are you hurt?" Lochlan's head swivels, taking in every inch of me, looking for damage.

"I'm fine."

"Where are your shoes?" Hayes asks.

"What were you doing?" Jackson asks at the same time.

"You're fine?" Lochlan asks in tandem.

My head swings between each man, and I don't know who to respond to first. I don't know why they're freaking out but now my little adventure seems like it was a worse idea than I thought.

"I went for a walk. I wanted to see the bears."

Lochlan throws his head back and turns away in disbelief. Hayes watches me warily, and Jackson still looks like he's checking my arms and legs for injuries.

"And, you didn't think to tell anyone?" Lochlan swings around to yell at me.

CHAPTER THIRTY-TWO

"I didn't think anyone would care."

"Christ, Jo. You have ten people standing on this property who care!"

"I'll clear everyone to go to bed," Hayes murmurs into his radio, nodding his head to Rain, who backs away quietly.

"Are you okay? Really?" Jackson asks, looking at me closely.

"I'm fine, I just needed to clear my head. But, I found this." I turn my pockets inside out, dumping the pellets onto the ground in front of me. "The bear that I saw was eating this. He wouldn't even look up. I think it came from the wrong side of the fence."

Lochlan's gaze snaps to the pieces at my feet, and he kneels, inspecting them. "Looks like rat poison."

"Only one bear was eating it, from what I saw at least."

He slides a hand over his face.

"I'll go drive the perimeter, see if there's a sign of anything," Jackson offers, giving me a 'good luck' glance.

"Where'd you find it?" Hayes asks.

"I don't know, I got all turned around. I started by the bunkhouse but somehow ended up over here. I left my shoes in the spot where I found it, though."

"Okay, I'll go check it out." Hayes steps away, leaving me alone with Lochlan, and my nerves return.

"Your feet are filthy," he grumbles, finally standing.

"It was easier to walk barefoot until I got here." I point to the rocks at our feet, and he nods.

He leans down and swiftly sweeps me off my feet, cradling me in his arms. He doesn't say a word as he walks us back up to the house, and all I can do is stare at the side of his face and the intensity of it.

"I'm sorry if I caused trouble," I whisper.

He doesn't say anything as he deposits me on my feet in front of my door, but he also doesn't move away. He braces his hands on the door on either side of my head and squeezes his eyes shut before looking at me.

"Don't *ever* do that to me again. You might've gotten me wrapped up in this fake engagement shit, but do not forget that I am your boss. I told you not to wander."

"I was just–"

"No! Don't use that pretty mouth to soften me up. Your adventure starts after you leave this place and not a second before! Do not forget who is in charge here."

He pushes off the door frame, and I watch his back get farther away through blurry eyes.

That's the Lochlan that I first met, and not the one I've fallen for.

Chapter Thirty-Three

Lochlan

"As her brother, I hope you weren't too hard on her. As Sheriff, I'm glad she wasn't out there when whoever threw the rat poison over the fence would've seen her." Jackson's bagging the pellets into an evidence bag, even though we both know there isn't any way to trace where it came from.

Jo scared the hell out of me, and I'm having a hard time reigning in my rage. I'm not mad at her, but I'm infuriated that my home isn't safe enough for her to walk around without worrying about her.

I'm furious that my first thought when I couldn't find her was that someone could have taken her.

This place should be secure, impenetrable. She should be able to explore every square foot of this property without consequence, but I can't make that a reality because some fucker wants to harm me. The bears. My grandfather's legacy.

"It's better that she's mad at me but listens to my rules rather than disobey and get herself hurt. It's the price I'll pay."

He glances at me, unconvinced. It's the same look Hayes usually gives me.

"When you thought someone had her, what was your first thought?"

"What do you mean?" I thought I was going to murder someone, but I won't admit that to him.

"Where did your mind go? Who was the first person you suspected? Even if it doesn't make sense in hindsight, our brain works in weird ways."

"First, I assumed it was whoever has been harassing this place. Then I thought maybe Frank, one of my old parolees, came back to mess with me. He always showed too much interest in her. Then I suspected that her parents sent someone for her."

"Why would her parents do that?"

"Ahh, well. She told them that she was engaged to me to get out of being set up with Conrad's campaign manager."

He blinks slowly at me, contemplating what I just said. "You're engaged to my sister?"

"It's fake."

"This place is turning into a soap opera." He sighs, shutting all of his evidence into the back of his SUV. "Well, fake or not, I'm counting on you to keep your promise about her safety. Even if she thinks you're a dictator."

"She can give me the silent treatment for all I care, I won't let a fly land on her."

* * *

"This is where my mother expected to showboat my engagement to Austin so all eyes will be on us. Try not to look miserable," she says slyly as we enter a giant garden party on the lawns of the Biltmore Estate.

This place is historical and fancy, and incredibly out of my element. Normally, I'd lean on her to carry us through an event like this, but as suspected, she hasn't spoken to me since the night she wandered off.

We're supposed to act like an engaged couple, but she can't even stand to look at me.

And, I can't stop looking at her.

She's as beautiful as she always is, dressed like every stitch of fabric and every accessory was made for her. She's also wearing the red lipstick that nearly brings me to my knees every time she wears it.

"We'll lay low, there are only a few people I want to speak to about donating, and then we can get out of here." She speaks as she glances around the crowded tent, still refusing to even face me.

The stuffy suit jacket she bought and forced me to wear is punishment, and I keep shifting my shoulders trying to dislodge it from my neck.

"JoAnna, so good to see you." A woman that I've never seen approaches Jo, and I tune out their conversation, looking for the bar.

"This is Lochlan Dane, my fiancé." Her hand touches my stomach, resting there as an intimate gesture one might do with someone they're in a relationship with, but I can't stop focusing on it.

Every touch is torturous.

Every fake nicety makes me wish it were real.

"You could at least pretend to be engaged in conversation," she accuses when we're alone, again.

"I don't want to talk to these people."

"I'm aware, but don't make me look bad just because you can't stop being a grouch for an hour." She huffs, stalking towards the bar as elegantly as she can.

I step up behind her as she's ordering her drink, and I feel her spine stiffen. "If you didn't want to be engaged to a grouch, then you shouldn't have put that ring on your finger," I whisper in her ear.

"And, if you didn't want to put up with my antics then you should have told me to fuck off," she hisses under her breath.

Gone is the woman who was ever intimidated by me, and in her place is a woman who can snap my neck with a look.

I hate to admit how much it amuses me.

My cock pulses and I have to step away from her so she doesn't accidentally brush against me. It's why I can never think straight around her, all my blood rushes downward anytime she's near me.

"A photo?" A man with a professional-looking camera asks us, and just as I'm about to say no, Jo agrees.

She slides her arm around my waist and places her hand back on my stomach, forcing me to inhale deeply. I don't take photos, I don't know what to do with my arms, but my palm finds her hip bone like a magnet while she smiles prettily.

"Great, now give her a kiss," he instructs, casually.

She looks at me with sadness in her eyes, already expecting the rejection, and it kills me. I wish I were a man who could kiss her in a crowded room like no one was watching.

My lips find her temple instead, lingering there while the camera shutters in front of us. "I'm sorry, darlin'," I utter

242

softly.

"Yeah, me too." She steps away from me. "When the photographer uploads his gallery from tonight, I'll post those pictures on my Instagram. My family will think it's odd if I don't showcase you on social media.

"I don't know what Instagram is."

"I know." She sighs, turning her back to me. She walks away and doesn't come back until she's ready to leave.

Not uttering another word to me the rest of the night.

* * *

As the late summer storms begin in the mountains, it's turned the property into a mud pit. Even when it's not raining, there is constant cloud coverage, preventing anything on the ground from drying up.

There have been flash flood warnings in effect all week and storms every night, resembling my mood perfectly. I've never felt more trapped behind these gates than I do now.

It was my choice to be here, to continue my grandfather's legacy, but I'm stuck in this place with no outlook, no future. And, it hasn't been as painful a realization until right now.

A harmless kiss wouldn't be destroying me if I simply had something to offer the woman asking for it.

"Hey, boss. Did you hear?" Ryker asks as I meet them all down by the bunkhouse. We've been attempting to lay down dry bedding and add some semblance of natural shelter for the bears all day, so they have a dry place to sleep, but we're all exhausted and covered in mud.

"Hear, what?"

"There's a tornado watch in effect."

"I'm not surprised." What else could go wrong?

"It's supposed to escalate within the hour."

Tornadoes aren't a common occurrence in the mountains, but it's not unheard of. Normally, flooding is the worst part, but the homes in this area aren't built to withstand damaging winds.

"Alright, let's get things wrapped up, and we can hunker down for the rest of the night. The bears will hole up where they can, and we can assess the damage tomorrow."

I don't know what makes me look, an itch on the back of my neck or a feeling in my gut, but I turn around, eyeing the guesthouse.

"Where's Jo?" Her car isn't here.

Everyone looks at me with wide eyes like they're afraid to answer. "I know she did not get through her day without chit-chatting with one of you fuckers." I'm past the point of being annoyed by her socializing with them; I've come to expect it. However, I don't accept anyone lying about it.

"She had a meeting at school with one of her professors," Jordy admits.

"When?"

"She left about an hour ago, and said the office hours started at six."

"Dammit," I mutter to no one. "Dammit!"

How am I supposed to keep her safe when she's a magnet for danger?

Chapter Thirty-Four

Jo

Two weeks from now, I have to present my thesis to my entire class, and my professor just ripped my project to shreds. I've heard that it's to be expected. The real test is the pressure they put on you in the final weeks to succeed, but it brought down my confidence significantly.

It's my fault. I haven't gone the extra mile to research my topic. With all of my personal drama this summer, I haven't been brave enough to ask Lochlan for another favor.

I reach the vestibule of the engineering building, and my steps turn sluggish. It's pouring rain.

It's at least a quarter mile walk to my car, and I'm wearing heels, of course.

I checked the weather, I knew to expect rain and brought my umbrella, but it's coming down hard and blowing sideways.

Oh well, I'll get drenched and have to drive the 45 minutes back to the sanctuary in wet clothes.

One more deep breath, then I'll walk as fast as I can and accept the misery.

Howling wind bursts my eardrums as I struggle to push the door open, hardly creating enough space to get my body through before I'm taking off down the sidewalk.

I can't jog, not with how wet the rain makes my feet, but even if I could, I can't outrun this weather. The heavy rain pelts the side of my face, soaking my hair down my neck.

I'm not watching where I'm going, but I know I'm almost to the parking lot, and unfortunately, student parking is way out in the back.

The water rushing along the curb is more like a river than drain water, and deep enough that it will soak my foot to my ankle. I'm preparing to leap when headlights sweep over me and someone honks.

My umbrella gets rocked by the gusting wind as I turn to look, folding inside out and blowing from my hand in the same instant.

"GET IN THE TRUCK!" Lochlan yells over the roaring wind.

Why is he here? It doesn't matter, I'm not passing up the opportunity for shelter.

He meets me at the passenger door, soaking his own clothes, and helps me in. As soon as he shuts me inside, the raging storm is muffled.

A burst of noise as his door opens, and then silence descends again, drowned out by the engine of the Bronco.

My clothes are sticking to my skin, and I'm soaked to the bone.

"What are you doing here?" I ask between deep, dragging breaths.

"There's a tornado warning, I didn't want you to get stuck in the storm."

"But, now you're stuck."

"Yeah, I guess I am."

"What about my car?"

"We'll get it later."

I slump back in my seat, relieved to be in the passenger seat. I don't need to control the ship, I'm content to be along for the ride.

"This is the outside of the weather system, it might get hairy as we get closer to home."

"This isn't the bad part?"

"I didn't want you to drive into the thick of it by yourself."

My head tips to the side to look at him, but he's staring into the rain. He tries so hard to believe he's a bad man, some evil person to be around, but he's not. He's the most reliable person I've ever met. His concern for my well-being never wavers, even when I have been giving him the silent treatment.

I want to reach out to him, to touch his arm and thank him for rescuing me, but I've been shut down so many times that I can't make myself do it.

He turns the volume up on the radio, tuned into some weather station, and drives into the storm. He was right, it gets worse the closer we get to Rollins County.

The radio signal gets fuzzy, and the rain is so heavy that we can hardly see.

"Maybe we should pull over," I mumble. My damp clothes are making me tremble, but I'm not sure whether it's my nerves.

"It's not safe in a vehicle. If a storm rips through here."

I'm just about to ask if he thinks there will be a tornado when the emergency alert broadcast interrupts the newscaster.

ERR ERR ERR ERR ERR. A Tornado has touched down in your immediate area. Seek Shelter, now. ERR ERR ERR ERR ERR. There is a severe threat to human life and property, with catastrophic damage. Immediately seek refuge in the safest location possible.

It goes on to list the affected counties, and ours is on the list.

"Lochlan," I whimper.

"I know," he breathes out nervously. I've never heard him sound nervous before.

The wind blows the Bronco harshly, forcing him to correct the wheel over and over as small branches blow across the road. One hits the side near my window, and I screech.

"Why didn't you drive one of the trucks?"

"This was the closest one, and I was in a hurry."

We're just outside of Lawson, the biggest town in Rollins, and I can hear the tornado sirens. This is bad, really bad.

He slams on the brakes, and my head nearly hits the dashboard until he accelerates again, throwing me back.

"I can't see shit." He swerves around a downed tree, and I throw my hands over my face, wishing I could stop looking. I peek through my fingers as he drives blindly down the freeway that no one else is stupid enough to be driving on.

He takes the corner that takes us to our mountain road when the rain suddenly clears and the sky goes from dark gray to... Green?

"Is it over?"

"We need to take shelter. Now." He speeds into the parking lot of the little carryout, jumping the curb, and my entire body lifts off the seat before bouncing down as he drives straight up onto the sidewalk on the side of the building. "Come on!"

He flings his door open, bracing against the wind as he pulls me across the bucket seat and into the ladies' bathroom. It isn't until he's struggling to shut the heavy bathroom door that I realize how truly not over this storm is.

"Get in the corner!" He yells, but I'm short-circuiting, I can't move.

He flips the deadbolt and throws himself my way, shoving me into the corner and crowding me with his body.

The wind howls outside the concrete building, and I hear the train horn, the roar of tornado-force winds. It sounds like the bathroom is going to collapse at any moment, as large debris is thrown against it.

Something crashes into the one tiny window, smashing the glass out, and I scream as glass particles rain down around us. Lochlan's arms circle me tightly, engulfing me while his back takes the brunt of the rain surge blowing in.

It's so loud, it never feels like it's going to stop. "Lochlan," I plead his name, screaming into his chest when thunder cracks loudly right on top of us and the lights go out.

"I've got you, baby. I've got you. I'm not going to let a thing happen to you," he murmurs in my ear, squeezing me tighter. His hand cups my head, holding it against his chest, and blocking some of the noise.

Focus on his heart.

Focus on his heart.

When I can hear his heartbeat, that means this is over.

His heart.

His heart.

His heart.

The erratic tempo of his heart beats against my ear, and I can finally breathe. I can't hear the wind; all I can hear is his heart beating.

"Is it over?"

"I don't know, I think so."

If he wouldn't have come to get me, I would have been in the worst of it, and I could have gotten myself killed.

My shaking arms squeeze his waist tighter, imagining that I could have had to endure all of this alone sends a wave of sadness over me.

I'm so used to doing it alone, I don't want to think about the day that Lochlan won't be there to save me.

He's always here to save me.

Chapter Thirty-Five

Lochlan

I'm afraid to let her go. As if the moment she's gone from my grip, the roof will cave in and I'll lose her. I'm not someone who can be scared easily. I've confronted 800-pound black bears without breaking a sweat, but just now, I was scared to death.

"Are you okay?" I smooth her hair away from her face, so I can look at her, and I mean really look at her.

Her hairline is clean of any debris, her forehead is bare of any scratches. My thumb traces across each eyebrow and down the bridge of her nose, along her cheekbones, and the length of her jaw. She's fine, not a mark anywhere.

She's okay.

"I didn't think it would ever stop," her voice wavers.

I pull her in again, kissing the top of her head. Breathing her in. "Come on, let's get out of here."

I give her just enough room to walk, keeping my arm anchored around her shoulders. I'm not sure what to expect when I open the door, but I brace myself for it regardless.

"Oh, no," she cries. "The Bronco."

Small branches are scattered atop the truck that blew in

from nearby trees, but the worst of it is a dent in the roof, and the quarter glass above the side mirror on the driver's side is smashed out.

Overall, not that bad. "It's okay, it's drivable."

She continues to stress about the state of the truck as I usher her in from my side. "Your grandfather's car. God, it's all my fault. You came to rescue me, and now it's messed up."

"It's fine."

"No, it's not fine. I ruin everything, I destroy everything I touch. Now, your car." She squeezes her eyes shut, and I think she's spiraling into a panic attack, but my truck isn't truly the culprit.

"Look at me." I grab her face and bring her in close. "Jo, look at me, dammit."

She does, blinking her wide eyes at my face until she actually focuses on me.

"I don't give a shit about the truck." She blinks once, twice. "I don't care about the truck. I would do it a thousand times over."

"What?"

"I don't care about the truck," I emphasize, pressing my forehead to hers.

"Okay." She nods, holding back her tears.

I tuck her into my side, holding her close as I back us off the sidewalk and onto the pavement, crushing limbs and trash under my tires as we hit the main road again.

It's dark now, and we're most of the way up the mountain when my headlights catch an obstruction in the road. "Shit."

"What?" She leans forward, finally noticing.

"Let me get out and look." A giant spruce tree fell across the roadway, blocking our path completely. There are culverts full of rainwater on either side of the road. I can't drive around, and this is the only road up to the sanctuary.

"What do we do?" She asks when I get back in the truck.

"I'll get the guys to bring chainsaws to cut it and tow it out of the way, but for now, we're stuck." I blow a breath out.

Any other day I might be pissed about this type of situation but I can't find it in me to care. After almost being blown away in a tornado, all I care about is that she's safe.

I call Hayes while I stare introspectively out the window at a tree that won't be moving anytime soon, and when I hang up, I realize how silent she is.

Her legs are curled up in the passenger seat, and she's hugging her knees, shivering from head to toe. Her clothes are still wet from being rained on, and now her adrenaline is waning.

"Come here," I demand, tugging her into my lap and cranking the heat. She comes willingly, curling up across my legs as if she's done it a million times.

I hold her, circling my arms around her like my life depends on it, because it does. Her comfort is more important than my need to breathe as I pull her tighter to my chest.

Even after the trimmers ease and I feel her body relax further into mine, I don't loosen my grip or wipe away the sweat trickling down the side of my face. If she's content, then I'm not doing anything to mess it up.

"Do you regret coming to get me?" She whispers suddenly. When I look down at her, she's already looking at me.

"Not at all."

The faintest smile crosses her lips as she swipes the bead of sweat off my temple. "I'm warm enough."

I don't immediately lean forward to turn off the heat, and

she reaches over to do it herself. Except she doesn't curl her hand back into her chest when she's done, she lays it atop mine, just over my heart.

"This is awfully big for someone who pretends like he doesn't have one," she whispers, curling her fingers into my shirt.

She's wrong, I don't have it.

It's already in her possession.

Before I can confess my unyielding obsession to the woman I'm only fake-engaged to, headlights sweep across the windshield, filling the cab with light.

Even after being drenched and wind-blown, she's captivating. Her dark lashes flutter heavily across her smooth skin as the warmth of her gaze loses focus.

I should get out and help the others, but I don't. I hold her for the hour it takes them to cut the tree into pieces and move it off the road, admiring her as she succumbs to sleep.

I manage to steer us home, but I would have sat in the roadway with my hazards on all night before I would have woken her up.

I'm considering doing the same thing once I park in front of the house, but she blinks awake when I turn the engine off.

"Is it all over now?" she mumbles into my chest.

"Yeah, it's over."

She sighs but doesn't move, and I don't want her to. Getting out of the truck means I go back to gravitating around her without actually being able to have her.

"Is it too late to watch a movie?"

"No, it isn't." I huff in amusement, glad that the silence I've suffered through for nine days and 21 hours is over.

She skips inside to the guesthouse as if we didn't just endure a natural disaster and picks out a movie, handing it to me before she finds dry clothes.

"Is this some sick joke?" I stare at the Twister DVD in my hand.

"I thought it went with the theme."

"I think you've finally lost your mind."

"Maybe." She ducks behind the curtain separating the bathroom from the rest of the room and starts peeling off her sticky, wet clothes, kicking them across the floor.

By the time she comes around the curtain, tying her hair into a damp knot on top of her head, I'm locked painfully inside my body.

She was just naked, less than ten feet away from me.

"Ready?" Her sweet, innocent voice has no idea the torture I endured while the thinnest of curtains separated her from my view.

"Yeah," I mutter, grabbing her hand and leading her across the stepping stones to the porch.

"Afraid I'll blow away?"

"Something like that."

I don't let go of her until she's settled onto the couch, but only to start the movie before pulling her back into my chest when I sit. After the night we've had, all my rules be damned.

Chapter Thirty-Six

Jo

I've never cuddled with a man, but Lochlan's arms will ruin me for all others.

I've seen this movie a hundred times, but I don't recall a minute of it. I'm solely focused on how our bodies are molded together.

His hand resting on my hip is searing me like a brand, and I spend a considerable amount of time slowing my breathing so my pulse doesn't give away my nerves.

"I hope that was the perfect ending to our fucked up day," he remarks once the credits roll.

"I don't know, it hasn't been all bad," I whisper, shyly, not brave enough to look at him when I say it.

He cups my cheek, turning my face. "You were almost ripped out of my arms by a tornado. It was fucking terrible," he insists.

His lips are so close, I can't help but stare at them, desperately wishing he would kiss me. But, he doesn't.

"You should get to bed," he murmurs, tearing his eyes away from my mouth, too.

My entire being deflates. "You're right, today does suck," I huff, jumping to my feet. The rejection stings no matter the reason for it, and I don't want him to see how badly it affects me.

"Jo," he pleads, catching up to me on the porch.

"Goodnight, Lochlan."

"Don't leave when you're upset."

"I'm not upset," I lie, staring out over the porch railing.

"I told you I couldn't let your first kiss be a fake one."

"Then don't let it be fake."

"What?"

"God, Lochlan, do you want me to beg? As if I'm not humiliated enough."

He steps up behind me, gripping the porch railing on either side of my hands, leaning in with his head next to mine.

"I don't want you to beg, darlin', but I want to be a man who deserves you," he whispers, breathing me in when I nuzzle into his neck.

"You deserve the world."

"I don't believe that, and neither should you." He takes a step back, and it rips the lid off of my tamped-down emotions.

"You told me that I was the smartest person you know. Were you lying?"

"Of course, not."

"Then take my word for it, and kiss me."

He turns to look at me, but doesn't take a step in my direction, and my chest heaves. "Dammit, Lochlan. Kiss me!"

The rumble of his inner turmoil escapes his chest as he erases the distance between us, threading his fingers into my hair at the nape of my neck, stealing the air from my lungs.

His forehead battles mine as the war rages behind his eyes and the muscles in his jaw strain against his indecision.

"I won't ask again. If you walk away from me now, I'm not giving you another chan– "

He claims me fiercely, his mouth capturing mine with enough force to send electricity through my entire body.

His lips are soft despite his intensity, molding against mine as if they were made of the same pattern. The fullness of my bottom lip is cradled perfectly in the seam of his and I feel the soft tug as if he wants to suck it into his mouth.

The pressure only holds for a second, though, before he pulls back, checking my face for signs of something as I blink up at him. Pleasure? Regret?

He won't see any indication of the latter.

"I haven't done this in a while," he whispers roughly, close enough I can feel his breath skip against my lips. "We don't have to…"

"Don't stop," I plead, bringing his mouth to mine, and his whole body reciprocates, pinning me to the porch railing as he crushes my lips with his.

It's hungry, starving even, but it's not rough. He's a brutal man, but he's tasting me like I'm the finest dessert, breathing me in while he explores my mouth, my lips, my tongue.

I'm dizzy with lust that I've never experienced, but his arms hold me steady, his muscles flexing as he cradles me against his chest.

His teeth brush against my bottom lip, and I gasp at the sensation, curling my arms around his neck to bring him impossibly closer until I'm weightless, floating as he settles me atop the railing.

Other than what I've studied while watching movies, I

258

don't know what I'm doing, but I want to do everything at the same time. His teeth nip at my lip again, and I mimic it, reciprocating with my teeth against his bottom lip.

The strength of his arms tightens around me until it's impossible for me to move, but I'm still not close enough.

I want him inside my skin and my legs spread on instinct, allowing his hips to meet the 'v' of mine. The hardness that presses my tender flesh is foreign, and I can't believe it is what I think it is, but I roll my hips against it anyway, dying to feel every inch.

His breath huffs against my mouth, and he freezes, squeezing his eyes shut as I grind my core over him.

This isn't kissing, this is more, but no part of me wants to stop. It feels too good.

The storm darkens in his eyes, but I know my time is coming to an end; his moral compass won't take anything more from me.

I wish I could throw it into the fucking wind.

His big hands grip my hips suddenly, holding me taut against him and halting my movement. But nothing can stop the throbbing that I'm experiencing at the apex of my thighs.

"I know, I know. You want to stop," I sigh, dragging the tip of my nose over his cheek, lightly tracing his scar.

"No." He shakes his head slightly. "I want you in the worst possible way, darlin'. We *need* to stop."

"Just because I'm a virgin doesn't mean you have to treat me with kid gloves."

He squeezes his eyes shut again, exhaling roughly, making his hips flex and push his hardness into me. "There is nothing virginal about you," he growls, claiming my lips again in a powerful kiss.

"Let me walk you home," he strains through his teeth with his eyes still closed.

"I live ten feet away," I whisper against his lips.

"Let me walk you home," he utters, a little more in control of himself this time, tipping my head back to kiss my neck. His stubble tickles my skin, making goosebumps rise on my arms and legs as warmth fills me everywhere else.

My feet hit the wooden planks of the porch, and he helps me regain my balance, but he doesn't let go. He wraps his arm around my shoulders, tucking my head into his chest as we walk down the four steps and eight stepping stone distance.

"Try to get some sleep tonight," he whispers against my forehead before kissing it gently.

"I don't know if I'll be able to sleep." I giggle softly, and he smiles. One of those rare smiles he usually hides. It sends my heart racing even faster.

"Yeah, me either." He opens my door for me and reluctantly lets his arm fall, brushing his hand down my back as he does. "Goodnight, darlin.'"

"Have sweet dreams, Lochlan." I smile as he waits for me to close the door, and press my back to it once I'm alone inside.

I'd squeal if I didn't know he was still right outside.

* * *

I'm not sure what the protocol is when you wake up the day after you kiss your fake fiancé for the first time.

I take my time getting ready, stalling, really. Do I walk right into his house? Do I pretend it isn't a big deal?

So many lines were blurred last night, and I don't want anything to bring down the cloud I'm on. I swear my lips tingled all night long, I fell asleep with my fingertips pressed against them.

Unfortunately, when I open the door, it's utter chaos outside. I don't know how I didn't hear it, but there are people everywhere. All the parolees, at least four cops and their cars, Jackson's here, and I see Lochlan standing across the gravel lot, pointing and talking to Hayes.

Something happened.

"Jackson, what's going on?" I ask him because he's the person nearest to me.

"Someone pulled one of the fence partitions down last night, tried to use the wind damage from the storm to cover their tracks, but you can see the metal's been clipped. Trail cams caught one of the bears getting loose."

"Oh no."

"Lochlan's leading the charge. They're coordinating a search party, and I'm going to head down the mountain, close the road so traffic can't come up this way until they catch him."

"I need to check on Lochlan," I mumble, and Jackson looks amused. He doesn't ask, and I ignore his curiosity.

Tension is thick as I approach Lochlan and Hayes. He senses me, though, turning as soon as I'm in arm's reach.

"Which one was it?" I ask right before he pulls me in like last night, kissing the top of my head.

My cheeks heat with the surprising display of affection, my eyes flicking to Hayes, who doesn't look shocked in the slightest.

Did Lochlan tell him we kissed last night?

I don't know which answer is good or bad.

"Dodie, the old fucker limped out of here on three legs like he was reclaiming the wild." Lochlan sighs, still keeping his arm wrapped around me.

"Do you need my help?"

"Nah, nothing we can't handle."

"I might have Jackson take me back to get my car once he's done here."

"Okay, let me know when you're almost back in case there's a grumpy bear roaming around," he says gruffly, but not nearly as angry as he'd normally be in this type of circumstance.

"Sure." I pull away to leave, but he tugs me back in, locking me in with a passionate kiss in front of Hayes, God, and everybody, until I'm breathless and slightly hazy.

I fumble my way back over to Jackson's cruiser, and I'm not sure how I didn't trip.

"Well, that's not what I expected to see this morning."

"It's… Complicated."

Chapter Thirty-Seven

Jo

I'm concerned with the state of the sanctuary as I enter, and if there is still a loose bear because I never got a response from Lochlan when I told him I was heading back.

It's relatively empty, though, no signs of anyone or any extra cars. So it must be safe.

I'm barely to the porch when I hear grunting come from behind me. It's late, just after sunset, and I freeze, preparing to avoid a curious black bear when I notice the hulking form coming my way.

Lochlan's arm is draped over Hayes' shoulder as he helps trudge him across the gravel. He looks inebriated, and Hayes looks exhausted, carrying his weight.

"What is going on?"

"Ah, he might have gotten a little shit-faced. Help me get him up the stairs." I loop his other arm over my shoulders and help Hayes get him up the porch steps and through the front door.

"Hayes, what happened?"

"He saw the 6 o'clock NEWS." He huffs as we continue up

the stairs to his room.

"They ran a story? I saw reporters at the bottom of the mountain, but I didn't tell them anything," I puff through ragged breaths.

"Oh, I know. They included that and a photo of the two of you, after they went on a smear campaign against him." He nods to a door and I help him through it to Lochlan's bedroom. "I got it from here, don't worry about it, Jo."

"No, let me help."

"He wouldn't want you to worry."

"Of course, I'm worried!" I yell at an appropriate volume as we dump Lochlan onto his bed.

"What did they say?" I ask with my hands on my knees, catching my breath.

"You should just watch it."

"Oh, God." He starts to take Lochlan's boots off, and I brush him away. "Please, let me do it. It's the least I can do."

"He'll sleep it off, he'll be fine by morning."

"Does this happen often?"

"No, not since you got here." I look at him, and he rolls his neck to crack it. "He stopped drinking so much when you started staying in the guesthouse. He wanted to be in his right mind every second of the day in case you needed something."

"That's ridiculous."

Lochlan mumbles something incoherent, and we both look at him as he slumbers in his bed.

"Not to him." He shrugs, "Are you sure you've got this?"

"I've got it."

Once he's gone and it's just me alone, I take in the gravity of the situation. Whatever was said was bad enough that he broke his rule with drinking. I should pull the blanket over him and leave him to sleep, but I can't get myself to move.

I sit on the edge of the bed instead and pull out my phone.

The blonde woman who approached me while Jackson was closing the road down comes up on my screen.

Second Chance Sanctuary is once again proving to be a danger to our community with an adult black bear on the loose near the outskirts of Langston and a troop of felons leading the charge. You might recall the man who owns the sanctuary and his scandal from nearly two decades ago.

Lochlan Dane is known for sexually assaulting his classmate, Bethany Summers, but denying his guilt in a lengthy legal battle. After being convicted and later exonerated of his crimes, some in the community welcomed him back, agreeing with his improvement to Second Chance Sanctuary. Others worried about the crime that seemed to have followed in his return.

Dane is to be married to the daughter of former Governor Montgomery. Sources speculate the courtship is part of an elaborate scheme to sway votes for Conrad Montgomery, who is currently running for Governor this election season.

Montgomery is known to be a major critic of prison reform, but many believe this relationship could encourage voters in the middle ground to vote in his favor.

Is reform as easy as it seems?

Or can a criminal really change?

The photo from The Biltmore that I posted a few days ago pops up on screen, and they highlight my follower count as if I'm using it to sway one hundred thousand people to an agenda. The final clip is the five-second conversation when she asked me for a statement, and I very professionally denied comments at this time.

Jackson warned me not to speak to her, but I thought I had it handled.

No wonder Lochlan's upset. It's my fault.

He's lived in the shadows for years, and I swooped in and wrecked it all because of the attention my last name brings.

"Hey, baby. You're home," he mumbles, sleepily tugging on my wrist.

My heart flutters at his voice. "I'm here, get some sleep."

"Lay with me."

"I probably shouldn't." Sober him would be reluctant.

"Come on." He tugs again.

But, sober him might be pissed at me tomorrow for ruining his life and I might not ever get this chance again.

I kick my shoes off and climb onto the bed next to him, barely having a chance to make it to him before he pulls me down onto his body.

He's half asleep, I should resist as he cuddles me into his chest, but I don't.

"You're so pretty," he whispers, caressing my cheekbone with his thumb. His hooded eyes are almost closed, and I can smell the whiskey on his breath.

"I'm glad you think so."

"Everyone thinks so, but they don't see you like I do." He kisses me slowly, softly, but sloppily, and I take it graciously.

"Go to sleep, sweet man. You're going to hurt in the morning." I brush his hair back, and he nuzzles into my hand, kissing my wrist.

He's either very affectionate when he's drunk, or it's because his reserves are down. I try to untangle myself, to give him space, but he holds me tight.

"Stay with me."

I could probably get free from his arms once he falls asleep, but I don't really care. I snuggle into his chest and let him hold me until I fall asleep.

Another first.

* * *

The first thing I realize when I blink awake is that I'm not in my own bed. The second thing is that Lochlan's arm is wrapped around my torso, spooning me tightly to his body. The third thing is that he's hard, *everywhere*.

His bicep is solid muscle, caging me in, and his chest is a brick wall behind me, but most concerning, or alluring rather, is the firm erection pressed against my ass.

I peek over my shoulder to confirm that he's sound asleep and also notice that he managed to kick off his jeans sometime in the night, and he's only wearing his boxers. His shirt is nowhere to be found either.

I'm not panicking because I'm afraid to be touching a nearly naked man, I'm afraid of his reaction once he wakes up and realizes what's happened.

But, I'm also slightly overwhelmed because *I am* touching a nearly naked man.

I do the only thing that makes sense at the moment, and tickle his arm lightly until his muscles twitch and he rolls off me lazily, flopping onto his back.

I release the breath I was holding before volleying upward, sitting on the edge of the mattress. I'm upstairs in Lochlan's house. I've never come up here, never been allowed. Technically, I shouldn't be up here now, but Lochlan is asleep, and he probably won't even remember I was here.

I hook my shoes on my finger and tiptoe out of the room, but stop when I realize there's no door to shut behind me. I do a circle, seeing the hinges, but no door is attached.

That's weird.

As I glance back at the bed, a smile stretches my lips. He's never looked so at ease. Both his arms are thrown back over his head, his legs are splayed across the mattress as he snores softly. The large bulge in his boxers elicits a lot of feelings in the pit of my stomach: curiosity, excitement, nerves, and shame for observing him without his knowledge.

I force myself into the hallway, finding the bathroom across the hall with the only door still in place. Down further from the stairs is a spare room, and when I peek inside, it looks like a storage space, three wooden doors are leaning against the wall, along with some of his grandmother's paintings.

The third and last room at the end of the hall is the biggest room, probably the main bedroom at one point, even though there isn't a bed anymore. There's a big desk, wider and slightly taller than a normal desk, a small love seat along one wall, and the rest of his grandmother's paintings along the other.

On the farthest side are two double doors that open but don't lead to a balcony; they're flush against the side of the house with a small railing to keep someone from stepping out.

Sheer curtains frame the doors, and I can only imagine how they blow in the breeze when they're open. It looks over the backyard and into the woods that surround the bear enclosures on the backside of the property.

This must have been his grandparents' room. There's still an art easel sitting empty in the corner.

My fingers dance across it as I move back toward the doorway, but then I spot the papers strewn across the desk. It's not a regular desk at all, it's a drawing desk. There's a handle on the front to angle the top.

I shift some of the papers to spread them out, observing the sketches that have been drawn recently. A bear moving through the trees, the moon in the sky surrounded by stars, and a replica drawn in pencil of the old barn, just like the one I kept in the guesthouse.

There's a close-up of a bear's face, its sharp teeth exposed in its wide-open mouth, roaring in pain.

I marvel at the accuracy of the emotion in the eyes and the attention to detail as I drag it aside, revealing the next one.

My breath catches in my throat.

Suddenly, I'm staring into a pair of eyes that are a reflection of my own. Even in shades of gray, I can tell they belong to me.

The flick of eyeliner and the curl of the lashes are mine, but more impressive are the smile lines that I've considered getting Botoxed and the tiniest solar flare that circles my pupil at the center of my dark irises.

He didn't only draw my eyes, the next sheet is a close-up of my smile. The next is another smile, but it's my profile and that dimple above my cheekbone that won't go away, no matter how much weight I lose.

I keep moving papers, finding outlines of my likeness, some shaded, some not. Some aren't finished, and some have probably been worked on for hours.

I recognize the lines of my body that I've critiqued in the

mirror my entire life. Different variations of a silhouette that aren't pornographic or voyeuristic, but rather beautiful interpretations of a body that I hate.

I'm already choked up seeing these pictures done by his hand, but when I dig my way through to the last one lying flat under all the others, I can't believe my eyes.

A portrait of a beautiful, carefree woman, throwing her head back and laughing as if nothing could hold her back.

It's me, but it doesn't look anything like me.

Not the me that resides inside my head.

This woman is uninhibited... And, happy.

"You weren't supposed to see those," Lochlan's voice startles me from the doorway.

I spin towards him, grasping the portrait to my chest. He's pulled on jeans, but he's still shirtless and barefoot, standing immobile, staring at me.

"I didn't know you liked to draw."

He doesn't speak, his head dipped in... Shame?

"They're really good," I remark, encouraging some sort of response.

"Something I picked up in prison," he says, avoiding eye contact completely.

"I'm sorry about the NEWS story."

"Don't be sorry. It's just a reminder of reality."

"No, it's not." I take a step towards him, but he turns his head, avoiding me again. "I'm sorry that I've dragged you into this."

I place the picture back down on his desk before I leave, silently begging him to say something, but he only stands utterly still, letting me go.

"This is the first time I've ever seen a photo of myself that

270

I didn't criticize right away. That never happens," I say over my shoulder after I enter the hallway. "Thank you, Lochlan."

I go back to the guesthouse, and can't get my thoughts to stray away from him. Imagining him drawing the delicate details of my face with such intent focus stirs heat in my belly.

My fingertips trace the lines of my body while I'm in the shower, wondering how long he had to have looked at me to get them depicted accurately on paper.

And what he would do if he saw more than my silhouette.

When I step around the curtain, there's a sheet of paper that was pushed through the gap under the door.

It's the portrait of me laughing with a note written in the corner.

If you could see yourself through my eyes, you'd never find a thing to criticize.

I fling the door open, hoping to catch him on the other side, but he's nowhere in sight. This closed-off, sweet, frustrating man.

He hides what he's thinking, feeling, and skills like this. A talent like this could be framed and sold.

Framed and sold.

That's it.

Chapter Thirty-Eight

Lochlan

After I slipped the paper under the door, I was not prepared to face my actions head-on and made it a point to stay busy on the other side of the property the rest of the day. My nightly ritual of capturing my favorite moments of hers in a drawing was my dirty secret.

My obsession has been under wraps, but now she sees the truth behind the distance I've kept from her. Hell, she probably thinks I'm a stalker...

The first time I put pencil to paper, pulling her likeness from my memory, I stared at the sheet of paper until the sun rose.

I am a stalker.

Thinking of her constantly, leaving gifts on her doorstep, and worst of all, pretending my feelings towards her are barely there.

Once I got a taste of her lips, though, I can't hide my need for her like I used to.

She slept in my bed.

I was drunk, but I was extremely aware of her sweet body molded to mine all night.

All my dreams were about touching her, tasting her the way that I really want to.

Jo makes me want to be a better man, a man of integrity, but she doesn't know all of the shades of morality I've dabbled in. Running a halfway program for felons isn't for the faint of heart, and I've ruled with an iron fist to prevent any real damage from being done. I've been known to enact principles of the prison yard here because it's a rule book they all understand.

I'm in charge. There's no debating it.

But the blood on my hands shouldn't go anywhere near her.

"I've been thinking," Jo says as she walks out my front door. Tonight is another event we have to be fake-engaged at.

She went inside to check her reflection in the mirror without a mention of sleeping in my bed last night or the drawings she saw.

I thought she'd be disturbed, but she hasn't said a word as I've been racking my brain for the right explanation for my madness.

"Thinking about what?" I ask, glancing over and getting an eyeful of her tanned and shimmery legs. She's standing right next to where I'm sitting on the porch steps, fastening her necklace around her neck.

She's wearing her lipstick. The one that looks like the ripest of wild strawberries, deep red, and sexy as hell.

Looking up at her at this angle is a damn tease, my face is so close to her thighs and the hem of her dress, I could drag my lips across her skin if I was a selfish man.

If my relationship to her wasn't fake, I'd make her stand here while I buried my face between her legs, ensuring that she's late to this shit event we need to go to.

"Don't bite my head off for this idea."

My eyes find hers, and she's watching me closely. I'd almost bet her mind is on the same wavelength as mine, but it's dangerous to get my hopes up like that. She let me kiss her, but she owes me nothing else. I won't take anything else from her.

Her firsts should be with someone better than me.

No matter how much the thought of that makes me want to jump off a cliff.

"I think we should sell your grandmother's paintings. I know an art broker, I've been in contact with her, and she thinks there might be a real profit in the collection you have." She sits down next to me on the porch and twiddles her thumbs, waiting for my reaction.

"What kind of profit?"

"Enough to get the cameras. Enough to stop dragging you to these parties that you hate."

"You're kidding?" I knew my grandmother had a talent, but I never expected the world to see it.

"I'm very serious," she whispers, leaning her shoulder against mine hesitantly. I've been so caught up with the shit in my head, I hadn't considered that she might still *want* to be near me.

"Let me talk to my sister. I'll make sure she's okay with it, or at least let her pick out any she wants to keep. Then they're all yours."

"Did you ever try to paint?"

"I did once, when I was young. My grandmother tried to teach me, but I didn't have the eye for it. She was a natural."

"Still, she must've passed down her talent. A normal person

can't pick up a pencil and draw the way you can."

"She told me once that all it takes to be an artist is to behold beauty and capture the way it makes you feel." I kiss the top of her head, and she exhales in relief.

I'm such an asshole. I don't deserve an inch of consideration from this woman on a good day, but she continues showing me grace. She thinks that I'm doing her a favor by being her fake fiancé, but she's the one who has changed my life.

Having even a window of time with her in this lifetime is a damn honor.

"I want you to have this." I fish the spare house key out of my pocket.

"Why? Your door is always unlocked."

"I only leave my door unlocked because you don't have a key."

She looks puzzled at my response, clearly never having thought about it.

"Jo, I live on a property with a group of ex-cons. Some who I don't know very well, who come in and out like a revolving door. Some are more like Frank and his drama, and some that aren't cut out for the rules that I enforce.

"I used to always lock my door, but the moment you started staying here, I wanted you to always have a way in. Whether you needed to do laundry or get a snack from the cabinet, but mostly because you're a drop-dead gorgeous woman, who is surrounded by men. Men who might not live by the same ethics that I do."

"You wanted me to have access to you in case someone gave me trouble?"

It's so much more than that, but I just nod my head at her.

She'll never truly fathom how much her safety means to me.

"I suspect things might get worse around here, especially after the NEWS story they ran. People who have a vendetta against this place might start coming out of the woodwork. We need to start keeping the doors locked again. I want you to be able to get into my house whenever you need to."

"You don't think it's safe enough here with all the guys?"

"I don't trust anyone with you."

"I trust *you* with me," she says, propping her chin on my shoulder.

"I'd put a bullet in my head before I did anything to harm you, darlin'."

"Lochlan, I just put this lipstick on and I don't want to mess it up, but I'm going to kiss you now." She leans in and whispers, "Don't move," before pressing the most delicate kiss to my mouth.

"One more," I beg, before she's even pulled back a millimeter. I sense her smile more than I can see it as she delivers another butterfly kiss to my bottom lip, and then the corner of my mouth, the scar on my chin, and lastly, the scar on my cheek.

Every time her lips touch me, my soul recharges, and I feel like a new man.

If only it were that easy.

Chapter Thirty-Nine

Jo

Sometimes I catch him looking at me closely, introspectively, and now I know he's imagining the lines he would draw to replicate the image of me he's seeing in this moment.

The curve of my waist, the flow of my hair across my forehead, or the dimple in my cheek.

When he watches me from across the room, he's capturing the illustration in his deeply mistrustful and closed-off mind.

I take up space where most others won't ever get a glimpse.

And it's a privilege to be his muse.

I shuffle and bounce around all of the bodies in this packed ballroom, making my way toward the man at the center of my mind. We're at the elaborate Biltmore Estate again, for an end of summer event that most people die to be invited to, only to see the legendary gardens and historic archistructure.

I can't seem to care to be here because all I can think about is the man so trapped behind his walls that he pretends to be a villain when he's really a savior with a bleeding heart.

Lochlan's sitting at the bar with the rest of the guys, staying as far away from the other guests as usual. I don't blame him for it, I like him the way he is in his big, standoffish brute ways.

He can hate everyone else. As long as he keeps his one soft spot reserved for me.

His grandmother's ring sits heavy on my finger, and the weight of this predicament hovers over me, but I've stopped being concerned about it. No matter what happens in the future, I know Lochlan won't hurt me.

"Are we celebrating?" I ask, shimmying between Lochlan and Seiver, where they sit on their bar stools. They all have shots sitting in front of them.

"Nah, we're just keeping the bar in business," Seiver says.

"This is an open bar."

He shrugs and laughs, getting up from his stool and offering it to me with a sweeping gesture. "I need to find some grub."

"Are you going to take your shot?" I set my empty cocktail glass on the bar top, sneaking the cherry out and biting it off the stem.

"I don't need it." He holds up his shot glass with his thumb and pointer finger, offering it to me.

"I'm not very good with shots." I throw it back anyway, my entire body cringing when the bite of alcohol shocks my system.

"Did just fine," he says, leaning in and kissing my bare shoulder.

"Be careful, people might actually think you like me," I whisper, placing my chin on my shoulder so our heads hover within inches of each other.

"That's the point, right, being my fiancé and all," he whispers against my skin, making me shiver. He smirks.

"I don't think anyone is paying attention."

"They're looking at you, I guarantee it."

"You're very good at this, you know?"

"What?"

"Acting like a man in love."

He leans back, and I think I offended him until he hooks his finger under my stool, effortlessly dragging me closer. "You're an easy woman to love... I'm sorry your family has made you think otherwise."

I rock back at his words, stunned by his admission. Am I that screwed up?

A little kindness and attention shown to me by a man is all I know of love.

"Hey, don't. I see your wheels turning in that big brain of yours." He cups my cheek in his palm, and I lean into it. "I was giving you a compliment."

"I'm so far behind. I'm not even sure what it means to be in love with someone."

"You'll know when it's right."

"How?"

"It'll be warm and easy, exciting but gentle." He sweeps a loose hair off my cheek. "You'll know."

"More wisdom from your grandmother?"

He chuckles, nodding in amusement. "My grandparents are all I know of true love, but my grandmother cussed like a sailor, and my grandfather grumbled about her constantly. So it might not have been easy or gentle, but it was warm and exciting. At least the parts they showed Becky and me."

"Well, you're better off than I am, then. My parents' relationship is probably the furthest thing from love."

"So, search for the opposite of what they have." He shrugs like it's that simple.

"You seem so sure that it's possible."

"I am sure."

I stand up from my stool, placing myself between his legs, and flush against him. His hands envelop my waist, sending a tingle down my spine. "So, what would you call this, then?" I ask, wrapping my arms around his neck.

"I believe that you're feeling lust," he murmurs, watching me under hooded lids.

Lust? Is that all this is?

This intense need to be near him as soon as my eyes open, and dreaming about him when they're closed. Fantasizing about how his lips would feel on every part of my body. Counting the days until my birthday, but dreading that number dwindling because it means I have to leave.

"What about you? You feel it, too, right?"

He grips my hips tightly, ensuring there is only one thing that I can pay attention to. His *lust*. "You know I do, darlin'."

I feel the words rumble from his chest, and it makes me want to curl up against him and never move.

"I don't think I want to be here anymore. Will you take me home?"

"Yes." He doesn't loosen his hold on me until I capture his lips with mine. He won't take much from me, but he's greedy with what I've already given him. Any chance he gets to claim my mouth, he does so eagerly and without hesitation.

A flutter of appreciation always fills my belly, and it makes me wonder what other things would feel like... Specifically, I wonder how they would feel with Lochlan.

The tension grows thicker in the darkened interior of the Bronco as we drive up the mountain. His hand hasn't left my thigh, clasping his fingers just below the hem of my dress,

280

inches from the panties I picked out earlier, specifically with him in mind.

My fingers trace the black lines inked across his forearm, paying special attention to each bolt of lightning and every vein.

We hardly speak, and I can hardly breathe because I'm suffocating in anticipation.

What's he going to do when we get there?

How will I handle it?

Will he throw me up against the car or over his shoulder?

Normally, I'd cry at the prospect of someone lifting me in any capacity, but Lochlan has a way of making me feel petite.

He pulls through the black iron gates, and my pulse batters loudly in my ears as he parks in front of the guesthouse.

His hand slides all the way down my thigh to my knee before he lets go and comes around to my side of the car to open the door for me.

As soon as my feet hit the paving stones, he wraps his arms around me, lifting me easily and walking me towards the guesthouse. He doesn't set me down, instead, he collides with my door as his lips crush mine, pressing his hard length against my belly.

I don't want to just feel it. I want to see it, touch it.

I want him to take me to his bed and show me how a man uses it.

His mouth is hot on mine, taking, consuming. I can't do anything but feel him.

I can't worry about what might happen next. All I see is him, right here at this moment.

His tongue teases mine, and I reciprocate, caressing his until he moans into my mouth. That sound turns me molten hot as the muscles inside of me pulsate. The new sensation is becoming dangerously addictive.

"Lochlan, I want more," I strangle out between his open-mouthed kisses.

His lips drag across my jaw and down to my neck, tasting me, biting my sensitive flesh. Except, he stops at my collarbone and works his way back up, forcing a whimper from my throat.

"More, more than this." I gasp when he bites my earlobe just above my earring.

His exploration stops suddenly, his forehead finding mine. "I can't, Jo."

"Yes, you can. I want you to."

"You're killing me, baby," he growls against my lips.

The door clicks behind me, my body following it as it opens, but I don't stop kissing him until my feet hit the wooden floor inside because he doesn't follow.

The lights are too bright in here as I blink up at him, but his eyes are shut painfully tight while he drags lungfuls of air in and out.

"Goodnight, Jo," he whispers roughly against my forehead. He kisses me there and retreats…

No, no, no!

I spin, flitting around my room in a flurry of chaos, kicking my shoes across the floor, yanking my zipper down my side, and digging through my suitcase until I find what I'm looking for.

He does not get to do this to me again.

The moon is high in the sky, lighting my path to his porch, and my bare feet don't make a noise as I bounce up the porch steps, stopping in front of his door. Should I knock?

CHAPTER THIRTY-NINE

Should I barge inside and demand he take me like a–

"Something I can help you with, darlin'," his low voice drawls from down the porch. It's so dark I didn't see him sitting in his rocking chair.

I'm much more aware of my choice of attire now that I'm being confronted with my actions.

It doesn't matter, I'm doing this.

His eyes watch me heavily as I pad towards him in my powder blue silk robe that barely hangs past my butt.

I don't stop until I'm standing between his knees, gripping the lapels of my robe so he doesn't notice my hands shaking.

"Why did you leave?"

He studies my face, intensely, not letting his attention fall below my chin. I'm practically chum in shark-infested waters, and he's swimming right by without taking the bait.

"You were drinking tonight. I didn't want the alcohol to inhibit your decision-making."

"Bullshit."

His brows tick slightly as if he wasn't expecting me to argue. "I could taste the vodka on your tongue, Jo."

"I had one measly shot."

"And, before that?"

"I had a Shirley Temple with extra cherries."

I see it the moment he realizes he was wrong. I had one shot, but that was it. I'm not anywhere near intoxicated.

His knuckles tighten around the whiskey glass resting on his knee, the two fingers of amber liquid sloshing gently from the force.

"Are you too intoxicated to make rational decisions, Lochlan?"

His other hand fingers the tip of my robe belt, smoothing

the material between his fingertips. "I haven't taken a drink since I poured it."

"Why not?"

"I wasn't ready to erase the taste of your mouth," the admission rumbles from deep in his chest.

"Take a drink and I'll kiss you again."

A faint smirk tips his lips. "What's under the robe?"

He doesn't wait for my response before tugging lightly on the tie, slowly unraveling the knot at my waist.

"My finely tuned argument for you to take me to bed." My voice wavers slightly, and I know he hears it because his gaze finds mine immediately. He keeps watching me as he pulls the belt loose completely, letting the ties fall to either side of me.

The silk drapes open, getting caught on my breasts, but exposing my bare belly and the matching blue panties underneath because I wasn't brave enough to go completely nude.

My nipples are tight with arousal, the points visible through the thin fabric make me feel as exposed as I would if I were naked.

When I don't run away after being revealed, his eyes wander down my body, sending flames wherever he looks.

He inhales roughly, making his nostrils flare when he spots my panties, gripping the arm of the rocking chair in his free hand to hold himself back.

I'm so tired of the restraint.

I pluck the glass off his knee, taking two steps back to lean against the porch rail, and letting some of the moonlight drift across my bare skin.

"If you're worried about the taste in your mouth," I start,

taking a small sip of his drink that burns all the way down. "Taste it on me."

He's up and out of his seat before I can set the glass down on the railing beside me, grabbing my head between his hands and kissing me brutally. His body forces its way between my thighs, crowding me until I'm sitting atop the wooden rail.

"You're gorgeous, Jo. So, God damn perfect." He peppers praise between his hot, open-mouthed kisses, making my head spin. "You're the sexiest thing I've ever seen."

"You think so?"

"Darlin', I think you're God's gift to this earth. A mirage of hope to be dangled in front of sinners like me."

"But, you weren't guilty."

"Doesn't mean I haven't sinned." He kisses my jaw and the soft spot under my ear.

"You're a good man, Lochlan," I insist breathlessly.

"You might change your mind if you knew all the things I want to do to you."

I shake my head. "Do it, do it all." I curl my fingers into his hair, forcing his mouth to mine again, giving him everything I have.

His hands find my waist, touching my nakedness for the first time, and making me gasp.

"More," I beg, but his fingers only tighten, and I pull back, forcing him to look at me. He sees the sadness on my face, and I can tell he can't stand it.

"Whatever happens between us, I need you to promise me something," he whispers, his forehead pressed to mine.

"Anything."

"You won't let this hold you back. Whatever happens, you leave this place behind after your birthday."

I search his eyes, wondering why he's asking this, but… "I promise."

He picks up his whiskey glass, and I think he's going to take a drink, but instead he tips the glass, letting the remnants trickle onto my chest. It makes me shiver as it travels down my sternum and the center of my stomach, only stopping once it reaches the cotton fabric stretched across my hips.

He lobs the glass over the railing, abandoning it in the bushes beyond before his mouth descends on my chest, tasting and sucking the liquid off my skin. Another gasp escapes me when he moves lower to the space between my breasts.

His tongue continues along the path of alcohol, swiping over my diaphragm, cleaning the evidence away before he moves lower, sucking the soft skin above my belly button into his mouth. I don't know what a hickey is, if what he's doing will leave a mark, but I hope it does.

His tongue swirls into my belly button, and I cry out in surprise.

"One word and I stop, baby."

"No, don't stop," I plead, widening my legs to make room for his shoulders as he kneels between my knees.

He tastes the skin above my panty line, and I can feel my legs trembling, but not in fear. In anticipation.

Then he does something completely unexpected. His nose presses into the cotton right above my center and he inhales, dragging the tip along my slit.

I'm too shocked to gasp or utter a single noise.

My head rocks back when his tongue follows the same path over my panties, his warmth soaking through the thin fabric, molding it to me.

His lips skim the exposed skin right above the tiny little bow at my waist before taking it between his teeth, and tugging it slightly until the dampened cotton caresses my sensitive flesh.

"Oh, fuck," I mutter, breathlessly.

Then he kisses my clit and a strangled sound escapes me.

Chapter Forty

Lochlan

I knew she'd be this perfect. Her arousal intoxicates my senses, sending blood rushing rapidly in and out of my heart, and swelling my cock to the point of pain.

I've become familiar with the pain. Months of following this beautiful woman around without having any intention of admitting my attraction... My obsession.

I'll continue withholding, giving her everything I can without taking what I shouldn't.

That's what I tell myself as I inhale the soft skin below her belly button, unable to stop my hands from climbing up the backs of her thighs and squeezing.

Her ass is as full and firm as I've dreamed about, and drooled over.

The rough pads of my fingers don't belong on her angelic body. I don't deserve it as they hook the top edge of her sexy underwear and drag the cotton centimeters down her hips.

My ears have never been given a better pleasure than her soft gasps and her quiet moans. And, I know my eyes will never witness anything better, so I lean back to make sure I get to see every inch of her gift to me.

Only, my attention is drawn to the dip between her hip and lower abdomen, and the tiny, almost invisible, outline of a heart. No bigger than the tip of my pinky.

"You have a tattoo."

"Barely," she breathes out.

"Who the fuck touched you, here?"

I glance up at the moonlight casting a halo of light around her face, and watch the shy smile stretch across her cheeks.

"I was invited to a brand event two years ago. A tattoo artist was there, providing their services as a party favor. *She* was very gentle."

I kiss the ink.

"I'll be gentle, too," I whisper against her as my fingers grip her panties once more, continuing their journey.

"Don't be." She gasps when I kiss her bare mound then again when I kiss the very top of her clit, letting her tiny threaded bow dictate my path downward.

My tongue is teased with the taste of her until I'm suddenly jerking away and jumping to my feet as a loud crash assaults our haven on the porch.

The gate explodes wide, slamming into the fence on either side as a truck comes barreling through.

It skids to a stop, illuminating the house and the porch where we stand, but reverses within the same second, tires spinning as they retreat.

"Dammit!" My arms flex protectively around Jo as she buries her face in my chest. "Get inside, baby."

She doesn't move, and I kiss the top of her head, "Get inside. Call Hayes."

"Where are you going?"

"After them."

* * *

The Bronco's engine roars as I speed down the mountain and after the shit box truck. They probably weren't expecting anyone to be home, or for anyone to come after them, but they did get a good head start. Just not enough of one.

I'm not letting this fucker get away.

My tires barrel down the road, barely seeing the faint glow of their red taillights ahead of me. There's only one reason to brake at this point down the mountain, and that's to go into the carryout.

I floor it, skidding to a stop near the gas pumps when I see Frank, the dickhead, step out of his truck. He's the only person in the parking lot, the only person who could have come from my property.

My foot punches the gas, and he's a deer in headlights watching me accelerate towards him.

My engine jets forward, barely stopping in time to merely pin him between my truck and his.

His hands are up, but his feet shuffle away from my bumper as I slam my door.

"You've been attacking my home!" I lunge for him, dragging him across the hood of the truck.

"No, no! It wasn't me!"

I toss him to the ground and regain myself. Beating him to a pulp won't get me anywhere. The clone of Jo sitting on my shoulder is keeping me from letting loose.

"You just destroyed my gate!"

He starts kicking his legs to scoot away from me, but I stomp on his shin to keep him immobile. "Fuck you!" He yelps.

"I gave you an opportunity to get back on your feet, and this is how you repay me? Men beg for a shot like this when they get out of prison!"

"You had everything," he screams, trying to dislodge his leg from under my boot.

"I've been through hell and back to get where I am. And, being where I am still isn't great."

"You got her."

Her? "Jo?"

"You told us we couldn't talk to her, we couldn't look in her direction, but I saw the way she looked at you. It wasn't fair," he slurs.

"You're confused and drunk."

"I'm not." He jumps up, blindsiding me with a rock. The stone pierces my flesh, and I stumble back a step, but he swings again, clipping my cheek with it.

I stare at him as the tang of iron coats my tongue and the warmth of blood trickles down my temple. My rational behavior goes out the window.

He charges me, attempting to take me down from my waist, but I hold him off easily, not letting him get me to the ground. When my elbow connects with his spine, he howls in pain and falls back onto the pavement.

"You're a stupid son of a bitch." I grab him by the collar of his shirt and throw punch after punch, the impact of my fist against his face sends blood spraying, but I don't stop.

It isn't until someone hooks their arm under my shoulder, preventing me from swinging, that I let my arm go limp.

"Dammit, Loch. You're going to get your ass thrown back in prison," Hayes scolds angrily. He drags me back to my truck and throws me up against the side. "What the fuck were you thinking?"

"He attacked us." I spit blood onto the concrete.

"Yeah, you better hope the law sees it the same way." He nods towards the road as the Sheriff pulls in. Jo must've called her brother, too, but I don't fault her for it.

An innocent mind like hers only goes down one path when it comes to inflicting justice.

"I need an ambulance to my location," Malec talks into his radio as he walks over to us. "Are you hurt?" He asks, surveying the blood covering me.

"He got me good on the side of the head, but the rest of the blood is Frank's."

Malec folds his arms and sighs. "Jo told me someone rammed the gates, and you went after him. Did he say why he did it?"

"He was angry after I fired him. He wanted Jo."

His normally cool exterior stiffens briefly at the mention of his sister, but if you blinked, you'd have missed it. "That doesn't make sense. He's not the instigator of all your trouble, then?"

"No, there has to be someone else."

"Let me chat with Frank. See if he's more forthcoming in a holding cell."

"What do you need from me?"

"Lay low. I'll have a lawyer get in touch about pressing charges. And, get some stitches in your head, you're bleeding like crazy!" He yells as he walks away.

This is the most blatant violence I've been a part of in front of a cop, but the most mediocre shakedown. He didn't even try to make me sweat or question my actions.

He believed me.

He and Jo have their perceptive tendencies in common, I guess.

Jo.

Chapter Forty-One

Jo

I trust that Lochlan can take care of himself, but I still don't want him to get hurt. I've paced across his living room floor until the pads of my feet hurt.

Finally, headlights light up the living room window as an army of trucks pull in, and I take off outside with the flannel throw blanket wrapped around my shoulders, faintly aware that I should have put real clothes on while he was gone.

The cool night air skates up my bare legs, fluttering the bottom of my robe as Hayes parks the Bronco right next to the house. Lochlan climbs out of the passenger seat slowly, and I gasp.

He's covered in blood. Dried patches across the side of his face and across his knuckles, and spots splattered up his forearms.

I meet him midway down the steps at his height, grasping the back of his neck in my hands, examining the damage.

"Who did this?" My eyes roam across his bloody temple and hairline, down his neck, and back up to his face, where I see an amused smirk.

"Worried about me, darlin'?" His hands grip my hips,

pulling me closer.

"Of course, I am."

"I'm alright, promise."

"Did you get the guy worse?"

"I did."

"Good," I say against his lips, feeling him smile again.

"Real cute, love birds, but he needs a butterfly bandage or he's going to keep bleeding," Hayes cuts in from behind us.

"Ah, right." Lochlan starts to pull away from me, but I don't let him go.

"I'll do it, show me where it's at."

He looks at me like he's not sure if I'm serious.

"Let me do it," I whisper, raking my fingers through his hair to cradle the back of his head.

The hands at my hips slide down a few inches just before he hoists me up, wrapping my thighs around his waist. Everyone is outside watching us, but I only look at him as he carries me inside and all the way up the steps.

He maneuvers us into the bathroom and drops down on top of the toilet lid, keeping me firmly in place on his lap. "The first aid kit is in the drawer," he rumbles, raising goosebumps on my arms.

The drawer in the vanity right next to me houses a small box with gauze, antiseptic, and band-aids of all varieties. There's even a needle and thread, but I choose to ignore its intended use for the time being.

"Wash it first, try to get some of the blood off," he instructs softly, nodding to the drawer with the hand rags. It's a small bathroom, everything is in reach, but even if it weren't, I think he'd bleed out before letting me go.

I wait until the water is warm before soaking the towel

and dabbing it across his cheek, slowly cleaning his skin. It's dried and sticky, and I'm probably being too gentle, but he doesn't interfere.

He's not in a hurry, and I'm determined to take my time.

He doesn't flinch when I re-wet the towel and dab at his cut, but he does close his eyes until I'm done. It's my only indication that he's affected by this at all. He doesn't seem concussed, though I'm not sure I'm qualified to give an opinion on that besides what I've seen on TV.

"Dry it off with the gauze and then do the antiseptic."

"Okay," I whisper.

"Thank you," he says softly against my jaw as I reach for the first aid kit again.

"What happened?"

"Frank."

"What? I thought he was gone."

"Hayes said he'd been hanging around the motel they dropped him at. Apparently, he got a hold of a truck and decided test his luck instead of getting the fuck out of town."

"Did you…?" I can't voice the word that comes to mind, not because he isn't capable of eliminating someone, but because I don't want to imagine the repercussions if he did.

"I hurt him real bad. That's all."

"Is this type of thing how you got your scars?"

"Yeah."

I touch the big one along his cheek, looking at him thoughtfully until he elaborates.

"I got jumped my first week in prison by an Aryan Brotherhood tweaker. They wanted to initiate me into their gang of racist scumbags, but I sent him to the infirmary."

"How long were you there?" I trace the length of the scar,

all four inches of it if I had to guess.

"They sewed me up and sent me back to gen pop within a day. I cut my hair off after that because I had a feeling it wouldn't be my last fight. I didn't let it grow again until I got out."

"How many more fights?"

"Plenty. They saw my size as a threat. Someone always had something to prove." He thumbs the one on his chin. "This is from Hayes."

My jaw drops. "What the hell?"

Lochlan chuckles. "At the time, he thought I deserved it. He found out he was sharing a cell with a predator. I would have done the same thing, so I didn't hold a grudge."

"Didn't he feel bad once he found out you were innocent?"

"He's paid his penance many times over, don't worry." He reaches up, pinching my chin in his fingertips softly, and looks at me. If he wanted a kiss, he would lean in, but he doesn't; he's just looking at me tenderly.

"Time for the bandage," I breathe the words out, blinking rapidly to clear the fog in my brain. It feels like someone turned on the hot water, filling the room with steam.

I carefully secure both sides of the butterfly strip before I'm brave enough to look him in the eyes, but when I do, I see the source of heat making it hard to breathe.

His thumb caresses my cheek, falling to my mouth and paying special attention to my bottom lip. "I'm sorry I ran out on you earlier."

"It's okay, it was important."

"You're important."

The breath catches in my throat, but I'm already struggling to get air in and out of my lungs. His dark eyes are intense, studying me closely.

The blanket fell from my shoulders to the floor the moment we arrived in the bathroom, and I let my flimsy robe join it, tugging on the belt to let gravity take over.

The silk slips down my arms, pooling on the floor at his feet.

His chest heaves, and I watch his throat as he swallows thickly. There's only a moment of insecurity in my head, exposing myself this blatantly in front of him, but it's not because I'm afraid he won't like what he sees; it's because I feel so unprepared and *inexperienced.*

His rough hands travel up my spine, bringing my chest close and nuzzling his face between my breasts as if he needs them to survive. My fingers find the back of his head, gripping his hair and holding on for my own sanity as he explores me further, gently dragging his lips across my soft skin.

When his lips reach my tightened peak, a soft gasp escapes my throat, and his fingers dig into my spine, holding me tight.

Another first.

He doesn't rush, memorizing the first nipple with his lips before doing the same with the second. It isn't until I'm molten lava on the inside that he tastes me, flicking his tongue across where I'm most sensitive and sucking me into his mouth.

He worships me with his tongue, and my hips replicate it, grinding languidly against his lap.

When he sucks my other nipple into his mouth I can't control myself. My hands are clutching and grabbing at him, rubbing down his chest until they find his belt.

I don't know what to do once I'm here, and I start fumbling with the buckle, not thinking even two steps ahead to what I'll do once I release it.

As soon as it pops free, his mouth stops moving, and I'm lifted into the air, losing the progress I was making.

It's only a few steps to his room where he drops me on the bed softly, staring ravenously at my almost naked body. His eyes roam over me, and he looks like he's struggling with where to start before he reaches for my blue panties, continuing from where he was interrupted earlier.

He drags them down my legs until I'm completely nude and frighteningly exposed, but I'm not worried, not with him. He makes me feel beautiful and safe, and more confident than I've ever been in my life.

"Spread your knees," his gravelly voice demands.

I shake my head. "Take your shirt off first."

He rips it up and over his head, dropping the blood-stained fabric on the floor as I take him in slowly. He's larger with every breath he takes, radiating with strength and unbridled chaos, and I hope he gives me all of it.

"Now, your pants."

He shakes his head no this time, and I frown. "If I take my pants off, I won't be able to stop. Pants stay on."

"I don't want you to stop."

"Darlin', I don't want to either, but you know how I feel. You can't sway me on this one."

My frown deepens, but he's too focused on my lower half to notice.

"Spread your knees for me, baby."

Like a voice-activated entry, my legs open at his command, baring myself to him completely.

"I knew your sweet pussy would be fucking perfect."

His words make me clench. I've never heard anyone talk dirty in real life.

Chapter Forty-Two

Lochlan

Of all the places I've been in my life, on my knees in front of this woman is absolutely where I belong. I've never felt like a slave to pussy, but I'd willingly shackle myself to her.

"I'm going to touch you now, darlin'," I warn her. "Try to relax."

I know she's never done this before, and I want her to be totally aware of what's happening. I want her to enjoy her first time.

"Tell me what you like." I kiss the spot above her clit. "Tell me when it feels good."

"How will I know?" She's nervous, I can hear it in her voice.

"You'll know, baby." I kiss her clit and she gasps. She doesn't have to say a word to tell me exactly what I need to hear.

I take my time, kissing her, giving her warm, open-mouthed kisses down her center until I swipe my tongue into her sweetness and she cries out. I do it again, earning another gasp and I'm fucking gone.

Hearing her reactions spurs something in me that I can't control, and I bury my face against her as my tongue consumes her. I reach her clit again, sucking it into my mouth more roughly than I should and she screams in ecstasy, sending even more blood rushing to my cock.

I'm in so much fucking pain but I don't care. I'll endure it all for her.

"Mmorre," she stutters out, and I reward her, sucking her clit again and moving it back and forth between my lips. "Oh, fuck, Lochlan!"

"You're doing so good, baby. I'm going to put my fingers inside of you." Her head flops to the side, and I sense her need to hold on to something. "Grab my hair. Push me away if it's too much."

Her fingers curl into the strands at the top of my head and she grips them painfully making my dick flex against my zipper.

My pointer finger enters her tight opening, and the feeling makes my entire body shutter in pleasure, my eyes closing in a fucking trance. She's perfect.

"That's one," I inform her raspily, struggling to hold it together.

"More," she breathes roughly.

"Two." My middle finger joins the first, slowly easing into the space so I don't startle her. Or, hurt her.

"That feels so good," she cries, tugging on my hair as I start pumping in and out of her, slowly.

"You feel so damn good, Jo. I'm not even inside of you and my cock's never been so hard in my life. Feeling you wrapped around my fingers is making me crazy."

My praise makes her whimper, and it only drives me mad. I rub her inner walls until her hips start twitching and then I find her clit with my mouth again, sucking and licking it until she's bucking off the mattress.

"Yes, baby. You're fucking close. Let me have it."

"I can't, I can't." Her head whips side to side on the mattress, and I know she's holding onto her last little bit of control.

"Scream my name, Jo. Tell the whole fucking mountain who's making you cum," I demand, fucking her with my fingers and groaning against her clit as her walls tighten around me.

"Yes... Yes... LOCHLAN, YES!" She screams, exploding around my fingers as her thighs clamp my head. Her climax rocks her intensely, and I'm right there with her, the breath stalling in my chest as if it were my own release.

I kiss her tender flesh until her muscles relax and her legs fall heavily onto my shoulders. I kiss my way up her thighs, and my lips don't leave her skin until I fall to the bed beside her, where she curls into my chest.

Her warm breath fans over my skin, and I think she might fall asleep, until I feel a trickle of wetness.

"What's wrong?" I cup her cheek, tilting her face upward. Her eyelashes are wet with tears. "What's wrong, baby?" I ask again, swiping the wetness away from her cheek with my thumb.

"Nothing, I'm fine. That was just intense. I'm all jittery and I don't know... Overwhelmed." She laughs softly, sniffling.

"Have you ever orgasmed before? By yourself?"

"Not like that. I think I've been doing it wrong if that's how it's supposed to feel," she huffs in amusement.

"There's no right or wrong way."

"That seemed like the right way."

"Sometimes," I begin, my hand traveling down the length of her stomach to her clit. She gasps when my fingers start

303

circling her sensitive nub. "It can be a slow build-up, almost lazy."

Her mouth finds mine, breathing against me while I pepper her softly with my lips, kissing her through her pleasure.

"You feel it in your stomach, warming you up, and making you feel weightless." She moans her response, clutching my neck desperately.

"There's no rush." I move my fingers down, dipping into her tightness to prolong her torture and tease her. "Sometimes sitting right on the edge of your release is better than tipping over."

Her nails dig into my throat, and a smile tilts my lips. My eager seductress doesn't seem to agree with me.

"Do you want to cum, again, darlin'?"

"Yes," she mumbles, her eyes squeezing shut tighter when my slick fingers return to her clit.

"What was that?" My hand works her rapidly, demanding her orgasm from her.

"YES!" She screams from her throat, letting go completely before slumping back into my chest. I kiss her forehead, wrapping her in my arms.

"I think you've changed my life," she breathes against me raggedly. "Can an orgasm change your life?"

"Yeah, darlin'. It can." I kiss her forehead again.

It only takes a couple of minutes for her soft breathing to turn into soft snores, and I keep her tucked tightly against me, pretending that I'll never have to let her go.

Because the truth is that she's going to leave, she has to. And, I'll be here in the same place I've always been.

She brought life back to me, and now I'll spend the rest of it suffocating without her.

I shift her onto the pillow and tuck her in under the blankets because my mind is too wired to sleep. Whenever that happens, I end up in the other room, drawing whatever it is that's keeping me awake.

From the day she arrived, it's been Jo. Before that, I would illustrate any encounter I had with the bears. Even after a lifetime of working with the animals, every glimpse is a sacred memory.

Now, she's the gift I admire.

I've drawn the lines of her body before, but never with great detail. I drew what she gave me, and that was her smile and her twinkling eyes. Her curves in every dress she wore was my only guess at what was underneath, but my imagination never quite did her justice.

I didn't dare mark lines on paper that weren't authentically her. Now, I know the shape of her breasts and where each freckle lies, how the curve of her waist meets her full hips, and the area between her thighs intimately.

I can still taste her on my lips. Smell her on my fingers. Remnants of Frank's blood still cover my arms, but I'm a sick man, and I don't want to wash away the evidence of *her*.

I draw until my head aches and the earlier events of the night catch up to me, ending with a sketch of the beautiful woman in my bed. I take it back into my room and lay it on my nightstand because if this is all I get to keep from my time with her, it's staying close.

Chapter Forty-Three

Jo

I'm not surprised to see this particular ceiling when I open my eyes, or the light that's streaming in through the window. I remember the exhaustion taking over and being held tightly in Lochlan's arms.

However, I am surprised at the warm tingly sensation happening between my legs as my stomach muscles clench in response. The thick, dark hair of the man responsible is buried between my legs, but my eyes are drawn to the way his hands grip my thighs, spreading me wide.

His knuckles are still cracked and bloody from last night; the roughness is a startling contrast against my soft thighs, but the sight of it makes my insides burn even hotter.

A man so dangerous is making me float on a cloud of ecstasy as he eats me for breakfast. His tongue flicks over my clit and a soft moan escapes me, making his grip on me more brutal, pulling me in tighter.

Every noise I make stirs him, encouraging his worship. By the time I cum, my hips have completely left the mattress as he holds me firmly against his face. "Fuck, fuck, fuck," I mumble, as his feast continues.

"I want another one," he demands gruffly, sucking me into his mouth. It only takes a few seconds of his back-and-forth motion to make me cry out again.

"You're so perfect, baby. You did so good," he praises, making all the warmth go to my chest as he kisses his way up my body.

"Is it normal for me to be so horny even after cumming twice?" I ask, watching a pained expression take over his face.

He clears his throat. "Yeah. That can be normal," he forces out roughly.

I push his shoulder until he's lying back on the bed, and I climb on top of him.

"Jo…" He warns, but I cut him off.

"Don't."

He's still wearing his jeans from last night, but my hands rest against his shirtless chest as I sit astride his stomach. His eyes cut to my bare pussy and where it hovers over him and I see his abdominals flex below me.

"I just want to lay on you," I whisper, laying my chest across his until I can bury my head in his neck. My body is flush against his torso, and I can feel his shallow breathing pick up speed.

His hands palm my ass, holding me firmly atop of him. "If you're testing me, just know I'm not doing well," he rasps. I'm not even sure if he's speaking to me.

"What?" I ask against his throat.

"Nothing." He squeezes my butt harder, kneading it with his fingers.

"I can get off of you if you want me to."

"No," he says quickly. "Stay put."

His rough palms massage my cheeks, spreading me wide down there, opening me up and exposing me in a way that I've never experienced before.

It isn't until he rocks the flesh of my hips ever so lightly that I realize how close I am to his hardness. The bulge of his jeans rubs against my pussy softly and he grunts at the faint contact. He sounds like an animal in pain.

His hands rock my hips again, but this time I linger a second longer, prolonging the feeling of his erection against me. He blows out a curt breath, squeezing his eyes shut as if he can escape the feeling.

My fingers find my favorite place on the back of his neck, tangling into the curls there, and I rock my hips again, watching the pain and pleasure morph his face.

It's exhilarating.

This time when my ass rocks back, I grind into him, rubbing myself over his stiff zipper.

"Don't. It won't– You shouldn't…" He clears his throat to attempt to speak again. "My jeans will hurt you, don't rub against them," he forces out, very reluctantly.

"Take them off."

His eyes pop open. "I can't." The restraint is misery on his face, he's struggling terribly.

"I won't do anything naughty."

"God, please. Don't say that. Don't use that word," he strangles through his throat.

I'll add *naughty* to my list of words to use again.

"Let me grind against your boxers. It's not as rough and it'll make me feel good."

He growls harshly, yanking his jeans down and kicking them off the end of the bed, and then he reaches into his nightstand and grabs a bottle.

"You have lube?"

"Jacking off to you morning and night was going to cause an injury," he states seriously, and I have to bite my lip to keep from smiling. He pours some of the liquid onto his fingers and cups my pussy, rubbing gently until I'm grinding against his hand because it feels so good.

"This isn't what I wanted," I say distractedly.

"Then stop fucking my hand, baby."

"But it feels good."

"Of course, it does. I was made to make you cum," he grits out, tweaking his fingers to rub against my clit. I'm already so wound up that a few seconds of that is all it takes to make me jerk my hips as I orgasm. Again.

I should feel bad about this unfair treatment, but *he's* the one holding out on me.

"Maybe I should leave you alone now," I say to the ceiling, still coming down from my climax. My slick pussy is sitting directly on his stomach but he doesn't seem to mind.

"Do you want to stop?"

"No, but…"

"Then sit on my cock and give yourself another one," he demands and I smile, looking down at him.

He's so tensed, he has a bead of sweat on his forehead, and I'm soaring.

"On your cock, you said?" I sit up and shuffle my knees back until I'm hovering over his boxers. It isn't until my fingers grip his waistband that he jolts up from the mattress.

"That's not part of the deal," he warns, gripping my wrists delicately.

"But, you're my fiancé. I should know what you look like."

His pupils dilate at my words, but he doesn't release me. "I just want to know how it feels to ride you, I won't try to put it inside of me, I promise." I place my forehead on his and push it gently until he releases me, and he falls back to his pillow.

His eyes watch me wildly like a caged beast, as I pull his boxers downward, freeing his massive cock. "Oh, fuck," I mumble.

He's a big man, I expected it to be big, but nothing could prepare me for how thick and powerful his dick would look. It could be studied. He's the ideal male specimen that masculinity should strive to be.

I've seen pictures, watched explicit scenes in TV shows and movies, but nothing compares to Lochlan Dane.

It reminds me how much of a grown man he is and how little I know what to do with it. No wonder he refuses to have sex with me.

My swollen flesh is enveloped with warmth as I sit, straddling his length, feeling him for the first time. It's steel beneath me, harder than I ever imagined it could be, and he doesn't falter as I settle my weight on him.

Instead, he groans when I make contact, throwing his head back on his pillow for only a moment before his eyes return to where my pussy sits on him. My hips tip forward the slightest bit, and his entire body flinches, exhaling roughly.

"I'm not really sure what to do…" I murmur.

"Just do what feels good," he says as I rock my hips like he was doing to me before, rubbing my clit against his cock. His eyes roll back in his head and he mutters, "Fuck."

His reaction spurs me, and I stop overthinking, grinding against the entirety of his hard length until the tingling feeling in my stomach starts growing. His hands grip my hips forcefully as I ride back and forth along his cock, feeling the muscles in his legs twitching against mine.

It's harder to reach an orgasm this way, with my muscles tensed and my momentum waning with exertion, but I'm determined. I plant my hands on his chest and use him as leverage, rocketing my body back and forth until I'm breathing heavily and I can't keep my eyes open.

"I'm so close," I mumble, as he starts rocking me harder against him, increasing my pace. It's right there, I'm right there, but I need–

His cock flexes, the ridge of his head bumping against my clit, and my entire body shudders, tensing with my orgasm. My eyes flutter open, seeing that my hands strayed to his throat.

My grip tightens as I ride out my climax and he gasps roughly, thrusting his hips as his cock pulses with his release, coating his stomach with the milky substance I've never seen in real life.

My shocked gaze meets his, and my breath only re-enters my lungs when his mouth drops open in silent relief.

I lean forward and kiss his bottom lip, biting it lightly when he doesn't reciprocate. "Did I do good?" I ask softly against his mouth, and I feel his slow smirk.

"Yeah, baby, you did good."

Chapter Forty-Four

Jo

"I need to take a shower. I would invite you, but I know you're sore and I don't trust myself to behave." He rolls off the bed until he's sitting on the edge.

We collapsed in exhaustion next to each other for about an hour. He even texted Seiver and Hayes to let them know he wouldn't be available until later.

The man who never takes a day off wanted to spend the morning in bed with me.

"I'm too tired to move anyway." I giggle, and he tilts his head to the side to smile at me. I reach out and trace the tattoo of claw marks tearing down his left shoulder blade.

"Be right back." He murmurs after my fingertips drop to the bed.

I can't believe all that we've done since last night. I finally feel like a real woman, taking control of my life and enjoying the touch of a man. A man of my choosing.

I flip onto my side, snuggling into the blankets, when a paper catches my eye. It's upside down on his nightstand, and when I turn it over, I smile.

He drew me. I'm naked, posed sensually with my hands in

my flowing hair, and my back arched, accentuating my hips.

The same hips that probably have bruises from his finger-tips because he never wants to let them go.

Maybe he'll let me keep this one.

A shrill honk sounds from outside, making me jump.

I crawl out of bed to inspect, recognizing the car and the person in it instantly.

Dread fills me as I scramble to find something to put on, but all I had when I came over here was my silk robe, and it's still on the bathroom floor.

I snatch Lochlan's T-shirt and boxers off the floor and hurtle myself down the stairs, slamming into the door before swinging it open.

"Mom, what are you doing here?"

Her sneer deepens immediately upon setting her eyes on me. I didn't check the mirror, but I'm sure I look crazy.

"I came to save my daughter from this barbarian, but I can see you've already ruined yourself for him."

"Don't call him that." I might not have much of a backbone when it comes to the woman who birthed me, but I'll stand tall for my fiancé. *Fake* fiancé.

"Look at you! You're a disgrace already."

"I'm not."

"What do you think you're doing? Honestly. Do you think this man is going to give you a good life? Provide for you? He lives in a farmhouse for Christ's sake. This isn't you!"

"*You* don't get to tell me who I am. You have no idea who I am."

For the first time in my life, I feel confident and happy with myself. I have no desire to seek her approval, and I don't care if she dislikes me. I don't need her.

"You can tell Dad and Conrad I won't be attending any more events. You can consider me no longer a part of your family."

"You've turned into a whore and lost your mind."

My head jerks to the side as if I've been slapped. I know it isn't true, but hearing her say that so crudely is like pouring alcohol on an open wound.

"Get the fuck off my property," Lochlan's voice booms from the top of the stairwell.

His steps are slow and calculated as he descends the stairs. He's only wearing a towel around his waist, and his hair is still wet from his shower, but he looks as menacing as always.

"I could kill you for taking her from us!" She seethes through her teeth.

Suddenly, I realize she's the ugliest woman alive.

"Then you better bring an army," he says over my shoulder, grabbing the door and slamming it in her face.

I stare at the stained wood until it's nothing but a brown blur before my eyes.

"The first thing I'm doing when we get the money from my grandmother's paintings is to get a gate that doesn't open for anyone."

I ignore his words, walking over to the mirror on the other side of the room to stare at myself.

My hair is messy and the curls have fallen loose, my makeup has mostly faded away, and I'm wearing Lochlan's clothes. She called me a whore, but I didn't feel like one until she said it.

I felt cared for and cherished, not used.

"Am I a whore?" My insecurities are forging forward, and the peace from this morning evaporates the longer I look at my reflection.

"What? Of course, not."

"She makes me feel so disgusting. All I can see are my flaws." I palm my stomach, dragging his shirt up and out of the way to look at the softness that I've always wished was toned. My forearm pushes my breasts that are too heavy, higher.

If I rotate my leg the light catches the cellulite in my thighs and my calves that are too wide.

A large hand covers my stomach, drawing my focus there.

"I'm not a man who knows much, but I know you are a woman who has no business worrying about her flaws."

"Of course, I should. If I know what they are, then I can hide them or pay to fix them. I've had a spray tan twice a month for almost a decade to hide imperfections, my eyebrows are micro-bladed to fit my face perfectly, and my mother made sure my entire body was lasered hairless when I turned 18. Spanx and–"

"What are Spanx?"

"The shapewear that you ripped off me at that event."

"That shit does not belong on your body."

"It flattens my stomach in tight dresses."

"That. Shit. Doesn't. Belong. On. Your. Body." He wraps his arm around my waist, pulling me flush against him. "You're practically wearing a potato sack with my shirt on, and I haven't been able to stop thinking about how much I want to fuck you."

My breath hitches in my chest. "I look terrible, right now."

"No, you look like a gorgeous woman with bed head, wearing *my* clothes. It doesn't matter what's on the outside, you're still perfect."

"No, I'm not." I shake my head in disbelief, refusing to meet his gaze in the mirror.

"Are you disgusted by me?" He tilts my chin back to center, forcing me to look at him.

"No," I respond in astonishment.

"Do these change your mind?" He points to the scars on his face.

"What? No."

"What about these?" He rotates his hands, showing his cracked skin and calluses.

"No, I like your hands." My cheeks flush pink in my reflection.

He steps back, and I turn to face him. "Do these bother you?" He points to old stretch marks under his shoulder where his armpit and outer chest meet.

"Of course, not."

"Does this disgust you?" He pinches the roundness of his nearly firm stomach. I shake my head and he drags an old wooden chair over that was sitting next to the wall, dropping down on it and jiggling the evidence of his beer intake. "How about now?"

"No, you know that it doesn't."

He loosens his towel suddenly, exposing himself to me fully. His dick is hard and heavy, and stands to his bellybutton as he reaches down to cup himself.

My throat is dry as I try to swallow, watching him spread his knees wide. "Would you have rubbed your perfect little pussy all over my cock earlier if you knew I had these?"

There are faint purple lines between his thighs from where his muscles have grown and stretched over the years that it took him to become this large and imposing man of the mountain.

316

"Yes, I would have." I shuffle towards him until my toes touch his. "Because none of that stuff changes how I see you," I admit, reluctantly, understanding his point.

"There isn't a single part of you that should change, Jo. No matter how long you pick yourself apart in the mirror, no one will ever compare to you, whether you believe it or not."

I don't believe him, not even a little bit, but if I could see myself through his eyes, maybe I wouldn't hate what I see so much. "You're pretty good at this fake fiancé stuff." I nudge his knee with mine, too shy to look at him.

"That's because it isn't fake fiancé stuff." He stands up suddenly, tipping my chin to look at him. Our bodies are hardly separated and his cock is stiff against my belly. "All I know how to do is be honest. That's what this is."

"Can I be honest about something?" I glance up at him because I can't stop looking at his hard length between us, but I don't wait for his answer. "I want to know how it feels to touch you."

"Jo," he warns.

"I want to experience life on my own terms, Lochlan. I want to do this."

"I don't deserve any more of your firsts. If you want to know how it feels to touch a man, then you should wait."

"No, not a man. *You.*"

His cock jumps, but his eyes squeeze shut and a mix of emotions sweep across his face. "And, if I say no?"

"I guess I can go ask one of the guys in the bunk–"

His hands wrap around my head in the blink of an eye, tangling into my hair and backing me up until my butt hits the back of the couch. "Finish that sentence, I dare you," he grumbles as his hardness digs into my stomach. "I told you, I don't share. Fake fiancé or not. If you're doing any experimenting, it's with me."

"Then let me touch you." I peer into his eyes, silently begging him to give himself a break. He's the only one who thinks he's undeserving. "I want it to be you."

He nods almost imperceptibly, and I grab the hem of the T-shirt I'm wearing, but he stops me.

"Don't take anything off. If you're naked then I'll have you bent over the couch with your virginity all over my cock before I can think straight," he grits through his teeth making me shiver.

I glance down at the intimidating monster between us. When I was grinding on him earlier, it wasn't as scary because my body knew what to do. I was doing it for my own pleasure, and my hips knew how to move to take it. This is very different.

"What do I do?"

"Anything you want, darlin'. There isn't a thing you could do wrong."

I bring the pad of my pointer finger to his crown, ever so softly circling the rich skin. I expected it to feel firm or tight, but it's smooth like the softest butter.

He sucks air in through his nostrils at my contact, fighting to maintain his composure as I explore down his length, traveling over every vein and memorizing them.

"Would I be able to feel these inside of me?" I ask, honestly. His fingers curl tighter into my hair at the base of my scalp.

"Not sure." His voice is raw, each word like gravel escaping his throat.

"Should I hold it like this?" My hand circles the underside of his girth, my thumb over the top, nearly touching the tip of my middle finger.

"Yes."

"Would it even fit inside of me?"

"It'd fit." I glance up at him, but he shakes his head. "That's still a no, darlin.'"

"You have impeccable self-control, boss," I murmur, moving my light grip down to his base and back to his crown, how I'd assume a man would jerk off, forcing a strained breath from his chest.

One of the hands in my hair slides down my back until it snakes inside his boxer shorts that I'm wearing and he grabs a handful of my butt cheek, squeezing it hard. "And, you're close to being punished, darlin.'"

Chapter Forty-Five

Lochlan

Her delicate touch is so feather-light, but I can barely handle it. If she tightens her grip even a little bit, this will be over.

Having her hands on me is one thing, but hearing her beg to touch me nearly killed me. A woman like her wanting me isn't something that I can fathom.

"Am I doing a good job?" She asks sweetly, always wanting to be the best at everything she does. My little overachiever.

"Yes," I grunt, trying to keep it together.

"Can I touch these, too?" Her hand has stopped moving at the base of my shaft as she stares at my balls. Their heavy and tight, ready to fucking explode.

"You can," I admit reluctantly. "They're sensitive, though. I can only handle so much."

Her hand moves downward anyway, cupping the rounded flesh that she has tortured for months. The days and nights that I suffered with the worst case of blue balls, all because she walked past me in the kitchen or mouthed off to me with a little more confidence than the day before.

"What do I do?"

"Hold them with your right hand. Jerk me off with your left hand." She switches hands at my instruction and starts pumping my shaft rapidly with her dominant hand, harder than she was before, and my legs start twitching as my muscles tense. "Fuck, baby. That feels good."

She gasps softly when a drop of precum beads up at the tip of my crown.

"Swipe it with your thumb... Rub it in with your hand... Yeah, just like that... You're so fucking perfect, Jo... Keep fucking me with your hand..." The praise tumbles from my mouth naturally as I stare at her in awe.

Her pretty flushed cheeks are nearly as pink as her lips that are hanging open in fascination while she stares at my cock. I tip her head back up, stealing her mouth in a kiss because I can.

From the moment she offered me her first kiss, I haven't been able to stop taking her lips every time she's near me. And, thinking about how badly I need them when she's not.

Kissing her ruined her momentum for only a second before she picked it back up, continuing to work me like a damn expert. Even if she had stuck with tracing me with her little finger, I think I would have came eventually.

"I'm going to cum soon, baby. Where do you want it?" I ask against her mouth before sliding my tongue against hers.

"Uh, what are my options?" She breathes out.

On your tits. All over your ass. Deep inside your sweet cun–

"I can catch it in my hand or I can lift your shirt up and I'll coat your sexy stomach," I respond, rationally.

"I want to taste it," she whispers against my lips, and my whole body jolts.

"Fuck me," I growl. Her eyes widen with worry as if she's

upset me, but that couldn't be further from the truth. "Get on your knees."

She drops to the ground at my feet and looks up at me with those big brown eyes that I love, opening her perfect full lips as she continues jacking my cock right above her mouth. It's the sexiest thing I've ever fucking seen.

I'll never be this lucky again until the day that I die.

"So close, baby." My thighs twitch and my hips flex on their own accord, preparing for another life-changing release brought on by this incredible woman.

And, then her tongue sneaks out, licking the underside of my head to the very tip of my crown and I fucking lose it, my cum rockets out and into her mouth with such force my knees buckle, nearly taking me down.

My cum fills her mouth until I'm worried I'll gag her, but her eyes only flutter, taking every last drop.

"You don't have to–" I start just before she swallows and licks her lips. "Fuck."

"If I had even an ounce of talent, I'd draw this," she states seriously from her knees with her palms planted on my thighs, gazing up at me dreamily.

My head falls back in laughter because I can't begin to understand her attraction to me or her reasoning for giving herself to me like this.

It doesn't matter, though, because she'll ultimately leave and never think about me again. She'll touch another man like this, she'll adore him, and she'll think that he deserves her.

But no man will.

"Time for your next lesson." I grab her under her arms and pick her up until she's flush against my chest.

CHAPTER FORTY-FIVE

"What is it?" She asks eagerly and it makes my cock stir.

"After doing something like that, you deserve proper treatment."

She tilts her head at me curiously, and it makes me smile in the way that only she can pull out of me.

* * *

"I have to be honest. I did not expect this," she says through a mouthful of ice cream. She's freshly showered, wearing more comfortable and clean clothes, and cuddled up on the couch watching one of her movies.

"Which is exactly why it needed to happen. You don't do what you just did to a man without being treated like a damn queen afterwards. That's the lesson, darlin."

"You're such a softy."

"Am not." I side-eye her, grabbing the blanket to cover her up. She curls further into my side and sighs happily.

"Are you sure you don't want some ice cream?" She holds the spoon up until I shake my head, and then pops it into her mouth.

"Actually." I grab her chin. "Give me a taste."

My mouth claims hers, swiping my tongue through her lips and tasting the sweetness on hers. I had no interest in the ice cream, not when she tastes better than any dessert on this planet.

Her surprise turns hungry, and the kiss intensifies until my body is slowly pulled to cover hers. She barely manages to find the coffee table with her bowl before wrapping both hands around the back of my neck and dragging me the rest of the way down.

Her cold fingers dig into my skin as I nibble softly on her neck, my hands lifting her hoodie up from the bottom to take her full breasts in my palms. I flick her tightened peaks with my thumbs, drawing her moans out.

"What are you doing?" She asks as I snag her spoon from the table, dripping the melted vanilla on her sexy tits.

"I told you I wanted a taste." My tongue laps up every bit, slowly and methodically, cleaning her skin off with precision. The special attention I pay to her nipples makes her writhe against me, and I keep torturing her. I suck on her sensitive points until she's grinding uncontrollably against my rib cage, seeking the relief she really wants.

"Please, Lochlan, I know you don't want to fuck me but I'm begging you. I've done the other stuff, and I've done so well. Don't I deserve your cock inside of me? Please," she begs, while grenades detonate against all of my self-control and willpower, attempting to destroy my integrity.

"Fuck, baby, don't say that," I mutter against her chest, kissing the spot over her heart. "You deserve everything in this world. Everything."

"Then why won't you do what I want?"

"Because it's not supposed to be like this."

She grabs my face in her hands and looks at me tenderly. "Like what? With a man that I want? Or a man whose ring I'm wearing?"

"That's not fair."

"Why? I forced this engagement on you, but I didn't force you to treat me the way that you do. You aren't faking the way you touch me, or the way that you look at me. You aren't lying when you speak to me more lovingly than anyone in my entire life has."

"This engagement is fake, and it has to be because if I make love to you the way I want to, then I'll never let you leave, Jo. Don't you get it? If you let me love you for real, then I'll die when you leave me. Because you *have* to leave. You can't stay here forever. Not when you have your entire life to live out there."

"Lochlan…"

"I'm sorry, this was a mistake." I push off of her, stumbling out of the house before she can get another word in because she sways me too easily with them.

I don't want her to see how truly and deeply in love I already am because I can never tell her, and I don't want her pity.

My fists hit the porch railing, and I grip it roughly, shaking the old wood until the whole partition rattles.

"FUCK!" I yell at the universe. It's such a sick twist of fate to put her in front of me, make me want her, and be forced to push her away.

I can't be the reason she stays.

A red SUV pulls through the wide open entrance, and a groan of aggravation rumbles inside my chest. Is there a sign that says we want visitors at the bottom of the mountain?

"Why are you out here looking all broody and sad?" Becky asks as she steps out of her car with Emory.

"This is how I normally look."

"True, my mistake." She hands Emory a bag, and she skips up the porch steps to hand it to me.

"I brought my fairy dress. Do you think Jo will play dress up with me?" She looks up at me so innocently, and my heart breaks all over again, knowing that Jo will leave Emory

325

behind when she goes, too.

"Oh, uh."

"I would love to, Em," Jo says from the doorway. She doesn't look at me. "Let me go grab some stuff from my room."

She hurries down the porch steps to the guesthouse with her arms crossed over her chest because she isn't wearing a bra.

Becky looks at me knowingly, and with even more little sister amusement.

"Don't start," I mumble over Emory's head.

"I didn't say anything."

"You don't have to."

"It's only 11 am." She smirks.

I hold up my hand and walk back inside, ignoring her.

Chapter Forty-Six

Jo

"Do you think it's okay for me to keep some of these even though she wasn't my real grandma?" Emory asks as we go through the paintings upstairs.

"What do you mean?"

"I know I'm adopted. She didn't even know me."

"She would have loved you, and I think she'd want you to have something of hers."

"How do you know?"

"Well, family is what you make it. Your mom and uncle love you so much, so I know she'd feel the same." Who wouldn't love the little girl I'm sitting next to, full of sunshine and glitter, dressed as a fairy princess?

"Did you know her?"

"No, I didn't. I met your grandfather once, though."

"He was nice, he played with me. Sometimes I wish I had a brother or sister to play with."

"I had an older brother growing up, but he was mean. We never played together."

"You didn't have a sister?"

"No, I do have another brother. I didn't meet him until

327

recently, though. He's nicer, he probably would have played with me as a kid." I shrug, feigning indifference when it really eats me up inside. I missed out on so many years with someone who could have been good and decent in my life, but now we're practically strangers, and it's a hard relationship to navigate. Especially since I plan to leave.

"Look at this one!" Becky says from the doorway, holding a canvas. We had all split off into different rooms to start divvying out the paintings they wanted.

The one Becky is holding is a dusky evening in the wild strawberry clearing that Lochlan had taken me to.

"It's beautiful." The grass and trees, and the vines of ripe fruit, are in varying shades of dark green, making the strawberries look like rubies scattered in the thicket.

"You would think this place held some sort of lost treasure the way Lochlan always safeguarded it."

"What do you mean?"

"He used to make me guess the password as kids before he'd let me in the clearing. It was his favorite place."

"Oh." I don't know what else to say. I haven't spoken to Lochlan in a few hours; he made himself busy and avoided me since our moment on the couch earlier.

"What was my favorite place?" He asks from the hallway. I can't see him, but I can imagine his look of concentration as he studies the painting she turns to show him.

"Do you want to keep this one?"

"No. I have the real thing."

I hear his steps retreating. "I'd like to have it. If you don't mind."

"Sure. Hey, Loch, go put this in the guesthouse for Jo." She hands him the painting, and a wave of embarrassment washes over me. I feel silly, holding onto memories of this place when he wants me to forget it altogether.

"I'll get the other ones loaded into your trunk," he grumbles to his sister.

"Are you sure this is going to help this place?" Becky asks once Lochlan is gone.

"Definitely. My friend is going to sell some of the originals as authentic one-of-a-kind, and the others will be distributed commercially. Money should continuously flow into this place as long as they're selling."

"That's nice of your friend to help us."

I shrug. "I have a lot of friends, none of whom call me Jo."

"Yeah, I get it. Anyone who calls me Rebecca is backhanded. In my mind," she clarifies, laughing as she thumbs through the paintings Emory has already gone through. "My mother's name is Rebecca. She thought it was quirky to name her daughter in her honor. Which is weird since she dipped when I was five."

"You never saw her again?"

"We saw her on holidays. When she wanted to introduce us to her husband of the month. She's never met Emory, and I plan to keep it that way."

"How old was Lochlan when she left?"

"He was nine. It was a lot harder on him, but he was brave for me. He always is." She sighs. "I was a mess at our grandfather's funeral, but he was stone-cold and just held me throughout the entire service. I came back the next morning to pick something up when he was still asleep, and the house was destroyed. He must've unleashed everything once he was alone. I cleaned up shattered glass, mopped liquor off the floor, but I never said anything and I never asked about the doors." She knocks on one that's propped against the wall. "I assumed they made him feel trapped, again."

"I can only imagine how much pain he carries from those years," I utter.

"He can't seem to escape it." She starts to say something else, but we both hear the steps creak as he returns to where we are.

"Jo, Jackson's here. He wants to talk to us." He leans into the doorway, looking at me finally, and my heart aches. His eyes are heavy with his burdens.

"We'll get out of your guys' hair." Becky ushers Emory out as we meet Jackson on the porch. I use my last bit of energy to keep up my facade, waving to Emory as they pull out, and letting my smile drop as soon as they're gone.

"What'd Frank have to say?" Lochlan asks immediately.

"It took him a few hours to sober up, but he finally admitted that he was blabbing his mouth in a bar, complaining about you and this place when a guy offered him 200 bucks to ram your gates."

"Someone paid him off?"

"He was too drunk to remember who it was, and after grilling him on it, I believe him. I think he was pissed off enough not to ask questions, and cash was cash. The truck he used was unregistered, supposedly part of the deal."

"Do you think it could have been my family? They're pissed that I'm here. My mother stopped by this morning," I admit.

"No, I think it's someone local. Frank was at a hole-in-the-wall bar. No chance your family would be there to randomly overhear him."

Lochlan's gaze is distant when I look at him for his input, but I'm too unsure of things between us to touch him and offer support.

"Randall Porter's local," he finally says.

Jackson's face turns stormy. "Please, elaborate. I've been trying to take down this guy's whole crooked family, and you could make my day."

"I don't know, he's a mayor. I never thought he could be involved with anything illegal, but his name is stamped on every letter concerning my license and property. He's made it known that he wants me to sell, and I've seen him in Conrad's ear."

"Seedy politicians," I utter. "Men who associate with Conrad are worse than criminals. They do horrible things and get away with it all the time."

"Let me look into it. *Don't* do anything unhinged." He points at Lochlan sternly. I've never seen him use his cop voice on him. "If Randall Porter is behind this, then I'll nail him."

He takes off in his SUV without a goodbye or a wave or anything. He's amped up about the possibility of getting this guy, but unfortunately, that means Lochlan and I are alone again.

"I need to go check the fences," he mutters, looking at my feet.

"Oh, right." His head tilts up, hearing the disappointment in my voice.

"Do you want to come with me?" He asks hesitantly.

The sweet man that he is. He can't stand to see me sad.

"I'd love to."

* * *

"Right there." His arm stretches past me, pointing to a tree fifty feet in front of us. "Look up."

We're in the enclosed side-by-side, deep into bear territory. When he said he was checking fences, I had no idea we'd be inside the enclosures with the bears, but I haven't been able to tame my excitement.

"Oh, oh. I see him!"

"It's a her. Minnie."

"Aw, Minnie. Why is she here?"

"She is mostly deaf after getting hit by a car. She was in treatment for so long that she got used to being hand-delivered food. They didn't think she'd reintegrate well back into the wild. We think she was the one eating the rat poison, but other than a few piles of puke, she's been fine." He drives on and I wave to the bear that gives zero shits about me.

"We might see Rocko, he usually hangs out near Minnie. I think he's tried to mate with her, but she's fixed, so." He shrugs.

"Why did they do that?"

"She was pregnant when she was hit by the car. Taking the cub out and attempting to save it ended up causing more damage. It didn't survive."

My lips droop as heaviness overtakes me.

"I'm sorry," he says softly, reaching over to squeeze my hand. He pulls away, but I hold onto it.

"I guess not all of us are meant to be mothers."

"Becky used to think that, too. Now she is one. There's always a way around roadblocks."

"I think I would adopt someday, if I was stable and established." I tip my head to the side, pondering it. "But, mostly, I'd wait until I was implicitly happy with my life."

"I hope that happens for you, darlin'."

"What about you? Are you happy?"

"I'm happier now than I ever have been, but not with my life." He squeezes my hand.

"You deserve a happy life, too."

"Maybe."

"Loch–"

"Look, right over there is Rocko." He points to a small gap in between some trees, and I watch the huge black bear amble clumsily through the brush. "His equilibrium is all off. That's why he walks like that."

"There's another one." I point in the other direction, barely seeing the black fur through the trees.

"That's Dodie."

"I'd love to get a couple of pictures. I wrote about him in my thesis."

He looks at me in surprise. "About what?"

"The effects of amputation in adult animals and their chances of thriving in the wild with prosthetics."

"I didn't know you were writing about the bears."

"Not just the bears, but I do highlight them. I didn't want you to be mad."

"Why would I be mad?"

"I didn't want you to think I was exploiting them."

"I'm sorry I've been such a hard ass." He shakes his head regretfully. "I've really dug a hole when it comes to you."

"You have a lot of responsibilities. You don't need to worry about my feelings."

"But, I do. And, I hate myself for every time I've made you sad."

"I've figured you out by now, Lochlan. The thing that

saddens me the most is how you treat yourself."

Chapter Forty-Seven

Lochlan

T*he thing that saddens me the most is how you treat yourself.*

I haven't stopped hearing her voice say those words all night. I've been so caught up in my self-loathing all summer that I never thought to ask her what her Master's thesis was about...

Not that I even knew what that meant until this afternoon, as someone who didn't get to graduate from high school and earned their GED in prison.

Jo steps out of the guesthouse, and I tip the rest of my drink into my mouth, accepting the burn of it down my throat. She tiptoes up the porch steps to where I'm sitting in my usual rocking chair and stops a few feet from me.

Unlike last night, which feels like a lifetime ago, she's wearing a silk nightgown under the silk robe. Fully clothed but dangerously tempting.

"Jackson texted me. He wanted me to let you know that Randall Porter has an alibi for all the incidents here. He's going to keep looking into it, though."

"My gut's still telling me he isn't innocent."

"I believe your gut, too." She looks at me thoughtfully, sweetly, but filled with uncertainty. All because of me.

I pat my knee, reaching out and pulling her to my lap without any resistance. She curls into me and lets me rock her while I struggle to gather the words to voice my thoughts.

No matter how much time I have, it never seems like enough to express how I feel in the right way. But she deserves more than my silence.

"I'm sorry for using our fake engagement to try to sway you earlier." She twists my grandmother's ring off her finger before I can speak. "It wasn't fair when you've been firm in your boundaries."

She tries to hand it to me, but I stop her, wrapping my fingers around hers.

"I told my mother that I'm done with the events and I'm done with her and my father. I don't need a safety net anymore," she whispers.

"Keep it until after your birthday, until you're sure you won't need it. It'll make me feel better."

She smiles softly and slips it back onto her ring finger. "I turn in my paper next week, and then that's it. I'm officially a Master's graduate."

"No cap and gown?"

"No, not when you finish your credits in the summer. I could come back and walk in the winter commencement this December, but I don't see the point."

"Why not?"

"I'd only be walking for myself, I wouldn't have any family in attendance."

"I'd come."

"You'd sit in a packed event center for hours to watch me

336

walk across the stage for five seconds?" She giggles like it's a ludicrous thought.

"I'd do a lot more than that for a glimpse of you."

She tips her head up to look at me. "It's when you say things like that… That's what makes me want to stay," she murmurs. "The way you touch me is a bonus."

"Maybe I should keep my mouth shut then and just batter you with orgasms until your next big adventure."

"I want to get the full experience of this one," she whispers against my lips.

I hold her tenderly and kiss her deeply, pouring my heart into hers because I don't have the words to do it properly.

Her lips elicit warmth in my blood, but the aching in my chest is heavier. I don't want to give her up, I don't want her to give the ring back.

I want every part of her while I can have her.

"Can I ask you for something selfish, darlin'?"

"Anything."

"Stay with me until you leave. Sleep in my bed, in my arms. If my lap is available, don't sit in any other seat."

She smiles, "Only if you promise me something in return."

"What's that?"

"Call me darlin' every day, multiple times a day, and don't ever use it on another woman. I want it to be mine."

"I can guarantee there will never be another."

"Is it selfish of me to be so happy about that?"

"It's never selfish as long as you're happy."

"I don't know if it works that way."

I shrug because she'll never convince me otherwise. "What's next? Your first stop once you pack your bags?"

Her face shifts, solemnly. "I don't know. I used to think I'd start driving and only stop when I found something to look at."

"But?"

"But that seems like a lot of driving and not a very solid plan," she laughs softly. "The closer I get to freedom, the more scared I am to do it alone. I've always done everything alone, but this seems different."

"I just want you to be safe."

"Maybe I'll spend a week at the beach, get a nice tan, and plan my itinerary. There's nothing the ocean can't fix."

"I wouldn't know."

"You've never been to the ocean? You live in a coastal state?"

"I've never really gone anywhere other than here and to prison."

Her jaw slackens, and she stares at me until she's convinced I'm not joking. "That's crazy. No, what's crazy is that I can't steal you away from all of your duties and force you to come with me."

A small smile tilts my lips at her thought. "Being taken by you would be a pleasure."

She tucks her head into my neck so I can't see her face and sighs. "I wish you were serious, but I know you'd say no, and I don't feel like crying tonight."

"You know I can't leave this place."

"I know," she utters the words so softly that I can hardly hear her.

I rock us silently back and forth for a long time, nowhere nearer to a solution. She's meant to leave, and I'm meant to stay here; that's the reality.

"Do me another favor… Go get a new phone so I can send you bikini pictures from the beach."

CHAPTER FORTY-SEVEN

My hand tightens around her thigh at the prospect. "Done."

"Take me to bed," she whispers against my jaw, kissing it lightly.

I lift her from our seat and don't let her feet hit the floor as I carry her to my bed. It's a terrible idea to keep her this close, knowing it's only temporary, but I don't want to miss out on a single second that I have her.

The silk that covers her figure melts against my skin as I hold her close and breathe in the scent of her hair. My fingers memorize every inch from her knee to her hip as my palm roams over her.

It isn't until she hooks her leg over my hip that my hand travels further and I find out that she isn't wearing anything under her nightgown, and I squeeze her ass appreciatively because of it.

My fingertips dance softly across her curves, following the crest between her cheeks to her slick heat. Her breath hitches when I graze over her pussy.

"Open up for me, baby." She lets her leg fall off my hip and spreads her thighs so I have better access to her, and I take full advantage, slipping two fingers into her hot center, making her moan.

I let the heal of my hand stimulate her clit while I fuck her with my fingers, letting my mind get away from me as I fantasize driving my cock into her this way.

"More," she breathes against my lips, taking my mouth in a desperate kiss. She takes what she wants, slipping her tongue against mine until I'm burning with reckless need for her.

My hips rock against her thigh in rhythm with my fingers pumping in and out of her, consumed by her. Her grip around my neck tightens as I make love to her mouth, breathing in every whimper and moan that escapes.

Her orgasm is coming, I can feel her inner walls tightening, and just before the spasm comes, I remove my hand, leaving her empty.

"Ahh, what? Why?" She cries just before I yank her tits free from her nightgown and suck her nipple into my mouth. "Oh, fuck," she mutters, forgetting her earlier complaints.

My hand tweaks one nipple while I feast on the other, soaking in the way her body writhes against me in pleasure. She keeps grinding against my cock through my boxers, and when I switch the attention of my mouth to her opposite nipple, she bucks her hips, involuntarily catching the crown of my dick against her demanding tight hole.

She freezes, feeling the blunt object push against her opening, and then she rocks against it purposefully, her mouth popping open in a daze as she fixates on it.

I can't stop watching as she bounces her hips up and down, practically fucking herself without penetration.

I should stop this.

But, I don't.

"You're such a good little tease, using my cock." She whimpers at my words, putting herself in a frenzy. "You're so wet for me, I'd slip in so easily, filling your tight little cunt. I'd fuck you until you couldn't stop screaming my name."

"I want to cum on your cock," she begs in near delusion. Her cheeks are flushed red with frustration and ecstasy.

"Rub your clit, focus on that, let me help you." I grab the base of my length through my underwear and push my head against her pussy, replicating what she was doing with her hips, letting her relax.

Her fingers find her clit and she starts working herself

rapidly, chasing her orgasm at a full sprint as I pretend to fuck her.

And, as I die inside, desperately wanting to take her for myself.

"I'm so close, Lochlan," she rasps out between breaths right before her head falls back in explosive relief.

I'm pressed so tightly against her pussy that I can feel the waves of her orgasm clenching the head of my cock, and it steals the air from my lungs.

It nearly kills me.

* * *

I dream about fucking her, all night I make love to her in my dreams, whispering praise and 'I love yous' in her ear, begging her to stay without consequence for doing so.

When I wake, imagining her mouth taking me, I'm not surprised. It played on repeat throughout my sleep, but when I keep blinking and the sensation isn't evaporating, my head launches off my pillow.

Jo's sweet ass is in the air between my thighs as she sucks me into her mouth as far as she can go and back up slowly. "Good morning, sweet man," she hums from beside my stiff cock.

All I can do is blink at her, no words forming on my tongue.

Her tongue circles my crown, and a strangled noise escapes my chest. Then she takes my head in her mouth, and my whole body shudders.

"Fuck. You don't have to do this, darlin'," I tell her

reluctantly, wanting nothing more for her to keep going.

"I want to." She dips her head again, her lips dragging down the length of my cock until she gags herself. "You don't have to do that either," I grunt.

My legs flex and the tingling at the base of my spine electrocutes me when she hollows her cheeks to suck her way back up. When strands of her hair fall into her face, I reach for them, fisting all of her hair at the nape of her neck so it's out of her way.

"Do you like it?" She murmurs.

"Yes."

Her response is to take me down her throat, again, squeezing her hand around the base of my cock where her mouth doesn't reach.

She takes her time, exploring my length with her mouth until I can't stop my hips from flexing, begging to take the reins.

"Tell me what to do." She's driving me wild already, but she must sense my need. I forget how inexperienced she is and how eager she is to learn.

"Do what you're doing, just faster. Don't be gentle."

She responds kindly, bobbing her head at a quicker pace and tightening her lips around my girth until my hips buck in response. "Oh, fuck. Just like that... You're killin' me, baby."

Her mouth pops off of me suddenly, as she sucks in a lungful of air, trying to catch her breath. "I'm sorry, I don't know how to do this and breathe at the same time."

"It's okay, you don't have to–"

"No, I want to keep going." She sucks me back into her mouth determinedly and I groan in appreciation.

My fingers tighten on her scalp, holding her head taught.

"Breathe through your nose. Don't worry about moving until you're ready." She hums in agreement as I flex my hips, fucking her mouth softly.

"Good girl. Now suck… Yeah, just like that. Flatten your tongue and swallow when I hit the back of your throat… Fuck… You're so fucking perfect, baby… Breathe, keep breathing through it…"

I'm in a fucking trance pumping my cock into her hot little mouth, I feel like I'm still dreaming.

"I'm not going to last much longer, darlin', you're too fucking good."

She hums happily, clawing my thighs with her fingers as she deep throats me farther than she's gone before, and then competes with herself, taking me down her throat repeatedly until I'm a fucking goner.

"Yes, baby… Fuck… I can't… Look at me, let me see those pretty eyes…" Her big brown eyes blink up at me with a mouthful of my cock and it's all I can take.

I explode down her throat before I have a chance to warn her, too dazed with pleasure as my cum fills her mouth and coats her lips, dripping down her chin.

"Shit, I'm sorry."

"Don't be." She swipes the evidence of my release off of her face and sucks it into her mouth making my depleted cock pulse.

I shake my head at her. "You don't even realize how fucking sexy you are." She shrugs, shyly, and I reach for her, pulling her down on top of me. "Beautiful, perfect, sexy, gorgeous, and dumb as hell for even giving me the time of day."

She giggles against my chest and kisses the place over my heart. "I don't know, I think it's the smartest thing I've ever done."

"Then come up here and sit on my face, let me prove myself."

She sits up and looks down at me sweetly. "You don't need to prove yourself, I know you are well equipped to take care of me. But, I also need to get to campus. I need to turn in some paperwork and take an exam."

"I would have woken up earlier if I had known that."

"In my defense, you do normally wake up before me, but you seem more inclined to ignore your responsibilities when I'm in your bed."

"Can you blame me?" I palm her ass in my hands, squeezing roughly.

"Three more days and then school is over," she whispers solemnly. "Eight days until my birthday."

"Then, let's make the most of it." I kiss her head, pretending like I'm not falling apart at the thought.

Chapter Forty-Eight

Jo

Lochlan kept his promise. He's woken me up every morning with an orgasm and put me to bed with them, holding me tightly until I fall asleep. It's taken so much stress off my life that I haven't been anxious at all about turning in my thesis.

Leaving campus for the final time is anticlimactic.

I earned my Master's in Biomedical Engineering, but I'm leaving with a lifetime of confidence and happiness because of the man whose ring I'm wearing.

I'm not sure it's a good idea to keep wearing it, but he didn't want it back yet, and I've been selfishly glad. I admire it every chance I get, imagining what it would be like to truly be claimed by Lochlan.

If he had given me this authentically, I know he'd never let me go.

A big part of me wishes he wouldn't.

I pull back into the sanctuary and feel a wave of sadness overtake me. I technically only have a few more days left until I should leave. I'll have the money from my trust to start over and do whatever my heart desires.

Unfortunately, what my heart desires the most is right here.

I know deep down he doesn't want me to leave either, but I don't think he'll ever forgive me if I stay. He'd certainly never forgive himself.

Even with my backpack empty of all my textbooks, I tread heavily to the front door, stopping when I see the hot pink sticky note stuck to it.

Emergency meeting with the guys. Come to the bunkhouse so I can fill you in.

Uh oh. Something must've happened. I leave my backpack sitting on the porch and hurry to the bunkhouse.

I fling the door open and jump back.

"*SURPRISE!!!!*" Everyone screams. The guys are clapping, and Emory is jumping up and down. Becky and Tessa are holding a cake. Jackson, Natalie, and her little brother, Dec, are holding a 'Congrats Grad' sign, but my eyes go straight to the tallest of the bunch.

Lochlan's standing to the side with his arms crossed over his chest, smiling at me. Proudly.

My heart does a little somersault in my chest, and my feet don't stop moving until I'm leaping into his arms. "Thank you," I muffle against his cheek before kissing it.

"Congratulations, darlin.'"

* * *

"I'm not going to be able to move for the rest of the night," I whine, slumping against the big sectional in the bunkhouse. I just finished my third piece of cake after eating two plates of the BBQ that Seiver made and way too many helpings of all the side dishes Natalie cooked.

We're hours into my surprise graduation party, and I can't think of a time that anyone has ever celebrated me, let alone this many people. I don't want the night to end.

"I'm sure Lochlan won't mind carrying you home." Natalie winks, and I laugh. Sometimes it's easier to talk to her than Jackson because there isn't the added pressure of being a long-lost sibling.

Lochlan's shooting pool with Hayes against Becky and Tessa, but when I look over at him, it's only a moment before he meets my gaze. His attention never wavers from me for more than a few minutes.

I smile shyly from across the room and focus my attention back on Natalie, who is smirking at me. "I have to leave soon," I remind her.

"Right. Well, if you want to leave and go to our house so you're still close to lover boy, let me know."

"Jo's moving in with us?" Jackson asks, sitting down with his own plate of cake.

"No, I'm not." I laugh. "I'm traveling for a bit, that's the plan."

"What does he think about that?"

"He wants me to go. He doesn't want me to stay here."

Jackson looks at me pointedly. "That might be what he's saying, but I can see a man who does not want you going anywhere."

"It's…"

"Complicated," he finishes.

I know I owe him more of an explanation of me and Lochlan's strange relationship, but I'm not even sure where to start. In reality, I don't know what we are either.

"Mrs. Sheriff." Emory comes running up to Natalie, who looks startled to be labeled as such. "Can Declan come with me to pet the mule?"

"Oh, um."

"Please, sissy!" Dec begs from beside her.

"I guess that's okay." Emory takes off running toward the door, but Natalie grabs Dec's arm to stop him. "Does she know you don't like to be called Declan?"

"Yeah, she's in my class." His cheeks grow rosy. "But, she can call me Declan if she wants." He sprints after Lochlan's niece, and Natalie looks at Jackson and me like an overly concerned but proud mom.

"Do you want a drink?" Lochlan asks from over my head, leaning over the back of the couch.

"No, I'm okay." I pat the seat next to me, and he comes around to sit down. I don't hesitate to lean against his chest, sighing contentedly.

"I don't mean to kill the mood," Jackson starts. "But, someone posted Frank's bail. They used a bail bondsman, paid anonymously."

"Whoever hired him to ram the gates?" Lochlan assumes.

"That's my guess."

"What should we do?"

"Well, I took the liberty of getting eyes on him. Seems like he skipped town. I don't think Frank's going to be a problem. It's back to whoever hired him."

"But you have a theory?" Lochlan asks. He and Jackson seem to always follow the same wavelength, even though they are the least chatty people I know.

"I still think Randall Porter is behind it. It's too convenient

348

that he has an airtight alibi for every single date and time that something went down here."

"He's paying someone?" I ask.

"Most likely. His family loves to get other people to do their dirty work. I'm building a case against his mother, Vanessa Porter, already. I think she was more involved with her father's crimes last year than she led on."

"He's the one you killed?" Lochlan asks, and I whip my head to look at Jackson. I didn't know he had been involved in anything like that.

"He was a twisted man," Natalie interjects, reassuring me.

"The lawyer we used to get custody of Dec is filling in for the prosecutor, she's helping me gather what I need before we press charges. I'd like to include Randall Porter in the lawsuit if I can get the evidence against him."

"What do you need from us?"

"I'm going to send her your way to get witness statements, start a paper trail."

The door to the bunkhouse slams open as Dec comes running inside. "There's a fire! Help!"

We're all out of our seats at warp speed, pool sticks crash as they're thrown down, and every person in the room sprints outside.

"We didn't do it, I swear!" Dec yells, running as fast as he can towards the little barn with the strays. "The hay just started burning!"

"Where's Emory?" Lochlan asks, while Becky and Tessa are running around, screaming her name. I don't see her anywhere.

"She was right here, she was letting all the animals out so they didn't get hurt." Natalie grabs him around the shoulders, holding onto him tightly as chaos erupts around us.

Everyone is splitting in different directions. Ryker and Arizona are the first to grab hoses, while Curtis and Jordy start tossing hay bales away from the flames before they catch.

Jackson's calling for Fire & Rescue, and when I turn to look at Lochlan, he's gone. I spin, barely catching a glimpse of his back as he runs into the burning barn.

"Lochlan!"

"He's making sure she's not in there," Hayes says from beside me, suddenly, grabbing my arm so I don't run after him. "She's not in any of the other outbuildings. Seiver went to check the main house," he tells everyone else.

"Rain, round up the strays before they get hurt. Spock, make sure the fire engines can get through the gate when they get here!" Hayes commands, one eye glued to the burning building.

"Hayes, it's getting worse."

"I know."

The fire catches the roof, and the flames grow brighter, sending more black smoke billowing out than before.

"Where is she?" Becky cries while Tessa holds her.

"She's not in there!" Lochlan yells from the opposite side of where he went in, coming back around to where we're standing. He has smears of soot across his skin, but other than that, he's unmarked.

I don't have time to be relieved that he isn't hurt when Seiver comes hobbling down the path between the barns. "The guesthouse is on fire, too!" He yells, coughing. "I tried to snuff it out, but it was burning too quickly."

"DAMMIT!" Lochlan yells. "I don't give a shit about the buildings. Let them burn. Find my niece!"

350

"Split up!" Hayes yells, taking control and divvying out roles to the parolees while Lochlan comforts his sister.

Everything is moving around me hypnotically as I try to rub two brain cells together to solve our problem... To fix anything that's happening.

"Are they all accounted for?" I ask out loud. Lochlan glances at me like he doesn't know what I'm saying.

"What?" Hayes asks.

My mind's reeling. "Rain, did you find all the strays?" I ask him as he walks by, pulling a goat.

"The chickens and barn cats have scattered everywhere. Goats are accounted for. No mule, yet. He must've taken off."

"That's where she is. She went after the mule. She had to have," I guess. "How well does she know the property past all the outbuildings?"

"She's been on all of these trails with me a hundred times." Lochlan's eyes are wild with worry, but I see the speck of hope my idea gives him. "Everybody take off down a different path!"

The parolees scatter in different directions on foot as Becky and Tessa run to the garage.

"Stay here, help Jackson with anything he needs when the other first responders get here." He kisses my head and turns toward the garage, but I grab his arm.

"I want to help look for her."

"I know, baby, but you don't know the property well enough. If you get lost and I can't find you, I'll lose my fucking mind. I'm holding on by a thread already."

I see the pain in his eyes. Emory missing is destroying him.

"Okay, I'll be here in case she turns up."

"Thank you," he utters against my forehead before running

to the garage. Becky drives the side-by-side out of the garage with Lochlan hot on her heels on the four-wheeler.

Chapter Forty-Nine

Lochlan

I've ripped the throttle, speeding down the trails between the enclosures and shouting Emory's name until my throat's raw.

Every time I cross paths with someone, they shake their head no because they haven't seen her. It doesn't make sense.

How the hell could she just disappear?

She knows she isn't allowed to be out here by herself, especially at night. But I guess she has that mentality in common with Jo, they don't fucking listen.

I'd give my very last breath for my niece, but I'm holding onto the frustration I have over this situation because I cannot accept that anything worse happened to her than wandering off.

I have a spotlight attached to the handlebars of the four-wheeler, and I use it to scan inside the bear enclosures. My stomach twists at the prospect of her little body being in the same cage as the bears... She's a little girl. She's my baby.

If my life hadn't been such a train wreck, I would have adopted her when she was left at my gates. But subjecting her to a lifetime of judgment because of my name would have been selfish, and I couldn't do it to an innocent baby.

Becky knew where my heart was and didn't hesitate to alter her life to add Emory to the family. I helped raise her.

Our legacy is her.

The bears haven't attacked anyone at SCS in over ten years, but that's because we give them their space, and we respect them. Their needs are met here, and they're not usually human aggressive, but they're apex predators. They're wild animals, and intruding into their environment is dangerous.

I take a corner, driving down a new path that no one else has gotten to, and slam on the brakes.

My headlights shine directly on my mud-covered niece, struggling to pull the halter of a stubborn mule.

She's okay.

Thank fucking God.

"He ran away, Lochy." Her bottom lip quivers like she's in trouble, and all of my earlier suffering evaporates as soon as I have my arms around her. My sweet baby niece is fine.

"It's okay, sweetheart. Don't worry about him. I'll have the guys round him up."

"Well, don't have that one guy do it. It's his fault."

"What one guy?"

"I don't know. He said he was a new guy. He slapped his butt and it made him take off once the fire started."

As far as I know, everyone who works for me was inside the bunkhouse at Jo's grad party...

"We need to go. Leave the mule."

* * *

I can't drive as fast back to the barns with Emory riding with me but I haul ass as safely as I can. I don't stop until I have to, blocked by all the first responders tackling the blaze of the small barn and the guesthouse.

There are four fire trucks, at least nine cop cars, and what looks like 20 other vehicles scattered about that belong to my family, the sanctuary, and other first responders, if I had to guess.

It's a fucking mad house.

People are running back and forth, dragging water hoses, and yelling into radios. I scoop Emory up so she doesn't get lost in the shuffle and sprint over to the first familiar face.

"Hayes, I got her!" I yell and he spins around, his body deflating in relief. "Get a hold of everyone else, let them know to stop searching."

"Got it."

"Where's Jo?"

"I don't know, last I saw, she was with Sheriff Malec." He nods his head towards the guesthouse fire, and I scan the crowd for Jackson. He's taller and easier to spot.

"I think whoever did this is here. Emory saw him." Hayes' eyes widen and then darken. "I need a fucking fortress set up in the bunkhouse. Get my family. Get them guarded by every single one of the guys. I need to tell the Sheriff. Take Emory." I hand her off, and the normally talkative little girl doesn't say a word, but I watch tears fill her eyes.

"It's okay, everything is going to be okay." I wipe her wet cheek and smile, even when it's the hardest emotion to pull off at a time like this. I nod at Hayes, and he takes off to the bunkhouse.

"Jackson!" I yell over the chaos, sprinting towards him. He

whips his head to find me. "I found Emory. Where's Jo?"

He relays to his radio that my niece was found, calling off whoever was searching for her on his end. "I don't know. She was coordinating with the volunteer firefighters. It turned to chaos, and she took control."

"He was here, the fucker who started the fire might still be here."

A roar of frustration rips from his throat before he relays into his radio again. "Be advised, an arson suspect might be on scene. Keep channels closed."

He wipes his forehead. "It has to be one of the volunteers. I swear I vetted all my LEOs, and none of them are involved in illegal activity. The fire chief feels the same about his guys."

"I need to find Jo. Now."

"I'll start looking, too. Listen, Lochlan… If you find this guy first…" He shakes his head.

"Be careful what you ask for, Sheriff. I'm not a man who will be held back by laws if she's in harm's way."

"I'm aware. Find my sister." He yells over his shoulder, delving back into the shit show around us.

Chapter Fifty

Jo

One hour earlier...
"Where do you need me? How can I help?" I ask Jackson, jumping out of the way when someone sprints past me, pulling a water hose.

There aren't fire hydrants this far up the mountain, and that means water is scarce. There are already three fire trucks on scene when a fourth pulls in through the gates.

There are too many cars and not enough room for the truck to get where it needs to.

"Start flagging all the volunteers to move their vehicles back into the field behind the house. We need this area cleared as much as possible." He speaks into his radio, splitting his attention between me, the other deputies, and the flames billowing out of the guesthouse.

Thank God, Lochlan insisted that I stay with him in his house. I pulled all my stuff from the guesthouse last week, so I didn't have to go back and forth.

"I've got it under control. Don't worry."

"Hey, Jo." Jackson stops me. "Be careful," he says offhandedly. I'm not doing anything particularly risky, so I know he's just saying it as an impulse, but it makes me wish I could be more helpful.

"Sure thing." I smile halfheartedly.

I don't really have a plan once I start directing the volunteer firefighters out of the way, but convincing people that you're in control isn't that hard to accomplish. I'm flagging people to where they can park and coordinating with a couple of guys who are setting up a makeshift drinking water station.

"Excuse me," a man's voice comes from behind me.

"Yes," I utter, turning towards one of the volunteers. He's wearing a firefighter's helmet and coat, and it's dark enough that I can't quite see his features. I have to lean in closer to hear him speak because of all the chatter around us.

"I was parking my truck when I caught my eye on a little girl. She's hiding in the woods and was too scared to come out when I called for her. I reckon she belongs to you."

I gasp. "Take me to her."

"She's right through here." He leads me a few feet down one of the paths that takes us away from the house, but it isn't until I shout Emory's name a few times that I realize how far we've walked. "I don't see her."

He doesn't respond, and I spin around, but my chest tightens...

He's removed his helmet, and he's looking at me with an amused grin on his face. It's creepy Jerry from the junkyard.

"What are you doing?"

"Luring you away was like dangling candy in front of a toddler."

"Luring me away from what?"

"Not from anything, but towards something." He chuckles, lunging for me and gripping my bicep forcefully before I can dodge him.

"What do you want from me?"

He yanks my arm, pulling me further down the path until my feet are stumbling over themselves. Every worst-case scenario is filtering through my mind...

Is he going to hurt me?

Did he hurt...

"Where's Emory? Is she okay?"

"Kid's fine."

Thank God.

"Where are you taking me?"

"Not too much farther."

His responses are so calm, as if what he's doing is at all rational.

"Lochlan will know I'm gone."

"He's out on a wild goose chase looking for that girl. I made sure of that."

My blood chills in my veins. This isn't a spontaneous impulse he's acting on, he planned to take me...

"You started the fires? And the barn fire a few months ago?"

"Fraid so, sweet cheeks."

"Let me go."

"No."

My panic increases as we get closer to the bear enclosure fences.

"Why are you doing this?"

"Because I was paid good money, and that's how the world works."

"It doesn't have to. You can stop whatever you're planning, and we can fix this. I'll tell them you had a change of heart, and it'll be fine."

"I think it's too late for that, but nice try." He pulls a chain out of his deep pocket and wraps it around my waist, pulling me flush against him to tighten it and lock it around me. "If you behave, I won't hurt ya."

"Behave?" Is he going to...

"Don't move." He loops the chain around the fence post and secures it loosely. I could escape. If he steps away a few feet, I could untangle the chain and run...

He grips the chain link fencing in both hands and peels a section back that he must've previously clipped, opening a doorway into the enclosures. He steps through after he grabs my chain, tugging me along.

"Come on, girl."

"You're taking me in there?"

"Looks like it, don't it?"

"It's not safe."

He rolls his eyes at me like I'm the unreasonable one. "Come on." He tugs me harder, making me trip through the hole, falling to the ground at his feet.

When I don't immediately right myself, he pulls my chain, forcing the metal to dig into my waist, and bite me with pain.

"Please, don't."

"Get the fuck up, I'm tired of being nice."

"Nice? This isn't nice!"

"Pretty girl like you probably isn't used to the real world, but guess what? Life isn't nice," he yells in my face, making me flinch away.

I'm too scared to fight as he tugs me a few feet along the fence line, farther into the bear enclosure.

My feet crunch through the dried leaves on the ground until my open-toe sandals squish against something soft and

360

moist. It's cold against my skin.

Jerry sticks a small flashlight into his mouth, holding it between his teeth while he secures my chain around one of the metal fence posts. I glance down with the extra light and squeal, kicking my feet.

Blood. And what looks like brain matter is scattered all over the ground, coating my toes in dark red. "What is this?" I scream, trying to get away from it, but he's tightened my chain around the fence post, and I can't move. I can only twist a few inches left and right.

"Stop being a sissy. It's ground beef and chicken livers."

"Why?"

"It'll attract the bears." He laughs from deep in his chest, and my jaw drops.

"You want them to eat me?"

"Something like that."

"I thought you said you wouldn't hurt me?"

"Well, I won't. Can't say as much about the bears."

"On no, no, no, no," I mutter repeatedly, trying to twist free from the solidly locked chain. He's padlocked me in. "Why? Why me?"

He shrugs. "My brother wants power, and this place is like a gold mine. He thinks this will do the trick."

"What?" My brain is not understanding his plan, and I don't know who his brother is.

"If Mr. Dane's fiancé gets mauled by the bears he cherishes so much, it'll finally get him to shut it down." He smirks, amused by this outlandish conversation.

"He won't. It won't work. He'll never give this place up," I cry.

"Something switches in a man when he loses the woman

he loves," Jerry murmurs.

"You've made a mistake."

"No, I don't think so. Chain, meat offerings, solid distraction." He smacks his fire jacket, smiling at me disgustingly.

"Lochlan doesn't love me. We're only pretending to be engaged."

His eyes narrow.

"I'm just his employee. I lied about being his fiancée, and he went along with it. That's it. He might be sad I'm dead, but he won't give this place up. I guarantee it."

"You're lying."

"No, I'm not." Tears stream down my face. I am trying to force him to see the errors in his ways, but I'm not sure I'm not lying...

I'm not really Lochlan's fiancée, and he's already planned to say goodbye to me. We've grown inseparable, but he's not in love with me. He can't be; he wouldn't allow it. He told me as much.

"It's a shame for you, then, I guess. Plan isn't changing. Sorry, sweet cheeks." He takes a few steps, and I realize he's leaving me.

He's leaving me here inside the enclosure completely defenseless and at the mercy of the bears. I don't want to be near him, but I definitely don't want to be alone.

"Please, don't do this."

"I have to. A man has to feed his family."

"I hope your family is ashamed of you."

"They probably would be if they knew what I was doing... But all they know is that the bills are paid and they've got food in their bellies. A rich girl like you doesn't understand something like that, but maybe these bears can show you what it means to be hungry." He laughs deeply, stepping back through the fence. He rights the chain link and twists it just right so it looks flush like it hasn't been tampered with.

"I'll scream until someone finds me."

"Go ahead." He rights his firefighter helmet. "But I'm headed off to start some more chaos somewhere far from here." He winks, holding a lighter and a small bottle of lighter fluid.

A sweep of light reflects off his face suddenly, and he drops, crouching away from it. Curtis walks around the pathway, sweeping the trees until he notices Jerry in his path and jumps.

"Damn, dude, what the hell are you doing out here?"

"I was searching for the little girl."

"CURTIS!" I scream, and his head swivels, searching for me. "I'm in here, help!"

His gaze finally finds me, but he's struggling to comprehend why I'm behind the fence. He opens his mouth to speak, and Jerry lunges at him, taking him down by his waist.

"No!"

Jerry tries to climb on top of Curtis, but he swings his legs, kicking him off before he can. A full-out brawl ensues as they fight for the upper hand.

Curtis kicks Jerry hard enough to give himself more space to get to his feet and swings a punch at him. I see the pain twist his features when his scarred fist connects with Jerry's jaw.

His hands are too damaged from his skin grafts.

Jerry stumbles to the ground, but when he stands back up, he's holding a thick branch in his hands like a baseball bat. He launches at Curtis, who dodges the first swing, but his head gets clipped the second time Jerry swings, sending him to the ground.

"Curtis! No!"

Jerry swings the branch down like an ax, striking Curtis in the back of the head, and his body flattens lifelessly.

"NO!" His blood pools around his head, and a guttural scream escapes me until my lungs run out.

My head is swimming as Jerry drops the branch and stumbles back a step, wiping the blood off his mouth with the back of his hand.

"What did you do?" I cry, banging the back of my head against the fence post.

"I didn't want to do that. I didn't want to fucking do that!" He yells. "Fuck!"

"JO!" My name reverberates through the trees, and there is only one person that it could belong to.

"Don't fucking breathe," Jerry threatens, yanking my hair through the fence. "Say a damn word and I'll light this place up."

I feel liquid soaking the skirt of my dress, dripping down my legs, and then the odor of lighter fluid hits my nostrils. He's dousing me in accelerant.

He empties the bottle along the fence line, spraying it back and forth along the path he originally brought me down, and then throws the empty bottle on top of Curtis' motionless body.

He fishes the lighter out of his pocket and waits.

Chapter Fifty-One

Lochlan

I heard her scream as if it was amplified inside my head. Every one of my senses is so in tune with her that I've convinced myself I could smell her scent if I got close enough.

Logic has no room in my mind when it comes to Jo. No one has seen her; she's been missing for at least an hour, and that's 60 minutes too long.

Someone doesn't scream like that unless they're terrified or they're about to die.

My boots pound the dirt until I'm cut off by the bear fences, but what really stops me is a pair of legs lying in the dirt before me.

Men's legs…

Curtis' legs.

Curtis.

"Take one fucking step and I drop the lighter."

My gaze pings to a man standing just ahead in the shadows of the trees. The moonlight isn't illuminating enough to show me his identity.

I don't really give a shit right now, anyways.

I keep scanning for Jo. I know I heard her.

My eyes sweep past the bear enclosures, and my body jolts, seeing her pressed up against the wrong side of the fence.

"DON'T!" He yells as he sparks the lighter in his hand. Jo's cries reach me at the same time.

"Listen to him, Lochlan. Listen to him, he sprayed me with lighter fluid," she cries breathlessly.

Every muscle is tensed to save her, to kill somebody, to fucking stop all of this madness.

"What do you want?" I grit out, not taking my eyes from Jo. The rage in my body is rattling my bones.

"I don't want anything. My job's done." I look just in time to see him smirk as he throws something into the trees and drops his lighter. The ground ignites, and he takes off on the other side of it.

"No! No!" Jo screams. "LOCHLAN!"

Her fear rushes over me in a wave as the trail of fire travels quickly, lighting the path towards the bear enclosure. I don't think, I just react, running and skidding through the dirt to cut off the fire before it gets to the enclosure. The flame catches my pants, but barely has a chance to burn before I smother it, smacking away the fire with my hands.

I cut off its direct path to her, but the fire is still burning brightly, catching the dry brush along the trees, and filling the air with smoke as everything begins to ignite.

It's going to start a wildfire.

"How'd you get in there?" I yell, smacking the fence until I find a loose spot.

"Right here, right here." She nods her head to a spot a few feet from her, and I grab it, pulling the chain link wide open in one tug.

"We've got to go, the fire is spreading." I reach for her, noticing the chain looped around her waist.

"Lochlan," she utters as my hands roam over her, looking for a way to free her. "Lochlan, look at me."

My eyes ping to hers. "It's too late. He threw the key."

"What?"

"He padlocked the chain. He threw the key into the woods. I'm stuck."

"No."

"Yes. He wanted this. He wanted me to get trapped here." She nods to the ground and the raw meat scattered at our feet.

"The bears?"

She nods stiffly. "Now, I'm going to burn and they're going to eat me like I was cooked over a campfire." She laughs humorlessly with streaks of tears running down her cheeks.

"No."

"Go, you have to go. You need to get help, or the entire mountain will burn."

"I'm not leaving you."

"You have to."

"No, the fuck, I don't."

"Lochlan. Please, go. It's okay, I'll probably be alright," she shrugs sadly, unconvinced.

I tug on the chain around the fence post with all of my strength until the entire fence line rattles. It's solid metal. There's no way to break it.

I would need bolt cutters and time. Neither of which we have. Even if I could run for help, I might get cut off by the fire and wouldn't be able to get back.

The thought of her being trapped here, burning to death...

367

"I'm not fucking leaving you here," I growl, tugging harder on the chain that's not going anywhere.

Her hands cup my face, forcing my attention upward. "If you stay, we both might not make it. You have to go."

Her big beautiful sad eyes don't have a fucking clue. I press my forehead to hers, feeling her trembling body against me.

"Darlin', if something happened to you, I wouldn't survive a moment without you anyway. But that's not going to happen because I'm getting you the fuck out of here."

"Lochlan…" She whimpers, seeing what I'm not over my shoulder. "The fire is getting closer. If it gets too close, I'll go up in flames."

"No, you're not." I feel down her dress, finding the damp spots and ripping the fabric clear from her body.

"It's on my legs, too."

My palms scour the ground for mud, and I fill my hands with it, smearing it up and down her legs, covering any remnants of accelerant.

"Nothing is going to happen to you. Do you hear me?" I demand, and she whimpers again, burying her head against my neck.

"I know you fix everything for everyone, me included, but you can't fix this. I'm still trapped here."

"I'm going to fix this."

The fire crackles through the dry brush around us as I try to fulfill my promise to her.

"Lochlan, can I ask you something selfish?"

"You can ask me anything."

"If I die, will you bury me here with your family? I don't want to go back to my family, but I don't want to be alone for eternity either."

CHAPTER FIFTY-ONE

"Stop. Stop it, don't say shit like that."

"And, maybe you could visit me every once in a while," she murmurs in my ear as I clutch her body to mine.

"JoAnna Montgomery, shut the hell up. You're not dying."

"And, if you don't mind dragging out the fake engagement thing… Will you put Jo Dane on my headstone… So I don't have to carry their last name forever. I like your family better than mine."

"Don't, baby."

"Please," she begs, wiping the sweat off my face. The fire is close, the heat of it is heavy on my back, but the flames are still far enough that we're not in danger of burning. Yet.

"Jo Dane has a nice ring to it."

She smiles, "I should have convinced you to fake marry me weeks ago so I could have gotten rid of my family name faster."

"If anyone could convince me to do it, it'd be you."

"Thank you for taking care of me all summer." She wraps her fingers around the back of my neck, tangling into my hair like she loves to do.

"You probably regret accepting the job right about now."

She shakes her head. "No, I think this was the big adventure I was looking for," she whispers against my lips, kissing me softly. "Do you regret falling in love with me?"

She uttered the words so softly I hardly heard her.

But I did hear her, loud and clear.

With a wildfire burning at our heels, and her eyes pleading for comfort from my words, I can't be anything other than honest.

"I have many regrets in my life, darlin'. That will never be one."

She laughs, but it's only joyful for the briefest moment before it turns sad. "Thank you for saying that." She nuzzles against me, hugging me tightly. "Now, please, go."

"No."

"Lochlan, please."

"We've been through this. I'm not leaving you here."

"The entire sanctuary is going to be destroyed if you don't get help. The bears will suffer."

"They're smart animals. They'll figure it out."

"You don't believe that. This is your life, your legacy. You need to save it."

"I don't care."

"Lochlan…"

"Let it burn, Jo. I don't fucking care. I'm not leaving you." I hold her face against mine, feeling her breath fan across my skin.

I need to do something, I can't let the world go on without her.

I step back, staring at the chain link fencing. It's 12 feet high with 12 feet between each post. It keeps the bears in, but it's not indestructible.

"I'm getting you out of here." I kiss her brutally and jump back through the hole I came through.

I pull the chain link webbing from the outside until the metal cuts through my skin, but I keep pulling. I don't stop until it breaks free from the posts and snaps back, falling to the ground.

"What are you doing?" She asks, her eyes bouncing between me and the fire in front of her. It's bright enough that I can see the beads of sweat on her forehead.

"Your chain is looped like a figure-eight around the post.

If I can get it down, we can slide you off and worry about getting it off of you later."

"It's metal and probably cemented into the ground."

"I didn't say it would be easy." I jump up, gripping the pole as high as I can and dig my foot against it, pulling the aluminum post until it starts to give.

It's metal, but it's hollow. If I can get it to bend just enough, I can get her off.

"Lochlan," she cries and then coughs.

The fire is getting closer, and the smoke is filling the air.

I jump up again, grabbing even further up the pole now that it's slightly bent, and I use every bit of strength to bring it towards the ground.

"Ahhhh." My entire body is screaming in pain, but it's still not enough. It's bending, but not enough to slide her off.

Not by mysel–

"LOCHLAN!" Hayes yells, riding in on the side-by-side, driving straight through a trail of flames. Jordy, Arizona, and the Sheriff jump out.

"Help me!" I yell mid-pull, feeling my biceps ripping from the inside out.

Jordy and Arizona jump in immediately, helping me pull the metal post, leveraging it with brute strength until it's almost low enough.

"Move, move!" Hayes yells, looping the tow chain around the top of the post. "Clear out, if it snaps back, it could take your head off."

Jordy and Arizona find a safe spot, but I go to Jo, wrapping my arms around her to cover her the best I can. "I've got you, baby."

"Lochlan, the fire," her voice rattles.

The flames are licking my back now, at least that's what it feels like. My shirt is saturated in sweat, and each breath feels like it's being forced through a bendy straw.

Over her shoulder, I see Jackson checking Curtis's lifeless body. He went down in the dirt far enough from the tree line to keep from getting burned up.

He picks him up and hands him off to Arizona, who takes off, carrying his limp body out of here through the only clear path through the trees. The fire is nearly surrounding us now.

"Heads up!" Hayes yells before throwing the side-by-side into reverse and pulling the pole.

My hands go around Jo's head, bracing for anything that might come flying her way if this doesn't pan out.

If this doesn't work, I'm afraid it might be over for us.

Us. Because I'm not fucking leaving her.

The metal post protests, screaming as it's bent towards the ground, and then the tow rope snaps.

It's like a whip cracking against my side.

"Ahh," I cry out involuntarily.

"Are you okay?" I feel her breath against my neck.

"I'm fine," I gasp as the pain radiating through my side blinds me.

At least it wasn't her.

Chapter Fifty-Two

Jo

He's absolutely not fine. The misery is evident on his face as he grimaces, but he doesn't slow down or hesitate for a moment when Hayes reverses back to the pole and jumps off.

"Let's go!" He yells, saddling up next to Lochlan.

Jackson and Jordy are there, standing on the back of the side-by-side, and I hardly have a moment to prepare before Hayes nods at Lochlan, and they both start lifting me into the air.

If I wasn't on the verge of death, this would be my worst nightmare.

They lift me until Jackson and Jordy can grab my arms, pulling me along the post as Lochlan and Hayes steady my legs. It's not comfortable, but they're maneuvering me off the post relatively painlessly as the fire crackles all around us.

"You're almost off, Jo. You might feel like you're falling once the chain slips off, but Jackson will catch you," Jordy informs me, holding my shoulders steady.

"Oka–" I don't have time to finish my word before it feels

like gravity is cut off, and I scream as my body tumbles off the end of the pole.

I land with a thump, safely in my brother's arms. Not really the family bonding I was hoping for, but I'll take it.

"Thank you," I breathe out.

"You really scared me there for a minute," he huffs in relief, handing me down to Lochlan on the ground.

"Just making up for lost time."

"No more near-death experiences," Lochlan growls, cradling me to his chest.

"Let's get out of this one first," Hayes says, as we load into the side-by-side.

Lochlan keeps me in his lap while Jackson and Jordy sit down in the back. Hayes guns it, driving directly towards a wall of fire that is our only way out. I curl into Lochlan's chest, squeezing my eyes shut as he holds me firmly against him.

I don't see when we're free, but I feel the shift as the air clears of smoke. We barrel down the path towards the barns and pass firefighters running towards the fire.

It's too narrow in the wooded area for the trucks to get through, and I have no idea how they're going to fight it. But my job is done, I survived.

The professionals can figure out the rest.

Hayes drives straight to the bunkhouse, but we go through the back door so I can't see what's going on with the rest of the property. I also don't think I have the capacity to see all the damage that was inflicted.

"Do you need a medic?" Jackson asks me, and I shake my head.

"You?" He asks Lochlan, who grimaces as he's still holding

me.

"No," he grunts, taking me over to the couch and sitting down. A strangled moan escapes him as we settle onto the cushions.

"You're hurt."

"I'm fine."

"Lochlan, we're safe. You can go get checked out."

"I'll be fine," he breathes.

"Let me off, I'm making it worse."

"Don't you fucking dare leave me." He wraps his arms around me tightly, grunting as he does.

Stubborn, sweet man.

"I won't leave, I promise." I scoot off his lap, and he's in too much pain to stop me. I leave my legs draped across his thighs so he doesn't fret, and hold onto his arm.

His hands are bloody and destroyed, making me gasp.

"Lochlan Dane. You need a medic!"

"I'm fine."

"Alright, fill me in," Jackson says, sitting down on the coffee table in front of us. "From the beginning, Jo."

"It was Jerry from the junkyard, I thought he was a volunteer firefighter. He lured me into the woods because I thought he had found Emory." I gasp, looking around. "Where's Emory?"

"She's fine. She's asleep upstairs," Hayes says from the other side of the couch, holding bolt cutters. "Becky and Tessa are with her."

I nod, gathering my thoughts as he comes over to snip the chain from my waist. It takes a few attempts, but he gets me free after about a minute.

"He admitted that he was paid to start the fires. He was

also paid to get rid of me so Lochlan would be forced to close the sanctuary."

Lochlan grumbles deeply beside me.

"I pleaded with him and told him that I wasn't really Lochlan's fiancée. It was all fake, but he wouldn't let me go." Lochlan's grip tightens on my legs as I continue talking. "He wanted me to be mauled by the bears per his brother's orders. I don't know who his brother is."

"I'm going to fucking kill him," Lochlan grunts as he tries to stand up but I press on his chest, stopping him.

"Don't leave me."

"Yeah, let's not make death threats out loud," Jackson mutters, and Hayes laughs. "Your word is all I need, Jo. I'll get a hold of the judge and get the warrant for his arrest."

"Just like that?"

"Jerry the junkyard owner will be in cuffs before dawn, and I'll find out who his brother is," Jackson confirms earnestly.

"What about Curtis?"

"He might not make it, Jo. I'm sorry. He lost a lot of blood, but he's on his way to St. John's Hospital."

"Oh my God," I cry, covering my face. "He was trying to help me. He tried to fight him off but…" I can't even utter the words out loud.

"He's a good man. He was a soldier. He knew what he was doing when he tried to save you. He wouldn't regret it," Jackson promises.

"Seiver and Arizona went with him to the hospital," Hayes adds.

"What about the bears? The fire?"

"They'll run from the fire. They'll be fine. If it gets too bad, we'll let them loose."

CHAPTER FIFTY-TWO

"Loose?"

"Better than burning alive," Lochlan utters, kissing my head gently as if we weren't in jeopardy of that only moments ago.

"Are you sure you don't want to see a medic?" Jackson asks Lochlan as he stands.

"No, I'm fine."

"Alright, you guys hang tight inside. I need to go check on the crews."

Once he's gone and everyone else around us makes themselves scarce, I burrow into Lochlan's neck, letting the weight of the situation finally hit me.

"Is there any chance Curtis will be okay?"

"He's a tough son of a bitch. If anyone can pull through, it's him."

I nod, silently letting the tears flow free that I've been trying to hold back. Lochlan's arm anchors me closer, eliciting a sharp intake of breath as he moves. "Thank you for staying with me out there and comforting me when I thought I was going to die," I hiccup through my sobs.

"I told you I wouldn't let that happen."

"You told me a lot of things," I murmur, resting my hand over his heart.

"And, I meant everything I said." He closes his hand over mine, pulling it up to kiss my fingers.

"But you still want me to leave after my birthday?"

There's a heavy, stagnant pause as I wait for his answer.

"My feelings towards you don't change anything."

I squeeze my eyes shut, but there isn't a thing that will stop the onslaught of fresh tears from escaping my eyes.

He loves me, but he wants me to leave.

The pain of that is worse than nearly dying.

* * *

It's dawn, I can see the light creeping in the window through my swollen eyelids, and I'm in Lochlan's bed, but I'm alone.

I check the room with his drawing table but it's empty and when I go downstairs, I check the lower level and don't see him. The only thing I see is a pink sticky note stuck to the inside of the front door.

Needed to help the guys. Keep the doors locked until I get back.

As I'm reading the note the door knob jiggles and a squeak escapes me as I jump back, but it's just him.

"I thought you'd be asleep," his voice is low and gravely, he's almost whispering. He looks exhausted, and he's still covered in the grime from last night. His blood.

He hasn't been to bed at all.

"I was looking for you."

He's standing in front of me, staring at me silently like he's unsure of what to do.

But he looks so tired and sad, I can't put any distance between us. Not when I'm one day closer to my birthday.

"Shower first or straight to bed?"

"Shower."

I grab his wrist because there's still dried blood in the lines and cracks of his hands, and I'm not sure how badly they might hurt, and tug him slowly up the stairs.

I help him peel his clothes off before I drop mine on the floor beside them.

His eyelids flutter heavily as he watches me, but he doesn't say anything as I pull him into the shower.

The bruise on his side from the tow cable snapping is black and blue, and bigger than a softball. I don't touch it, but I run soap over him everywhere else, cleaning yesterday away.

"Rinse," I instruct, but he doesn't move back.

He steps forward, wrapping his arm around my waist and backing me into the shower wall where his other hand pillows the back of my head. His lips take mine in a desperate attack of sorrow, terror, passion, all the pent-up emotions that he bottles in so well.

He kisses me like this might be the last time, but I'm determined not to let that happen.

He's hard-headed, but I'm stubborn.

My hands trail up his chest to his neck, careful not to put any weight on him, and I slip my tongue between his lips, feeling his moan against my hands. His cock grows harder, bobbing against my stomach as I make love to his mouth.

I'm so in love with him, it hurts inside because it doesn't seem to matter.

It seems as if we're destined to go our separate ways.

Chapter Fifty-Three

Lochlan

Almost losing her has me all twisted up in my head. Hearing her beg to be buried next to my family is a feeling I can't describe.

I don't want to think about her name on a headstone at all, but every time I've imagined it, it's etched in stone next to mine.

It's delusional.

But it's the only thing that feels right.

I'll be buried in an unmarked grave before I put my name on a stone without hers. That's how meaningless my life feels without her.

I tighten my arms around her, letting the dull pain radiate through my side. Over the course of the last few hours, the pain has been constant, but the sharpness has dissipated slightly.

Still hurts like a bitch. Which means there is no hauling her to my bed like I want to. Not without making her worry.

She notices my pain anyway. "Is it your ribs?"

"Hayes thinks I bruised my spleen."

"He's a medical professional, now?"

"No, but he's smart like you and he's seen a lot of injuries."

She sighs because she knows I won't budge about seeing a doctor. "What can I get you?"

"Ibuprofen. And, a shot of whiskey would do the trick," I utter against her neck.

"Go get in bed. I'll be right behind you."

As soon as I settle onto the mattress, my pain eases. When I'm relaxed, it isn't nearly as bad, and I'm exhausted.

I could sleep for days, but days are all I have left with her.

"Three ibuprofen and one shot of whiskey. I'd normally discourage this type of mix, but I think you've earned it."

I swallow back the pills with the burn of the alcohol and breathe through the aching in my side. When I open my eyes, she's kneeling on the bed, staring solemnly at my bruise.

"Come here, darlin'."

"How badly did the fire spread?"

"It burned through about two acres before they contained it."

"And, the bears?"

"All accounted for. The guys got a temporary fence put back in so they can't escape."

"The guesthouse?"

"Nearly cooked down to the foundation."

"I'm sorry, Lochlan. What a disaster." She cuddles gently into my side.

"It could've been worse. We'll manage."

"If there is anything I can do to help…"

"This right here is what I need." I kiss the top of her head.

"Just that?" She asks, tipping her head up to kiss my jaw.

My mouth finds hers, and I kiss her slowly, gently, letting the warmth of her body heal me more than the whiskey ever could.

"Do you think you will feel better in a couple of days?"

"Hopefully. Why?"

"Because I know what I want for my birthday."

"What's that?"

"You."

"You already have me, darlin'. I'm hooked around your little finger." I lean back against my pillow and close my eyes.

"I want you to make love to me, Lochlan."

My eyes ping open, but I can't respond.

"Don't tell me no."

I still don't speak because no part of me wants to tell her no. Not anymore, not after everything that happened last night.

"I know you were hesitant before because you were trying to protect me, but there is no one I feel safer with. And, maybe you still think I'm young and naive, but I know what I want. I want my first time to be with a man who loves me. A man that I'm in love with, too."

My whole body jerks off the mattress as I pin her underneath me. "Ow, fuck." I grumble as the pain eases. "Don't play games with me, Jo. Don't tell me what you think I want to hear."

She smiles at my urgency. "I'm not playing any games. I know you want me to leave this place after my birthday, but I don't want to go without loving you completely. There was the briefest moment when Jerry was dragging me into the woods that I thought… That I thought he might…" Her bottom lip trembles.

"Fuck, baby. I'm so sorry I let that happen." I kiss her lip, soothing it.

She shakes her head. "Life is too short. Bad stuff happens too often, and I want to live without regrets."

"You think one of those regrets might be me?"

"If I don't spend every last minute showing you how important you are to me, then yes. I'd regret that for the rest of my life."

"I don't deserve you, Jo. I never have deserved an ounce of anything you've given me. But if you want me to make love to you, it'd be an honor. I'd cherish the privilege for eternity."

"I know you would," she whispers, kissing me deeply.

"I'll make it special, I'll take care of you."

"I know you will." She giggles.

I swallow thickly, painfully. "When do you leave, exactly?"

"The morning after my birthday."

"Well, until then, you're mine."

"I wouldn't have it any other way."

* * *

"Jackson and the lawyer will be here in an hour." The words are whispered against my neck, and it stirs me awake slowly.

The kiss that lingers there is what forces my eyes open.

"What time is it?"

"Nearly 6 o'clock."

"Mmm, so dinner time."

"I guess." She shrugs.

"Come sit on my face."

She gasps, "What?"

I throw the pillow away from under my head. "Straddle

my face with your sexy thighs and let me eat your pussy."

"Lochlan, I can't..."

"I can't lay on my stomach and give you the proper treatment, darlin'. Don't let me starve until your birthday." I reach down as far as I can and palm her ass, squeezing it roughly.

"Okay," she utters breathlessly, crawling up the bed, slowly. She's not trying to be sexy but she's damn effortless at it regardless.

"Are you sure this won't hurt?"

No. "Yes."

"Nightgown on or off?"

"Off. I want to watch your tits bounce."

Her cheeks flame red as she pulls the silk over her head. I'm going to miss her bed attire.

"Grab the headboard."

She grabs a hold of it and swings her leg over my head, putting her perfect cunt right over my mouth.

"Now, sit."

"But..."

"Let me taste what belongs to me," I demand, making her breath hitch. As soon as she's low enough, I swipe my tongue across her clit and she moans, sitting further and giving me exactly what I need.

My hands palm her ass, grinding her pussy against my face as I devour her. I fuck her with my tongue until my cock is hard enough to burst.

She's so warm and tight, the thought of what it will feel like to bury my cock inside of her is nearly enough to make me cum in my boxers.

Then I swipe my tongue up her slit, circling her swollen

clit and she makes a sweet sound, whimpering in pleasure when I suck it between my lips.

"Yes, Lochlan, yes!" She screams when I do it harder, and my hips jerk. I love it when she screams my name.

Her thighs start twitching against my head and I squeeze her ass harder, suffocating myself with her pussy as I demand her orgasm.

She's right there, mumbling incoherent words of satisfaction when I nip her clit gently with my teeth and she explodes, grinding against my tongue as she rides out her orgasm.

"Oh my God," she mumbles and then jumps, "Oh my God." She raises her hips as if she forgot where she was.

I know my face must be a mess, but as she smiles down at me, all I want to do is kiss her.

I want to kiss her every minute of every day for the rest of my life.

Chapter Fifty-Four

Jo

"Jo, this is Liv Greenwood," Jackson introduces us, leaning against the porch railing to let us talk.

"It's nice to meet you, Liv." I shake her hand, marveling at her natural beauty. She's almost as tall as I am, but slender like all the Pilates teachers I've ever had. Her suit is designer and tailored to her body impeccably.

She's the type of woman that even straight women have a crush on. Me included, but her shiny engagement ring stands proudly on her finger, screaming to the world that she's unavailable.

"Is Liv short for something?" Lochlan asks from beside me. It's an odd question for him to ask, and when I glance at him, he's looking at her peculiarly.

"Just Liv." She smiles elegantly, professionally even. Her teeth are perfectly white and straight, aside from one lateral incisor that's slightly tilted.

It somehow makes her smile more beautiful and unique, almost endearing.

I think I really might have a crush on her.

Lochlan's clearly not feeling the same confusion I am, his

386

furrowed brows are slightly more tense.

Not that it's completely unnatural for him. I shrug it off.

"You guys will be happy to know that Sheriff Malec apprehended Jerry this morning, and about two hours ago, his prints came back and confirmed his real name. Jeremiah Porter, Randall Porter's brother."

Jackson's smiling smugly off to the side. He's finally got the people he's been after.

"We'll keep him in custody and appeal to the judge that he shouldn't have the option of bail due to his history of criminal behavior and violence. Randall Porter is being charged, however, he'll likely post bail and be on house arrest until we can put them on trial."

"That's great news. What will you need from us?"

"Well, this is going to be a huge case with a lot of evidence. I imagine it will take almost a year to get to trial. I want to make sure we get it locked down and nothing goes wrong because I only present solid cases."

She's not being cocky, she's all confidence.

"Sheriff Malec will prepare witness statements for you both, and you'll likely need to go on the stand to testify, Jo. You're the main witness to Jeremiah's crimes here. I was made aware of your niece seeing him as well." She motions to Lochlan. "But, I prefer to keep children off the stand."

"I'd prefer that as well," he agrees gruffly.

"Good. I'm glad we're all on the same page. I don't need anything else from you all tonight, I mostly wanted to introduce myself so you could put a face with a name. We'll be in communication over the next few months, but please, if you have any questions, call me." She hands me a business card and walks back down the porch steps towards her car.

"I'm leaving town in a couple of days. Will that be an issue?"

"Jackson filled me in. It shouldn't be an issue as long as you're here for the trial."

"You can stay with us," Jackson offers.

A part of me waits for Lochlan to offer the same, but he doesn't. Liv looks at me tenderly as if Jackson filled her in on more than my plans to travel.

"Hey, Loch," Hayes calls from the side of the house, walking towards us.

My attention stays on Liv, though, as her shoulders tense. She blinks at me without really looking at me. Her eyes are seeing right through me.

Hayes comes a few steps closer and stops suddenly. "Olive?"

Liv's pristine tan disappears in front of my eyes as the blood drains from her face. "I've got to go. It was nice to meet you. Call me if you need anything."

She turns, jumping into her Jaguar, and in a split second, the engine roars to life.

"Liv!" Hayes yells, running towards her car.

She peels out, kicking dust into the air, and Hayes yells, "FUCK!"

He sprints to the garage, and I look at Lochlan with wide eyes. "What was that?"

"I think the lawyer just saw a ghost," he murmurs.

Hayes comes flying out of the garage on his motorcycle, speeding past us and through the gates.

"I'm going to assume he knows how to drive that thing," Jackson utters, staring up at the sky in exasperation.

"Even if he didn't, he'd learn real quick before he let her get away."

I stare at him, wondering about this big mystery that he's clearly privy to, and why I'm not good enough for him to chase.

Why won't he fight for me like that?

He won't even ask me to stay…

"Before I get your witness statement about last night, I need to tell you something."

"What?" Lochlan says, tearing his eyes off me. I was so deep in thought, I didn't even realize he was looking at me.

"Randall Porter was pretty loose-lipped when I arrested him. He was looking for any way to escape his charges, but it was too late for that. I just didn't mention it until he purged himself."

"What did he say?"

"He admitted that Conrad was the one who gave him the idea…"

"What?"

"He confided in your brother that he had plans for the sanctuary." *Your.* Even Jackson doesn't want to claim him, and he shares his DNA. "Conrad suggested getting rid of you was the best way to sway Lochlan to do what he wanted."

"That fucker," Lochlan grumbles.

"It's hearsay. I can't charge him with anything, but I thought you needed to know. You already mentioned that you planned to cut them all off, but I'm here for you. Whatever you need."

"Thank you, Jackson." I smile sadly at him.

He stays an hour, getting our statements, and when he leaves, a pit settles in my chest. He feels like the only real family I have left, and now I'm supposed to leave and miss out on more time with him.

It feels like I'm losing more than I bargained for.

"Hey, you okay?" Lochlan asks, coming up beside me on the porch.

I shake my head and melt into his chest.

"I know he hates me, but how could he be so cruel?"

"Your brother is scum of the earth, darlin'."

"I don't know what I ever did to my family that was so wrong."

"You didn't do anything wrong. They never deserved you."

I laugh, sadly. "I don't think they see it that way."

"Fuck, em."

"Yeah, you're right."

"It's all the wisdom in my old age."

I slap his chest. "You're not that old."

"Old enough to know better," he murmurs against my head.

I ignore his loaded statement because I don't have the energy to argue with his moral compass tonight.

"What if I go to the media? Tell them the truth about Conrad and my dad both abandoning children..."

"That'll ruin your clean break from them, darlin'. If you drag them through the mud, they'll put you through the ringer, I guarantee it."

"I know, but what else do I have to lose? I don't have to worry about my parents' approval anymore. I have nothing to lose. No one."

"You always have me."

"You want me to leave."

"I don't *want* you to leave."

"But, you're insisting that I do."

"That's different. I've been trapped behind these fences so long that I know how selfish it is to ask you to stay."

"It's not selfish if I want to stay," I whisper against his chest, and his arms tighten around me.

"That's exactly why you need to go."

"Even though you love me?"

"I can't let this place be all there is for you *because* I love you."

It's the first time he's said it outright, and I can't help but tip my head so I can look at him. "When did you know?"

"That I was in love with you?"

My breath hitches, hearing him say it with conviction. "Yeah."

"When I watched you pick pieces of grass off my grandparents' headstone."

My lips part. "But that was so long ago."

"I don't think it was soon enough, honestly. I was just too stubborn to admit it."

He's loved me for half the summer...

"I don't understand... You acted so..."

"Grumpy?"

"Well. Yeah."

"You're the best thing that will ever happen to me, and the hardest thing I'll ever do in my life is watch you walk away."

"Lochlan..."

"It's okay, Jo."

"No, it's not."

"Baby," he starts.

"What if I don't go?"

He reaches up to cup my cheek in his hand. "Then I'll spend the rest of my life worried that I stole your youth. I know what that feels like, darlin'. I can't do it to you."

He's comparing prison to this place as if it's equal, but I can see in his eyes that he can't be persuaded. His mind is made up. All I can do is cherish the time we have left and pretend like I'll be able to move on when I leave.

"I love you, Lochlan. Always will." I nuzzle my head into his palm.

"And, I hope for your sake that isn't true."

Chapter Fifty-Five

Lochlan

"I have something special planned for your birthday tonight, but I need your curious eyes preoccupied until it's done."

She smiles up at me from the kitchen table, dazzling me with her beauty, and my heart nearly stops in my chest.

Her anticipation about tonight has been buzzing through her, though, and I'm trying not to feel the pressure.

But, fuck if I can't wait to have her.

If my bruised side wasn't so tender the last few days, I probably would have let her take advantage of me, but the last thing I want to do is mess up a special moment for the most incredible woman I've ever met.

"I need to go to the bank and make sure I have full access to my trust and home to pack the last of my things."

"Are you sure that's a good idea?"

"It won't be pleasant, but it'll be fine."

"I can go with you."

She stands from the table, wrapping her arms around my neck. "You worry too much."

"You have a tendency to walk face-first into danger."

"Of course, I do. I know you'll always be there to protect me." She smirks and leans into me further when I snake my hands under her skirt to palm her ass.

"Until the day I die, darlin'."

She tries to hide it, but I feel the sadness sweep over her. We both know that tomorrow, she won't be here for me to protect.

* * *

Jo: I told them what Conrad did, and they don't believe me. They're taking his side.

   Jo: They took my car. They won't let me leave.
   Lochlan: I should have come with you.
   Lochlan: Jo?
   Lochlan: Missed Call
   Lochlan: Missed Call
   Lochlan: I'm coming for you.

The twisting in my gut increases every mile closer I get to her father's estate and every minute that I don't hear from her...

They wouldn't hurt her. They wouldn't.

Politicians are the worst type of criminals.

Would they hurt her?

I'm not taking the chance. I've already almost lost her this week, and I refuse to let a hair be harmed on her head.

Her BMW is sitting in the driveway when I pull up to the gates. They're more secure than mine, with a guard standing in a booth.

"How may I help you, sir?" The guard asks. He's an older man, wearing a ball cap over his graying hair.

"I'm here to see JoAnna."

"Ah, friends with our Jo girl, huh? I haven't seen her much this summer."

"I'm her fiancé."

"Well, I'll be. Why didn't you say so?" He buzzes the gates, and they swing open. I nod him my thanks and drive through.

Pulling the fiancé card might have been unnecessary, especially since our charade has come to an end, but it rolls off the tongue too easily.

I meet more resistance at the front door, except this man is wearing a suit. He's either a nicely dressed security guard or a butler of some sort.

"How can I help you, sir?"

If one more person asks me that damn question before I set my eyes on Jo, I'm going to lose my fucking mind.

"I'm here for Jo."

"JoAnna?" He asks curiously as if he's never heard her nickname.

That's all the reason I need to push past him, forcing my way inside. He calls after me as I stride down the long marble hall.

Raised voices are coming from a room with double wooden doors, and I don't hesitate to blow them wide open.

I find Jo first, sitting by herself on a small sofa. Her father is standing behind a desk, her mother standing behind him on one side, as her brother paces in front of the desk.

They all stop speaking to look at me, but I only see her. "Are you okay?"

She tips her head and smiles, looking at me in relief. "I'm

fine."

"What the hell are you doing in my house?" Her father grits through his teeth.

I ignore him, closing the distance to Jo, stroking her cheek with my thumb. "Ready to leave?"

"Yes." She gives me her hand and I pull her to stand.

"We're discussing this, NOW, JOANNA!" He booms, and I watch her flinch.

But, before I can give this fucker a piece of my mind, she steps in front of me. "I'm done talking. I've said my peace."

"We'll take your trust fund," her mother rattles, through a handkerchief as if she's been crying.

"If you try, I'll have my lawyer obliterate you. I'll take you all down, starting with Conrad," she threatens calmly, nodding at me confidently as she struts out of the room like she owns it.

"WE'RE NOT FINISHED!" Her father yells.

"She's done and she won't be back." I hold his gaze until he loses his nerve and blinks away. My murderous glare finds Conrad next. "If you utter her name or so much as breathe in her direction ever again, I'll fucking kill you."

"And, what gives you the fucking right?" Her father asks after I turn my back.

"She'll be *my wife. My family*," I thunder, watching them blanch. "You don't have the right to her anymore," I finish calmly.

The yelling continues as I leave the room, but I let the doors slam behind me. All the noise drowns out once I set my eyes on her.

"I called for a rental car. You didn't have to come rescue me."

"I did. Even if you didn't need saving, I'd still lurk behind you, making sure you're alright." I wrap my hands in her hair, holding her tenderly.

"It's not really lurking when you storm the castle," she whispers, smiling softly.

"Well, there's a time and place for everything."

"I guess this worked one last time, huh?" She puts her left hand on my chest, tapping her ring finger against my sternum.

I grab her hand in mine, rubbing my thumb against the gold band, and the pit in my stomach twists for entirely different reasons than it was an hour ago.

"I hope they didn't ruin your birthday," I say, instead of all the other things trying to claw their way out.

She shakes her head as I walk her to the truck. "They don't get to ruin any more of my days."

"Proud of you."

"Thanks." She smiles brightly, scooting over to snuggle into my side once we're inside. "I couldn't have done it without you."

"I don't think that's true…"

"You believed in me enough to make me believe in myself. Because of you, I don't look in the mirror and see all the things I hate. I see all the things you love about me. It might seem silly to you, but it's changed my life."

"You've changed my life, darlin'." I kiss her temple, cherishing the way she relaxes further into my side, ignoring the twinge of pain it causes.

The pain in my heart far outweighs it.

"Take me home."

"As you wish, my princess." I nuzzle her cheek until her

smile turns to a full grin. She no longer belongs to the people of North Carolina… Only me.

For now.

Chapter Fifty-Six

Jo

I nstead of parking the Bronco by the house, he continues driving past the bunkhouse and down one of the larger paths. The anticipation of what he has planned is making me tingle with excitement.

"Happy Birthday, darlin'." The path opens up into the wild strawberry field, the deep green vines are dark with the dim light of dusk, and it's nearly too dark to see.

He parks in the open grassy area where he's set up a blanket and cooler next to a pile of logs in a makeshift fire pit. He comes around to open my door and pulls me out and into his chest. "Don't worry, this fire will be contained for the entirety of the evening, no threat to life."

"Thank you for the disclaimer." I giggle, letting him lead me to the blanket. He strolls around the fire pit, lighting it and all the candles in small buckets that I couldn't see. The citronella smell hits me as he creates a barrier around us to ward off insects.

"I brought wine, but I don't want you to drink on an empty stomach, so cheese and crackers or a cupcake are your options," he says, digging through the cooler for his loot. He's so casual about it as if this isn't the grandest romantic gesture that I've ever experienced.

"Cheese and crackers, please."

He doesn't pour my wine until I've started eating, and when he does, he gives himself some too, which surprises me.

He takes a drink and cringes. "Yeah, no, can't do it."

"Doesn't burn enough?" I laugh as he pours it into my tumbler.

"I only have a sweet tooth for one thing." He glances at me and smirks at his cheesy joke.

The butterflies in my belly flutter, but there are also nerves, deep down.

"Come here." He must sense them, pulling me down beside him on the blanket until we're both staring at the sky, listening to the fire crackle.

"You see that bright star right there?" He points to a star that outshines the ones around it, and I nod against him.

"That's yours."

"You're really laying it on with the sweet comments."

He chuckles. "No, I mean it belongs to you."

"What?"

"I bought it in your name... No matter where you are, you can look up and find your star and know that I'll be looking at it, too." He's looking up at the stars, but I can't help but stare at him.

"How?"

"Jordy helped me." He shrugs.

I don't understand how he thinks I can find anything better than this. Than him. The love he gives me defies gravity.

It's bigger than the universe.

Tonight will be the best night of my life. Tomorrow

morning will be the worst.

He tips his head to look at me, and his brows scrunch. "Why are you crying?"

"They're happy tears. This was such a special gift, thank you." My lips find his, and they don't relent.

I want to kiss him for all the times he's made me feel special.

And, beautiful.

Cherished.

Loved.

I want to kiss him for all the time that I'll miss out on once I leave.

I bite his lip roughly, and he growls, covering my body with his.

He devours me as I open my thighs wide to make room for his hips, and my dress pools at my waist. The moment his hardness presses against my panties, I'm grinding against it, begging for it.

"You can still change your mind, baby."

"No. Make love to me, Lochlan. And, then fuck me, all night. Please." I gasp when he bites my neck, but then he sits up on his knees, leaving me.

He hooks a finger under the strap of my dress and tugs it off my shoulder, exposing my bare breast, and then he does the other, letting the cool night air pebble my nipples tightly.

"Beautiful," he murmurs, filling his palms and grazing his thumbs across my sensitive peaks. "I wish I had a picture of this, I'll never be able to capture it perfectly in a drawing."

"So, take a picture."

He looks at me curiously until I reach to the edge of the blanket to get the new phone he secured this week. His eyes darken fiercely.

I have no idea what I truly look like, my hair is probably a mess, and I can feel the heat of the fire against my flushed cheeks, but I know that he loves what he sees, and that's all I need to know.

He snaps a photo and I know he's satisfied because I can feel his cock flex against me.

I take his free hand and drag it up my stomach, cupping my breast with it. "Take another one."

He shudders a breath, squeezing my soft flesh in his hand and taking another picture.

"One more?" I suggest, pulling his hand higher, sucking his thumb between my lips. I'm not even sure if he had time to press the button before he throws the phone to the side and attacks, claiming my mouth in a brutal kiss that sends heat coursing through me.

My fingers drag the bottom of his shirt high up on his torso, until they brush across something that's not on the side that his bruise is on.

"What's this?" It's bigger than my hand.

Our noses are touching as he just looks at me, silently.

"Did you get hurt again?" It's plastic and distinctly bandage feeling.

He kneels again, not saying a word before ripping his shirt off over his head. "I'm supposed to leave this on but..." He peels the tape off his side, exposing a new tattoo.

I gasp, launching upward to look at it. It's...

Me.

The last drawing I saw that he had laid on his nightstand. It's simple, only the outlines of my figure, and nothing more graphic. I'm nude, but it's not overtly sexual at all; it's abstract and beautiful.

"Lochlan, I can't believe…"

"I told you I didn't want to get rid of you, darlin'. You're branded on me, now, but you're already burned into my soul forever."

"You're going to make me cry again," I whisper against his lips, squeezing my eyes shut to ward off the tears.

"Then let me distract you." He kisses me, pushing my back until I'm lying on the blanket again, and then he slips my dress off my body. My panties are next, he slowly drags them down my legs, leaving electricity in his wake.

The light of the fire dances across my skin as he stands to remove his pants, his eyes never leaving my naked body.

I'll never be more confident in any decision than I am giving Lochlan my virginity. Not because it's some sanctimonious virtue I've been holding onto, but because I'll never feel safer sharing this vulnerable moment with anyone but him.

His cock stands proudly, and I still can't fathom how it will fit inside me, but I'm aching to find out.

This time, when he kneels between my legs, a wave of nerves crashes over me. I expect him to line himself up to take me, but he doesn't. He leans over me, kissing me gently, letting his lips trail across my jaw and then down my neck before he pays special attention to my breasts.

I'm so wired by the time his tongue swirls my nipple that I feel an orgasm building. He bites it gently, and a whimper escapes me.

"Lochlan, please, I feel like I'm on fire…" I mutter, flopping my head to the side when he sucks my second nipple into his mouth.

The faintest brush of anything against my clit is going to send me over–

403

His middle finger dips into my pussy and when the heel of his hand presses against me, massaging me as he fucks me with his finger, it's not even a minute before I explode, rocking against his hand as I ride out my orgasm.

"That's it, baby. Now, give me another one." His second finger enters me while my pussy is still clenching, making me feel fuller than I've ever been.

His fingers curl, rubbing my inner walls until I feel the pressure building again, but from somewhere deeper. He fucks me with his fingers until my legs are twitching against his body, and then he goes harder, rougher, taking me and stretching me more than he ever has.

He hovers over me, kissing me fiercely as I writhe against his hand. "You're doing so good, baby. You're almost ready to take my cock in your tight little pussy. I just need a little bit more, I need you to be ready for it."

"I want it, please," I mumble as he fingers me until my core shakes, and another orgasm rips through me.

"Yes… Fuck yes… You're so sexy, darlin'."

My head falls back against the blanket, and I stare up at the sky, catching my breath when I hear the cooler open and a bottle cap click.

When I glance at him, he's pouring lube onto *three* fingers.

"One more, baby."

"Finger or orgasm?"

"One more finger, endless supply of orgasms."

I giggle breathlessly and then choke it back when the cold lube touches me *there*. It feels the same as before, but as soon as his third finger is added, I realize how unfull I was before because now I'm stuffed.

"Relax for me."

"I don't know if I can."

"You will because I need you to. I need you ready for me because I can't wait to bury my cock inside you… Good… Good girl… I knew you could do it, you're so fucking perfect," he praises me endlessly, swelling my heart.

I'm drenched down there, but I don't think it's the lube; I think his words are soaking me wet.

His thumb circles my clit suddenly and I moan, already nearly zapped for my next climax. His fingers inside of me aren't moving much, they're taking up space while I grind against him, chasing the high of the pleasure that he gives me.

"Show me how much you want my cock, darlin'. Fuck my hand… Yeah, you're going to take my cock perfectly, I know it… Give me what I want…"

"Fuck, Lochlan!" I scream into the dark sky, gasping for breath as my release hits me. The way my pussy pulses around his fingers makes me grind against him harder, greedy for more.

His fingers slip out of me so fast my torso jerks up off the ground. He wraps them around the base of his cock, squeezing his eyes shut painfully as he braces himself above me.

"Lochlan…"

"Don't say a word," he grumbles, breathing deeply for a moment before he finally blinks his eyes back open and looks down at me. "I was about to fucking cum and your voice almost set me off."

"Sorry," I smirk at him unapologetically.

"You still want to do this?"

I nod, keeping my eyes on his.

"More lube?"

I shake my head.

He comes in closer, lining his hips up with mine and drags his head through my folds, up and down my slit. I should lay back and focus on feeling it, but I can't tear my eyes from him.

Everything is slick and the crown of his cock circles my clit easily, forcing my senses into overdrive because of how sensitive I am. He raises it a few inches, leaving a stream of precum still attached.

"That's what you do to me, baby. I'm a fucking mess every time I'm near you."

"I'm ready, Lochlan," I beg, watching him line up the tip with my opening.

He barely presses against me a centimeter, and he's blowing a deep breath out. "Fuck." He breathes deeply again, pushing a bit further.

My lips hang open in utter disbelief at the sensation. Disbelief that this is even happening.

Watching him put his cock inside of me ignites something primal inside of me that's been waiting to explode. My hand grips the back of his neck, pressing our heads together as we both watch him enter me another inch... Then another.

It feels amazing...

It feels like I'm stretched deliciously full...

Until an ache blossoms around inch four.

I ignore it.

At inch five, I angle my hips to try to relieve it.

Inch six is nearly painful...

"I can't..." I utter under my breath before he can get to seven.

He stops immediately, pulling back slightly.

"No, don't stop. I just need a second."

"Hey, we have all night, I'm not rushing this," he whispers breathlessly, kissing my cheek.

"I want this to be good for you, too."

He huffs a laugh. "Jo, I'm doing everything I can not to embarrass myself in front of you by cumming too early. Don't worry about me."

"Tell me what to do, how to take more."

He clears his throat like he's struggling to think straight. "Uh, I don't know. I've never been with a virgin before. And, I really don't want to fucking hurt you."

"I can take it," I insist, and he smiles gently.

"I know you can, baby." He kisses me slowly, softly running his tongue across mine until my needy pussy sheathes itself back to six inches. The bite of pain is slightly less than before, but I can still feel it shooting through my nerve endings.

His thumb finds my clit and my muscles immediately respond, clenching and relaxing with his efforts. Each time I tense, I open up a minuscule more, hardly noticeable, but I feel it. I take him the tiniest bit more, and my pride swells.

I might not be the only woman he's ever had, but I'll be the best.

It aches, but I take two more inches like a fucking champ.

"Slow down, baby."

"I can do it," I breathe out.

"I know, but I'm grasping for my sanity here."

I blink up at him, and his serious face, with his brows furrowed in concentration, and sweat dampening his forehead. He's losing his mind, and it's the sexiest thing I've ever seen in my life.

"I love you, Lochlan," I utter between breaths, forcing his attention on my face. "I love you," I whisper once his eyes are on mine.

His hand finds the back of my head, and he lays me back against the blanket, covering my body completely with his. "Until my dying breath, baby." He tweaks his neck slightly, preemptively with guilt, before filling me to the absolute brink.

A squeak of pain escapes me, and he captures it with his mouth, gasping his regret.

"I love you," he utters. "I love you." He kisses my mouth, my nose, my cheeks, and my eyelids.

The burning pain inside of me eases to an ache after a multitude of 'I love yous', but I'm dizzy from all of his affection.

"I love you," he whispers, trailing his thumb up my cheekbone.

I nuzzle into his palm, letting it ground me. "Until the day that I die," I vow, shifting my hips against him.

Chapter Fifty-Seven

Lochlan

Her hips tilt against me, and a torturous groan escapes my throat. Being inside her is better than I ever could have imagined, but hurting her to get here thoroughly wrecked me.

If I wasn't positive that the pleasure would come to her, I'd have stopped everything the moment she twinged in pain.

"Use me until it feels good, baby. I won't move until you're ready," I promise, reaching down to rub her clit, determined to give her ecstasy after the pain.

She pivots her hips hesitantly, grinding against me until small moans tumble from her lips. Her pace quickens, and my fingers follow, and when her fingers thread into my hair at the nape of my neck, I know she's enjoying herself.

"You're doing so good, baby. Cum on my cock, I want to feel you pussy clench every inch of me."

"I'm so close," she pants, her twitching hips keep throwing off her rhythm, but I feel the moment she locks in, tipping over the edge with her orgasm.

Her walls grip my length and all of my muscles tense. The sensation fucking rocks me.

"Oh my God. Yes…" Her hands clutch my hips, and she pulls me impossibly closer, forcing the slightest movement inside of her, and my eyes roll back in my head.

"Oh, fuck," I mumble.

"I'm ready, Lochlan. Show me what it feels like," she begs sweetly, pulling my body in until our faces are aligned.

"Once I start moving, I'm a ticking time bomb, baby. Won't be but a minute," I warn her, hoping I'll even last that long.

She smiles. "Then you can show me, again, and again, until the sun comes up," she whispers her words against my lips and then claims my mouth in a kiss.

It's tender and gentle, and I mimic it, pulling out of her tight heat only a few inches before pushing back in.

We both moan into each other's mouths, and when I do it again, pulling back further and pushing back inside of her faster, she gasps.

"Okay?"

"Yes," she breathes, sliding her tongue against mine.

I pull out until just the head of my cock remains and bury myself back inside her to the hilt, capturing her cry of surprise in my mouth.

"More?"

"Yes, yes," she mumbles, flattening her hips to take me deeper. And, I lose it.

I take her hungrily, pumping in and out of her until she can't control the noises coming out of her mouth, and I can hardly breathe, attempting to hold back my release.

"Lochlan," she whimpers my name, biting my lip, and it's like I've been zapped with a lightning bolt. My cum explodes out of me, filling her until she's flooded inside.

Her eyelids flutter, and she heaves breath in and out of her lungs as she takes in the feeling for the first time.

I'm fucking speechless.

She asked me once if an orgasm can change your life, and I wasn't lying when I said that it can, but I think I underestimated just how much she would be able to tilt my world on its axis every time it happened.

"That was better than I could have ever imagined," she whispers.

I laugh, breathlessly. "Thank God, because that was the best thing that's ever happened in my life."

She giggles, wrapping her arms around my neck and sighing happily.

"I'm sorry to do this, baby, but it might hurt again when I pull out."

"Then don't."

My cock twitches inside of her and I see her brows twinge. "If I don't do it now, it'll hurt worse. I'm sorry."

I sit up on my knees, removing myself from her as she groans in discomfort. My cum leaks from her pussy and I get lost staring at it for a moment. All the manhood in the depths of my soul is fueled by the sight.

Mine.

She shivers once she loses my body heat, and I toss two more logs on the fire before wrapping her in a blanket and pulling her to my chest.

We were both looking forward to this moment enough that tomorrow seemed like a distant thought. Now, it's almost midnight, and tomorrow is nearly here.

"Give me some time to recover, and then I'm doing that again," she states softly, letting her eyes shut.

I kiss her forehead, chuckling silently as she snuggles

further into me. As suspected, within a few minutes her breathing deepens, and she's fast asleep.

She can rest as long as she needs.

I won't be getting a wink of sleep tonight.

* * *

She jerks up from the blanket as I'm snuffing the fire out. Dawn just reached above the trees, giving me enough light to pack up.

"I slept all night... No," she cries, burying her head in her hands.

"You needed sleep."

"I needed you."

"I was right beside you all night, darlin'." I drag my thumb along her cheekbone. I ran my fingers through her hair and memorized the way her body felt against mine. I didn't take my eyes off her for a moment.

She stands, keeping the blanket wrapped around her shoulders, and I wrap her in my arms, kissing the top of her head. "Come on, let's get back to the house. You smell like a campfire."

She doesn't say anything as I help her into the Bronco or on the way back up to the house. She doesn't even utter a word when we go inside, and I follow her up the stairs.

She drops her blanket and steps into the shower, walking directly under the stream to wash her hair. I watch the soap drip down her back until it's rinsed clean because I'm afraid if I take my eyes off of her, she'll disappear sooner.

She peeks at me from under her wet lashes and scrunches her eyebrows. "Aren't you coming in?"

I undress, and her eyes travel the length of my body, paying special attention to the tattoo on my side and to my growing cock.

"I still can't believe you did this," she says under her breath, tracing the lines of her body on my ribs.

"I was going to wait until you left, I wasn't sure how you'd feel about it, but Hayes had the tattoo gun out yesterday and I couldn't wait any longer."

"How is he?"

"Not sure, he didn't talk much. But he'll fill me in when he's ready."

"I guess I won't ever find out what the drama was about," she laughs sadly.

I pull her into my chest, feeling the exact moment her warm tears mix with the hot water streaming down on us.

Just tell her to stay.

Beg on your knees.

Don't let her leave.

Once the water turns cold, I usher her out, drying her with a towel until it's damp.

"Take me to bed," she whispers, kissing my chest.

"Jo, it might hurt…"

"Everything already hurts, Lochlan." She looks up at me with so much sadness in her eyes, and I know they're a reflection of mine.

I can't give her the world, but I can give her this one last thing.

My lips take hers, and I lift her, wrapping her thighs around my waist, carrying her to my bedroom one last time.

413

I don't drop her on the bed, I lay her down gently, covering her body with mine as if it will kill me to separate myself...

I just need to taste every part of her... One last time.

My lips skim down her neck and across her beautiful breasts, sucking and biting her soft skin until she's squirming beneath me. I lick down her stomach and moan when I taste her sweet pussy.

My tongue swirls her clit and then I suck the nub into my mouth and she gasps, grinding against my face.

Her fingers grip my hair, fucking my face with abandon when my tongue fills her tight hole.

A switch has been flipped this morning. This isn't soft and gentle like last night; this feels urgent.

Desperate.

"Fuck me, Lochlan," she begs, but I keep devouring her, soaking her pussy with my tongue because I know if she tries to take my cock, the repercussions from last night will sting.

"Cum for me first, baby." I fuck her with my tongue, rubbing her clit erratically until I know she's about to burst.

Her hands claw across my scalp and her hips buck, "Fuck, fuck, fuck," she cries out, squeezing my tongue with her orgasm.

"Good girl." I get to my knees in front of her, lining our hips up, and she watches in fascination as I spit. My saliva drips onto the head of my cock where it's braced to enter her, swirling it around her opening. "Take a deep breath."

I watch her chest heave, and I drive into her, filling her to the hilt.

"FUCK!" She screams, her eyes rolling back in her head.

I don't move, I wait for her to adjust, and when she blinks up at me, I pull out and do it again.

CHAPTER FIFTY-SEVEN

"Tell me to stop," I beg her, needing her to right my self-control.

"No, harder."

"Jo…"

"Harder!" She insists, meeting my hips when I drive into her with more force.

"Fuck, baby." I breathe through the pleasure, because if its the last time then I'm lasting to the very fucking end.

"Fuck me, Lochlan. Give me everything." She looks up at me with such pain in her eyes, not a single thing I do physically could hurt her worse.

I cover her body with mine, kissing her with all the love that I have for her as I pound into her intensely, deliriously.

We're both closing in on oblivion as we breathe in each other's gasps of pleasure and sorrow. She pulls me in as tightly as I'm holding her until there is no space between us.

Her walls clench my cock as her climax rips through her, and her teeth anchor into my bottom lip, forcing my hand.

My release explodes out of me and she finally lets go of my lip, gasping as my cum shoots inside of her.

Grief sweeps over me immediately.

There's no honeymoon period after an incredible orgasm when it's meant to be the last.

My hips retreat an inch, but she shakes her head. "Not yet."

I stay firmly rooted in place, holding this beautiful woman who owed me nothing but gave me my life.

Who finally made me feel like living.

Chapter Fifty-Eight

Jo

The burning in my nose travels to my sinuses, and it's all it takes for the tears to spring from the corners of my eyes.

"Don't cry, baby."

"I can't help it, I don't want to go."

He drops his head to my chest in defeat, as if he's a failure for making me want to stay.

"I don't want to forget," I whisper, sliding his grandmother's ring off my finger. He stops me.

"Keep it."

"I can't. It should stay in your family."

"My grandmother would want the love of my life to have it even if I can't have her," he tells me with a lifetime of sadness in his eyes.

I push his shoulder, forcing him to roll off me, and he goes willingly, sending a pang of hurt into my chest when I see his crushed gaze. But when I crawl on top of him, his eyes flare back to life.

I don't check to see if he's still hard before I reach down and line my pussy up with his cock, but he's primed and ready as

I sit on it, ignoring the sting as I take him fully in one motion.

He grunts in surprise, blinking up at me.

"Tell me to stay."

He squeezes his eyes shut in pain.

I don't accept that as an answer, and I start grinding on his lap, using him.

"Tell me that you love me."

"I love you, so fucking much," he utters, gripping my hips in his hands.

"Tell me to stay," I demand, riding his cock like a woman unhinged.

"I can't," he whispers.

My hands grip his throat and I feel his rumble of appreciation as I fuck him.

"Tell me to stay!" I beg, feeling the tears stream down my cheeks.

"I can't!" He forces out, as I crush his windpipe. He doesn't bother pretending to fight me as he sits up, letting my hands stay wrapped around his neck as he threads his in my hair. "I can't tell you to stay," he utters miserably.

It's as if a balloon bursts and my entire being deflates. My whole body stills.

"You're really going to let me leave?"

"I have to."

"No, you don't."

"I do."

"Dammit, Lochlan." I jump off of him, stumbling off the bed. "You're breaking my heart."

His eyes shut, again, and he hangs his head. "I know, but you'll forgive me one day."

"No, I won't." I feel the pieces of my rational self fall apart

417

one by one as he sits there in silence. "You promised that you wouldn't hurt me."

"You weren't supposed to fall in love with me!"

"But, I did! And, if you let me leave here, then this isn't what I thought it was. You're just another person to use me and throw me away." I storm out of his room to his grandparents' old room, where my suitcase is.

"Jo!" He calls after me, but he doesn't follow me.

I expect him to chase me, but he doesn't, and I sink to my knees, wrapping myself in my arms. After everything I've gone through this summer, I still only have myself…

I'm all alone, again.

* * *

I picked myself up off the floor, and he didn't come check on me.

I dusted myself off, got dressed, and he didn't come.

I got ready for the last time in this house without a single bit of protest from him.

My heart is shattered because of it. The pain feels so real, as if it's truly breaking into a million pieces.

When I step into the hallway with my suitcase, you could hear a pin drop, and that's when I realize he isn't even in the house. I check all the rooms upstairs and down, but he's gone.

The rental car company will be here to pick me up soon, but he's nowhere to be found. His Bronco is still out front, but he's not on the porch or in his rocking chair.

CHAPTER FIFTY-EIGHT

He really had me fooled.

I sit on the porch steps with my giant suitcase and wait because I'm the only one I have left. I'm too embarrassed to call Jackson and let him hear my heartbreak, and I don't want to go searching for one of the guys who have become my friends and stumble upon the man who doesn't even want me…

A man who would let me leave without saying goodbye.

I left the painting of the wild strawberry clearing inside. No need to carry reminders with me.

I wait and wait, letting the pit of despair crash over me in waves. I'm going to miss Emory, Becky, and Tessa. I'll miss seeing Jordy go off to greater things, Seiver and his old man charm. I won't hear how Curtis is doing. No more bears, no more feeling of home.

A car pulls through the gates, and I stand, breathing back more tears when the man I'll miss most of all comes running up from the bunkhouse.

I can't even look at him.

I drag my suitcase over to the car, but just as the driver pops the trunk, Lochlan slams it shut. "Who the fuck is this?" He growls.

"It's my rental car."

"Go, get lost." He slams the top of the hood. "Get the fuck out of here!" He yells at the terrified man in the driver's seat.

"I just waited 20 minutes for that. And, it's not his fault, you don't have to yell at him." I kick my suitcase and let it topple over as I storm back over to the porch.

"I don't have swim trunks."

"What?" I throw my hands up because what the fuck is happening today.

"You said you were going to the beach. I don't own swim trunks."

"What?" I squeak out this time.

"I told you I couldn't come with you."

"I know, the sanctuary needs you."

He waves me off. "I thought I could watch you walk away. After everything I've sacrificed in my life, I thought I'd be used to it. I was determined to let you go."

I blink at him, trying to process what's happening.

"But this place doesn't need me the way I need you."

A breath of relief escapes my chest.

"You believed in me before you ever knew me, and you gave me my life back. You saved me when no one else would, and if you're asking for a life with me in it, I'm going to take it and never let it go. I'll never get a chance like this from you again, and if I lose you, I won't survive, darlin'." He closes the distance between us, clutching my head in his hands.

"You want to come with me?" I'm still not sure I'm hearing him correctly. His life, his grandfather's legacy, is here.

"I offered Seiver a pay raise. Hayes will handle what he can't. I called Becky, and she threatened to smack me on the back of the head for not telling you all of this sooner. She'll handle the admin stuff."

"You're coming with me," I confirm, watching a smile tilt his lips.

"I'll have to come back from time to time to check in and make sure there's still something left for Emory to take over, but wherever you go, I'll follow. If you want me to."

"Lochlan." I squeeze my eyes shut this time to ward off happy tears. "I do want to travel, I want adventure, and I'll buy you swim trunks... But I like it here. I want this to be my home. I want to have pizza with Emory every weekend, and I want to get to know my brother better. I want to have a life with you. Let's go anywhere, everywhere, but bring me home. Here."

He kisses me with his entire being, wrapping me in his arms this time with no expiration, and I finally let the tears escape, feeling whole for the first time in my life.

"Promise me something, darlin'. Don't take that ring off until I can get you a bigger one," he whispers against my lips.

I shrug in his arms. "I like this one just fine."

* * *

"JoAnna Dane," the dean of the engineering department, reads my new name, and I step onto the stage in front of a sea of other graduates.

The gown swishes around my calves as I walk confidently across the stage in my favorite sky-high heels to retrieve my diploma.

The thunder of applause and a few whistles that I recognize draw my attention to the audience and the section of seats closest to the graduates' seats.

Jordy, Arizona, and Seiver are standing up cheering for me. Jackson, Natalie, and Dec are in front of them, and Emory, Becky, and Tessa are beside them. And, in front of them all, standing proudly, is Lochlan.

He claps thunderously, watching me walk to my seat with a twinkle in his eye.

Love, it's love.

He's loved me thoroughly and deeply every moment of every day, and he's shown me what the real meaning of life is all about.

Love, peace, and family.

He's tried to buy me a new engagement ring, but I refuse to take off his grandmother's. He insists on giving me a big wedding, surrounded by people who love us, but I didn't want to wait.

I made sure his last name was the one I'd carry on my diploma. A wedding can come later.

He says I gave him his life back, but mine only started when I met him.

I used to want the white knight in shining armor.

But I needed the scorned prince who would let his kingdom burn for me.

Epilogue

Lochlan

"I got a graduation present that I want to show you."

"From who?" I ask as she steps between my legs.

"Hayes felt bad he couldn't make it to my graduation, and said he owed me."

Hayes has been caught up in some shit since the day he saw Liv on my front steps. He stuck around while Jo and I were bouncing around from place to place, but the moment we got back, he's been gone more than he's here.

I don't fault him for it. I always wanted him to get out of this place, but I'm worried about what he's involved in. We've been watching each other's backs for years, and I know when something is wrong.

My new fancy security system tells me every time he comes in and out of the gates at all hours of the night.

He's only keeping it from me because he thinks he's doing me a favor, letting me enjoy my newfound happy life with Jo.

I have been enjoying it. More than I ever thought was possible, but I'll always remember where I've come from. I want Hayes to get as far away from our past as I have. Even if that means he doesn't work here anymore.

"What did Hayes get you?"

"He didn't *get* me anything."

"I'm worried about what that tone means."

"He did something for me. One of his hobbies."

"Oh, God." I can only imagine Jo on the back of his bike or something more deranged, and I brace myself for what she has to say.

"See." She pulls up her silk nightgown, and I'm not sure what she's showing me because I can't stop looking at her standing nearly naked in front of me.

She lifts it higher, showing me a small strawberry on her rib cage beside her breast, no bigger than a real one.

"You let Hayes give you a tattoo right here." I grip her waist, pulling her onto my lap.

She rolls her eyes. "He's your best friend, I knew you wouldn't kill him. I also had clothes on. I just had to move my shirt up a bit. It took like two seconds."

I growl, pulling her in closer. "You're lucky, I think it's sexy."

"Oh, yeah? And, if you were scandalized?"

"I'd have to punish you."

She smiles widely. She knows damn well I'd never be able to do anything to her slightly resembling punishment.

"I guess you don't want to see my other one, then?"

"What the fuck? Where?"

"Right here." She tugs down the waistband of her panties and points to her tiny heart that I can just hardly see in the moonlight. The heart has an 'L' in the middle of it now.

"For me?" I ask in surprise, and she giggles.

"Well, yeah, of course. Hayes said you can come get a 'J' whenever you want, but…" She puts her hand over the tattoo

424

of her on my ribs and smiles shyly. "You don't have to, it's just a formality."

"I'll get it on my fucking forehead, fuck formality."

She bursts out laughing, leaning into my chest. "I love you, but please, don't do that."

"Whatever you say, darlin'."

Thank you for reading! The next and final installment of the Chance Encounters Series will be about Liv and Hayes. You'll find out why the ghost of her past sent her running...

About the Author

Amber Cassidy is an independently published author and full-time SAHM to two beautiful little girls. Writing has been a passion of mine since childhood and has enabled me to maintain my sense of self while in the thick of motherhood.

I am passionate about romance in any genre, but my current focus is small-town romantic suspense.

You can connect with me on:

- https://www.tiktok.com/@ambercassidy_author
- https://www.instagram.com/@ambercassidy_author

Also by Amber Cassidy

The Chance Encounters Series: Small Town Romantic Suspense, Interconnected Standalone Novels. Available on Amazon & Kindle Unlimited!

First Sight

Book One of the series introduces us to the crime happening in Rollins County with Nathan and Callie's unlikely meeting and their struggle with corruption.

First Touch

Nathan's little sister, Thea, is a small-town librarian struggling with trauma from her past. She never expects the mysterious new stranger in town to be the one to tear down her walls, or how they are connected more than either of them realizes.

First Surrender

Sheriff Malec is a reluctant hero, stepping into tackle the dangerous crime plaguing Rollins County because he wants to do right by the people. Natalie only cares about one thing: her brother, and she won't let the stoic sheriff get in her way.

Book 5

The last book. The release date and title are TBD!

www.ingramcontent.com/pod-product-compliance
Lightning Source LLC
Chambersburg PA
CBHW030539260626
47157CB00006B/2105